The
IMPERIAL
WIFE

ALSO BY IRINA REYN

What Happened to Anna K.

Living on the Edge of the World:
New Jersey Writers Take on the Garden State

The
IMPERIAL WIFE

IRINA REYN

Thomas Dunne Books
ST. MARTIN'S PRESS ❧ NEW YORK

THOMAS DUNNE BOOKS.
An imprint of St. Martin's Press.

THE IMPERIAL WIFE. Copyright © 2016 by Irina Reyn. All rights reserved. Printed in the United States of America. For information, address St. Martin's Press, 175 Fifth Avenue, New York, N.Y. 10010.

www.thomasdunnebooks.com
www.stmartins.com

Designed by Anna Gorovoy

Library of Congress Cataloging-in-Publication Data

Names: Reyn, Irina, author.
Title: The imperial wife: a novel / Irina Reyn.
Description: First edition. | New York: Thomas Dunne Books/St. Martin's Press, 2016.
Identifiers: LCCN 2016001230 | ISBN 9781250076038 (hardcover) | ISBN 9781466887367 (ebook)
Subjects: LCSH: Women art dealers—Fiction. | Painting—Collectors and collecting—Fiction. | Catherine II, Empress of Russia, 1729–1796—Fiction. | Self-actualization (Psychology) in women—Fiction. | Self-realization in women—Fiction. | BISAC: FICTION / Historical. | FICTION / Contemporary Women. | GSAFD: Historical fiction. | Biographical fiction.
Classification: LCC PS3618.E95 147 2016 | DDC 813/.6—dc23
LC record available at http://lccn.loc.gov/2016001230

ISBN 978-1-250-10978-1 (Canadian edition)

Our books may be purchased in bulk for promotional, educational, or business use. Please contact your local bookseller or the Macmillan Corporate and Premium Sales Department at 1-800-221-7945, extension 5442, or by e-mail at MacmillanSpecialMarkets@macmillan.com.

First U.S. Edition: July 2016
First Canadian Edition: July 2016

10 9 8 7 6 5 4 3 2 1

For Sonya

If I may dare to use such terms, I take the liberty to assert on my own behalf that I was an honest and loyal knight, whose mind was infinitely more male than female.

—CATHERINE THE GREAT, *MEMOIRS*

The

IMPERIAL
WIFE

Tanya

The Burliuk is a fake. To make sure, I flash the ultraviolet light closer to the surface. No doubt about it—the form's flat, the red way off. The image has no depth, and the tentative, choppy signature floats. These are not at all the artist's confident, swirling lines. The painting's canvas is made of Masonite, a material Burliuk would never have used in 1911. And most damning of all is the bucolic subject matter in keeping with his later, American period. Oh, well. Disappointing, but at least I made the catch before slotting the piece into the catalogue.

"It's a stunner, isn't it?" The consignor's voice slices through the dim light of the viewing room. "I fell in love as soon as I saw it."

"I can see why you were drawn to it." This was supposed to be my showstopper, my top star. A Russian-period Burliuk is rare, much less one from 1911. But I manage to maintain a cheerful demeanor.

I've got to hand it to the forger; apart from slapping the wrong date on the thing, he did a decent job. The reproduction has its own energy. The farm is vivid, the horse and ducks rendered in the playful vein of the master's later work as an immigrant living on Long Island. Of course by that point, Burliuk's most important Futurist work was long behind him, these lucrative if mediocre farm scenes probably aimed toward the tastes of American art collectors.

I imagine a struggling immigrant in Leipzig or Queens copying, line by line, the style of some blown-up original. The love and patience that requires, to apply one's hand over another's intention, to reach back hundreds of years in search of connection.

I'd prefer to stay in the dark forever. But the catalogue deadline is looming and I've still got nothing pressworthy. I flip the light switch.

"If you haven't guessed, the Russian market's sort of new to me. You know how it is. Never sure what you're getting half the time." The consignor, Mr. Brooks, is an unassuming-looking man with mild blue eyes, razor-thin eyebrows, and flushed cheeks. A gallery owner from Greenwich, another innocent American wading into the dangerous waters of Russian art, trusting the expertise of others, discounting all the danger signs. I'm tempted to shake him, to offer him the following advice: just stay away from the Russians!

But because he's considering consigning other, presumably authentic, pieces to Worthington's, specialists are never to sound the alarm right away. Instead, the matter must be handled with subtlety and delicacy, infusing a fruitless situation with a spark of hope so the relationship continues. One of the worst parts of my job is collusion in this limbo, like a doctor cheerfully recommending further testing when she knows the prognosis is no good.

"You're right to be wary," I say gently, warmly. "The market is flooded with fakes. In this case, it might be best to leave the painting in our care."

"Really? Why?" There it is again, a reed of distress in his voice. A part of him must know. The bony knobs of his knees are pressed together in tan plaid slacks.

I place the flashlight down on the coffee table where our past auction catalogues are fanned out. I'm reminded of the deadline again, the front page that would now have to feature the Goncharova Spanish dancer. That one was a coup, but it's no neoclassical-style, turn-of-the-century Fabergé hardstone inkwell like what Nadia Kudrina's got over at Christie's. And in this climate, in this depressed market, clients want rarity above all. The kind of property they can't get anywhere else. To guarantee the highest bids, it should be a work that's fresh to the market, rediscovered, that no one even knows exists.

"We may have a bit of a historical contradiction here. As a courtesy, we would be happy to bring in our restorer to look it over in greater detail."

"What do you mean by a contradiction?"

"It's the subject matter, that's all. Just raises a small question in my mind."

"Oh, no. Really?"

"It should take just a week or two. We'll get it back to you." I say this in a conclusive way. But always positive. This is just an obstacle to be surmounted.

Mr. Brooks rises off the couch, his hand resting protectively on the frame of the fake. I reach over to reassure him in some way, a pat on his shoulder, a handshake, some human interaction he may remember later in the depths of his distress. I know he's paid over two hundred thousand for it and he's not getting that money back. Just as my fingers settle on the wool shoulder of his jacket, I notice my assistant Regan in the door waving frantically to me.

"Excuse me, I'll be right back." The door claps shut and the light brightens. I breathe in, exhale.

Regan is waiting down the hall, in the corner of the floor carved out for the Russian art department. Because our specialty is still relatively new, our area's an afterthought. We're an island surrounded by East Asian and Middle Eastern, a row of desks squeezed between mahogany bookshelves and a cemetery of broken ergonomic chairs. My friends always expect the Worthington's offices to look like coolly curated galleries or at least the blankness of a modernist museum. How lucky you are to work there, they tell me. If they only knew! The space is a disheveled jumble of extension cords and books and articles and spreadsheets. On top of one of the bookshelves sits a ransacked box of chocolates next to a wilting bouquet of yellow roses. Most of the specialists' desks are littered with electrolyte water bottles, teacups, or clear nail polish. Like everything else at an auction house, beauty here tends to be for public consumption only.

"Good timing. What's up?"

"Someone's in the paper," Regan sings, holding up the *Financial Times* "Diary of a Somebody" column. In red ink, she has circled the pull quote:

Between a looming Russian art auction, a
fund-raiser at Sergei Brin's, and her husband's

best-selling novel, Worthington's Russian Art
specialist Tanya Kagan Vandermotter hobnobs
with the most important businesspeople of
the world. But despite all the fabulous parties,
she is "just a simple girl from Moscow" whose
dream is to see more Russian masterworks
returned to their place of origin.

"Booya. Read it and weep, Nadia Kudrina. This is coming in at the perfect time."

I wave it away, but I'm secretly pleased. "Let me see that."

Most of it is embarrassing me as I read it in print but I'm tempted to walk it straight up to Dean. *See, you can't cut the Russian department now!* I turn on the computer to find an in-box flooded with congratulations and e-mails with subject lines like "Hey, Simple Girl from Moscow!"

I call my parents to celebrate. They're thrilled.

" 'Diary of a Somebody' must mean you are a Somebody," my mother says. My father promises to find a copy of the paper in New Jersey. If he has to cancel a client for a trip to Barnes & Noble, so be it.

I think about calling Carl, then I picture his pained face, the one he's been wearing lately. The flutter of his eyelashes as he levels his gaze on me, trying to puzzle out my motivations. The way he asks "Is that you?" when I step through the door in the evening, as if connecting the possibility of a stranger with the person invading his space. The oblique angle of him through mirrors. But I dial his number anyway. The phone goes to his voice mail and I leave a message seeping with exclamation points.

"Let's all have dinner tonight!" Then I hang up.

When the *Financial Times* first called about doing the column, I'd wanted no part of it. Those columns made me squeamish for their subjects. They portrayed art experts as jet-setting glamour-pusses that engineer million-dollar deals at Art Basel by day but fly back to their London town houses just in time to bake their children perfect biscotti from scratch. Who say things like, "Heli-skiing really helps me unwind." Beautiful specialists in modernist homes with handsome, curly-haired Mediterranean husbands or WASPy blondes in organic caftans and chunky jewelry. Always photographed in black against a somber background or their noses dipped into the rim of a wineglass. The idea of being in those pages among that company was laughable. A Russian immigrant whose parents live in a two-bedroom house in New Jersey? Who has no idea what heli-skiing is or how rugby is even played, a million miles away from penthouses in the Time Warner Center and weekend jaunts to places like Mustique? Who was promoted only because her former assistant, Nadia Kudrina, decamped to Christie's? Who was nobody when she first met Carl Vandermotter?

But the company insisted I do the feature. The *Financial Times* was an opportunity for Worthington's to stand out among our competitors, my boss Marjorie informed me. This was our PR opportunity, a chance to finally conquer a Sotheby's whose board was being challenged. But I could read between the lines—the future of the Russian department is on the line. Why pump money into Russian art at a time like this? Why not look toward China or the safest place of all: contemporary? Most galleries in the world support the contemporary market—Warhol, Koons, and Hirst are always a safer bet than Burliuk and Goncharova.

"Why don't you want to do it? Isn't your husband's last name on that wing in Beth Israel? I'm sure your in-laws would expect it," Marjorie said, catching me between meetings. She probably assumed she was being tactful the way she was laying it on about Carl's family. "And didn't he write a best-selling book? Think of it as extra publicity for him."

"It was at the bottom of the list for two weeks," I protested, wary of both topics. I was not about to explain to my boss that the Vandermotters are cheap. That their money is tied up in trusts and real estate, doled out to us in tiny increments, that my husband did nothing to help the publisher earn out his advance and makes less money at his new job than Regan, that for most of his twenties and early thirties, he'd been a graduate student. That we live in a one-bedroom railroad apartment that hasn't been renovated since 1977. But the idea of them reading the piece and sharing it with their friends was a good point. With the Vandermotters, what you projected to the world was everything.

There I stood before that slumping, bearded reporter, a young man wearing a T-shirt that superimposed the phrase RAW BROOKLYN over a picture of a bleeding steak. He seemed shocked by his modest surroundings, as if he had trekked all the way uptown for a subject more identifiably ethnic, someone glitzier, out of a New Russian reality show. He was clearly expecting gold fountains, jeweled tubs, bedsteads lined with Swarovski crystal, a balcony onto Central Park.

"Is this your primary residence then?" He looked confused as he scanned our galley kitchen with its pans dangling on hooks above the stove, our bathroom with its chipped black-and-white tile, our walls cluttered with photographs, posters, and the odd expensive gift from clients, our mid-century reproductions and flea market finds. He kept checking his phone as if to make sure he had the right address. *Why am I interviewing this lady again?* I saw it in his eyes.

"I'm just a simple girl from Moscow," I explained, but then it occurred to me that I could be misquoted into a version of all the other insufferable "somebodies" in these pages ("I am so used to having a trainer that the machines daunt me. It's as though my whole morning is devoted to trying to work out how to program the StairMaster"). I started again.

The real secret to being the best specialist in an auction house is understanding the psychology of your clients, I told him. You have to know how to entice reluctant bidders to get into the game, intuit who says he wants privacy but doesn't mean it, whose privacy is so crucial that his very life depends on it. It's a skill divorced from art expertise. Your job as a specialist is to know without being told, to penetrate the brains of busy people and extract their deepest desires.

I watched him take notes between sips of black coffee, enjoying the texture of the words on my tongue. When my husband came home, the reporter practically fell on him, insisted on watching him type some sentences on a computer. From the fascinated way the guy skimmed Carl's books and notebooks, it seemed like he was a frustrated writer who would have preferred to do the feature on Carl, not me. And who could blame him? Who cared about a Russian art specialist when there was a best-selling writer in the house? The reporter asked many questions about Carl's "process," then moved on to America's strained relationship with Russia, grilled him on whether the next Cold War was brewing.

"Why don't you talk a bit more with my wife? Isn't she the subject of your profile?" Carl asked him, pulling apart a nectarine.

The reporter was so pushy about wanting to peruse a marked-up draft of my husband's manuscript of *Young Catherine,* that it was Carl who finally had to kick him out. We were both relieved when he was gone.

"Asshole," Carl said, disappearing into the alcove that we had turned into his office.

"Just give me some good news, please," I say to Regan now. "I need it."

A coven of assistants and interns gaggle, a whole group of recent college graduates I can't tell apart. Working at Worthington's is like being at a place like Smith College in the 1950s, all that hair and cashmere and hyacinth scent and girls fantasizing for their true lives to begin. Regan was such a relief because she didn't fit this profile. I liked her aggressive resilience, her Ph.D. in Slavic Languages and Literatures, the tattoos she didn't bother to hide, her unconventional style: a blazer over a 1950s-style dress, oversized costume clips in her ears, her hair swept into a French twist. Why did I need another competitive oligarch's daughter or fragile flower working for me? At a place like Worthington's, with the kind of clients we work with, you need someone on your side.

Regan can't hide her grin. "Natasha at the Hermitage called. Guess what they're busy authenticating? The Order . . . wait for it . . . that belonged to Catherine the Great. The consignor says it's ours if we want it."

I can't help myself: "Holy shit."

"Can you believe it? I can't believe it," Regan says.

"Can we get it into the catalogue?"

Regan squints, a grimace of disapproval. "She says authenticity would be contingent on this one Catherine historian. He's famously slow with his written evaluations. But he's cautiously optimistic."

"I think we have enough for now. Let's move forward." I lower my voice. "We might not have another opportunity. You know the situation."

"Yeah, but won't it take some time? What kind of assurances can we make?"

I talk it over with Regan, calculating what we'd need to do—photograph, draw up copy, get it shipped here in time for the preview. "But it looks pretty much okay to Natasha, doesn't it?"

"She counted the stones with the old weight and cut and compared it to the court records."

"And the box?"

"They think it's original. Their gut impression is it's right. But this guy is the final word on Catherine relics." Regan eyes me skeptically.

"Great. Let's do it. It's our top star. It's huge."

"Really? Are you sure? We've got the Goncharova."

"Are you kidding? This is much better. This is also a good news story." I ignore Regan's caution. It's a moment every specialist dreams of, a moment that occurs only once or twice in a career. We're all archive rats who dream of uniting a work of art with its provenance and this is one hell of a provenance because it belonged to Her. I felt it when I first laid eyes on a digital image of the medal, this radiating milky heat, as if Catherine herself were sending me a private message across the ocean. So her Order exists after all, not buried with the royal dead as the research implied. I perform a little dance on my toes.

One of the girls unearths a lukewarm bottle of prosecco from her desk, another offers to fetch Marjorie, but the panicked face of Mr. Reed William Brooks peers out from the square window of the viewing room.

"Uh-oh," I say. "Better get back in there."

There's a round of protests from the girls. *It's practically the weekend!* Even Regan says, "Come on, how often does this happen?"

"You know what? We should celebrate with real champagne. Where's the one Medovsky sent over?" I'll bring Mr. Brooks a glass too, it's the least I can do. I give him a signal to wait just one tiny moment.

While the foil is unpeeled, while one of the ladies struggles with dislodging the cork, pointing it toward the books and away from the canvases and sculptures, I call Carl again.

His phone rings and rings, his voice mail once more assuring me that he will return my call. I leave him a message to meet me and my parents at a restaurant in the neighborhood.

A few of the girls are arranged around desks like rose petals, heels hooked around the legs of chairs. The last of the chocolates are consumed. A knock, now loud and insistent, is coming from the direction of the viewing room. The champagne is poured into plastic cups, warm and overflowing with foam.

Before returning to one of the many clients who always seems to need me, before leaving the girls with their cardigans, their pearl earrings, their diamond engagement rings, among whom I will never, ever belong, I quickly drain my glass and grab the cell phone. In case Carl calls me back sooner than I expect him to.

"It looks like it's Catherine the Great's. Ekaterina Velikaia." As the sparkling water is being poured, I'm wondering if I hadn't been hasty arranging the foursome in a spontaneous spurt of pride. My parents are not restaurant people, have never grown comfortable with fussy service and the constricted nature of a meal among music and noise. My mother is wiping a perfectly clean knife on her napkin while my father pushes away the bread basket and asks for raw vegetables to dip in olive oil.

The lighting is too dark, so they're squinting at the picture of the Order, passing it from one to the other. As usual, I fixate on their approval, their excitement. I've never understood why I still need them to be impressed with me, as though in order to repay them the immigration freight of passage, I had to prove my successes justified their decision to uproot us to America. For as long as I can remember, from grade school to my marriage to my job, I've been repeating ever-escalating versions of "Look, Ma, look, Pa, look what I've done!"

"And what is this I'm looking at?" my mother asks.

"An order. You know, like a medal she'd wear."

"Catherine the Great wore this?"

"Peter the Great established this honor for women marrying into the royal family or as gratitude for some great accomplishment. I think his wife got the first one. Catherine got hers when she committed to marrying

Peter's grandson. There aren't many of them around, much less one that has been proven to be Catherine the Great's."

"It looks like an ordinary necklace."

"How can you say that? Look at that sash of scarlet moiré, the silver star encrusted with diamonds."

"And people actually believe this trinket was really Catherine the Great's? Americans are so gullible," my mother persists, fully enjoying herself.

"Are you ready to order?" the server says.

"We're waiting for someone." I turn back to my parents.

My father is the mediator as usual. He has finished reading my profile in the paper. "Your mother is joking. We are very happy. This means your auction will be good, yes? You were worried."

My father is spreading butter on a roll. He hands it to my mother. For himself, he dunks a carrot in oil and bites off a chunk. Olive oil and protein and a regimented eating schedule are his secrets of eternal youth. I like seeing them together, the way my father takes care of my mother, the tiny acts of making sure she is lacking for nothing.

"Well, of course we're happy for you," she says, taking the bread as if challenging the idea that eternal youth, if it means forgoing rolls and cookies, is not worth it. Her fingers are a pianist's, an eagle's. "I just don't know why anyone in their right mind would pay millions for this thing. Are you sure it's not a fake? Did they say it was definitely hers or did someone just make it in their basement? But either way, it is very nice that you can finally show that Kudrina a thing or two. She is very annoying on television, always showing off how she is the only Russian expert in this country. As if my boopchik doesn't even exist."

Why must my mother also bring up Nadia Kudrina? But I work very hard to flash an insouciant smile, then fold away the digital scan in my tote. Carl walks in. He is wearing an eye-popping coral button-down that rarely makes it out of his closet, his blond hair still wet from a shower. His breath is unhurried.

"You're always late," is on the tip of my tongue, but I swallow it. Better to be encouraging, praise the victories, not the shortcomings. Four years of marriage have taught me this. "Nice shirt," I say instead.

"Thanks." He kisses my parents hello, then me. He smells of the shampoo he favors, a barklike lemongrass. I still can't believe a Jewish girl like me married someone this light-haired, this at ease with the world's accommodation of him. The servers flap about him like butterflies.

"*Kak dela?*" he asks, unfurling his napkin. The question, in his charming secondhand Russian, seems to be directed at all of us at once. My mother beams. In the end I wonder if this isn't my greatest success in their eyes. Not my job, my education, my apartment. But to have married someone this American, this effortlessly charming.

"You heard about Tanya's great coup?" my father asks.

"Papa, let's order first, okay?" I flag down the server. My mother and I decide what healthy dish my father will order, and settle on the poached trout.

"Coup?" Carl turns his calm, almost hazel eyes to me.

"The *Financial Times* came out. Hey, it's not as horrible as we thought it would be. Isn't that great?"

"Oh, well, that's good, isn't it?"

I pass him the newspaper. I'm not ready to tell him about the Order after all. This is Catherine the Great we're talking about and there's still this tension around us after the book. When something awkward and unsayable enters a marriage, it plants its feet right in the middle, folds its arms and refuses to budge. Our voices are still unnatural in each other's presence. Too high, too friendly, too easygoing.

I imagined the restaurant would eventually turn bustling and jammed with people's voices, but other than a single couple tucked into the back near the kitchen, we occupy the only other table in the dining room. There are all these hopeful pale blue candles flickering on empty tables, illuminating decapitated heads of hydrangeas. My every word is magnified.

"But what is really exciting is the auction," my father says. "Why aren't you telling him?"

Carl finishes chewing. Unlike us, he observes strict protocols of mealtime decorum. "That's great! Did the Burliuk come in?"

"The Burliuk was a fake." I make way for my salad. The plate drops before me with a ceramic thud, a gnarled mess of arugula. "But we did get validation of something else from the Hermitage's curator of eighteenth-century Russian decorative arts."

"Ekaterina Velikaia! Just like your book!" my father proudly interrupts. "Wasn't she wearing it on your cover, Carl? This is romantic coincidence, yes, Vera? They are both . . . how we say it? Catherine-heads?"

"Romantic," my mother repeats, her eyes more observant. I can tell she is worried. She knows I don't summon them from New Jersey to eat at restaurants on random Friday nights. But I'm continuing to smile, to ride the swell of celebration.

A mother and son walk in, and are seated near us. A family of four is right behind them. Now the door is revolving, voices pervading the empty air. The weight of my choices lightens.

"Oh, yeah? What'd you get in?" Carl asks. His interest is so sincere, so well-meaning.

"It's her Order," I say. I keep my voice high and bubbly, an extreme version of the recent me. "Isn't it exciting? We'd be looking at seven million at least, and that's just the guarantee."

A slight smile crosses my husband's lips. I want to read it as genuinely pleased for me—for us—laced with nothing more ominous. My entire body swells with hope that the worst is over, the last of the new marriage wrinkles are ironed out. I do something uncharacteristic in front of my parents. I reach over his grilled squid and kiss him on the lips. I linger there for what feels like hours longer than necessary. In case he can focus solely on me.

At home, we are incredibly kind to each other. I brew him a cup of decaf without his asking, and settle next to him on the couch with my glass of wine. We watch his choice of show, then rinse our glasses in the sink. He gets to wash up first, tolerates my checking my e-mail in bed without complaint. I keep smiling; studies show pessimists give up more easily than optimists. Optimists see minor hiccups for what they are, temporary and surmountable.

"You should wear bright colors more often, you know," I say, watching him peel off the pink shirt. "They suit you."

"You think so?" His finger brushes my cheek slowly. I close my laptop. That's how he usually initiates sex, a light touch somewhere on my face or neck. But he has found on my chin an eyelash. It's one of the smaller ones, black and curling. It rests in the middle of his index finger.

"Make a wish."

I do. Then I watch it blow away. But instead of disappearing into some mythical eyelash paradise of fulfilled wishes, I can see exactly where it comes to rest, on top of the sheet. The eyelash's reappearance unnerves me. Does he still want sex? That was one of the victims in that blip early on in our marriage. For Carl, sex is the direct expression of his feelings. For me, sex is an escape from them. It's where I allow myself to get obliterated, to neither think, nor, for once, to lead.

"Hey," I joke. "Can you make a second wish on the same eyelash? How does that work anyway?"

"I don't think so. You get only one chance at a wish." Carl leans back against the pillow, his Grecian profile dipping into his book. Then, just as abruptly, he shuts it. His lips outline the rim of my ear and I allow him to diffuse my entire day, a day more stressful than I can admit even to myself. I try to sink into feeling only, but the mental collage is of a frowning Marjorie, Mr. Reed Brooks seeking rescue from the submarine of the viewing room.

"You're so beautiful," I breathe as if my words will transport me where it matters.

"And you," he says. "And you." But in it I detect a mournful spiral.

The next day, the Museum of Modern Art is less crowded than usual because of a dripping March rain. Carl and I run in soaked and dump our jackets in the coat check. Since I'm a corporate member, we enter the museum for free, two tickets handed to me once I flash my Worthington's ID. I hand one to Carl.

I love museums the way my husband loves libraries, for their civilized silence, the generosity of their gifts, that they can make you see familiar work in a new way depending on the curatorial point of view, the angle of the historical context. I love being surrounded by thousands of strangers yet encased in our own cocoon, the sound of our wet shoes tapping the floor in rhythm, the murmur of self-confident opinions around us. I pay partial attention to the show, but mostly it's about the pleasure of ambling, of peaceful interaction with Carl. No demands from clients, no pressures from Dean's office. A rare Saturday with my husband.

"Okay, so I've got the new novel all mapped out," Carl says, veering me around dutiful scrutinizers of section labels. *The exhibition brings together many of the most influential works in abstraction's early history and covers a wide range of artistic production.*

"Really? Tell me."

"Okay, so picture this. It's set in St. Petersburg in 1911 at the Stray Dog Café. You know, the one where Mandelstam and Akhmatova and Tsvetaeva argued and read poetry and drank red wine. It was a famous hangout for the greatest poets of the era. Before the Revolution. It'll be like a Russian *Cabaret.*"

"Uh-huh."

"What do you think? Does it sound viable to you?"

I have no idea what he's talking about, but pretend I do. It's always sobering how much more Carl knows about my own history. He pulls back each finger, chapter by chapter. "It'll open in the 1960s with Robert Frost visiting the elderly Akhmatova in Leningrad and move back in time."

"That sounds amazing," I say, probably too loudly because a few people without headphones look up at me, irritated. We are all standing in front of a map that links people and countries, slashes of red connecting Picasso to Liubov Popova and Vanessa Bell.

"It's just in the research stages right now," he insists. "But doesn't it sound fascinating?"

"I can't wait to read it. Whenever you're ready."

"I might show it to someone else first. If that's okay."

I pretend that the suggestion of this arrangement is perfectly acceptable, even as it stings.

Carl is letting his hair grow longer, the preppy 1980s way it looked when I first met him. That impossible golden flax, pin-straight, straining over his ears and collar. I note that he's made the style decision without sharing it with me. When we first got together, he would ask for my feedback on the most minute things: loafers or the Top-Siders? The paisley or polka-dotted umbrella? Even matters of diet: should I eat this late if we're having an early dinner? Should I skip the fries? Will the salad fill me up, do you think?

I suppose after four years of marriage, it's natural that our minds will take turns back to an independent consciousness, occasionally skipping over the needs of the other. But it's striking. I flap out some of his hair between my fingers, air-drying it. I imagine his students—that Victoria, in particular—focusing on the way that my husband's hair moves during a long lecture on fiction craft or one of his digressions on the Acmeist poets. He's the kind of good-looking that takes itself for granted, that even at thirty-four doesn't fully understand the extent of its power. Even now, women linger on his face as they move past him to get to the corner with all the watercolors.

We move deeper into the show.

"Seriously. Tell me more. Where's the love story?" I pull him out of the way of a guided tour bent on its systematic survey of the art. But he's already thinking of something else, I can tell by the distracted way his mouth slacks open.

"Hey, I think I really need to see it for myself." He leans down, hand around my shoulder. He pushes a fistful of hair behind my ear. "Can I come in to the office?"

I pause, genuinely confused. "See what?"

"The Order. It's incredible, right?"

My heart stumbles, trips. "Yeah, it kind of is."

"So it exists. God, to touch the thing. That she wore it. Ekaterina Velikaia."

"But what do you need to touch it for? I'll show you a digital."

On the wall behind Carl, I read out loud a Kandinsky quote: " 'Must we not then renounce the object, throw it to the winds and instead lay bare the purely abstract?' "

"Seriously, Tan. A digital is hardly the same thing. I just feel like I have to touch it with my own hands."

"Of course. But the consignor was very adamant that no one but a serious buyer should even breathe on the thing."

"Are you serious?"

"I also have an incredible Goncharova, just stunning. A very rare *Spanish Dancer*?"

"Jesus. Why am I even surprised?" He brushes by the art with barely a glance and for a moment submerges into the sea of the tour group. I feel a numb devastation, then perform my cognitive tricks to recover. *Everything's fine, everything's fine. A bad situation is a momentary setback, nothing more.*

I look for him on the other side of the crowd. "Look, you should come to the preview. You can see it then. It'll be behind glass and there's going to be so much great art. You'll love the Archipenko too."

"You don't want me to touch it. You don't even want me to be anywhere near it. You want to keep me apart from it. It's yours. It's all yours." Before I know it, he's an entire room ahead, staring neither at the Kupka nor the Picabia. He stuffs his hands into the pockets of his pressed khakis, then takes them out. His hair is still wet, stubbornly wet.

My friends warned me about the beginnings of marriages, like clumsy fumblings of any new skill. "Those first years are the worst, believe me," my best friend Alla warned me. "You think you made the biggest mistake and will want to run from it every single day." But her statement seemed so counterintuitive that I dismissed it right away. What about its opposite, the wearing off of bliss, the slow understanding of the person you married?

"That'll never happen with us," I assured Alla. Carl was perfection. Exotic, voluminous, firebird perfection. I had somehow managed to trap it, convinced it to fall in love with me.

As I'm deciding on how best to approach my husband's mood, I glimpse a client's shock of gray hair. My first thought is to try and avoid him, but he's already seen me and is steering his wife over. A specialist is a salesperson first; she can't be seen ignoring her clients. This man happens to be one of my favorites too, a grandfatherly bon vivant who reminds me of my own grandfather, who once wore suits and bow ties and effusively greeted random ladies on the streets of Rego Park ("Ciao, beauties") as if he were Marcello Mastroianni or a flaneur in Malta. He had not lasted long in America.

I'm forced to summon Carl over for introductions. *Come, honey! Meet Jeremiah Gruber.* The man's wife is a petite, fragile-looking woman with a fit physique and two gold knots dotting her ears. Carl hesitates, but then obeys.

"You wrote a novel, didn't you?" the wife asks Carl. She is looking at him with an admiration I'm used to by now. My husband belongs to that species of handsome, tall male writers. "I'm almost positive I read about it in *People*. Catherine the Great, wasn't it?"

"We just got the news that it'll be translated into Italian." I pull my husband closer, offer his hand a brief, conspiratorial squeeze. There's no response. I feel only bones surrounded by a film of flesh.

"I can speak for myself, thanks, Tanya," he says in my general direction.

"Maybe we can entice you to come and meet with our book club," the woman says to him. She is rooting around in her snakeskin handbag for a pen or card. "We often have writers drop in and answer questions about their inspiration."

"She's in three book clubs," my client says.

"That's wonderful," I effuse, filling in the space. "I wish I had time for reading."

My husband folds his museum guide, signaling an end to the conversation. He's gotten more polite at deflecting requests like this, but people are always unpleasantly surprised when he refuses to take part in self-promotion. He's a classic pessimist like my mother, convinced everything good that happens to him is a mistake and everything bad is part of an unshakable narrative. "I don't think so. Thanks for asking though."

"Oh." The card is frozen in midair. "I guess you must be busy on the next book."

Carl is examining the vivid Sonia Delaunay painting before him, the slashes of swirling color meant to imitate the electric lamps new to the streets of Paris. "That's right. I'm busy on the next book."

My client comes to the rescue. "They're a handsome couple, Tanya and Carl, don't you think?"

"He's thrilled at all the attention that book's gotten, we all are," I say. I take the wife's card since someone has to. "I'll write you both for the auction preview. You'll go crazy for the early Komar and Melamid, Jeremiah. It dates right before they dissolved their partnership. Lovely to see you both."

When they're out of sight, I turn to Carl. His jaw is tight, his eyes flashing steel. *You want to run from it every single day.*

"Oh, honey, they meant well."

"Yeah, I know. You meant well too, didn't you, Tan?"

"Of course I did. I do."

"Okay, keep telling yourself that."

He strides out of the gallery, those long deerlike steps, his shoes inaudible on the parquet floors. My eyes are filling and I blink frantically to keep them dry. It's just the typical bumps of a beginning, two individuals learning to be a couple, wedging themselves into their proper places.

I make an effort to take in a bit of the show but falter in my usual concentration. He's gone a long time. I dash off a few e-mails on my phone. But fifteen minutes go by, then a half hour, then forty-five minutes. I take a seat on the bench in front of the restrooms. Man after man is expelled, none of them him. The rainstorm must have ended because the galleries are clogging with visitors.

I text—*where are you?*—then another one right after that in capital letters: *ARE YOU STILL AT MUSEUM?* I take the escalators and check the benches in front of each restroom. Tourists filter in and out, shaking out umbrellas from a flash rainstorm. When the flood subsides, I exit into the outdoor sculpture garden with its Calders and Picassos speckled with water. Families are circling around black mesh chairs, scooping gelato with flat plastic spoons.

Throngs are descending the staircase through mirrored glass but he is none of the men. I think I catch the flash of his trench, the wheat of his hair, but it's always someone else, a mirage. My calls, frantic and multiplying, go to voice mail. After what seem like minutes but must be at least two hours later, guards announce the museum is closing, and the chatter around us begins to subside. When I turn in my number at the coat check, his trench is missing.

"How can that be when it's my husband's," I say. "My number is for both our coats."

"Sorry." The lanky young girl has wide, apologetic eyes, overwhelmed by the long line behind me. "The guy said he lost his number so I gave it to him."

My phone vibrates inside the purse. Carl has written: *I'm at TJ's empty place. In Queens.*

"All right, sure," I say into the phone, as if he can hear me, as if he had only informed me of a late night's work. A coat I recognize as mine is handed to me.

I step out onto Fifty-third Street in a daze. The city ebbs and contorts, a discordant jumble of zigzagging bodies in yoga pants and floral blouses, baseball hats and suits. A row of vendors in fingerless gloves hawk reproductions of van Goghs and tribal masks to the last of the day's customers. The sky is a hazy, noncommittal blue. Down in the subway, the faces are heavyset, too bundled for the weather, feet encased in tall rubber boots, entranced by screens of their phones and tablets and oblivious to their neighbors. An angry swell rises like heat through the car, a series of jabbing purses and elbows, when the lurch of a long-awaited train heaps bodies against one another.

When I emerge at my stop, even my own block doesn't look familiar, and it takes me several minutes to realize I was heading in the wrong direction, on Amsterdam and not Broadway. I pass stands piled with bananas, mangoes, plums, and other impossible fruit yanked too early from the warmth of its homeland. When my building rises before me it may as well have been summoned there by magic.

I want to walk in on indulgent laughter at the punch lines of Russian anecdotes, Carl and my father gorging on pickled tomatoes, spreading out a newspaper with the peeled skin of dried fish. I can almost hear Carl's voice, his impressive idiomatic Russian.

"Where'd you go?" I'd chide, but in a nonjudgmental, loving way.

Carl might laugh, enfolding me in his arms. "Did you really think I went to Queens? Did you really think I'd leave you?" Husband. In Russian: *muzh.* Short for *muzhik,* a man, a wise, noble man.

The next morning, I'm woken by a repetitive thumping sound in our alcove. *Oh, good,* I think. *He's home.* He's had a night away but now he's home. I throw on a robe and pad barefoot to the alcove.

"Hey, that you?"

I peek around the corner to see Carl's tossing his Russian history books and a smattering of mismatched clothes into duffel bags. It's a useless array of items he is carting—staplers and belts and shoe polish—like a college kid moving to a dorm room. His face is slick and shiny, his shirt wrinkled.

"What are you doing?" It is a numbed shock that spreads through me, the kind that separates mind from body. I'm dimly aware that outside it continues to rain. "Honey?"

Carl looks older. His haggard exhaustion is centered about his eyes. He doesn't pause his packing, the entire bit emerging from him as if he's been preparing for this confrontation and has memorized his lines. "You know what? I realized in Queens that I need more time to think about us. That's all this is. Okay?"

I find myself standing between him and the bags, pulling closed the sash on my robe. "Wait a minute. We should see someone, right? I'll get a referral to a therapist. All we need to do is approach this with the right attitude."

Our eyes meet in the long static of silence. "The way he looks at you," my best friend Alla used to say, enviously. "I wish someone looked at me like that."

And it was true. He used to look at me as though the world turned gauzy around me, placing me in relief. We would be in a room full of people, but I'd feel the force of his attention. He might introduce me to someone at a party—"This is my wife, Tanya"—and it came out sounding as if he were the trusted caretaker of some magical force he didn't fully understand. At night, we read his favorite poetry out loud—Brodsky or Blok—until one of us grew too sleepy to continue and neither of us remembered the gist of what we read in the morning. In public, Carl called me *kotenok,* his Russian kitten. We held hands past the time our friends had dissolved their own intimacies in favor of their newborn children. Children. We had originally planned them for a year ago, when I was thirty-one, and he thirty-three. It seemed like the ideal age, not too early or late. Sometimes, I worried that he loved me too much to see my true self, that he saw my character through rose-colored glasses. But I liked his interpretation better and who even knew what my true self was anymore?

The Look is not entirely gone in his eyes, but it's flagging, tired, focusing on the tasks before it. "It's temporary, a place for me to work."

"You can work here. I'm gone all day." From his face, I see I have to approach it from a different angle, so I take his hand, feeling my way around the inner pouch of his palms. There is a small bump on his thumb, a callus or wart he never got around to checking out. "If we communicate, we can easily pull through. But you have to talk to me."

"I know. I hope so." He leans over to kiss me. A real Russian woman would have taken advantage of this kiss. She would have opened herself like a flower, kept him tethered under the guise of vulnerability. She would have stopped at nothing to keep him—phantom pregnancy, guilt, threats. A real Jewish woman would have decided this was the end of the world. A husband taking time to think would be nothing less than disaster because life makes the most sense through a lens of fear, caution. But in being both of these women, I am neither.

"Babe, I'll make us an appointment with someone who uses positive psychology approaches in marital conflict."

He flings the duffel back over one shoulder, a tote bag filled with books over another. "Tan, think about it. How can you love someone you don't respect?"

"Oh my God. Is that what this is about? I totally respect you."

He shakes his head.

It is filling my mouth, getting ready to erupt. *Why?* But I can't utter the word. If he tells me right then, something irreversible will be made real. Isn't it better to take him at his word, to treat whatever this is as time to regroup while I come up with a solution?

In the kitchen, I surreptitiously blow my nose. *Live like you expect miracles,* I think. *One foot in front of the other.* "You want some tea?"

He's leaning against the lintel, the Look flashing and receding. He displays the hesitation of changing his mind, like he might collapse me into his chest at any moment. But then he gives up. "All right. Tea. That would be great."

We drink it side by side at the round kitchen table, two steaming mugs of Earl Grey all the way to the bottom. He is staring into the watery depths of his cup while I keep chattering away, drinking liquid that tastes of wood. I tell him about what Regan wore the other day—a purple wig, frilly apron, fishnet tights, and combat boots. How Marjorie looked her up and down but said nothing. I refill our cups. I tell him about a client of my father's, a ninety-one-year-old man who gets a regular massage. When my father tries to slot him in for the following month, he always says the same thing, "But how do I know I'll still be alive a month from now?" "You can't die because if you miss an appointment with me, you'll get charged for the visit," is my father's response.

The kitchen clock ticks on, merciless, while the preschooler twins who live above us are loudly evading their mother's efforts to dress them. I set out a plate of leftovers from last night. What Russians call "bird's milk" but is actually a version of yellow marshmallow covered in a crisp chocolate veneer. It's usually his favorite treat.

Finally, he gets up. "The car's by the hydrant. It's packed with stuff. I should probably go."

Why? I want to say again, and again, I swallow the word. The toddlers are gone and the quiet is more terrifying than the noise had been.

After he leaves, the apartment has never been so deeply vacant. It's as if all the items I once took such pride in—the swan-necked lamp I found at Housing Works, the Lucite coffee table I bought cheap on eBay, the Art Deco–style bar I unearthed at a flea market—have been stripped of their essential essence. Fingers trailing the surfaces of things, items I thought we had amassed together when, in retrospect, it had been I who'd picked up tapestries and vases in bazaars. Furnishing our lives. But it's what he wanted, wasn't it—me making the decisions?

Eventually, I make my way to the bookshelves, an entire array of left-behind Russians on what I call Carl's shelf: the Bunins, the Brodskys, the Babels. And an entire untouched row of *Young Catherines*. I take one out, run my thumb along the decorative edges, the portrait Carl insisted should be its cover. The grand duchess in the yellow dress trimmed with white lace, ears draped with heavy chandelier pearls, the Order of Saint Catherine proudly slung across her slim torso. By Carl E. Vandermotter. I turn to the first page: *Sophie glimpses the comet's head, a blaze of fire rippling across the vastness of the sky, and implores them to stop the carriage. The entire procession comes to a halt.*

Catherine

Sophie glimpses the comet's head, a blaze of fire rippling across the vastness of the sky, and implores them to stop the carriage. The entire procession comes to a halt. Word of the famous sight had been spreading throughout Europe. "Maybe we will glimpse it on the road," her mother had said while they were packing. But none of the rumors adequately described the agitated beauty above her.

The comet appears to hover close to the ground, like a folding fan imprinted onto the night. It flashes six fingers out of the frozen, snowless earth before its tail is swallowed by blackness. She pulls the fur of her collar closer around her throat, not for warmth or out of any fear, but in rapture. Even though the horses tip their noses toward the stars, the view exists for her benefit alone, a private performance mediated by God. *The comet is me*, she thinks. Nature sends signs to the chosen ones. It is that simple: this journey, the comet, is me.

"Isn't it marvelous, Mother?"

"I see it, I see it. It's marvelous." Her mother is already back in the carriage, having taken a sideways peek by her side. "You'll catch your death. Get in, Figgy."

Sometimes she wished her mother were in possession of an affectionate tale for how the family nickname had been conferred, but Sophie guessed it meant nothing more profound than a shortening of the Fredericka in her name. Sophie Fredericka Augusta. Figgy. "Coming."

It is colder than cold, the wind whipping her head back and forth, drawing its force through her hair. She can see her mother huddling under the blankets, her face dipped under layers of sable. She is either beckoning in Sophie's direction or shuttering the curtains, her face a mask of perpetual grievance. But Sophie cannot look away from the sky. She sees the comet as a summons from above: fingers beckoning for her to come closer, to merge with this explosion. When the light bows and recedes, in its residue she sees a covenant, a confirmation. What she is undertaking will be a one-way trip, and there will be no return to Prussia: not to her father, her beloved governess, Babette, the siblings she never needed, and yes, even George, with eyes that never settled on a definitive color between sleet and grass and arms that had so recently formed a rim of love around her.

"You were meant for greater than life with your uncle," George said by way of farewell, pressing a perfumed letter into her palm. His eyes were rimmed with red, threaded by its pathways. His nose was buried in her hair. Just a fortnight ago, they stood by the lake, gray with early frost. She wept then, pummeled the slope of his shoulders, promised him an eternal identity as his true wife. When she arrives in Russia, she will suffocate him with correspondence, she promised.

He yanked out an errant curl near her ear as a keepsake, wound it around his thumb, then folded it into his coat pocket. His eyes were woolly, filmed over, and she found it impossible to meet them. The excruciating parting seemed to go on for hours.

But it was a relief when the sound of his horses finally retreated from the courtyard and, in her mind, she was packing for the journey. Sophie is not the sort to be sad for long; dwelling on the vanished is not intrinsic to her nature. Sophie is a dreamer, not a nostalgic. George was right. Life with him meant a garrisoned existence close to the bitterness of her mother. What lay ahead was the exotic East, the adventure of a famously lively court, a place where her singular voice would be heard. Also, the companionship of the grand duke, though she hopes he has grown more charming since her first unpromising encounter with him.

George's proclamation—*you were meant for greater*—thrums with truth now against the sky inflamed by a six-tailed comet. She climbs back into the carriage, and they continue their long eastward journey.

She expects a magnificent Russian palace, a Versailles of the East that she has read about in travelers' accounts, but they pull up in front of a sagging wooden building painted in bright, primitive colors. It is foreign, backward. It lacks luster. This oversized hut is Empress Elizabeth's court? Her mother sniffs in disappointment at the sight of it. Half of it is draped in darkness, a few windows illuminated as if in anticipation of unexpected guests, a row of frozen tree stalks framing the entrance, the stairway chipped, the first step already crumbled to dust.

But then the silence of the road is shattered, their carriage surrounded by a flurry of chamberlains. Their doors are flung open, and they are greeted with a jumbled mix of languages, German and the guttural buzz of Russian. Their baggage is being transferred from hand to hand until it disappears into the entryway. Sophie struggles to remember court protocol. Are they to wait for bows? Are they to follow a particular person into the palace? Darkness cedes to candlelight. She feels disoriented, miniature. Young.

They descend from the cabin, her mother solemn and ceremonial, draped on the hand of some field marshal or other. They are being welcomed, passed off to other welcomers, taken to a set of garishly lit rooms at the end of a hallway. The interior is slightly more promising, the occasional flicker of inlaid gold, expensive brocade hangings in the French style, crystal chandeliers dangling overhead, mosaics drawing patterns across the floors, mirrors stretching floor to ceiling. The wood floors are missing a few panels, but shiny with oil. Servants dressed in deep maroon bring glasses of wine on gold trays, bid her to sit. But she is agitated. Everything brims with exotic, folklike charm.

When they are left alone, mother and daughter stare at each other in a kind of disbelief.

"So here we are," she says, if only to seal the air with sound.

But her mother is already pulling up violet powder from her portmanteau. "No rest for us tonight, Figgy. We must be prepared to impress Her Majesty."

For Sophie, her mother is as unknowable as the severe steppes they have just traversed, always enshrouded in complaints and negative observations. The tenor of the grumblings is always the same: if she had only not agreed to the terrible match with Sophie's father who stuck her in dull provinces far from any shred of glitter or excitement. If she had only insisted on Frederick's intervention at the crucial moment before the nuptials, she might be a player on the world stage herself. Now she has worked her own family connections to the very bone in order to subsist on Sophie's future success. Sophie is not allowed to forget that she is in debt to her mother's sacrifices, that elusive promise of happiness.

Her mother crosses the room, a cool thumb fanning the surface of Sophie's cheek. "We should tidy up. We may be introduced to the grand duke any minute now."

Just as her coarse braid is loosened, the doors swing open. The boy who will be Sophie's husband ambles in, all bony legs and elbows.

"I had to see you. I could wait no longer." He is speaking German quickly, frantically, with an odd thick accent, marching from one end of the room to the other while her mother's lapidary hands work to reattach the headdress to her hair. His flushed face is illuminated, then wiped clean by evening's shadow. He exudes a confined energy, a horse sprung free from the stables. What should her response be? Sophie glances at her mother for guidance, but her mother is standing mutely by the chair, the hair around her forehead ascending like flames. They are waiting for something else to happen.

A brief examination proves her future husband to be barely taller than he was four years ago. On his person, there are few signs of maturation or masculinity. His skin is the lifeless color of parchment, a face punctuated by the faintest of chins. Sunshine seems to have eluded him. She wonders if some token of affection would be appropriate, if she should at least be smiling or curtsying or speaking German to him. Her mother has already recounted to her the fate of this boy, grandson of Peter the Great but happily raised in Kiel, plucked by the empress as her heir and reluctantly bundled off to Russia.

"You cannot imagine how glad I am to have a playmate at last, a fellow German speaker, a friend," he blurts. One of his cheeks is tinged yellow, as if almost healed from a recent bruise.

"I am very glad to be here." She curtsies, just in case. The German language seems to put him at ease. Back in Zerbst, one thing Sophie never lacked was tact, an instinct for the tone of an occasion. When her parents entertained her mother's influential relatives, she was always invited for the musical portions of the evening, the guests commenting on how far beyond her years she appeared, how witty and wise for such a wee thing.

A man enters their apartments; he is announced as M. Lestocq, the empress's surgeon. His wig is a surge of voluminous curls cascading past his shoulders. A brownish residue of his most recent meal dots his bottom lip. He bows but not too deeply. Her Majesty, the Empress Elizaveta Petrovna Romanova, is ready to receive them.

Sophie performs a quick, nervous survey of her wardrobe. She is wearing a dress of pale pink silk. The dress is not nearly as elaborate as her mother's, she notices, even provincial in its simplicity. She smooths the fabric at her waist and finds at her throat faint beads of sweat.

"Am I not poorly outfitted?" she hisses to her mother. But there is no time to improve her jewelry, to assess the state of her coiffure. As they leave the chambers, she looks behind her at the boy who will be her husband, who is receding, framed by the door, slumped and alone. Should she have said a proper farewell? She feels a trace of his need and the nascent shreds of affection, a sign to her that she must be experiencing the blossoming of romantic love.

The way to the empress seems to take as long as the trip to Russia itself. They file down a series of long corridors, the faces of welcoming ladies and gentlemen flickering in candlelight. Sophie feels herself gulped by them, her every crevice examined. They make no pretense of hiding their curiosity, examining her figure and hair, their eyes boring into her back. She tries not to return their shadowy stares, not to compare their mode of dress to her own. A friendly face shines up at her and she pauses before its singular expression. A girl exactly her age, a silver dress that pins her narrow waist.

"*Bienvenue, princesse.*" Her kind voice is the whispering of dandelions.

She stops before the girl. *"Merci, vous êtes gentille."* But her mother's hand presses at her back, pushing her onward.

They turn a corner and continue on this endless path of scrutiny. Then they are stopped short by the sight of an imposing woman lodged directly in their path. Sophie makes out vivid blue eyes, skin made whiter by the contrast to her hair. Her gown seems to fill the entire palace, her ample breasts smothered by jewels. Half her face is shrouded by an enormous black feather that loops over from its origin deep in her hair. All Sophie can see is this figure of a woman, too large, too majestic, too languorous to take in at once.

Her mother is kissing the woman's hand, bowing between a long string of *mercis*. A hand reaches out, and Sophie is plunged into a bodice, her face indented into that voluminous bosom. "My own blood is not dearer to me than yours," the woman is murmuring, all perfumes and motherly embraces. She leads them inside her state bedroom, where Sophie can only make sense of gold. Gold letter opener lying on a gold-rimmed dressing table, brocade curtains threaded with gold, gold-lacquered wardrobe.

In better light, she can assess the contours of the empress's beauty, all the feminine attributes one would desire: an ideal rosy pallor, defined lips, cinched waist, snowy skin. She allows herself to be examined, but says little apart from complimenting the empress on her superlative taste in décor. It is always best to say less, to assess the situation and meld herself into her surroundings. She is ready to take her place beside this woman in gold lace, with her white teeth and thick black hair dotted with diamonds as plentiful as stars. Over her mother's chalky curls, the empress watches her with icy eyes, takes Sophie apart into pieces and puts her back together.

"A dinner has been set up for you. You will excuse me if I dine separately."

"Of course, of course," her mother says, tripping over Sophie's hem in her attempt at servility.

"I trust everything is suitable."

"Suitable? We have never been so well treated in our lives. We are living like queens!"

"Are you."

The tone is dry, and Sophie is burning with shame. Her mother comparing herself to a queen! Mortifying, her mother. She inserts something of her own about the supreme generosity of Her Majesty's welcome, which seems to please the empress.

"For both the princesses, we have established a coterie of ladies-in-waiting," the empress announces before retiring to her rooms. The ladies from the hall come forward and Sophie is happy to see the girl who had welcomed her standing among them, a single star in silver. Her first Russian ally.

Tanya

PRESENT DAY

In the east midtown offices of Worthington's Auction House, the phones continue to ring. *Is this a terrible time to sell? First-time buyer here—any good deals to be had on Soviet nonconformist? I heard New York is getting out of the Russian art business, is that true?* Even the richest of clients are skittish. They trust nobody and who could blame them? The Russian economy is plummeting, everyone is lying low, paintings are going missing, and the sanctions are making life difficult. *Have you heard,* they gossip, *it's getting bad back home, the ruble is weak and getting weaker, another fake Kandinsky at the Tate, and do we know how this Ukraine nonsense is going to end? We are just going to wait this one out— our businesses are hemorrhaging.*

Regan, sporting a carefully messy topknot and blood-orange lipstick, is arguing into the phone in fluent Russian.

"Look, we know the climate, but we're really excited about some rare lots this time around." And later, "No, we can't put aside a piece just for you. An auction is open to everybody."

The girl is almost six feet tall, with a booming voice that commands the room. She turned out to possess the right temperament for working with clients like this, clients who believe auction company policies are drawn up for everyone but them. Who are always angling for a shortcut, a loophole. *What is the first rule of working with the special wealthy Russian client?* I grilled her during the interview. Regan, unblinking: *We never ask them how they made their money.* What is the second rule? *You never know who's on the other end of the line.* Hired! Regan gestures for me to pick up the phone, pointing to the bar of skin above her lips. It's our sign for the Big Fish.

He's the very definition of Russian oligarch: Berezovsky, Abramovich, Khodorkovsky, and finally, Medovsky. One of the originals, worth untold billions, Ukrainian-born Jew, the eternal expat in London, owner of a minor rugby team, of five properties around the world including the requisite penthouse at the Time Warner Center, a mansion in Knightsbridge, a villa in Monaco.

"Sasha! Where have you been? It's been dull without you around here." Do I sound hearty enough? Since Carl left, they've all noticed it at work. I'm late in the mornings, I lose the thread of discussion at meetings. These days, I'm riveted by the construction outside my window, the soothing repetition of jackhammering.

"Business, always business, Tan'ka. Counting down until Monaco."

"You're a lucky man, Sasha. I'm vacationing in New Jersey this year."

"That is crime, we will see what we can do about that. I know this is early, but I wanted to make sure you have right phone number for auction. I will be back in London after all, so use British cell."

This is how my clients operate: initial chitchat but then right to business. But this is Alexander Medovsky and I'm not about to lecture him on manners. It's because of Sasha's contacts that I finally started a client list to rival Christie's, a list that gave me a chance to compete with Nadia Kudrina. It's because of Sasha that I received my first bonus this year. But until he turns active, until more of his friends sign on, my job might be as fragile as my predecessor's. That woman lasted exactly sixteen months in the job, I'm on month thirty-nine. It's as though I've been working toward this very auction for almost ten years.

I repeat the digits, the London area code and the rest of it, crisply and succinctly. Medovsky is satisfied. He must be anxious for a particular lot. The catalogue not even printed yet but the art world is insular and those within it follow the careful exchange of objects.

"Sash, don't worry. I'll be on the phone personally making sure you're as informed as possible." I try harder for maternal this time. They like that, my clients, the feminine touch, the myth of a warm, female bosom to cushion them. Physically, I fit their ideal of a "real Russian woman," not too tall, demure, slender wrists, voluptuous. "You know how to wear that dress," these clients tell me. If they must work with women, the aura must be pleasant, topiary.

"I know you will, Tanyechka. I have absolute faith. You've earned it."

I consider: ask about the wife or the mistress? By now, I've met both. The former, Lena, is an intimidating powerhouse of spiky, asymmetrical hair with impressively toned biceps, the latter, a reddish-haired waif barely out of gymnasium with tiny lips and practically no eyebrows. In the end, it's always wisest to settle on the wife. "How's Lena? Did she get her boutique up and running? Anything I can afford?"

Medovsky laughs, but in a distracted way that tells me his attention has already clicked to another piece of business. "I doubt it, Tanyush. But you should see store anyway. Right smack on New Bond Street. Gorgeous things. Stop by next time you're in town."

"Absolutely. Give her my love, will you?"

"And you to that Vandershmotter of yours."

"Thanks," I say brightly. "I'll pass it on."

Alexander Medovsky may be one of the reasons I've remained head of the Russian art department rather than one of the many specialists in the womb of the nineteenth-century Impressionist and Modern Art department where I spent thirteen lovely years, floating among the reliable stability of the sun-dappled landscapes and flushed domesticity. My former boss was as placid and vibrant as the paintings, and I bobbed on the surface of his clear expectations, happily checking off one task after the next, writing endless reams of catalogue copy. ("The present lot underscores the artist's talent for depicting the atmospheric qualities of the treacherous sea and man's struggle against nature.")

I was grateful for the job, for the surprising tenderness I felt for the pieces that appeared and disappeared from the office. At times, I could feel the artist's beating soul, could transpose myself into his (because it was almost always a "his") century. Through his brushstrokes, through his eye on the world, I sensed his celebration or ambivalence of industrialization, a fear of nature destroyed, naïve wonder of foreign cultures, of

Tahiti, or Japan. I thought I would never get any further, that my immigrant success story would end right there, as a respected, invisible member of a large team.

But then one morning, the pavement still steaming on the soles of my shoes, armpits damp with subway exertion, jittery Marjorie Carlyle called me upstairs into her office, unveiled something masquerading as a Larionov, handed me an ultraviolet light, and said, "Who's this anyway? And is this fake or not? Now that Kudrina quit with zero notice, you're the only Russian we've got." I didn't miss a beat: "This piece is in Larionov's Rayonist style, dated 1905. Which is impossible since Larionov created Rayonism in 1913." Marjorie said, "Fine. How do you feel about working with your people?"

And what could I say? The fierce oligarch's daughter was finally gone. And no one else at Worthington's knew Russian art like I did. On the other side of the world lay a vast country in turmoil and, like it or not, it was the country of my birth, the country that shaped my first seven years. And I felt it needed me to save its art in this volatile time, to return it to the place it once belonged before it was sold off for tractors by Bolsheviks and Stalin. I wanted to return it to those who would love and appreciate it. Who understood it with their very souls, the way I did. It was to be my destiny. It also crossed my mind that, as head of a department at Worthington's, I would be deserving of Carl—if not his social equal, then at least possessing the proper veneer of respectability.

I realize Medovsky hasn't noticed my flagging attention. He's describing the staircase in his wife's boutique, the woes of eternal renovations, the perils of shipping marble from Florence to London.

"Mm-hm," I hum as if deeply engrossed. What I didn't expect when taking the job were the people with whom I'd now be dealing, more concerned with their homes, their lavish lifestyles, with outdoing their friends than saving Russian art. And now I was intertwined with these men, my future tied to theirs.

"Sasha, I never asked. Is there a particular lot you've got your eye on?"

"The Order of Saint Catherine, of course."

"How did you find out? We only just got it in."

"Natasha at Hermitage told me. You know I have to ask. No chance is fake or didn't belong to the queen?"

I pause, in a delicate situation. These Russians gossip; to inject any doubt would kill the sale. Yes, the documentation hasn't yet been verified by the historian, but we are going forward anyway. In my old professional life, the one that seemed to have ended when Carl left, my conscience would have dictated telling Sasha the truth. But I'm a great believer in signs and portents. What if Catherine the Great is some ghostly yenta, bringing me and my husband back together?

"Tanyush?"

I stall with a sip of water. And it's probably fine, isn't it? Natasha at the Hermitage was very certain.

"I'm here. It's a nice choice. A very special piece. As you know, it was gifted to young Catherine by Empress Elizabeth so the value is really priceless. The provenance is very promising. Sold by the Bolsheviks through China. In 1926, Norman Weisz, an American diamond merchant, bought it at Christie's in London and resold it to Wanamaker's department store, where it was bought by a steel tycoon who gifted it to this famous silent film actress right before he died of a sudden heart attack. No indication he even knew it belonged to Catherine the Great. Now the actress's granddaughter in Chicago got it appraised by the Hermitage and she's selling. Don't you trust us?"

"I trust you. You're the only one in this rotten business to trust. The only one with any integrity. Maybe you can do what you can now to discourage the other bidders, because I'm set on it."

I smile. It's typical for my clients to conflate my integrity with the expectation of bending the rules.

"You know that trust is the most important part of this business. I don't take it lightly, Sash."

My job is to make Medovsky feel comfortable with me and, by extension, the auction house. Not that there's any doubt he will win the auction, a man of bottomless resources, a man who bought three hundred acres in Dartmoor from a dining companion who had no idea he'd be selling off his beloved property by the time dessert arrived. If Medovsky

goes against a few other determined bidders in the auction, I'll get a bonus. I'll be made vice president. In the eyes of those who matter, I'll be
an actual "Somebody."

"You know, Sash, I just thought of something. I can already imagine
the Order at the Hermitage, the plaque reading 'a gift from Alexander
Medovsky.' How wonderful would that be? Have you ever considered do-
nations to institutions?"

"Actually, I intend to gift it to our president."

I try not to let the frown seep into my voice. He must know the Russian president is hardly popular around here. "Really. Well, you know a
museum donation—the museum Catherine actually founded—would
make the same point. Even better, really."

"No, no. This is not joke, Tan'." He sounds annoyed now, a warning
for me to back off. "I have promised him this."

I quickly switch the subject to Medovsky's rugby team, the acquisition of the new scrum half who will be starting the Amlin Challenge
Cup. I have no idea what any of those words actually mean.

"*Ladno,* got to go. *Obnimayu.* Oh, and don't forget to book your tickets to Monaco. May tenth. Get there by sundown."

"What? Monaco? Sash, what are you talking about?"

"Are you or are you not vacationing in New Jersey this year?"

"Yes, but."

"No buts. They tell me New Jersey is paradise on earth, but Monaco
is not too shabby either." He explains the event: a fund-raiser for the Tel
Aviv Museum of Art at his house, friends Oleg and David will be there.
Do I know who they are? They are Very Important Men, and if I want to
know more about them, their names and histories are actually linked on
the Wikipedia page under "Oligarch." "If you want to be a player, Tan,
you have to drink with players. You know this."

I could call Carl and ask him to come with me as a kind of truce. But
Carl disapproved of my clients' lifestyles so I'd been underplaying the
outlandish details of my business trips. This trip might delay, rather than
accelerate, our reunion. *Book tickets NYC–Nice.* I jot down the date and
pass the stickie to Regan.

Regan's voice has amplified. "No, Mr. Meskin, we don't give discounts on art, this is not a sample sale." Then Marjorie's head is framed by the door, a face made even more yellow by the overhead lights. "Off the phone?"

As always, Marjorie's look is disheveled and blocky. Squares of conflicting color in her peach pants and burgundy blouse, cinched at the waist but not complementing her body, an unflattering bird-feathered haircut. *Do you think we're all afraid of her because she looks like she doesn't give a shit in a place like this?* Regan has said, not once. There is something unnerving about a person who makes no effort to appear polished among women who wear pearls and Lilly Pulitzer prints unironically, men who sport speckled bow ties and double-breasted blazers. This, or the position etched onto her door, or her brusque manner, or the fact that she never entirely trusted me, thought me too green for the job while trying to promote twenty-five-year-old Nadia Kudrina.

"What's up?"

"First of all, nice article in the *Financial Times*."

"Did it sound on point?"

"Hey, all publicity is good. It was a little chipper, even for you. But we're glad you did it."

"The reporter mangled a few of my quotes but I thought Worthington's got a nice boost."

"Dean's happy with it. So I heard about the Order. It's been verified, right?"

"Pretty much," I say. Admitting anything less than ironclad about the Order's authenticity might push an object off this auction. And I'm convinced that this auction will be deciding the future of the Russian art department, of my job, maybe even my marriage. When you pull off a major feat in one area of your life, it radiates outward.

"Fabulous." As expected, Marjorie hears what she needs to hear. She rises, pacing, tablet in hand. "This is just the news we needed. No one even knew the thing existed, right?"

"Right. The timing is perfect too because of Russia's renewed interest in the Romanovs."

"Oh, yeah? I didn't hear about that."

I find the article on my tablet, prepared to underscore the Order's importance. "They're inviting all the Romanovs back to Russia actually: 'The return of the descendants of the last Russian tsar to their historic homeland will contribute to the smoothing of political contradictions in the country, remaining from the time of the October Revolution, and will become a symbol of revival of the spiritual power of the peoples of Russia.'"

"Yikes, okay. And I hear Medovsky's going active. You clearly have a way with these people."

What was wrong with Worthington's and the way they always classified me as one of "these people" just because I happen to be Russian? Another way Worthington's pushes me across the border from those who belong, the unspoken demarcation between *us* and *them*. If only they knew that I'm neither *us* nor *them;* unlike Nadia Kudrina at Christie's, I'm no insider among the oligarchs, and unlike Carl, I'll never be truly American. What they don't know is that I exist elsewhere, in a third, unmarked space.

A sudden spray of afternoon sunshine slashes across my eyes. I watch its reflection chime against the glass skin of the skyscraper across the street.

"I hope I've got a knack for this by now, Marjorie. I've been doing this for some time."

Marjorie lowers her voice. "You know how important this auction is. You've probably heard what happened in Decorative Arts."

"Has the entire department been let go?"

"Between you and me? Yes. French furniture, English silver? There's no coming back for it. Not in the near future anyway."

"And us?"

"You know all the action's in Europe. If this auction's lackluster, we might have to consolidate the departments in London."

As quickly as it strikes, the light fades away, the office swabbed in sickly green. On the very day we were sipping prosecco for the Order's discovery, seven people were packing up their offices.

Marjorie returns to her chair, descends into it heavily. "Those people, they're not easy for most of us here to understand and that's why it's important you know we value your ability to build relationships. It certainly helps that they think you're on their side, reuniting them with their national art and all that."

Again, "those people."

"Very kind of you to acknowledge my efforts, Marjorie. Perhaps you can pass word of your thoughts to Dean. I think the U.S. office is very important for this company. This will be the department's biggest yield, not to mention all the revenue we're creating by collecting the seller's commission and not waiving the buyer's premium. I've gotten many phone calls about quite a few of the pieces. And now that you bring it up, I'd love to schedule a meeting to discuss some thoughts. I'm bringing in extraordinary people who are signing with Worthington's because of my relationships . . ."

But Marjorie is fidgeting. She's done with me. "Fine, fine, call Karen and set that up." A hint of anxiety crosses her face. She's likely having a very different conversation with the director of Southeast Asian, whose five major buyers just dropped out. The three Ds. Death, divorce, debt: the blessing or curse of any market.

When Marjorie leaves, I get ready to go for the night. Outside my window the spire of the Empire State Building injects white into the turbid lavender of evening. "Good night, Regan." The next time I glance up at the young woman's screen, Facebook is exchanged for the vividness of Goncharova's *Spanish Dancer,* the painting conservatively estimated at one point nine million.

"Don't forget to friend Mr. Meskin," I call out.

"I won't!" comes the sheepish reply. Caught.

Next to the viewing room is the storage room, and a pull compels me to the knob, to the back wall where the safe is kept. Past a small sculpture by Jacques Lipschitz, a Joseph Cornell etching, and I turn the knob of the safe tucked into the back wall. Next to a sapphire necklace worn by Grace Kelly and the rare 1913 Liberty Head five-cent piece, the Imperial Order of Saint Catherine sits on its velvet tray, its embedded diamonds winking, fresh from its intercontinental voyage. A medal of honor for female friends and relatives of the court. And, of course, awarded to all new Romanov wives. Carl would have loved to see it, to touch its face with his own hands. Why didn't I let him do that?

In the center of the pendant, Saint Catherine sits wrapped in her cape, holding cross and wheel. On the ribbon the embroidered words "For Love and for the Fatherland." I imagine the almost-fifteen-year-old future queen bowing her head as it was wound across her chest. The recent immigrant from Prussia who had no dynastic right to be an empress. Carl's Catherine who became mine too for a while.

Reluctantly, I drape the order back into the bloodred leather box and seal it under a tomb of chamois leather.

In the elevator, I step next to my old boss from Impressionist, as always tucked into a pressed Italian suit, a silk tie. How comforting it had been to watch his manicured hands in meetings, to simply follow orders rather than give them. To be commended, "Nice job on that catalogue, Tanya."

"Going to the event on five?" he says, a shellacked pinkie encircled by a heavy garnet ring pressing the already illuminated button. White teeth, impeccable suit, a man whose cosseted reality is incomprehensible to me.

"I've got my own later this week."

"Well, good luck up there with Eastern Aggression. Call me if I can help."

You'd think that U.S. relations with Russia being what they are, there'd be awkwardness about my position at the company, but luckily, auction houses are apolitical. They take advantage of the market unless there's a possibility of bad press. We had to say no to a charity auction by the president of Uzbekistan because of the country's record of human rights violations, but the only thing that truly changes the strategy of an auction house is if the money dries up. I've tried to use this to my advantage to show that Russia is not a simple, evil nemesis, that there are many important people who are fighting for change, operating for the good of the world.

The doors open and he steps out before I can assure him that I'm a boss now too, and everything's under control. I call after him anyway. "We're actually doing great, thanks."

Before the elevator doors close, I see that another gala is under way. The company still reeling from the recession and the galas give the impression of turning fortunes. But the champagne is cheaper, the band signed for free, its lead singer a nephew of one of the vice presidents. The director of Southeast Asian tries to wave me over. I glimpse blue tulle, crisp white blouses, caterers gliding around the floor with trays, behind them all the jagged lines of a Picasso drawing taking up an entire wall. I'm sure if I got off the elevator, I would find my single colleagues, all young women who ferment in these surroundings, who wait with a glass of white wine until an older male client sidles over, proposes marriage. So many girls here: deboned, pale, waiting for the man to pluck them alongside the art they're selling.

Outside, Third Avenue fades to a blur. The rushing bodies heading down to Grand Central, groups of tight jeans and huddled blacks, masses of suits spilling out of the Lipstick Building, couples slurping oysters in windows, the new generation of New Yorkers with their long, mussed hair and booties and bee-stung mouths. I was one of them once, rushing from gallery to dry cleaners to party to drinks with friends to whatever final place cradled me for the night. Those days of my twenties were vivid as Technicolor, wedging myself into crowded bars, leading an army of girls to subterranean dance parties, stumbling home at dawn. Responsible to no one but myself.

"Hi, honey, just checking in," I say into Carl's voice mail just before heading down into the subway. He'll pick up eventually; I just have to be loving, persistent.

Marriage stops time for lack of markers like this. Marriage, a thing that had once felt so inevitable, so stable, was now turning out to be the biggest mystery of my life.

Catherine

As the grand duke's birthday ceremony drones on, Sophie is staring at the best-looking man she has ever seen. He is wearing hunting insignia and is handsome in the soft, easy way of recent aristocracy, as his hands are rough and callused and his fingernails are studded with dirt. As he passes to the empress the red ribbon on which hangs the Order of Saint Catherine, he winks at Sophie. It gives her strength, this show of commiseration from the empress's favorite.

Sophie and her mother are now "princesses of the blood, my blood," declares the empress, swinging the medallion over Sophie's head. It dangles over her left nub of a breast, clanging against the bone of a non-existent hip. She examines the medal's center, stares at the seated woman portrayed there. The fair-haired saint appears to be watching her, approving. The history of the honor is briefly explained to them: established thirty years ago by Tsar Peter to honor his wife, Catherine, for rescuing kidnapped Cossacks with her own money, the Order is bestowed by the court upon every woman of high rank who either performs extraordinary acts for the love of her country or marries into the royal family. Surely the German princesses are familiar with the martyr Saint Catherine of Alexandria, a woman who dared to challenge a pagan emperor in order to save doomed Christian souls?

"Of course," her mother chimes in even though the question is directed toward Sophie.

In the middle of the explanation, the empress loses her footing, and Sophie notices that this Razumovsky, as she hears him called, rushes to steady her. His hands, his fingernails rimmed by those soiled moons, fall at the small of her back. The empress leans into him, a brief suture of skin, and a vague frisson of yearning courses through Sophie.

In the far corner of the palace hall, Sophie sees her future husband whispering with one of her ladies-in-waiting, a series of unpleasant laughs ringing through the hall. This merriment is to be expected of a man the day he turns sixteen, she supposes. And he does look more attractive in the light of day, the snowy paleness not as noticeable, his uniform lending him an appearance of height. She wonders if she will lean into him in that same catlike way, and if such an insubstantial frame contains enough strength to bolster her. Next to Razumovsky, the empress looks relaxed and happy. She whispers something in his ear.

And the ceremony welcoming her into the Russian court is over. Sophie waits for further instructions. "Come," or "Follow me," Razumovsky finally gestures to her. She is bidden to follow the procession toward the bells of a nearby church past the frozen corpses of trees, the famished earth, the faceless row of soldiers. As they trample, Sophie notices the empress's brown silk hoop skirt is pressed against his thigh and wonders if this is marriage, two bodies constantly intersecting.

The church is inundated with smoke. Swirls of incense make it hard to look around properly, but when the fog dissipates, she finds the place beautiful. So much more ornate than what she is used to, so different from the austere rigidity of the churches she has known. Entire panels of icons lined behind the nave, the blinding gold of the candle stands. She finds the music pulsing with emotion, the incantations of the priest might as well be poetry. In the sanctuary, the empress opens her mouth to accept the Sacred Gifts, and Sophie can envision herself in the same place, the spoon plunging inside her own mouth, the Mother and Child watching her serenely from golden frames. The image is so natural, so inevitable, it unnerves her. Then she overhears her mother's lady-in-waiting whispering in German: "I expect the princess will take no issue with conversion. I understand Lutherans do not hold to the apostolic succession, isn't that so?"

Silence, please, she wills her mother. She is about to step in, protest that she sees no great conflict between the faiths, not that it is this woman's business to inquire. The proper retaliation is forming in her mind, taking shape in her mouth. But for once, her mother is too busy craning her neck at the ceremony.

"How did you enjoy the service?" Peter says, when their paths conjoin in the church garden. She is aware of his attention solely on her now, a fresh interest to his gaze. In the gauze of the afternoon, the yellow smudge on his cheek is more evident as a bruise and, underneath it, she notices tiny red bumps beading from chin to ear. She wants to share with him the extent of her rapture, show him the place inside her where this country's beauty has already nestled. Her fingers are making their way there, up her rib cage to the place her heart beats the loudest.

"Actually . . ."

He leans in. "Barbaric, is it not? Lutheranism is so much more civilized, orderly. Do you not find it to be the case? Even so, back in my beloved Kiel, they had to drag me to church by my heels."

Her fingers flutter down and away. *Idiot,* she thinks, then allows the word to dissipate. Instead, she looks down at the dangling face of Saint Catherine. She can feel the resolve of this saint coursing from her rib cage all the way to the top of her head.

"There she is. Let me make the proper introductions." The empress is steering her away from Peter and toward a group of older women. And Sophie is swallowed by them: does the young *princesse* have a talent for music? Does she play faro? Because that is how they pass time between Lenten vigil services until the amusements are allowed to begin again.

"I am utterly devoted to faro. Back home, I am called the 'philosopher of faro,'" she says. And they are all laughing and nodding and agreeing, so she must be charming them with her excellent French. Was it not the king of Prussia himself who turned to her at dinner to say that her intelligence and wit were surprising in one so young? It is then it occurs to her: she will earn her Order of Saint Catherine. For now it was gifted to her for marrying Peter, but she *will* perform extraordinary acts for this country. The comet told her so.

Yes, she answers them now. She is passionate about dogs and horses. Do they ride? She finds it simple to say silly things expected of her, to hide the scope of her true intentions. *You were meant for greater,* George said to her. In fact, it is almost too easy.

Tanya

The Order of Saint Catherine is enshrined in a glass box in the center of the room, the red moiré sash rippling around the pendant on its bed of black velvet. It radiates brighter than any of the surrounding pieces. I'm aware of this preternatural glow even as I'm rushing around this auction preview greeting the arrivals at the elevator bank.

The Worthington's fifth-floor gallery is dappled by silk-covered knees and shiny elbows, chandelier earrings, matte lips. The sparkle of precious stones. Once in a while, I hear someone trying to pronounce the consonants of a Ukrainian artist and giving up. Guests are holding effervescent wines and our catalogues, eyes scanning the centerpiece, then turning to the sculptures and the landscapes on the wall.

The preview is my favorite part of the season, when I can catch my breath and survey the art I've gathered, arduously, piece by piece, from far-flung corners of the world, arrayed before me in all its breathtaking glory. It makes my heart constrict for Russia, for the brilliant minds that have lived and been destroyed by it, for all that suppressed risk and innovation, the lines, the colors, the earthly and the sublime. Each year, I feel Russia slipping away, growing more dangerous and foreign. Once, as a Russian, I was the enemy in this country too.

Interns are dispersing printed catalogues to newcomers, iPads displaying the downloaded catalogue are tacked to walls. The preview is important because it allows buyers a firsthand glimpse of the art in person. The art is hung as though in a museum, whetting buyer appetites and attracting the kind of press we need for a decent turnout. And our job is to parse the serious buyers from the party hoppers, to entice the uncertain into bidding at the actual auction. Marjorie, clueless to guest hierarchies, is wasting her time on celebrities and nonbuyers from the Upper East Side who come to these parties to be photographed in structured dresses and coral lipsticks, while Regan is smartly occupying the art bloggers from Art World Salon, passionate art-historians-in-training who actually appreciate the significance of the show.

My parents arrive and are hovering next to the Archipenko bronze at the entrance, pretending to scrutinize its patina. They look uncomfortable here among the coiffed, the self-assured, the multigenerational New Yorker buyers. An Archipenko bronze is as foreign to them as penthouse apartments overlooking Central Park, but aware of their role as my parents, they move stiffly, with studied admiration, among the art. I'm relieved that my father's not wearing his tracksuit, my mother having forced him into a short-sleeved shirt. I hug them, inhale my mother's perfume. She is wearing all black, as if the very color will protect her from the intimidating crowd.

She feigns confidence around the sculpture's amorphous body. "Nice piece."

"Isn't it amazing?"

"This one I like," she admits. She once asked me regarding a Rothko, *Can you explain to me why this is art?*

"But I want to show you something really special." I lead them to the glass case, to the Order of Saint Catherine. "This is what I told you about at dinner."

How lovely it looks preening in the center of the room, her tiny oval alone in all that space, the diamond-encrusted cross, the staunchly seated woman surrounded by symbols of faith and martyrdom.

"That *barokhlo* a queen wears? It's even shabbier in person," my mother says, squinting into the glass.

"It's not so bad," my father says. "It's old, that's for sure."

"You're kidding right, Yash? I saw something very much like this at Century Twenty One in the jewelry section."

I try not to take offense. My mother is pessimistic in the way she sees both herself and the world. Good things happen by accident and bad events come about due to personal shortcomings. She's a classic Russian Jew. Which is a shame because my mother is beautiful, the luxuriant hair she crops too short, cobalt eyes never handed to me, a sorrowful Modigliani face. I think my mother is more beautiful than Isabella Rossellini, who is now in front of the Goncharova laughing with Jeremiah Gruber and his wife in a voluminous shawl draped over a pair of complicated dungarees.

"Whoever buys this ugly thing is idiot," my mother continues. "Do these rich people really think this belonged to that queen? The Hermitage probably hired someone last year to forge this."

"Shh, Ma, please keep your voice down. It's not fake."

"How much you want to bet that Hermitage person was paid off to say that?"

As usual, my mother injects the proper amount of fear into me. I've been trying not to think about that possibility, but how could you not with the world I'm navigating? If it's discovered to be fake, my reputation might be ruined, not to mention that Medovsky's wrath, like so many of my clients, carries in it real mortal dangers.

I swallow and repeat, "It's not fake. Why don't I get you drinks. Champagne?"

A man standing behind us moves closer to the sheet of glass so his face recedes and refracts between the panels. "Such an incredible, incredible piece.

"'The Order was gifted during the Imperial era to what Peter the Great originally referred to as extraordinary persons of the feminine sex.'" He's quoting the words of my catalogue copy in a Russian accent and, indeed, the tome rests in his hand, one finger thrust deep into its spine. My mother flickers to the man's bare ring finger, then back to his face, and I realize that all my peppy evasions—Carl's swamped in midterms, he's on major deadline—have not been entirely convincing.

The man is astoundingly tall and tan and attractive, three uncharacteristic traits for your standard Russian male. "I see you estimate it at seven million."

I feel a faint sensation of recognition. Have I worked with him before? Have I seen him around the galleries? "Depending on interest, it may go for a lot more. One never knows at auction."

"I can imagine. Still, it is a Russian treasure, isn't it?" His finger, ringless, dappled with curly, black hairs, leaves prints on the glass.

"You know then that it belonged to Catherine the Great."

"Of course, that is precisely what interests me. Nostalgia for the Romanovs has never been my thing, but Catherine was different, wasn't she? She was a very special kind of monarch. A special kind of woman." My parents, having long ago lost interest in the conversation, move to the Grigoriev, a risky gouache and watercolor that will probably never make estimate when oligarchs prefer oils.

I switch to Russian. "Will you be bidding?"

"Posmotrim." We'll see. He exudes a Mediterranean ease, his skin tanned, his body lanky, deceptively athletic, that of a basketball player. So different from the delicate sensitivity of my Carl, but then they all are, hailing from a land where men are men, women are women, everyone slotted in their proper place. Once I resented that old-world patriarchal division of roles but a few years of marriage to Carl have made me rethink its shortcomings from time to time.

So this particular man is a somebody then. For a minute, I allow myself to hope that this one's here to repatriate Russia's art, to do more with it than embellish his own power. "Wonderful. Why don't we take down your information so you're in our system."

"I would rather it be over lunch. Four Seasons?"

"Monday?"

"Perfect. I fly back Monday night. I don't suppose you can bring the Order with you? I would like to examine it."

"You're welcome to, but here in our offices. The consignor's clause states it cannot leave the premises without prior consignor agreement."

"I thought in my case, you might make an exception. But by all means, vet away."

Yet another loopholer who thinks himself an exception. Still, is he flirting? They do that, my clients, their arms sinewing around my waist at these functions, complimenting me on my curvaceous figure, volunteering their hotel rooms after lunches, offering to fly me to their homes in the south of France. At thirty-two, I know I'm way too old for them, their mistresses twenty, twenty-three tops, but they insist they're enamored with my exoticism. The Russian who is not quite Russian. The Jew who left the Motherland, who can spot a fake in seconds.

"I'm afraid we cannot make exceptions."

"Until Monday then." He places his untouched glass on a tray and disappears inside one of the elevators.

"Nice looking." My mother sidles over, pretending what she just said was a disinterested observation, pretending she was not making an allusion to Carl's mysterious six-week absence. But now her attention is caught by a man crowned by a shock of white hair striding across the gallery with long confident steps. "Is that Steve Martin?"

And, in fact, it is Steve Martin, and the fact of it is hard for me to believe sometimes. The Manhattan borough president, Liv Tyler, Isabella Rossellini, Naomi Campbell, Jerry Saltz, all at my party. When I started in the industry, I was a mere witness to all this, a mousy drink-fetcher, a coat-gatherer, a flight-booker. Shyly standing by the wall with a carafe of water and a stack of catalogues, sitting at the RSVP table and marking off names, I dreamed of becoming what I am right now. But when did I ever enjoy the process of becoming? When would I finally be satisfied with what I've achieved? At each juncture, there was always more to want. More ways to be the most competent person in the room.

Near the bar, I notice that wine has spilled onto a pristine white coat. A squeal rings out across the room, a call for me to contain the confusion, to treat the stain with seltzer and a stack of napkins. I'm needed everywhere at once—a collapsed installation, another new client wants to register, the last bottle of red gone, Isabella Rossellini wants to introduce me to a potential client—and I forget my parents' champagne in the frantic mill of the party's conclusion.

"Tanya," Liv Tyler's circle greets me when I manage to inject myself among them. "Your dress is gorgeous. So unusual. Did you get it in Moscow?"

"I did, yes."

"I have to get out there soon."

When I glance back at my mother, she and my father are huddled on a trio of folding chairs that belong to catering. They probably wish they were home in New Jersey, among friends, in comfortable clothes, and for some reason the realization carries with it a sting. Once, I imagined my professional successes would bring them the deepest delight, but at some point I realized I've gone too far, achieved too much, striven to become too entrenched, American. I needed to take steps to curb all that ambition. Because in overreaching their expectations I've turned myself separate from them, foreign.

The party over, tables are wheeled out, and the cleaning crew is collecting trays of lipsticked glasses and balled-up napkins. The colleagues who helped take the heavier pieces off the wall are gone.

"You sure it's okay if I get out of here?" Regan asks, already shrugged into a canary-yellow vintage coat. "My girlfriend's doing that open mic thing with Eugene Mirman at Union Hall. It'll take me at least an hour."

"Go, of course, go."

One by one, the lights on the floor are extinguished. I collapse into one of the chairs being stacked by Special Events. Night shrouds the building.

Across the street, an office floor is still illuminated, lone workers animated by screens. "Would you just look at those corporate drones." Carl used to point to them when he picked me up for dinner. "What a waste of a life."

"Maybe you can afford to think that," I said, hurt. Wasn't he implying I was one of those drones?

I unlock the glass cabinet where the Order is draped. What was it the mystery man said? *I don't suppose you can bring the Order with you?* The saint gazes at me with the same unflappable expression, the skies in the background an unperturbed blue: For Love and for the Fatherland. Checking that the gallery is truly empty, I slide the order over my head. It is thick, hefty, not as light on the body as I expected. Just in case, I scan the room for witnesses.

I've not intentionally stolen a thing in twenty-two years.

Even now, I don't consider what I once used to do regularly as stealing—it was a child's logic, a kind of immigrant magical thinking. I was just ten years old, just a few years in America, and allowed to roam alone on the streets of Rego Park. At first, my parents hired a Polish babysitter to pick me up from the bus stop and feed me dinner, but after a few months, Agnieszka started skipping hours and days, and it was agreed that I was old enough to care for myself. My parents, distracted by the need to make money, to learn the intricacies of a new language, sprung me free among thrift stores, worn-down supermarkets, Korean delis, Russian hardware stores, the busy spokes of numbered streets that intersected Queens Boulevard. The extraordinary circumstances of immigration meant I was kind of an adult now, my mother explained when Agnieszka disappeared from our lives. She held my gaze so I understood. *In Russia, girls younger than you are responsible for their brothers and sisters.*

It was frightening at first, this sped-up graduation to adulthood, but what was the point of being a child when yeshiva did its best to exclude me, to separate me from the American Jews and the Israeli Jews, when there were no friends with whom to pass the long after-school hours that bled into evening. There was nothing to do but make peace with loneliness, make the best of it.

Daily life was just me and the city. Plunging into the music of honking cars, the coarse Russian language tossed about on the streets, the gangs of kids prowling Queens Boulevard, the thrum of subway underfoot. I felt the city whispering in my ear. *You're special.* The world as through tinted glass, dim and contorted, the neon of bars and movie theaters, stores hawking the silliest, expendable things like greeting cards and coffee, sequined bandannas and fingerless gloves. Wandering through a cacophony of languages that made no sense at all.

I dipped in and out of local bodegas, appraised their aisles. In Moscow, there was so little to buy, to want, and here, it seemed as though desires were so much greater than one's needs that there was a persistent ache in the heart. The impulse to take came on suddenly, but naturally. It would be up to me to care for my mother and father and ailing grandfather. At yeshiva, the rabbi droned on about the imminent arrival of the Messiah, and the Hebrew teachers passed me without even a glance at my essays on the *mitzvot* of the Torah, the foundations for Talmudic life or how to *kasher* a chicken. At home, my parents counted the dollars between them, ordered ribs from the Chinese takeout place for dinner, and stayed up all night arguing like they've never done before or since. My grandfather's medical bills, applications for services they were not sure existed. My Jewish moral life and real life were split in two.

I began with candy bars, then rolls of bread, then bags of soup noodles. And those items were easy to cart away, what with my angelic features, hair parted in the middle, enormous bows tethering my ponytails, neat flared corduroys. I never shoved things surreptitiously in my bag, but brought them out of the store in broad daylight, daring someone to stop me. *Look,* I wanted to tell my parents, *I can take care of us all.* But instead, unable to admit what I did, I ate the food in private, quickly, with trembling fingers, stuffing my mouth with bread and stale chocolate and unripe pears. Or I would feed it to a grandfather whose head lolled, whose eyes glassed over, and who called the bread "cotton, nothing more," and spat it all out.

One day, I targeted a store called Ninety Nine Cent Things. It was smaller than the faceless superstores I preferred, a cluttered hodgepodge of plastic items piled high in metal baskets with no particular order or organization. The inventory seemed to be stocked by a kid barely older than me, his cherrywood complexion and rapid speech on the rotary phone pinned him as hailing from somewhere in the Georgian Republic. I stalked the aisles, calculating, picturing the missing provisions of our bathroom cubby, soap or shampoo. "How thoughtful," my mother would say when I present the soap, two no-brand white rectangles stuffed into the pockets of my jacket.

Outside the sun was blinding for April, my eyes adjusting to the dizzying sear of it. There was the satisfying bulge of the soap in my back pocket, and then if I rushed home, I would catch the end of *He-Man and the Masters of the Universe* ("I'm Adam, Prince of Eternia, defender of the secrets of Castle Grayskull"). But the kid's face materialized before me, soft, caramel eyes on mine, his spiraling eyelashes, his hair the flat color of black ink.

"Young girl, wait," he was saying, "*devushka*. Stop." Why was he calling me young, when I was practically an adult? Couldn't he see I was special, older?

He held out his hand. We both stared into that palm, faint lines dividing it into three smooth sections. Then I looked up at the moon-shaped scar above his lip. I could see a different expression on my father's face now, one of shock and disappointment in me. *We are educated people, we don't do these things.*

Reluctantly, staring at the laces of my sneakers, I placed in his palm the bar of soap. How absurd it looked in daylight, a cheap carton, the glue of one flap coming undone. A diminishment returned to me, the feeling of my insignificance. At school, there was daily talk of punishment and victimhood, of God's disappointment and Jews' abandonment of God.

"Are you going to get me into trouble?" I asked dully.

On his face was forgiveness. He lifted a finger to his lips and just said, "Shh. Between us," and he left one of the bars in my palm, pleated my fingers over it, one at a time.

How could I possibly admit this version of me to Carl? He who loved me as untarnished, buoyant, moral? Corporate drones, he'd said; to him, it was an insult.

The last of the cleaning crew disappear at the elevator banks. I slowly take off the Order. Before I return it to its tray in the safe, I flip the medal to its back and read the inscription one more time: "Aequant Munia Comparis." *By her works she is to her husband compared.*

Tanya

2005–2010

Can you even imagine an immigrant girl who finds herself in a gilded auction house, a junior cataloguer trainee in a palace of glass and white walls, adorned by somber rugs and saucy milkmaids framed in Baroque gold? Just imagine what it's like to daily enter a shrine to beauty that gleams with two sides: the spotless external veneer and the hidden heart of it.

From my first day of work, from my very first interview with human resources, it is made clear that I am a visitor, a tourist, an outsider. This is obvious from my very appearance, the poignant effort I put into its composition while insiders wear their expensive clothes nonchalantly like second skin. I am asked where my people are from, but I know fully well that "my people" are the wrong kind of people, and in any case, any affiliation with "my people" grows more tenuous with each passing year.

I toil away at my trainee position, but am unable to scratch past the impervious façade: the doorman who directs me through the revolving doors, the greeter in his gray suit and tortoiseshell glasses, the security guard who scrutinizes me head to toe as I slip inside the lobby like a thief. In the elevator, I wait alongside women in flared skirts with matte, unblemished skin, a mysterious group of women flitting in and out of the office whose titles are "special events coordinators," who spearhead "private event groups": socialites whose sole job is to publicize Worthington's events to their Hamptons and Greenwich and Aspen set, a milieu I can only conjure in my mind as wonderlands of outdoor decadence, a string of established connections linked by name and university and pasts already lived and concluded. And above all, the mysterious proliferation of Hermès scarves: casually flung about shoulders, attached to coats, draped on the backs of swivel chairs. Imagine a Russian Jewish girl from the scruffy immigrant shtetl of Queens, who now lives in Ramsdale, New Jersey, with her massage therapist parents, arriving every day to a temple where no one speaks of money but simply exhales it.

Through a series of internships and interventions by Slavophile professors, I'm lucky enough to be hired in the Nineteenth Century Impressionist and Modern Art department, the bastion of respect. Who can argue with the perfection of water lilies and ballet dancers, the sun dappling on flexing swimmers, mothers toweling off rosy, bathed infants? My parents are thrilled: all dutiful Russians, cultured Russians, know their Degas and Monet and Mary Cassatt. And I am breathless with the desire to work among such beauty, the art that I idolized on trips to museums every weekend, the landscapes I admired on overhead slides in the courses of my art history major. I naïvely imagine placing the art where it will be most appreciated, where it will give its viewers joy.

But if my parents ask what my work actually entails, I have to admit that I see few Monets and Cassatts. I admit that my interaction with art is not allowed to be worshipful but monetary, tuned in to the needs of the market, the company shareholders, and the fickle client. Mostly, I have to invent titles for paintings with no titles, titles that will fill buyers with a fuzzy sensation of yearning and transport them to bucolic landscapes and cozy domestic scenes. The mother sponging that baby in a tub could be named *Bath Time with Mother and Child,* a couple strolling down a wooded lane, *Lovers in the Forest,* a vague blur of hyacinths next to a broken loaf of bread: *Rustic Supper, with Flowers.* I long to sit with a few of the paintings, to examine the artists' intentions, their strokes of genius, but there is no time for that. I measure canvases, pore over catalogues raisonnés and type condition reports until late into the night, until the last train to New Jersey. And still the inner world of Worthington's remains inaccessible to me.

Lonely, I try to befriend my colleagues, fresh out of art history M.A.s from Williams and Columbia and auction house certification programs. I think they may share my awe for the objects in my care. They are friendly, but eye me through the gauze of their separate lives. They sport American settler names like Martha and Edith and are pert and blond, hair falling in long, expensive layers. From time to time, they include me in drinks gatherings after work, midtown wine bars and Upper East Side Irish pubs, and they seem fascinated by my tales of arriving in New York with four suitcases and no English, my entire family crammed for a year into a cousin's living room on Avenue I in Brooklyn. But eventually, they lose interest in my incomprehensible past and swap stories about the mutual acquaintances of their cosseted lives, they reminisce about boarding schools in Connecticut and New Hampshire, about escapades at farms and house parties where parents disappear for months and horses wait for them in stables.

"Oh, sorry, Tanya." They remember me, that pathetic smile on my face, unable to share my own memories of drug-fueled parties on inherited estates or drunken hijinks at equestrian camp. I dare not admit that I received my education at Forest Hills High School and Rutgers College and, until I moved to New Jersey, worked evenings slicing salami at Monya's on 108th Street, cutting at an angle, into white globules of fat. I feel depressed, as if I might as well quit.

Then one day, Edith is standing over my desk with a tall, elegant-looking guy with expressive shaggy eyebrows, his overgrown blond hair threaded with red. It is his face that arrests me because it may as well have emerged from one of my untitled paintings: hazel eyes with a smoky clarity of quartz, a dash of bangs, the hint of sideburn. He may as well be the protagonist of my prep-school fantasies, the ones culled from old 1980s movies I watched with such fascination as a teen— sensitive boys with logos of eagles and mysterious Latin phrases sewn onto their blazers, clean, scrubbed boys out of movies like *Class* and *School Ties* and *Dead Poets Society*, who were full of passion and rebellion but were cruelly held back by rich and distant parents, tucked away in cavernous Westchester mansions.

"You're going to love how she names paintings. It's like a talent," Edith says, not bothering to introduce me, as if my purpose in her life is one of performance.

"Really," he says. He runs slender fingers through his bangs, as if unconsciously, but the hair makes a beeline for its original position. To my surprise, he doesn't exude arrogance or entitlement, but a guileless curiosity. He's encouraging me with a smile, and I try to focus on the painting placed on the floor beside me. In it, a woman is haggling with a blind merchant at a Turkish bazaar, while a group of men watch in amazement.

"What should we call it?" he says, an interesting use of pronoun. His clothes display the confidence of that fetishized privilege of my imagination—a rumpled, expensive-looking button-down with real cuff links, the shade of pink only investment bankers and members of his class can wear with any confidence, pressed khakis, black Docksiders. But one of the cuff links is missing, the shirt somewhat messily tucked inside his waistband.

In my attempt to return to reality—because those prep-school boys may as well be phoenixes or firebirds for all their foreignness—I scan the image. "*Haggling with Blind Man at Turkish Bazaar*?"

"Not so sexy, don't you think?"

"*Woman Does What Men Cannot*?"

"Don't forget the buyer is male."

"*Hand Over That Goddamn Rug*?"

"Something soothing. Can you see your Nigel with that stamp of a gavel, announcing, 'And now on the floor, Lot Four thousand forty-four, *Hand Over That Goddamn Rug*'?"

I laugh at his mock British accent, which is actually pretty decent. "How about we try for simple. *At the Bazaar*?"

"Perfect."

Edith watches the back-and-forth with bemusement, the iconic "Rachel" shag I envied feathery and effortless and perfectly, expensively executed. She whisks away the painting, along with the boy, and I assume I've seen the last of him. But at the end of the day, he's leaning over my ledge, cocking his aquiline nose in profile, a trench coat open at his waist. "So what would you name me?"

My body is humming, then palpitating. I want to say something cheesy: "*Hottie in Burberry*?" But I'm terrified of his disgust, his condescension. Instead I offer a breezy, "*Portrait of an Ambitious Man*?"

For a minute he looks elsewhere, blinks rapidly, then returns to meet my eyes. "You're good, Kagan. Is that what I'm reading on your tag? Am I saying it correctly?"

My face turns plum, the way it does when the First Settler Girls pronounce my name as though it were an ethnic food, vaguely distasteful.

"Kay-gan, yes."

He says, "Do you happen to hail from the former Union of the Soviets? I don't detect a Boris and Natasha accent but your name certainly implies such a provenance." He is being arch, I understand that much. But there is still a fear of a knife wiped of evidence. *Where are your people from?*

"Why, yes, I do hail from the cold steppes of Russia. Unlike Boris and Natasha, who, I should point out, hailed from Pottsylvania. And may I ask how you are related to our dear Edith Rhinelander-Jones?"

"Hey, listen, I hope you don't think that I'm Othering you or anything. I'm actually a scholar of sorts, of Russian history. It was my major in college and I'm doing a Ph.D. in Slavic Languages and Literatures. That's why I asked if you were Russian. No offense intended."

"A Russian doctorate? Why on earth would you do that?" I ask, lowering my armor of self-protection. I've never considered the beautiful prep-school boy out of *Dead Poets Society* holding anything but T. S. Eliot or Walt Whitman, much less Gogol. As I'm packing up for the night, Carl tells me about his obsession with Russian writers. That when he cracked open his first Dostoevsky, he finally felt understood. That early Tolstoy made him cry because of his deep well of empathy. That Nabokov's wordplay inspired him to try writing in the first place. His green eyes are set unevenly and close together, which lends him a raffishness among all that symmetry.

It turns out his last name is Vandermotter, a name shared with a wing at Beth Israel where my forehead was once sewn back together after a kid tripped me on the stairs of the yeshiva. So he does hail from the unlikely world of the Settler Girls. As the office winds down for the day, I can almost glimpse a hand reaching from the other side of the Worthing-ton's wall, a door creaking open to a place beyond the Irish pubs and wine bars, to a world where people populate Beaux Arts town houses in the East Sixties, where they smoke alongside stuffed moose heads in brown-paneled libraries, where their faces are recognized at the kinds of clubs that serve exorbitantly mediocre Cobb salads. As Carl talks, it is as if America itself is welcoming me inside.

I'm a tense, pessimistic, anxious person with a one-track mind for single-minded success, until my friend Alla brings me to a yoga center in west-ern Massachusetts. It is to be a weekend of yoga and hiking, girl-bonding over kale salads and lentil daal, sneaking out to town for glasses of wine. On the bulletin board hangs a daily schedule and a lecture title catches my eye: "Harnessing the Power of Optimism to Achieve Your Dreams."

The main lecture speaker is a professor of something called positive psychology and he is at the door summoning us inside. Alla laughs it off and heads to yoga class, but I pull up one of the chairs in the back of the auditorium. The man is tall and clearly Jewish, familiar. His eyes are transparent blue. He is armed with PowerPoint presentations packed with research. And in a breathless hour and a half, it is as if he tells me about myself. I create narratives of negativity, I perpetuate my reality because of my pessimistic perceptions of the world. Deep down, I think I'm un-deserving of a happy life. Optimistic people are healthier, happier. They get what they want in life and they enjoy it more. The only thing that holds us back is the narratives we construct about ourselves.

"What's your narrative?" the professor asks each of us, and I flash to the girl in pigtails, a girl who had once excelled in chess and math, lost in Queens. The girl who stole soap and was now being outperformed at work by interns. "Don't you see that the narrative can be reframed, that your life can take a new course?"

As soon as I return to New York, I screw up my courage to call Carl Vandermotter.

I bring Carl to a gathering of the First Settler Girls at O'Grady's, and they size me up anew, as someone by Carl Vandermotter's side, someone they would have to reconsider. Gin and tonics and margaritas appear and disappear, and with Carl as my cultural translator, I feel a greater intimacy with them. For the first time, I speak up. Betsy Rankin admits she found me self-contained and strikingly alien, that she was sometimes intimidated by me. Edith Rhinelander-Jones says all the girls know which painting descriptions are written by me because of how I manage to bring the particular essence of any painting to life in words. The girls are newly kind, the circle opening to accommodate me. The bar turns wavy as the night wears on, their compliments press past my barriers and doubts, my outer-borough immigrant insecurities. Curtains part to reveal verdant landscapes pocked with golf and cricket and polo and other sports foreign to me. I allow myself to drink a bit more than I normally would and relax into the shorthand of their conversations. When they talk about attending a wedding in Newport with a robber baron theme, I reveal that when my own parents married, my maternal grandparents arrived on an overnight train from Ukraine to Moscow with a wedding gift of two dozen freshly killed bloody chickens. At the time, chickens were a huge treat, not a single chicken to be found in Moscow, and the guests feasted on them for an entire day. But a few chickens had to be set aside for bribes. After a secret ceremony officiated by a rabbi, my parents gifted neighbors with chickens so they did not turn them in for holding an illegal religious ceremony. I'm aware of speaking too much, of saying the word "chicken" too often and too loudly, my voice catching with emotion.

"Wow," Betsy Rankin says, tilting a mojito in my direction as if in salute. "That's wild."

The entire night, I'm sure Carl Vandermotter will be leaving with Betsy or Sutton or the one who calls herself Gigi. But then I remind myself to expect more from the world. Reframe the narrative. He will stay with me, I repeat in my head. And he remains by my side, unmoving.

There are long weekend afternoons in museums, in cavernous wine bars with tall candelabras, cold ferry rides to Staten Island and back. I find myself stealing sideways glances to affirm his presence by my side, am aware of being careful around him, of presenting myself in a proper fashion. I'm acting more confident than I feel, not at all the girl who never made the first move with guys she found attractive, who performed dutiful lap dances cellophaned in absurd lace teddies for my first boyfriend because he asked me to and because I liked his frayed IRON MAIDEN T-shirt and his cocky smirk. For Carl's benefit, I edit my life story for its most laudable moments; I imagine that guys like him with lineages to protect, long strings of names affixed to family trees, eighteenth-century jewels passed on from mother to daughter to marrying son, expect a certain deportment in suitable partners. After all, what am I contributing to the relationship? An absence of history, an American invention. My jewelry dates back one generation at most, and even that I wouldn't be caught dead wearing—a thick Soviet ring inscribed with ruby hammer and sickle. A shoebox contains sepia-toned photos of murky, unknown ancestors, dark, stern shtetl-dwellers that populate an erased family tree. But he doesn't seem to mind, peppering me with questions about the singularity of the Russian people. Is it true they distrust you at first but then embrace you for life? Is it true that they're funny and melancholy and can recite Akhmatova by heart? They really are brilliant, passionate people, aren't they? How he wants to go to Russia and find out for himself, he says. I'm charmed by his earnestness (my parents having long ago abandoned Akhmatova for *Real Housewives of New Jersey*), by the inferno in his eyes that would ignite whenever the topic of "Russians" was raised. And he seems amused by the way I elbow to the front of a line for coveted tickets, when I point out discrepancies in service to managers.

"I guess I'm the kind of guy that stands in line like everyone else," he says, hanging back. The way he looks at me. He seems to take in all of me, the crown of my head, my overripe breasts, the curve of my hip. I feel like an animal of wild plumage, flown in for a special viewing. Under his gaze, I burst into bloom.

And he always pops by the office holding catalogues with paintings for me to name.

I point at each one. *The Harem. Barren Tree. Piscine Plunge. Sultan and His Tiger.*

"You're amazing," he says, flashing a hand with rolled-up sleeve, long fingers the color of heavy cream.

"Feel free to elaborate on your argument."

"I'm serious. It all comes so easy for you. You should probably write my thesis. I bet you'd finish it over the weekend."

"I'd need at least three days for a dissertation. Can I have one of the long weekends? Columbus Day? Memorial Day?"

I'm not yet used to acknowledging any talents, but I'm working on it. I am still very much a junior cataloguer trainee, sharing a desk with two half-day summer interns, one of which is Nadia Kudrina.

Carl Vandermotter becomes such an integral part of the group that to celebrate his dissertation defense, the First Settler Girls throw him an after-hours party in the gallery. Bottles of rum and single-malt scotch and mixers are snuck into the office, streamers, noisemakers. The girls stretch party hats over their heads. It's my first time at the auction house at night, and the space takes on a new, friendly valence free of the people I fear. The art glows gold in ornate frames, the pieces showing themselves intimately, free of artifice. All the imposing elements—the long, walnut tables of the greeters, the library of Worthington's catalogues going back seventy-five years—grow friendly, accessible. We drink like party-throwing teenagers with out-of-town parents and mingle underneath paintings of seaside bathers and fields of irises. As the night progresses, stylish friends show up with more drinks and I clap and turn up the music and try to whistle. I grow bold and climb on top of a conference table to rattle off a toast to Carl entirely in Russian. Most of it would have been incomprehensible to a native Russian (before my transfer to the Russian department, my grasp of my own language is still crude, unpracticed). But after my speech is over and I stumble with little grace to the relative safety of the carpet, Carl swings me into a sloppy dip. When I unbend, head pounding from the rushing blood, his lips are pressed against mine.

"Aww," the girls say in a single envious voice.

He's as eager and adventurous as I am to explore this city together, to walk around the Brooklyn everyone is moving to, catch underground performance theater, dance in underground nightclubs, try the street food cropping up all over town. I sense that for him—a native Manhattanite, nose-to-the-grindstone student of Trinity, then Princeton, then Columbia—these activities in the city's hidden craters are as novel and as transgressive as they are for an outer-borough, bridge-and-tunnel former Soviet defector.

I even like his careless way around sex, one day methodical trial and error, the next uninhibited and creative. A scientist microscopically examining tiny strands of DNA or a teenager making exuberant discoveries. Cheerfully, he brings in bondage and then forgets about it, his messenger bag stuffed one day with silk scarves, the next with lingerie, the following with fleece socks and a cotton nightgown. I realize that before Carl, I approached sex like a good student eager for As, and with him I allow myself to be selfish, to take and moan and giggle. Afterward, I love tackling the mechanics of a Saturday together with its individual compartments of pleasure. Coffee, paper, walk to the park, dinner. I start to relax, grow bolder. I buy *Learned Optimism: How to Change Your Mind and Your Life* and a bag of similar books. I underline them, hide them.

Of course, I notice chinks in my boyfriend's perfection, but there are ways to caulk them over until they become invisible. For example: he judges people who make lapses in moral judgment.

"But what if it's your best friend who needs the money? Wouldn't you want him to know about a good opportunity?" I would tease after we watched a news segment about a disgraced insider trader. (In any case, my Russian family never could wrap their minds around this as an actual crime; of course you'd pass along to your loved ones any useful financial information!)

"I don't care. I would never talk to him again. He broke the law."

"You do realize you're dating a Russian, don't you? We're not known for our morality."

"You, my dear, are the grandest of the Russian spirit," he says between kisses, and I absorb them even if I wonder if he's simply naïve, unworldly. I couldn't tell him about the bag of cherries I never paid for at Whole Foods: they never charged me and I said nothing. Or a few bags of cherries after that. Those were forgotten on the cart's lower shelf until after checkout.

"You could use a piece of art here and there. We can probably get you some photographs for under three hundred dollars," I suggest, fingers flat against his white, rented walls.

He brings me one of his mongrel wineglasses, the rare expensive-looking one with his initials bezeled into its side, clears a pile of papers from a wobbly metal chair. We are both mostly naked as we so often are. Covering our bodies seems an act of cruelty to the other person.

"I'd love it if you'd be my decorator," he says, artfully avoiding the subject of money. He's wielding that new-couple voice, one octave too low, suggestive. Stretched on the couch in need of fresh upholstery, an odalisque among student papers feathering his feet. He pats a small, uncluttered space beside him. "And I'd been meaning to get art, but had no idea where to begin. The only paintings my parents buy are these depressing Dutch portraits."

"I'll scout around for you. I just saw a lovely one of early spring buds in the ground."

"Would you? But none of your fakes, please. Originals only."

"You deserve nothing less than authenticity, my dear."

The kisses are intense, spontaneous, indifferent to audience. His arms, so long, as though they could wind around me three times. So what if I prefer settling in the hazy zone of grays while his world shines in impassioned black-and-whites?

"Tanya. Tanyusha. Tanyechka," he breathes late into the night, tracing the contours of my face with those delicate fingers. I wonder if he has read way too much Pushkin in translation, if he has internalized the intensity of Dostoevsky a bit too literally. How can I impose my messy, amoral Russianness on someone so entrenched, so unsullied, someone who chose me against all odds of logic? And there is the charm of that Upper East Side street his apartment overlooked, squares of forgotten New York where even the night's silence emits a genteel quality. And if I crane my neck from the bedroom window, the East River makes itself available to me, flashing mercury in moonlight.

The thing, the book, makes its first verbal appearance at an Italian restaurant in Brooklyn. We're seated at a corner nook, a location deemed
"intimate" by a hostess who led us to the table with an air of spontaneous generosity, as if to say, you will thank me for this when you're married. The place itself seems erected for nights whirling with snow flurries
and brutal wind, when inside is brick and fireplace, candle and dark wood,
low Tudor ceilings. We slide inside, bent over a single menu ("They're
printing more across the street as we speak"). A breathlessness of novelty, of being in a faraway borough, sitting so close to a creature still
more myth than man. Inhaling long tendrils of pappardelle, the second
bottle of red newly opened. His smell so clean, it engages with the spice
of each dish, morphing from lamb ragù to the lemony spice of green
beans. Then there's the symmetrical perfection of his features, his Ralph
Lauren handsomeness enhanced by a cable-knit sweater straight out of
a preppy catalogue, the delicate slenderness of those fingers as he expertly maneuvers wine into glass. He's a man thoroughly at home in his
skin, slowly working on his pasta, pleased with anything I share about
myself. And then, of course, there's the Vandermotter name that hovers
over us, sprinkling pixie dust of fascination.

It's over the final glass, the glass that was two glasses too many, when
I lean over and say, "Tell me more about your work at the foster care
agency. I think that's so incredible that you do that."

"I love it. I'm not a trained social worker or anything. I just help my
mother with administration. She's on the board." A pair of dessert menus
are placed before us, the printing problem resolved. Carl helps the waitress clear the last of the cutlery, wiping the table for crumbs. When she's
gone, he leans closer. "Actually, I've started a novel."

"That's great."

"I didn't want to say anything, but you're Russian, so . . ." He speaks
quickly, that vivacity exploding in his eyes. He doesn't seem to notice
that the restaurant has become bottlenecked with people waiting for our
table. "So get this. No one's written the book focusing on Catherine the
Great, before she was Catherine the Great."

"Is that right?"

"Not a good one anyway. So this young Prussian girl comes to the Russian court, marries this buffoon who can't even get it up for her. And she winds up with the crown. The queen of the entire Russian kingdom with no dynastic right to the throne! Not as regent, not as consort, but as empress and, to top it all off, one of the greatest monarchs in history. A foreigner."

"And?"

He's taken aback. "Doesn't that seem incredible to you?"

"Sure." Except it doesn't, not even remotely. Of course she would wind up with the crown if her husband was a useless *razmaznya*, I think. An immigrant like her with all those ambitions? But my instincts tell me not to say any of that out loud.

The door blows open with a fresh gust of wind and a large group files in. I'm aware of women blowing on their hands, coned in birthday hats, the hostess gesticulating in our direction. The servers are hovering around us, waiting for a decision on dessert so the table can be released.

The last thing I want to explain to Carl is the inner life of the immigrant. By now, I'm sick of mining my tale for narrative curiosity. I'm tired of my "exotic" story. Yes, it was very hard to not speak the language. Yes, for a long time, I had no friends and American kids tormented me for my accent and granny clothing. Yes, I cried myself to sleep most nights, afraid I would never belong here. Yes, my parents cried too because they were afraid they had made a terrible mistake. That a language was already dissolving on their tongues, that they would never lay eyes on their home again. I knew enough to make it easy on them and stuck to zoned schools, close and cheap schools. That I wish I were a Vandermotter instead, a path of privilege spread wide open for me. But what is the point of going into all this in an insanely busy, sexy restaurant on a Friday night, when the main choice is tiramisu or *pot-de-crème*? Our table, the server reminds us, has been promised.

Carl's face is still steaming from the heat off his plate, a perfect Nordic face crafted by angels. "Anyway I've been working on this thing forever. If something comes of it, they might hire me full-time at Ditmas College."

"I'll help with the Russian parts, if you like."

"Wow. I don't want to essentialize and say there's something unique about Russians, but I think you're amazing," he says. He's used that hyperbolic word before—"amazing." It thrills me almost as much as it worries me. Is he seeing me or some heroine out of *Doctor Zhivago,* a fur stole around her shoulders, melancholy blue eyes staring deeply into the expanse of icy steppes? Does it matter? "I could tell from the minute I saw you studiously naming those frankly ugly paintings behind your desk. This girl, I thought, is the opposite of complacent. She glows with fire. I have to tell you, I was pretty drawn to it." Reaching over the corner of the table, his hand is warm on my wrist. It burns a hole in its center. There's that Look I can't define, filled with reverence.

How grateful I am for that Look. How much my wobbly confidence needs the fire of all that admiration. I place a trio of fingers on his forearm. "Hey, you know what? I want to read your book when it's ready. I'll love it. And I can help you with any Russian words."

"Would you? It's kind of getting killed in this workshop I'm taking right now, but the only thing people understand in workshop is short stories. It's a waste to even put it up for workshop." He bends his head to mine in an arc of conspiracy. "But I've got a feeling you'll inspire me. *Moi kotenok.* Am I saying that right?"

The restaurant has more people standing than sitting, waiting their turn. All that waiting makes me feel at the cusp of uncultivated possibility. "Tiramisu and two forks," he tells the waitress. How confident he sounds ordering for us both. A sprinkle of cocoa powder, the moistness of rum, two forks meeting in the center. The last time I was this happy was when I won the third-grade spelling bee and overheard parents whispering that I'd only arrived in the country nine months ago.

When the bill arrives, the tiramisu not reflected on the final tally, Carl makes sure to call the server back and inform her that she forgot to charge for the dessert.

"Your man is an honest one," the woman says, and brings us a decadent complimentary bread pudding even though it will enrage the hostess and all those hungry people, and extend our stay here together, indefinitely. *Your man.*

Eventually, the day arrives when he says, "Are you ready to meet the Vandermotters?"

It's an invitation for which I've spent years at Worthington's preparing. I know only this much: his mother likes to be called Cece, she will expect a thank-you card after the dinner, and I'm to eat as much as possible before heading over because there will probably be little food on offer.

"Ready," I say, instructions memorized. I can't possibly eat, my stomach flip-flopping.

The weekend before, I spend an entire paycheck shopping for the occasion. Entering Bergdorf's department store is not unlike entering Worthington's, where the salespeople instantly appraise your worthiness of their solicitude. A store where dresses hang far apart from their neighbors in neat rows, sleeves queued up like soldiers. So different than the usual places I shop—the Russian-preferred discounted jumble of Loehmann's, the bins of sample sales and clearance racks of Century 21. At Bergdorf's, even the sale signs, when they crop up, are so discreet and tiny, they almost dare you to scrutinize them.

In a dressing room the size of my bedroom, I tremble into dresses of pink floral patterns and absurdly expensive blue and white cotton twill, and hold my breath at the exorbitant price tags.

"What is the return policy?" I ask the saleswoman. She assures me it is sixty days with receipt so I buy the Chanel blazer and bag and conceal the sales tag in one of the pockets.

As the day draws closer, I rifle through my mother's drawers for jewelry that looks most like pearls, trying out two of Bergen County's fanciest salons for elaborate up-dos and leaving looking less like Ingrid Bergman and more like Emily Dickinson. I research New Jersey's best dessert and flowers and wine as if my Russian manners would translate in this sphere, as if the Russian emphasis on culture would register as familiar to them.

"Wow." Carl appraises me when I'm standing at his door in an approximation of "old money" attire. I look like a headmistress of some decrepit British institution.

When I left the house earlier, my mother stared at me in bewilderment. "What did they do to your hair and why in the world did you buy that overpriced housecoat?"

Carl says, "You didn't have to get so fancy. I told you they're pretty casual. You should have just worn what you always wear."

"Are you saying I look hot?"

"You always look hot, baby." He tries to nuzzle near my chin before withdrawing. "But I'm afraid to touch you. You're like a doll in a store or something and you smell like fabric softener."

"That's Chanel No. 5, hon."

"So you like smelling like laundry?"

"I figured that's what your mother wears."

"First of all, she hates perfume, and she'd never buy any Chanel except at consignment," he says, enfolding me in his arms. I am amazed that he truly doesn't understand the source of my anxiety, that he's probably never felt its equivalent. "Second of all, you're trying way too hard. You should be yourself."

Be myself? What does it even mean to be "yourself"? Isn't life a series of situational personas? I'm internally working the freshly acquired tenets of optimism (*an outcome of a single situation does not dictate who I am and what I am capable of becoming*) but in reality, I'm too nervous to come into contact with anything, to rumple or stain. A rapid agitation worms inside my belly. Carl dresses in his usual pleated pants and rolled-up navy button-down shirt. His process is the opposite of mine, an impression of indifference when the result is unstudied perfection. He runs a lazy brush through his hair, then pours himself a glass of water, squeezes a lemon down its side. He kisses me at the corner of my mouth.

"Aren't we late?" I ask, by now wanting the whole thing over. I'm holding a box inside which, I'm convinced, is a squashed vanilla butter cream cake.

He insists we take the subway so he can better point out the signposts of his childhood. I don't want to admit that my new shoes are digging into my heels with each step; I can feel two slicing lines across the back of each foot. With each gingerly step, I feel burdened by the stiff layers, the jewelry choking my neck.

Down into the station, the heat of the Chanel blazer suffocating, I am weighed down by the effort of staying erect in a crowded train, the fabric of the dress stiff and unyielding. I catch a glimpse of my reflection in the train's window and can see how he compared me to a doll, all square and painted, the quilted handbag drooping like a piece of excess skin, the clownish pink lipstick.

Out of the subway, evening is settling. We walk away from the frenzied rush of Lexington toward the stillness of Park, where the pain of my feet has faded into a pleasant dullness. For me, the East Sixties may as well be an alien landscape. We turn on Madison, where boutiques are locking away jewelry for the night, expensive children's clothing stores are displaying a single style of cashmere, past delicate pyramids of chocolate squares and watches with flat, empty faces. We encounter the kind of people who live here and work at Worthington's, dining outdoors even though the air still carries the chill of spring, ponytailed mothers in sailor stripes pushing prams. Little girls eating sundaes at glass counters and Bendel's bags swinging between legs. Each block as manicured as my colleagues at work. Pampered in all this understated grace and beauty, this land of expensive boater shirts and anorexic mixed greens. I feel a burst of envy that Carl got to grow up here, taking all this for granted. Once my father got an especially large massage tip and in a burst of triumph and a hunger that could not be sated, my parents and I ordered more dishes from the local Chinese place than we could possibly eat, the remains of ribs like a cemetery of bones piling high on our plates.

In the lobby, past the greetings of the suited doorman, I try to forge some kind of confidence. But my heels are killing me and the string of the cake box is digging into my skin.

"Don't worry so much," he says. "It's no big deal. Trust me." He's patting his pockets for something, but his hands emerge empty.

I stall him, a hand on his wrist. "Do they know I'm a Russian Jew?"

"You're being silly," he snaps.

This is the first time he stops using our new couple voice. I knew that time would come but it's unexpected, a turning of the page, the end of a particular phase. I wonder if I've shown too much of myself, if my insecurity has risen to the surface despite all my work at changing my cognitive patterns. His sharpness is surprising, this sudden coldness that freezes the expressiveness of his face and turns him into the subject of a portrait.

"Of course you're right. I was just joking," I assure him. We ring the doorbell.

His father ushers us inside a living room that appears to be the beginning of a long maze, vertiginous ceilings sheltering incomprehensible places like pantries and linen closets. The very immensity of the space is wrong, unnatural for Manhattan, but I inwardly focus on breathing exercises and present Carl's father with the cake.

"Not necessary," he says, not in a polite way but as though he means it. It really is unnecessary. The vanilla cake goes off to the side and I never see it again.

"Ah, there you are." Frances Vandermotter appears in a cardigan and neat, pleated pants, highlighted hair pulled back into a bow clip. A sliver of blue skin is camouflaged under her eyes. She presses a single cold cheek against mine and is speaking loudly and exceedingly slowly. "You'll. Want. A. Tour."

My impulse is to assure her my English is fluent. "That would be great."

I had pictured a home chic and preppy, pointillist and perfect. But there's a mismatched quality to the place, the furniture pieces not in proportion with each other, too big or too small. American and English antiques clutter the tops of Queen Anne cabinets, faded cotton chintz curtains. I summon my charm and unleash it on the art as planned, except the art is not very interesting or varied, a series of Dutch nautical landscapes, a portrait of a prim Puritan woman.

"Carl tells me you're an intern at Worthington's. I'm afraid the art will disappoint you," his mother says.

"No, no, I love landscapes." I meet Carl's eyes over her shoulder. He shrugs in apology, mouths, *I swear I never said you were an intern.*

"And this one was inherited from an elderly aunt. Your boss in Nineteenth Century might be interested to appraise it sometime." You pass the pursed-lipped woman in a white cap, her eyes steely with resolve.

"It's well executed." I'm aware that by pretending to some kind of authority, I'm actually wielding it. "It's got great depth, actually." Next to the Puritan lady, a set of worn Princeton fleeces are framed, and the bureau holds an army of brass ship bells. Everything needs a good dusting but you can tell each item has importance, that its placement in relation to its neighbors is not incidental.

"Those bells belonged to the schooner that brought Armand's relatives from the Old World. So you see, you and Carl are both immigrants of a kind," she says. She is gesturing toward a cabinet, a glass shrine to silver. "These over here are Paul Revere."

"Paul Revere," I repeat, squinting at a creamer and a pair of sugar tongs, the words conjuring some vague horseback figure from high school history. I realize I will have to brush up on its significance with Lucas in Early American. "How wonderful."

She is telling me about some ancestral privateer who helped with the blockade of Boston, but then a voice drifts in from the living room, from a place that seems miles away. "Drinks, Cece, bring Tanya around, will you?"

"Tanya," Frances says, ushering me out. "Is it short for anything?"

"Tatiana."

"Ah, of course! I always loved those indexes in the back of long Russian novels where the various names are explained. Everyone had so many different names. Every time a character popped up, you had to consult the glossary to make sure you haven't met them before. Remember, Skip?"

From what seems like entire countries away, Armand calls back, "Ask your son. He's the Russian scholar. Do you know how old I must have been when I read *War and Peace*? Nineteen, twenty? And how old am I now?"

"Okay, we get it. You're old." Frances winks, two ladies making the best of their men's shortcomings. "Wine or something more interesting?"

As the evening progresses, I stop wondering why a man named Armand is called Skip. After some initial small talk about Russian literature, they don't ask me questions about the immigrant experience or about my parents in New Jersey. They drink and nibble, and discuss recent auctions and reminisce about fabulously rustic summers in Maine where reams of cousins hike, wait in line for the outhouse, and jump-start cocktail hour at four. And I feel bold enough to peel off the heat of my Chanel jacket with its carefully pinned price tag and laugh along with them at experiences I could only faintly imagine: pool parties where no one swims, with names I am expected to recognize, after-hours charity shopping to benefit children's foster care, family lacrosse games, a sport that never made sense to me, a house in Maine that sounds romantic even if I imagine my mother wondering why rich people like this couldn't afford a house with indoor plumbing. It is wading into a beautiful, cold pool, the water bracing and shimmering. But Carl hasn't said a word.

I notice a vagueness in the man I'm besotted with, as if Carl's not related to them, as if we're two arbitrary couples socializing. On our way back from the tour of the apartment, Carl and his father sit at an angle on their chairs across the extensive dining room table. Carl's only contribution is about the foster children's organization he and his mother oversee. He asks about the funds, about particular kids, if they have remained with their families, if there had been successful adoptions, which ones have aged out of the system. He insists on photographs and smiles only when he recognizes the faces of the kids, beaming or wearing tight smiles of artifice, flashing their baby teeth. He plays basketball with two of them on Saturday mornings, but only now does the importance of the organization in his life become clear to me.

How different it is compared to my raucous family dinners, where everyone's business is splayed out on the table next to the food, where I'm teased about finding a "normal job" or a "husband, finally." How different this Vandermotter exchange on culture and outdoors and sport compared to the drunken squeals of the Russian wives, the costume parties where the men dress as women in wigs and fake boobs, the swaying guests belting accompaniment to an impromptu piano recital. I'd been embarrassed by most of that, actually, by an immigrant lack of polish and sophistication, by its clannishness, the simple, peasant food. I find I like the coolness, the calm way Carl's father has of putting together drinks, deliberately, ice cubes first, the careful splash of lime, the neat shaving of citrus peel, and the way his mother wafts from room to room with her narrow, limpid eyes replicated in Carl.

"Another?" his father asks by the bar, and I say yes, yes to everything offered, and I hear my own voice colonizing the space, making it mine.

"You know, speaking of names, Carl tells me I'm an expert namer," I say, and launch into the story of how we met.

"Really? We had no idea. Whatever can that mean?" His father announces this as if relieved that somebody's talking, that they can all pave over Carl's silence with their chatter.

"I name paintings."

"You mean those titles are made up by people like you? I thought the artist named his own painting."

"Sometimes, but many times they come in untitled so it becomes our job. Titles sell paintings."

"Yes," Frances says. "I'm sure they do."

"Your internship sounds fascinating." Armand pops an oyster cracker in his mouth, scalloped and dotted with salt. "When we come by Worthington's next, we'll be sure to look you up."

"Oh, yes," Frances says.

"I'm actually not an intern. I'm an assistant cataloguer."

"Oh?" Armand says and, through the murk of wine, I'm convinced they're impressed, that my position has been elevated in their eyes.

And when they plant good-night kisses, I say a million thank-yous and return to the cherry stateliness of the elevator, I feel Carl coming back to himself, returning to focus.

We emerge into the night, and I admit to relief at being free of that building, at chucking my shoes and gingerly navigating the warm concrete with bare toes. "I think that went well. They seem nice."

"Well, it's what I got," is his odd reply. He hails a cab to drop me off at Penn Station and no amount of pressing convinces him to elaborate. It's the first time he disengages from me like this, barely a peck on the lips and then he waves to me from the corner. But he shows up at my office the following day with a warm falafel sandwich from my favorite Middle Eastern place. He's the same enamored Carl.

A week later, we're engaged.

"*Gor'ko*, to the happy couple," my uncle cries, and Carl and I are made to kiss, an exchange of pomegranate-infused vodka on the tongue. The guests are once again shoveled around a table built for half the bodies, the music loud enough for the merriment of forgetting. "Turn it down," someone is directed and then ignores. The television competes in decibels, kids swirling underfoot, a cousin's younger daughter smudged with poppy-seed jam from head to toe.

It's instantly apparent that at my parents' house, Carl comes alive, transforms into more of himself. The men are winking at Carl, pressing vodka shots on him. He brays at every punch line even if he later admits that he didn't entirely understand the content of the joke. Women rib him gently, eyebrows plucked thin and high. They speak English out of deference to his nativity, his conquering of their adoptive land. The house steaming with herring buried under thinly sliced onion and tongue fanned out next to marinated cabbage, buttery baby potatoes and singed beef and chopped beet salad. And Carl helpless before the refilled shot glasses placed before him, his hand unsteady after the next toast. By the end of the night, he becomes disheveled from exertion.

"Watch out, Carl, hope you know you're dating the CEO over there," a cousin named Mitya calls out. "That Tanya always ordered us around, even when she was a little girl."

Inevitably, my mother arrives to the rescue—"Don't say that, Mitya"—afraid that the suitor will be scared off.

No man wants a daunting woman.

No man wants a woman who earns more than him.

No man wants a woman who is too opinionated.

No man wants a woman who values career over family.

No man wants a woman who is vocal about being confident, who makes the first move, who picks the date activity, who makes a reservation, who has male friends, who does not greet him in full makeup, who serves her own food first, who wears sneakers, who admits to being hungry, who reads too much, who drives while he's in the passenger seat, who doesn't cook, who's messy, disorganized, complains, confronts, acts like a martyr, plays sports, watches sports, lounges, remembers past slights, fails to forgive. Women are very particular things here.

As the night deepens, Carl appropriates the term himself. "Come here, CEO," he says, pulling me closer, confronting the approving hoots of the guests with a bashful smile. "What? I like that she's the boss. That's why I asked her to marry me." Those words still so fresh, so tentative, feel like bathing in the petals of the most aromatic of flowers. It was a proposal as simple and unexpected as Carl himself, a nighttime excursion to the top of Rockefeller Center after hours, a buddy of his pulling strings to keep the deck open. The entire city was enflamed before us.

"This is where you belong, on top of the world," he said, before pulling out his grandmother's sapphire. It didn't fit, the oval was roomy enough to accommodate two fingers.

Right there, in front of my parents, I embrace my fiancé tightly, bury my nose in his neck. I'm afraid he doesn't really know me and might be mistaking me for another woman inside his own head, but right now it doesn't matter. I might detonate with all that love, all the excitement for the life that awaits.

And I watch my mother gulp down her protests, pass us the plate of chicken thighs sprinkled with dill. Her hands worrying the edge of the tablecloth, clumping it in her fists and then letting it go.

Catherine

FEBRUARY–MARCH 1744

Less than a week at court in this strange land and Sophie already knows to proceed with caution. All around her is plotting, whispers behind corners, sometimes within earshot. She can hear her name reverberating in the halls in harsh, foreign Russian. That Sophie. Have you seen that bony, oval-faced Sophie? That pale, raven-haired Sophie? That provincial princess? At least that is what she imagines is being said about her in Russian. She is aware of how her fleshless shoulders pop out of sleeves, aware that her dresses are far from the latest style. She has only three or four in a court that changes gowns three times a day. She perceives her hair to be wrong here, is convinced the maids spread word that she uses her mother's bed linens. She is probably deemed not pretty enough, plain and Germanic.

The place is impossibly cold, impossibly foreign. Outside her window is perpetual winter, stark and thick, the wind so strong it barrels into her room. If it were not for Katerina, lovely, loyal Katerina, her friend in the silver dress, she would be lost, awash in a sea of solitude. She calls for her. Katerina! Is Katerina near?

And here she comes, her Katerina, whom she already calls Katya. A kindred spirit who speaks German, who understands her jokes. Whose eyes she can trust. How lovely she looks rushing into her chambers in that unassuming way, her simple unadorned gown, a single strand of pearls, the modest chignon. She brings with her the sewing that is their pretext—the court must believe their many meetings are about practicing her Russian or sewing a decorative pillow for her groom. It is best not to admit confidences; already she knows the empress's temperament, her watchful eye. The empress may not want Sophie to have allies, she may want to isolate her, keep her far away from outstretched, helping hands.

"What are they saying about me today?" she murmurs to Katya as soon as the girl settles into the love seat with the sewing.

"That they are still hoping for the Polish Saxon Marianne."

"They want to get rid of me."

"If they only knew your temperament and tact, how lucky they would consider themselves."

"Bestuzhev is at the helm of this thought, I suppose?"

Katya keeps her eyes fixed on the stone floor. The cold, unforgiving floor.

"Never mind," Sophie says, hurt. She steers the subject to fashion, a topic she cares little about herself but knows her friend follows with interest. "Let us discuss your mantua for the banquet. It can be trimmed with silver silk."

Only Katya knows her worries about her future husband, her role in this vast unknowable land. That her future husband is beginning to repulse her. Peter, pronounced Pyotor. She has to practice saying it, her lips curling with the unpleasant maneuver of it. Pyo-tor. *Vashe Velichietvo, Pyotor Tretii,* His Highness.

But the girl is tactful and allows Sophie to change the topic. "I adore silver trim. It is elegant, especially on one of those dresses where the drapery parts to reveal the skirt. But my mother warns it is too naughty."

The wind laps against the window, fierce and swirling.

"I cannot go back, you know," Sophie says. The thought has just formed itself inside her; if Bestuzhev's campaign succeeds, she will be redundant. "I will not go back to Zerbst."

Katya looks up from the fine underlay of lace. "Oh, my dear."

They hear steps outside the door. The girls look up and it is Sophie's mother who has descended into an armchair, her powdered hair smoothed over her left shoulder. "I demand to know what they are saying about us at court. I've only a minute."

There is a long silence, the girls look down at their sewing again. There is only the wind rattling against the drafty windows. "I am sure I have heard nothing but admiration for your ladyship," Katya says. She is shrewd, Sophie thinks. Is it possible to encounter a sister in just a short month? As her mother closes her eyes, presses her fingers to her temple, the girls exchange a brief look.

Sophie says, "It is remarkably cold in here."

Katya smiles, her fingers dancing over the needlework.

"I detest that woman." Peter leans over the carcass of his fowl. The discarded bones are barely stripped of their flesh. Sophie drags her attention away from his plate but then she becomes aware of his too-long fingers on the table, the curvature of his spine, the outline of his thin mouth. For the sake of the long table of guests watching them, she is careful to retain her smile.

"Which woman do you speak of, Your Highness? My mother?"

He picks up a wing, then flings it back to the table. "My aunt, of course. The wretched empress. If not for her meddling, I would still be in Holstein. This country is backward, loathsome, filled with rude, parochial creatures. I detest it. You will find it to be so."

"Oh." She thought she was finally making an impression on him. She ascertained that her body was angled toward his.

The musicians enter, begin the process of unsheathing their instruments. The empress leans over to one of her ladies, whispers in her ear, and the woman scurries to fulfill some command.

Sophie follows the empress's every move. The woman's gaze slides over each guest, missing nothing. "I find there is much beauty in this land, this language. I look forward to being fluent very soon. I'm studying with your tutor."

"I am proud to say that despite his best efforts, Teodorsky taught me nothing. Nothing! And I would fight it too if I were you. Hold on to your German and your religion. The Russian language is ugly and so is their crude, backward Orthodoxy."

She wonders if the future king should speak this way of a realm he will someday inherit. Outside the window, she hears the first sign of fireworks and she longs to ignore propriety and run out to watch the show.

"In that case, I shall interpret Russian for both of us."

Peter slumps down in his seat. "I suppose I will have to marry you since She wishes it. But I want you to know I love another. Her mother was sent to Siberia as soon as the witch found out about my affections."

Sophie pretends to take great interest in his confidences, the pickled goose oily and slick inside her belly. She can see the empress turning to watch them, so she bends closer to her husband-to-be, inhales his sour breath of wine. Another firework explosion startles the party. The sound is sharp, sudden, tinting the window green with artificial light.

He says, not unkindly, "I hope you understand that I confide in you because you are my second cousin and I am simply being truthful."

There are needles poking at her heart. Her tongue is momentarily trapped in the cave of her mouth. "You are very right to do so."

"Would you look at them together, how perfect they are in each other's company," her mother says, bending toward the empress. Her breasts are in danger of spilling out of her gown's décolletage. "What a handsome pair they make."

Sophie sighs. So many meals to attend and the empress demands they drag on into the morning hours and turn into dance parties. She is dizzy from exhaustion. Birds arrive whole and return carved. Plates whisked away. Music followed by cards followed by gossip. The empress can outstay the entire court, reluctantly retiring to her bedchamber as dawn breaks. "Rouse yourself," she commands, to anyone that dares nod off in her presence. Sophie wonders when the actual governance of the kingdom takes place.

Now that she examines the castle more closely, all the furnishings, so opulent on first inspection, reveal their flaws. Chairs missing legs, doors hanging off hinges, the bottom of drapes dirty and fringed, bronze handles of cabinets broken. Glossy on the outside, rotten underneath. Marred, decaying.

The next time she sees Peter, it is only ten in the morning, but he is already trembling with two glasses of wine and has lined up his toy soldiers for the practice drill. They are made to stand at glassy-eyed attention in their blue military uniforms. "We're drilling formation today," he explains. Sophie drapes herself over the settee the way she saw her mother do, examining her pale arms, the light hairs dotting her forearms. She tries not to look up at the ceiling where a row of rats dangle by their necks, poor creatures executed for unwittingly playing the role of disobeying officers.

Peter is marching back and forth. Without his wig, he appears even slighter, barely more imposing than his toys. They make kings of men like these? But she is starting to understand that simply waiting for a spark in his affections is foolishness; she must play her own game, parallel to his.

"I thank you for your trust in me the other day, Grand Duke." She bows. "You can rest assured I will safeguard your confidences."

He pauses, lifts his eyebrows. "You are my only playmate here. We must be allies."

"Allies, of course I trust that's what we are."

He has transferred his concentration to his Holstein soldiers, the precision of their stance. Not a single toe out of formation. "Don't you love their flintlock muskets? Isn't Prussia an amazing place? How I wish I were back there."

Her voice softens. "Yes, I imagine it is hard for you, to be so far from home."

Of course he has asked her nothing about her own ennui, her homesickness. He appears to her from time to time, George, her uncle. Watching her bowing in the chapel, his head leaning against the doorway. She sensed his approaching footsteps as she kneeled, no prayers emerging from her mouth. Knowing instantly the slow approach belonged to him, his particular leonine stalk. Frozen, unmoving. His voice, when it darted across the walls, flung like silk on the surface of her skin. "I have said it many times, you are very pretty." At times, she wished her destiny would have her satisfied with a man like that, a man whose intellect she was already on the verge of surpassing.

She rose, turned to face George. "Clever, you mean. Or arrogant and prideful if you listen to Mother." Whether he possessed intellect or not, she has never seen eyes like his. Two changing sapphires.

"No, but pretty. A man would be very lucky to call you wife."

"What about my pointed chin?" Dimly, she was aware of the cross behind her, the sound of cartwheels rolling over the cobblestones in the square. His hair was tightly slicked back, his moustache draped over his lips like a hasty arrangement of bedclothes.

"I do not find your chin wanting. It is the chin of perfection."

She edged herself closer to the corner, a thin pain of dizziness overtaking her. Back in the privacy of her bed, she liked to adjust a pillow between her legs, achieving a related sensation. She was aware of the lowering of their voices, the vapor of their words compared with the substantial shuddering inside. She tried a saucy: "How do you feel about the return of Communion vestments? Are you in agreement with our new monarch on the issue?"

He was stalking closer, the room suddenly smaller. She held her breath, held her gaze on the looming cross. "Sophie," he said, his hand reaching for her chin, the overly pointed one, her mouth greeting his.

A clanging series of knocks returns her to the room with Peter. Her betrothed.

"Ah, at last. Here you are." He opens the door, the servants on the other side dressed in the same uniforms as his soldiers. They stiffen before him in a neat row, these human replicas of toys. Peter assesses each one individually for appearance. "You. Your pigtails are the wrong length. You are demoted to musketeer. And you. You better improve your firing time or you will be demoted too. Let us begin our military exercises." He turns to Sophie with a definitive clearing of the throat—you may go.

"May I stay and join you?" she attempts, but he looks at her as on a madwoman. But she has achieved her goal. His trust. Allies. A small step, but a step nevertheless.

She fetches her riding habit and meets her friend at the stables. Katya is a remarkable horsewoman. She is remarkable in all ways, but is confined to the tight boundaries of her gender. Sometimes, Sophie wants to push her to read, to think outside the vapor of love and balls and fashion, but Katya gently steers her back to her own interests, to the way their two worlds intersect. When will a betrothed love you? What are a wife's responsibilities? Whom do you find more handsome: Razumovsky or Volokhin?

Now, she admires the balance of her friend's sidesaddle position, her ability to give all of herself to the horse, an instinct for when the creature softens beneath her touch. Rastrelli's overwhelming Summer Palace recedes behind them in the usual contrast of glorious and fetid: the majesty of its sweeping Venetian façade at the bank of the foul Fontanka Canal. Sophie is relieved when she can barely see it. She breathes into the depths of her fur. It is an off-putting February; still no snow, only the placid whiteness.

"So the rumors are true? He just plays with soldiers all day?" Katya says.

"And he starts drinking early in the morning." Only with Katya does she allow herself the wrench of self-pity.

"You poor dear. But he must outgrow it. From what my mother tells me, men are like this, children. He needs a woman to set him straight, and who better than you?"

"But he is no boy. He is fifteen years old, Katya! Next in line to be monarch of all the Russias. When will he grow up?"

The air is piercing, clawing at her face, the wind slapping her cheeks. The gun rests, futile. Not a single duck when usually she shoots at least three by midday. But as she trains her head toward the sky and the possibility of prey, it occurs to her that Peter is only the beginning of her story. She has watched how the court treats Peter as dispensable symbol and perhaps a fool is preferable to a wily despot. It did not take long to see that his behavior is being ridiculed at court, that the empress has hoped Sophie's arrival will mature him. That everyone at court pities and respects her at his expense.

She feels a new burst of hope that might be her first political realization at court. Of course, she thinks, it is so simple, and yet she keeps forgetting it in her childish search for love. It is the one who reigns on the throne who holds all the power. She must focus her energies on the empress. She pushes her horse onward.

"Look at me, Katya," she cries, and swings a leg over the seat so she is riding the horse like a man.

"Should you? Oh, you shouldn't!" her friend cries. The canter is choppy, tides of cold air gripping at the throat. It is time to head back, she can hear them calling for her to turn around, but she ignores the cries and presses on, farther, farther from the gleaming complex.

That night, she tries to dress for dinner but cold is shivering up her body, making it spasm, convulse. She alternates huddling under soaking sheets and pulling them off in order to breathe. She should have never gone riding in the chill, she thinks. She is not accustomed to the Russian climate. Then she loses the thread of the idea. Her mother is speaking—*we're late, the grand duke is waiting for us*—but to Sophie, her face is swimming, distorted. *The empress has gone to the monastery, so there is no need to play the convalescent.*

"Please," Sophie says, the ache deeper now, somewhere at her side. This infection, whatever it is, has wormed itself to her very bones. "I would like to return to bed."

"Then I will attend alone," Johanna announces. She is dressed in the most spectacular brocade gown and is appraising the folds beneath her eyes in a gold hand mirror, a gift from the empress. Sophie tries to hoist herself up in bed in order to allow herself to be dressed—she can imagine how her mother will translate this illness to the mercurial grand duke— but the pain strikes below her right breast. She gives herself over to it.

Fine, fine, go without me. Sophie lies back down, wraps herself in covers, draws knees to her chest. She is cold, her very flesh exposed. If she could only sleep. A rapid scan of the room confirms her mother is gone. Sleep demolishes her, then she awakes to a cavalcade of faces. George returns through the waves of cold pulses. He pulls her behind the door, against the wall. The silver edge of her favorite tapestry of armies straddling earth-colored horses is scratching at her cheek.

"You shall marry me. My sister will be pleased."

"I suppose so. Johanna will at least be rid of me. Would I not make an ideal wife?"

"Indeed, most ideal."

He plants a kiss to her nose, to the swell of her earlobe. Then the scene shifts and it is that final night at home before the eastward journey. Downstairs with the nurse, she hears the voice of her little sister, a bubbling over of baby glee. In a wedge of the opposite wing, her father scratches at papers on his secretary desk, accepts visitors into the library, a long trail of appointments sprinkled across walnut chairs. The entire castle runs on schedule but there is an air of impending change. Sophie is leaving but she is not sure who knows about it. Her father does, yet he is buried away in his office. Babette was not told. Babette, innocently urging her to the Corelli on the violin with those soft fluttering hands. She certainly would have wondered at the commotion but was too afraid of Johanna to inquire.

"The idea of it. Being rid of you." Submerged in her neck, George's lips tracing some distant moon behind her ear.

She awakes and sleeps again. She is aware of arguments taking place beside her bed. Her mother is pressing some case with doctors, Katya is patting cool cloth to her forehead. Even Peter appears above her as concerned observer. The pain in her side worsens, radiating to the rest of her body. Her sheets are soaked with sweat. So this is dying, she thinks. A messy struggle, this.

She moans and is shushed. "Suffer quietly," she thinks her mother commands her. "What kind of report do you want to reach the empress?" Her jaw is inflamed, so tight and filled with fire she imagines it snapping off onto the floor. Humans or ghosts populate the room, she is not sure which. Strange, she thinks, that death stands on no ceremony, conveys no formal invitation. It simply blocks her view of living. Eventually, she feels herself placed into a substantial lap, an expansive bosom, finds herself under the caress of warm, pliant hands. She looks up to find it is the empress herself. She is murmuring, "My dearest, I will not let you slip away," and she is commanding someone, "Bleed her at once."

"Please. No bleeding." She can hear her alarmed mother. "That is how her little brother died." But her voice is extinguished, pushed back.

"She will be bled. Right now."

The prick begins with arms but attacks various points in her body—the feet, thighs, her posterior. She slips in and out of consciousness. Lestocq is gone, another doctor in his place who speaks Russian in a thick Spanish-sounding accent. And the empress never abandons her side, replacing the wet cloths on her forehead, holding Sophie's head in the crook of her elbow. There is a continued litany of comfort, a soothing string of words whose meaning she has only begun to learn. She jolts up in bed and vomits, a long expulsion of her insides. She imagines it as a fury of blood.

"I will fetch the Lutheran pastor," her mother cries, but the heat of Sophie's body is subsiding and she is becoming sensible to her surroundings. A tableau of people occupy every inch of the room, some are wringing bloodstained handkerchiefs, others just gaping at her. But she stares up into the worried blue eyes of the empress and remembers. The one who reigns holds the power.

She clears her voice. "What is the use of the Lutheran when I mean to convert? Send instead for Simeon Teodorsky. I will be happy to speak with him." There is a stunned silence and the generous bosom does not move from her side; if anything, it presses itself closer. Exclamations of joy wash over her.

"What a charming accent our little pupil displays. She has been studying her Russian," the empress exclaims.

"An unusually adept and eager student," Teodorsky confirms when he arrives, giving a nervous laugh. He looks more skeletal and pared away than usual. He might be frightened for his own survival.

With fresh lucidity, Sophie examines the empress's face. It is blotched and discolored by sun spots, lined with age. The empress is human. The woman has been crying out of fear for *her* health, Sophie's! She clasps the empress's hand, presses it tightly to her cooling cheek.

"It is you who healed me, *matyushka*."

"Oh, my darling." The empress is covering her face with relieved, exultant kisses.

And Sophie allows herself to be lowered back inside the foul-smelling sheets. No one will be sending her back to Zerbst. For now.

Tanya

PRESENT DAY

When I enter the Four Seasons restaurant, Igor is seated at a corner table by the window. It's the oligarchs' favorite table. A potted tree hides these particular men from the other patrons but allows them a view of the pool in the center of the room. He stands, pulls out my chair, and continues to dress somebody down over the phone. A loop of his finger brings us sparkling water and a tray of lime.

By now, I know the identity of the man sitting across from me. Igor Yardanov, multibillionaire real estate developer, media darling. A graduate of Mendeleev Institute, a child of engineers, trained as a mathematician. His story parallels that of many other younger oligarchs after the fall of the Soviet Union: he made his fortune by seizing a majority share in the country's aluminum production, settled into his wealth by becoming an owner of a chain of restaurants in Moscow, a movie studio, an avant-garde ballet theater, and a soccer stadium in St. Petersburg, a new development project in midtown Manhattan. A close confidant of Russia's president. Embroiled in a well-known rivalry with former partner Alexander Medovsky, according to a series of high-profile court cases in London over the carving up of the empire they launched in 2000. The only detail that sets him apart from the rest of his cohorts is his single, childless, never-married status. It is this, in addition to his scathing, bronzed looks, that tends to receive the lion's share of press, the speculation about his girlfriends, a swarm of rotating models draped over him at openings.

What my predecessor at Worthington's never understood, what Marjorie always found so mysterious, was that clients crave personal relationships. These are men with hundreds of daily supplicants, these are men sold to constantly, who sit on the receiving end of demands from colleagues, enemies, wives, and mistresses. When I first meet potential clients, I don't try to sell my expertise or the prestige of the company or why they should choose Worthington's over Sotheby's. Do they enjoy their home in Greece? Did they make it to Formula One this year? If Jewish, do they travel regularly to Israel? Only once the wine is flowing, a rapport established, can I gently move toward, what kind of art are you drawn to? Are you considering building up a collection? What period excites you? Anything in the London auctions that appealed lately? From the answers to these questions, I can size up the kind of man I'll be working with and tease out allies in preserving Russian culture.

Our table is arrayed with appetizers, slivers of duck prosciutto resting on feathers of wilted greens, morel mushrooms dotting a shallow bowl of asparagus soup. A pair of glasses arranged in front of us, a bottle of wine uncorked. He gestures for me to begin eating.

In the early days, I was less cheerful about these lunches, disturbed by the coarseness of the men sitting across from me. I'd have to suffer an entourage of goons passing around porn videos on their phones between courses, or berating the waiter for not bringing him "the best" this or "the top-of-the-line" that. Luckily, there are fewer of those around; the old guard is being replaced by those who know the best is not the flashiest, who have slowed their gorging after a lifetime of deprivation.

Igor finally hangs up and turns to face me. "We were not properly introduced at the party. Igor Mikhailovich Yardanov."

"Is it the Hudson Yards development that brings you so often to New York, Igor Mikhailovich?" I ask. New York: always a good starting point. Begin with New York, then turn to the beauty (or if the client prefers, the pollution/congestion/traffic) of Moscow, then end with their homes in the south of France. Like dogs that have been cooped up in cages, then so recently set free to roam, these men love talking travel.

"There is some of that, yes. But now I am here to bring back the Order of Saint Catherine." The wine is poured, he tastes, then dispenses with the ritual with a brief nod. "Yes, that is my sole goal for being in New York this time around."

I like how he puts it, the "bring back." Is he a fellow conspirator, a preservationist? I try not to worry that we have not yet heard back from the famously slow Catherine historian. I taste the asparagus soup without actually tasting it. "I should warn you, there's serious interest by very determined people."

"Medovsky."

"I really can't say."

"Listen, all that bastard wants is to curry favor with our president. It would be such waste to have this Order fall into his hands. I have plan for it that is not self-serving, if you know what I mean."

"I don't need to tell you that it is an open market." I vacillate between ordering the halibut and a duo of rabbit, whichever will be daintier to eat.

"You can trust me, that Medovsky's a bastard."

"I'd prefer not to discuss clients," I say, an unexpected protectiveness of Medovsky creeping into my voice. "But just out of curiosity, what would you do with the Order? If you did win the lot, I mean."

He adjusts his chair. His face is like a piece of paper smoothed of creases. I can make out the red pinpricks of a recent Botox injection on his forehead; the furrows between the eyebrows so prominent in Medovsky are completely absent here. He's a stretched canvas. Still, in the splash of sunshine, there's no doubt he's more handsome than in pictures, if a bit waxy, sepulchral. His hair is too neatly combed and pressed down to his scalp, his neck unnaturally moist and hairless. Centered above a starched button-down shirt is a violet silk tie. Only his teeth are a hint to his former life: jumbled, dotted with fillings.

"Tanyechka, can I call you that? I've asked around about you and what I hear is that you are of utmost moral character. People who trust no one, trust you. That *Financial Times* piece did not do you justice."

"So you read that." On the plate that has just arrived rests a tiny fillet on a bed of wilted watercress, the plate elegantly smeared in green. Maybe Marjorie was right after all. That article has resulted in more business. I fold a napkin across my knees. "That's very flattering. I'm honored if that's my reputation."

"That is why I thought you would help me. I want Order for good cause I am sure you would approve of."

My gut says it's authentic, and it's been wrong just once before. My fork sinks into the meat of the fish. "Which is?"

"Look, I don't want to say too much right now. You know Medovsky's character. If he is determined, there is no outbidding him."

The fillet of bison is cooling on his plate, all that brown of the foie gras and truffles contrasted with the milky sheen of his nails, the thin layer of clear varnish. "In that case, we have other lots you might be interested in. If you would tell me a little bit about an artist or two that impresses you."

"I'm more than happy to buy a few other things." He takes out the Worthington's catalogue from his briefcase, flips through it. "Like this, no offense intended, crappy Grigoriev. Throw that in."

"Igor. If I may." So he's like the others after all, always working to entrap me, to trick me into bending the rules. Would Carl like this guy or hate him? I realize how accustomed I've become to my moral compass pointing in the direction of his opinions. "There's really nothing I can do if you choose not to bid higher than the highest bid. But I will be your supporter, your friend, the entire time. We can be on the phone personally during the auction if you like."

"Medovsky won't stop if he wants something. You may have realized this already."

"I'm sorry. Like I said, there's nothing I can do."

He leans his chin on his hand in a theatrical gesture of defeat. C'est la vie! My plate is removed and an apricot crumb cake appears, a strawberry soufflé in front of him. He dips his spoon in the custard and holds it out to my mouth. "To sample, yes?" The spoon is dangling inches from my mouth, his eyes focused there.

I politely decline a bite from his spoon. "You know what, Igor? I'll be in Moscow previewing the lots. Why don't we meet there and speak further?"

"Excellent, yes. I will then be able to personally show you my plans for the order. This soufflé is lovely, yes? Light, not too sweet."

"Delicious."

He's smiling, now. Everything in this environment is perfect, just right, the touches scrutinized, chosen with intention. Sitting here, you feel like the most important of humans on the planet. The staff's sole job is to facilitate your triumphs, smooth away all obstacles. Once in a while, in places like this, the awed immigrant in me resurfaces. The impossible luster of the pool. Unmarred glass, the starch of flawless linen, the discreet scent of food. Silver trays without blemishes, chocolate truffles imprinted with a single lavender bud. Half a bottle of outrageously priced wine unfinished and abandoned on the empty table. And Igor slips his own credit card into the bill folder, even when I remind him the company's reimbursing.

"I cannot allow it, a beautiful woman to pay," he says.

It is so simply stated, as fact. A beautiful woman. Somehow, I've forgotten that I ever belonged to this category. Has Carl ever called me a "beautiful woman"? He was not one to spell out his feelings. His adoration for me was implicit in the Look, the tone of his voice, in the way he waved over to me in public places as if I were the only face in the world that mattered, in the quiet care with which he folded my laundered clothes and tucked them away in their proper places. But for all his Russophilia, he was determinedly American when it came to gender relations. *A couple should be partners,* he insisted on our honeymoon, while the very idea was ridiculous to my mother. *Partners?* she said. *If it makes him happy, no harm to let him believe this.*

Igor escorts me out the door to the street and lowers me into the backseat of a cab. His kiss on the cheek lies differently than that of my other clients. It's an incursion, an imprint. I swivel around to watch him on the curb. He stands immobile, patiently waiting for my taxi to fall out of view.

"How'd it go?" Marjorie calls out when I pass her office.

"Great. He's really interested in the Order." But of course what she's really asking about is numbers, projections, promises she can make to Dean upstairs. "Should go pretty high since he's bidding against a motivated client."

"That's fabulous." Marjorie's desk is invisible for the paperwork and digital printouts; she looks rather lost among them. "I suppose it's no secret that with the political and economic climate being what it is, the Russian department is on the chopping block. But you might be able to convince us with this auction that we can sustain the New York office."

"No pressure, right?" But Marjorie is holding up a pair of scissors as if confused about the object of incision.

Back in the Russian art area, I'm surprised to find the kiss still there, ingrained below the surface of my skin. I survey Regan's list of missed calls, but the names float away, meaningless. None of them are Carl's. What is he eating? I wonder. I picture him foraging for pretzels, his friend's tiny galley kitchen a mess of open Chinese food containers, frozen pizza. His desk strewn with papers. After we moved in together, we had to adjust for our two bodies in the same space, two conflicting schedules. I would be in the gym by seven in the morning, while he slept on. He would be watching nerdy television shows while my eyes drooped at nine o'clock. That first year was moving away from politeness to showing one another where we placed our limbs, the nature of our true routines. But I never did allow myself to relax. I was always attuned to external expectations.

The *Financial Times* with my photo at the column's head is doubled over beside my keyboard. "Great profile. Never thought of you as a simple girl. Congratulations," is written on a stickie note. Signed by my old boss in Impressionism, in his looping handwriting. I pick it up. My cool, unsmiling face is staring back at me.

"Regan, book my tickets for Moscow today, will you? Here are the dates. I've got to run to one of my Jewish lectures tonight." The tip of the girl's auburn head is the only movement in her cubicle, but her fingers dash over the keyboard.

At my sliver of window, the corner of Third Avenue and Fiftieth Street is filled with the sound of drilling, men belting out orders to other men. My hand hovers over the phone to call Carl. Instead, I dial the number of a Georgian restaurant around the corner from the address he gave me and order Carl a delivery of kachapuri and lula kebab.

After a few minutes, Regan cries out, "Done."

"We live in a world where God is hidden and we are fully responsible for our own actions. In the absence of accountability, human action turns to destruction. The challenge to our secular Russian Jews is this: take power, connect yourselves to the generations of history, perfect the world a little at a time." I pop into the room while the rabbi's in the middle of his lecture and find a seat behind Alla. The man next to me has his chin lodged upright in his palm, openly snoring.

"We're now fully aware that many Soviet Jews who were subsidized for yeshiva had a difficult time with integration. But if you delve into that experience, you will find that the education provided you with a necessary foundation . . ."

Alla passes back a note that says, "Rescue us!"

We're poised to clap, to acknowledge the climactic plea, but the rabbi turns the page of his talk and we slump back in our seats. "So you see, Russian Jews, despite having lived under a regime that tried to eradicate their Jewishness, can still play an important role in transforming the world because we are all part of a partnership between the generations. Through the Bronze Age, through modern civilization, through the chain that continued with your grandparents who did their share."

I sit among a row of crossed legs, a file of black pumps and logoed necklaces, polite manicures resting on Fendi bags. These are supposed to be my people, Russian-American professionals carefully selected by the Jewish Community Center to bring religion back to our wayward former-Soviet brethren.

Alla leans back in her chair and I'm enveloped in citrus perfume. "What's going on with Carl? Is he done with his thinking or what?"

"It's been less than a month," I whisper.

"Babes, you're in major denial."

Even though she's also married to an American, Alla belongs to my mother's philosophical school of gender relations—a Russian woman doesn't wait, a Russian woman acts.

"It's temporary, Al. Don't worry about me."

"I'd check out someone promising here if I were you."

"I thought you were the one who said to hang in there. That the first two years were the tough ones. And now you want me to just find a new guy here?"

"Basically, at least to scare Carl a little. He's taking you for granted, thinks you're going to just wait around while he makes up his mind," Alla says. She is unclasping her purse and checking her lipstick in the mirror.

"I don't think that's what he's doing."

The rabbi continues, "So our task is to tune in, not to transcend the secular nature of your Soviet past, but to harness it. We cannot depend on miracles from heaven."

The organizer of the night is cuing him to wrap up by noisily arranging the wineglasses in neat rows by the bar.

"What about that one?" Alla points to the sleeping man.

"Carl needs some time for himself, he's coming down from a lot of work stress. He'll be back any day now. You know better than anyone how much he loves me."

Alla leans back in her chair, purse in lap, tawny hair voluminously arranged around her shoulders. A brooch of inlaid sapphire and gold is carefully attached to a violet silk blouse. She's the kind of Russian woman I'll never be. "So what the hell's he doing then? Is he really 'thinking' about your future? If that's really all he's doing. I bet one of his cute new students is helping him think."

"There is no new student. You're being ridiculous."

"Don't wait too long, Tan. You've got to take matters into your own hands." I feel the softness of my friend's hand on my wrist. "I'm just telling you how it is. No more waiting around. You might be losing him right now."

I sharply pull back my arm and press a flushed cheek against the tall glass windows. My heart is flexing, contracting. Below me, along the FDR Drive, a blurry string of unmoving lights wait in the final gasp of evening rush hour.

The rabbi begins to notice the restless noise in the audience, and opens the floor for questions. The sleeping man is the first to raise his hand.

"Can you please explain to us where is the virtue in unconditional love?"

The rabbi is puzzled. His lecture probably said nothing about unconditional love. "Of course, when we think about Moses descending from the mountain with the commandments, he discovers his people have betrayed God with the golden calf. No doubt there was the initial temptation to abandon them . . ." The man sinks back to his original position. No one else dares raise a hand.

"Let's drink," someone calls out.

The rabbi, left alone, seems confused by the milling crowd. A flourish of silver hair glistens in the incandescent light. I find him lingering by the door as if deciding to eat or go, to run away from this crowd or hang around and make himself available.

"Rabbi, excuse me. First of all, thank you for the talk. That was very informative."

His dense eyebrows lift in welcome. "Well, I certainly hope I galvanized some of you."

"This is a bit off topic. I was actually wondering whether there are any actions we can take—you know, as Jews—to hasten a favorable outcome in a marital disagreement?"

"If you're talking about whether Jews believe in karma, the answer is we believe in *hashgacha*—providence. It tells us that we can ask God to change, to alter what came before and even repent. Even if what we have done in this relationship may have consequences that are unchangeable. Acting with pure, warmhearted intention's important. Focusing on what you can control in yourself rather than trying to influence others. There's *teshuvah*, of course, the doing of good deeds."

I think about how best to phrase it. "Actually, that's not exactly what

I meant. I was wondering when being proactive is preferable to being patient. You see my husband left and I think I know why . . ."

But Alla's approaching with the sleeping man tucked under her elbow and the rabbi takes his opportunity to slip out the door. I watch him in the hallway stabbing fruitlessly at the elevator button.

"So let's cut to the chase," Alla says. "This is Grisha. Meet Tanya. Tanya, meet Gregory. You're both sort of unattached. For the moment."

You've got to do something. A Russian woman acts. I look at Grisha. He is almost entirely bald and dressed in violet jeans looped by a fabric belt. A tight, white button-down shirt reveals a proud smattering of chest hair. A gold hand dangles from a necklace.

"So what do we have here?" he says, looking me up and down.

"I'll get you a both a cocktail." Alla floats away with an apologetic smile.

Grisha's kiss of greeting is the opposite of Igor Yardanov's, a wispy nothing scraped against my skin. He's inserting an abridged autobiography into the gaps of my silence. CEO of a development consultant firm, maybe I've heard of it? Plays tennis three times a week. Have I stayed at Koh Samui in Thailand? Have I seen the Gauguin show at the Met? Which other boards do I belong to? The lectures at the JCC's Emerging Leaders' series is really strong this year. Isn't it?

He escorts me to the buffet, offers me rolled-up roast beef, a wedge of knish. A hand continues to linger at the small of my back as if to guide me or keep me from tripping. I feel hot and uncomfortable and find myself staring at his downy arm hair. I see Alla lingering nearby, but I'm at a loss as to how I'm supposed to be. Like I'm single? Like I'm open to a date? I've forgotten all the steps, the push and pull of enticement, the small touches of his arm, the flirty repartee.

My phone rings, and I think, Saved by *hashgacha*! Carl probably thanking me for the takeout food. "I know how you love the lula," I'll say. And that will be the first step. That's how our fights usually ended, one person sublimating an irritation in an act of kindness.

But it's Regan with an emergency, a lot pulled at the last minute. I want to weep with the disappointment of it, not to mention the additional work it will entail. *Don't give in to learned helplessness. Don't catastro-phize!*

"I'll take a cab and meet you in the office?" Regan says, over a ca-cophony of drumming.

"I'll try to change his mind on the way. Just a case of cold feet or did he get a better deal?"

"Who knows? Good luck with that. I'm heading over."

"You rock. See you soon."

I find Grisha on my way out but he's already deep in conversation with an elegant woman in a hot-pink skirt. Her entire body is coiled into him, rapt with attention. He turns to me with a shrug, as if to say, *You snooze, you lose. You think I care that you're the CEO type? You think that'll make it easy for you out there?*

"I'm so sorry, but I've got to run." At the bar, Alla is frantically mim-ing a square in the air, the act of taking it out of a purse. Reluctantly, I add, "So, can I give you my card?"

"Well, *poka* then." Grisha pockets it. And he turns away.

Catherine

"Any doubts?" the empress says. She is perched on the settee, watching the maids' efforts. It took three of them to work the red material over Sophie's head.

Strange: the night before the formal betrothal, Sophie slept well for the first time since her arrival in Russia. Until this one, every night had been pocked by interruptions. The very slither of a mouse across the floor startled her awake. Her dreams were nothing more astonishing than reality transposed—Peter refusing to carry out his duties as husband, the disfavor of Her Imperial Majesty, the arrival of her charming rival Marianne from Poland, forgetting all her Russian during her confession of faith. But the night has actually been still, unmarred. She is refreshed. Filled with the keenest impatience.

"Doubts? I have written my father about the matter of the conversion. He has reservations as you know, but my own mind is at peace."

The empress looks taken aback and Sophie wonders if she meant doubts of a different kind, perhaps about the actual union. The empress is kneading the material of her skirt. "This is very expensive fabric, you know. Gros de tours. It holds up nicely over the course of a day, especially after all that kneeling."

The dress is strapped onto Sophie, her body made to conform to the stiff fabric. The empress is wearing the same dress, but hers is embellished by brilliant jewelry while Sophie's only options for accessories are a smattering of pendants gifted to her in the aftermath of her illness.

The pause in the conversation is long, unsettling. Sophie turns to the empress and looks directly into the woman's eyes. "This is the most beautiful gown I have ever had the privilege of wearing."

"Yes, yes," the empress says, distracted. "This must be an exciting time for a young girl." Again, she seems to want to impart more, a longer disquisition on conjugal bonds and duty perhaps. Sophie wonders if the empress will speak in greater confidence about Peter's character. But whatever moment she was trying to fashion between them is lost to the rush of logistics. They are telling her that the time has come to form the procession.

The palace chapel is thronged with shrieking onlookers, but for some reason, kneeling at the cushion, Sophie is not nervous. The chatter behind her continues even as the archbishop begins speaking. She has studied the intricacies of the conversion ceremony with Teodorsky, and is pleased to find she anticipates each element. The oil arrives on schedule, is dotted on the forehead, eyes, neck, and throat and just as quickly dabbed off with cotton. When it comes time to recite the faith, the Russian words unspool easily in her mind and off the tongue. Her dear governess Babette would have wept with pride. My little sheep has talent for recitation, her nanny might say, kissing her forehead. She wonders what Babette made of her sudden departure, if she wept or sensed something was amiss. She wonders if Babette found a new post. Sophie finds Katya's face among the maidens.

When her new name is first spoken around—Ekaterina, Catherine— she meets Katya's eye. In name, they are true mirror sisters now. When the empress first told her the plan for her renaming, she had initially been dismayed.

"May I ask the reason?" she asked. "Is my name not amenable to the Russian language? I have met several Sophias here."

"No need to regale you with the full story," the empress said, "but that was the name of my father's half sister, and the less said about her the better. My mother's name will do quite nicely. She was a marvelous person, *matyushka*, smart as a whip. I sometimes say my father was truly 'great' due to her influence."

Ekaterina. The name, spoken aloud now, turns Sophie into a new invention: an Imperial Highness, the Grand Duchess Ekaterina Alekseevna. Even her patronymic is a lie, her father's name being Christian August, the "Aleksey" chosen for its royal heritage as the patronymic of the empress's mother. All Catherine knows of the first Catherine, the one responsible for the precious order she wears at all times, was that she was exceedingly beautiful and of a luminous disposition. She had started off as a housemaid, then became Peter the Great's mistress and wife before becoming empress after his death. Catherine likes that she has landed in a realm where this is possible, the elevation of housemaid to empress.

Where she and the first Catherine part ways though: she will not be achieving the throne as mistress. She will not be making her Peter a "great man." His inability to rise to that moniker is apparent already.

They are now formally engaged to be married. Catherine is vaguely aware of the empress pinning a diamond pin to her shoulder, her very chest glowing with the blue of sapphires.

As soon as the betrothal is over, they are kids again, playing blindman's bluff. Peter is It. They cannot help laughing at the figure he casts swatting about the apartments in search of victims. His underdeveloped body spasms with laughter; through his uniform, she can make out the ribs of his chest. When he senses someone to tag he pretends to be lost and then lurches forward. But Peter's talent in the role of It seems to be limited to catching prey, Catherine notes. He is hopeless at properly identifying the person, thus is forced to remain It round after round. Catherine whispers to his equally daft courtiers to give him some kind of hint so the game might finally conclude.

It is the summer of little oversight, as if the entire palace belongs solely to them and their games, but Catherine never forgets that she is future companion to a king. When the merriment crosses inappropriate boundaries, when they become too loud or disturb the empress during her daytime sleep, everyone relies on Catherine's discretion.

"Quiet," she commands now in a new, imperious tone. The day before, she was on her way to collect portraits of herself and Peter, when she overheard the empress conversing with the doctors.

"Another year? Are you sure?" The empress was in one of her impatient moods. Catherine could hear her skirts brushing across the floor planks. "But we've already done the conversion."

Lestocq's voice, consoling: "A year passes quickly."

"But perhaps he can father a child sooner, perhaps the outward signs are deceiving."

"It is unlikely. His, how to say this, anatomy, is very much a boy's . . ."

Catherine considers tiptoeing her way back toward her apartments, but Bestuzhev is marching down the hall and he caught her flustered countenance outside the door. His eyes narrowed at her. She rushed away, peeking nervously over her shoulder. For the remainder of the day she rolled the precious word around in her mouth. "Year." A year is an eternity.

Now, to bring this silly game to its conclusion, she plants herself directly in Peter's way in order to finally be caught. He has detected her presence. She notes that the thin threads of his muscles tense, readying for the pounce.

"What are you doing? Get out of the way!" screeches Evdotya, the least intelligent of her ladies, who, at seventeen, should know better than to squeal at her mistress like that.

"Got you." Peter's hands are on her shoulders. She can smell the wine on his breath, the residue of charred duck he had for supper. Behind him, their group is convulsed in suppressed laughter, waiting for his conjecture. If he guesses correctly, she becomes It. How she wants him to succeed in this moment, to seize this small victory. He feels the contours of her cheeks and chin with his stubby fingers.

Finally, he says, "I've got it. I know who you are. You are Evdotya. Or should I check lower down to be sure?"

Screaming, gales of it, surrounds her. She pretends to join them in their good humor. Evdotya is clutching her stomach, spasms of laughter convulsing her body. Zhenia wipes her moist face with a handkerchief, the revolving courtiers (what are their names? They are always changing) are patting Peter on the back. She finds none of it funny.

"You are mistaken, it is your future wife," she says. She pretends to be included in the joke, but her whole body flares with shame. Evdotya is not even pretty, with a lumpy, misshapen chin and ruddy claws for hands. So it is as she thought—Catherine has not managed to make him love her and probably never will.

Tanya

Turning the corner with my bag of warm bagels, I see a man sitting on my parents' front steps. He's stout and overdressed for the weather, a ribbed sweatshirt zipped to his neck, a pair of wool slacks riding up his calves. Obviously Russian. Beside him rests a frame wrapped in butcher paper. I freeze, but there's no escape, just a smattering of trees along a long stretch of suburban openness.

Visiting my parents in northern New Jersey is a minivacation for me and I'd been enjoying a quiet morning stroll through Ramsdale. Panera Bread, Dunkin' Donuts, Krazy Bagels, Asia Express. Starbucks filled with teenagers, their heads bowed over their cell phones as if in devout prayer. Gas station attendants pumping gas, leaning back against the pumps to count the bills. Here, on the warm pavement, the world reveals its secrets. The Russian pharmacy with its Polish hand creams, Ukrainian homeopathic drugs, intricate Czech perfume bottles glistening in the window. The Soviet souvenir store—bobble heads of Krushchev next to cheap *matryoshki* in ascending order flashing shellacked gums in their painted-on red kerchiefs. The streets are splashed with young runners, senior citizens pushing before them metal carts. My people everywhere, shifting about with cotton mesh bags, locking SUVs with a decisive beep, lining up for dry cleaning. The spring colors, which glowed dull this morning, now pulse in shades of kaleidoscopic possibility. Ramsdale.

In the 1990s, leaving Queens for New Jersey was upward mobility for a Russian immigrant. No more tenement apartments riddled with ants and cockroaches and neighbors burning pungent foods, no more lumbering buses emitting gas into your window or the bedroom view of a courtyard with overflowing trash cans. The indignities of the Soviet Union were magnified in New York but New Jersey was America in miniature. The civilization of a house, the private dignity of a car, a mall with its neat, spacious clarity. Costco and its promise of deprivation's opposite. New York City was always there when you needed it, and when you lacked the energy to battle the traffic to cross the bridge to its cultural institutions, you watched the Russian television program *Kultura*. ("Our people on the move: *Kultura*.")

The show is anchored by a breathless pixie of a woman who seems to attend every play, opera, and gallery opening in New York City. With textured pleasure, she details to her viewers an unreachable world just over the George Washington Bridge peopled by Russian luminaries: the Misha Baryshnikovs and Anna Netrebkos and Vassily Grigorievs. Her talent is verbal transportation, the dissemination of myth. All of Ramsdale watches the show with bursting pride, the subject always someone's nephew or cousin or patient who's made it. *Our people on the move.*

A few months into my new job as head of Russian art, I got the call to appear on the show. I was strangely proud of the invitation, as if the entire community were a microcosm of a mother's pride. My parents alternated between delight and fear. I was somebody now, but for Russians with a long memory, visibility comes with a sheen of danger; I was in the public eye and vulnerable. My parents' paranoia was not altogether unfounded because after the show aired, strangers began showing up at my parents' house with a parade of masterpieces magically unearthed from ancient relatives. And here is another one.

"If you would just make an appointment at my office," I plead with the waiting man.

"I saw you on show." He's already unwrapping the painting, peeling off strips of brown paper and twine. I set down the bag and look. The subject is a wooded landscape, a silver brook splitting two rows of trees, the final rays of sunlight receding behind clouds. I move in for a closer inspection.

The man notices my flicker of interest. "That's right. I knew if you would only lay eyes on it. Very special Shishkin. You can't argue with quality."

I scan down the canvas for pigment and brushstroke. The first impression is good: it does seem to have age. The painting is typical of the Düsseldorf school, and Ivan Ivanovich Shishkin did study at the Düsseldorf Academy so this type of scene would be typical for him. The front door opens, and my father waves us inside. "Come in, come in. Tea is ready."

My father and the man exchange nods of recognition, of mutual respect. The man, it seems, owns one of the bigger Russian stores in town. He's a minor celebrity in Ramsdale who refers the occasional customer to my father, which means I have to take him seriously. My mother clears the table. The man and I are alone in the dining room with the painting.

"It's not particularly good, is it?" I say, making an effort to camouflage my excitement. Shishkin is a real coup. He is to Russia as Edward Hopper is to America, a painter that can move a true Russian to tears. My clients recall their days as schoolboys when they took excursions to the Tretyakov and encountered their first Shishkin. When I consider quitting my job, I think of what I do as reuniting these men with a dear friend they feared they would never embrace again.

"I would say it's a minor work even if authenticated," I say. Experts must always downplay the work's importance. A closer examination of the surface confirms it: it is a true nineteenth-century.

"Okay, so it's not a masterpiece. Must a genius always make masterpieces? But when I was six years old, I remember it hanging on Tyotya Sonya's wall. Her grandfather knew Shishkin's father from the army ..."

The man's story turns florid around the siege of Leningrad, then flows into a ribald autobiography of three tumultuous marriages, a poet brother arrested by Stalin but then released after interrogation, distinction on a collective farm plucking turkeys, modest fame as a Soviet author of children's nursery rhymes, and now part owner of a chain of

Russian stores in Bergen County. He lifts the painting as I work, tipping its face into the overhead light.

"Please don't do that," I reproach him.

"It's a beauty, yes? I spent years adoring this Shishkin hanging on my auntie's wall, and right before she died, Tyotya Sonya promised to gift me the painting. 'Save it for a day you need a little extra cash,' she told me."

"If you would allow me to handle the painting myself." I stare pointedly at his fingers until they let go of the frame.

In any case, stories like this can never be taken seriously. This kind of seller pulls out almost identical sentimental tales of Soviet wartime. He trots out the same dubious letters from an Aunty Sonya or Aunty Valya dating back to the 1930s that never fail to mention something like, "And by the way, I happened to pick up this special little painting from the studio of a most interesting artist . . ." By now I know better than to get suckered in. Still, this is no fake. The canvas is not lined, the craquelure is right for the era.

I'm overjoyed. I picture Vitya, one of my favorite clients, how he asks every time we're on the phone, "Please, Tan'ka, tell me today is the day you found me a Shishkin."

The description of Tyotya Sonya's final surrender to throat cancer turns gruesome when I interrupt, "Let's turn off the light and take a better look." I scoop out the ultraviolet light always in my bag for just these occasions, and examine the pigment more closely.

The man plucks a chocolate-covered *zephyr* from the dessert tray and bites down. "From my store," he says, holding it up. "Am I right or am I right?"

How this business can always surprise; sometimes, there's nothing less likely than authenticity. "I'll need to show it to my restorer but this is looking good."

"Wonderful, wonderful, Tanyechka." He is onto his second *zephyr* now, praising my mother for the real strength of her brewed tea, none of that weak American crap they call tea. My mother is bustling, blushing with pleasure. The service is set out to perfection, our best tea set, a perfect pyramid of sugar cubes.

"Your father, Tanyechka, is a perfectionist. My customers always say, 'he has magic hands,'" the man says. "Your beautiful mother is the queen of the office. Everyone looks forward to simply sitting in the waiting room and staring at her."

"*Nu,* enough already with your flattery. Shall I splash a little?" My father holds up a bottle of cognac.

"Splash, splash. Who am I to resist?"

Celebratory glasses are handed out. As I wrap the painting, I notice it in the corner. At first it looks like it could be a root from one of the trees, a brushstroke, a flourish in the earth. I shine the light closer. The Shishkin signature is not embedded in the pigment, it hovers on top of the canvas. On closer inspection, the signature is poppy, pretty, lacking in depth. The mark, then, the errant bark I noticed earlier, must be the original painter's name scraped away. Of course. The man purchased a Hans-somebody from the Düsseldorf School for five to seven thousand and is now trying to pass it off as a Shishkin.

I sigh. "Actually, I'm afraid there's a little problem with this Shishkin."

"What problem? What are you talking about?"

My parents have stopped moving in the kitchen, and the only sound we hear is the sound of a television program upstairs: "Ukrainian siblings Sima and Sonia Dodyk were among thirty-eight Jews who lived in a cave during World War Two for eighteen months, thus surviving the Holocaust."

The guy puts down the *zephyr,* his face gathering color. "I told you, my Tyotya Sonya has owned this painting her entire life. I thought you were this great expert."

I think about Carl—on the subway, he would lean back against the door and embrace me through the fits and starts of the train—and a torrent of unexpected sadness overwhelms me. I think I might cry right here, in front of this man and his fake Shishkin. But I swallow. "I know this must be a huge shock. But I'm afraid that although on first inspection it looked so encouraging, you'll see that under the trunk of that tree, there are the remnants of an original signature."

The man meets the eyes of my parents as if to say, *Can you believe this? Who does she think she is?* He is shrouding the face of the painting in reams of butcher paper, a series of angry strokes. "Five minutes of expertise and it's already got a problem? That's all I get? I was just speaking to Nadia Kudrina at Christie's and she says this is an important work. And come to think of it, did she not sell that record Shishkin last season? I guess I should go and see her after all."

The door is slammed shut and we hear the furious roar of an engine blocking our driveway.

"Are you sure you're correct?" my father asks. He looks shocked. "Is there any chance it really is a Shishkin?"

It's not the constant flood of fakes that get to me in this job; I'm used to them by now. I've been shown "early twentieth-century" paintings where the paint was still wet. Respected gallerists thrusting before me canvases baked in an oven to give the impression of age, second cousins at birthday parties asking me to appraise posters sloppily wedged into frames. That doesn't bother me anymore. It's the presumption that travels with me everywhere: I don't deserve my position, my expertise is nothing more than an accident of luck. My parents immigrated with someone who could not rise in the New World. Who is incapable of doing whatever it takes to make something of herself.

I heave, then the tears come in earnest. "I'm the specialist!"

My mother drops the dishes and hurries over. "Come here, hand it to me."

She cradles my head in her elbow, thumb working at the muscles in my neck. When as a child I was tormented by a nameless panic, a horror I could not pin down, my mother used to say, *Hand it to me.* And it always worked; once I voiced my fears to my mother, once I displaced that tumor of confusion from my own mind onto hers, it never failed to vanish. So now, in the pauses between a fresh wave, I hand her all of it: the fear of an incomprehensible new life, losing Carl. And the deepest, unvoiced one of all: that my marriage is falling apart and the fault is mine.

My mother listens, nods, takes in all my ramblings. I'm impressed that she asks no questions about Carl, offers no advice on what a woman has to do to regain the affections of her husband. She strokes my cheek.

"Don't worry, Tanchik. We won't be shopping at this man's store anymore."

As if to reinforce the dawning of a new era, my father grabs the entire bowl of chocolate *zephyrs,* and with the flourish of a former soccer player, flings the contents into the garbage can and slams down the lid.

Catherine

Peter's skin burns to the touch but he refuses to retire to his room. The objective of this particular game is to take turns telling the truth.

"I hate the empress's birthday fetes," he says. He strings up one of his puppets by the neck and hangs him from a bedpost. He is unusually pale and sluggish today. "I find it unbearable the way she outfits herself like a young lady, which she is not. She is old and a whore. Your turn."

"You look ill. Get some rest." Catherine sighs. In the distance, she hears the singing of the matins, probably coming from the ladies in her antechamber. She is not deeply devout, but his complaining on a Sunday is particularly grating. "Please, for the sake of your health."

"Must I? But I'm so bored," he says, then, brightening, "Did I tell you I retained a dwarf? He's extremely loyal to me."

She feels the plane of his forehead, then pulls back. "You are burning with fever. I will send for Lestocq. Now go."

At last, he shuffles off to his chambers, and she is left alone. She tries to practice the harpsichord but manages only a few halfhearted notes before worries engulf her. How sick is he? Should he be truly ill, her situation would be shaky. As it is, the long engagement is making everyone impatient, her role not yet cemented. A year, the empress said. What seemed before like freedom is now an extended purgatory.

She bursts into her mother's rooms. Johanna is in the middle of writing letters, but puts down her quill. These days, this is where mother and daughter are in unison. Their heads are bowed together on the settee, fingers clasped. They whisper a mutual language of comets and plans, their breath warm, intermingling.

"Let us change you into one of your more somber gowns and inquire after the grand duke," Johanna suggests. Once Catherine has on her gray daytime dress, they rush down the hallways of the wooden palace. At the door to Peter's room stands Count Brummer. He is blocking the entrance, and they can hear a flurry of agitated voices on the other side of the door.

"We are here to inquire after the health of the grand duke," her mother says.

The past year has brought a new imperiousness to her tone, an imitation of the empress's. She pushes their way forward but Brummer holds his place. A rivulet of sweat runs down each temple. If the grand duke dies, Catherine supposes he too will be sent back to Germany.

"Please, no farther," Brummer says in that thin, whiny way of his. "Smallpox sores have appeared on the body of the grand duke."

There is an intake of breath. Catherine comes forward. "Can I see him?"

"No, Figgy, are you mad? No!" Her mother pulls her away. "Death is looking him over. We must get out of its way." This is not the friend of the settee, but a frenzied creature dragging her away by the hand.

When they are out of earshot, Catherine says, "It seems wrong to run. Am I not neglecting my duties?"

"Don't you understand? Your sister's death. It would all be for nothing."

Just a week before, the letter came. Her two-year-old sister was dead of smallpox. She died in dreadful pain and motherless, a sacrifice to their royal ambitions. They have funneled all their fortunes into the scrawny, ailing boy on the other side of the door.

She summons the words they are both thinking. "But Mama, what if he dies?"

Outside the window, snow is being added to more snow. From time to time, a lone wolf comes into view, a speck of gray fur. Other than sledding or the occasional ride in the carriage, she has been confined to the palace for days. They watch the messenger to the doctor climbing into his sled, shaking his black coat from the onslaught of flakes.

She does not want Peter to die, she knows that much. Is it love, pity, or a stubborn projection for her future? She has no idea.

"We'll go to Moscow," her mother decides. "Send your Katya to pack our bags." This is her mother at her most regal. In moments of crisis, she sees clearly what must be done, arranges all the details. She will have them settled before nightfall. This is the part of her mother Catherine hopes to forge in herself.

"What if he dies, Mama?"

They are flying up the stairs, ready to disperse to their chambers and begin the work of leaving. And before disappearing to her wing, Johanna adds, "We need him alive but we need us alive more."

"Shall I send him a note, a few kind words?"

"Yes, that would be strategic," Johanna says, in the breathy way of having remembered a crucial item for the journey. "Reiterate your affection, prayers for his full recovery, those kinds of sentiments."

In her rooms, Catherine sits down at her desk. These days, when she sets her mind to writing, she finds that words are materializing in Russian just as frequently as in German. She has always loved jotting thoughts down on paper, her favorite exercise being describing herself: proud, not unattractive, lively eyes, practical, busy, not as patient as she would like, hungry to learn. She can picture her future self exchanging letters with the foremost philosophers of the day, who would take her seriously for the incisive, fluid nature of her prose. They would be impressed that a woman shared their curiosity about the world, despised shallow political intrigue, and loved frank, military character. They would read the contents of her letters at dinners, quote them to eminent friends. She will be at the helm of salons, she decides, bringing together European luminaries. Her library will be the largest in the world. Not to mention art. Standing before Peter the Great's sole Rembrandt, featuring the two men and their sad parting, she felt a new thirst for acquisition.

Then she remembers that all this glory hinges on Peter not dying. Should he die, her words will not be read, her library unformed, no philosophers would be gathered in her drawing rooms. Who would want to pore over the memoirs of a common princess from Zerbst?

"My dear Grand Duke," she begins, conjuring up that weak chin, those doggish, mercurial eyes. Her mind is blank. She plays with the handle of the dressing table, slides the drawer open and closed. The knob twists loose in her hand. Under the empress's distracted care, the entire palace is an underbuilt mixture of extravagance and filth. If she were empress, she would call in European architects immediately. She would be ashamed to call this her home.

"My dear Grand Duke. I pray for your recovery." She crosses this out. A banal repetition of her mother's words. "I long to fortify the mettle of your soul." Strikes this out too.

Her mother stands at the door. "The carriage is ready."

She is already in her fine coat, the heavy brocade one; underneath she wears her blue velvet gown lined with silver and silk. Behind her glows the face of her too loyal Katya, armed with their bags and dressed for the journey.

Catherine rushes along the page. "Each day, I will await news of your recovery. I will pray for your health and light candles in your name. My future husband, my dear friend, cousin. The companion of my life. My love." She struck the last part out, then reinstated it. Should this letter be intercepted later she will seem adequately attached.

Ekaterina, she signs at the bottom. As if to say: this name will not be taken away from me. A contract must be honored when it is committed to paper.

While she waits for news in Moscow, there is music and dancing and cards. Also visitors from abroad, familiar faces she knew back in Germany. The one she has been eagerly awaiting is Count Gyllenborg. He is sipping tea across from her while the Swedish diplomats are gathered around the faro table in animated conversation about someone named

Colley Cibber and an anticipated London production of *Papal Tyranny in the Reign of King John.*

"Do you know the plays of Mr. Cibber?" Gyllenborg asks.

"I'm afraid I haven't had the pleasure to acquaint myself . . ."

She blushes, deeply. More and more she is reminded of being in a far-flung land, far from the centers of culture. If she were empress, she thinks, Colley Cibber would perform the play in St. Petersburg or, better yet, she would send promising Russian playwrights like Sumarokoff to London to cultivate their talents. Her mind is racing: rather than merely importing culture, it is crucial to encourage it to flourish at home. Except for art. That must be imported; there was barely anything to look at in this country apart from that Rembrandt.

"Cibber's actually a vain fool, nothing in the world would entice me to see work that is in conspicuously bad taste."

"Oh," she says, even more mortified. Cibber will not be invited then, she notes to herself.

"No need for meekness. You must exercise your mind first and foremost," Gyllenborg is snapping. The orchestra is playing a pleasing medley of Italian concertos but the noise drowns out the possibility of intimate conversation. The entertainment was her idea, a way to impress upon the man that her taste for music is discerning, but now he is leaning forward to make himself heard over the din of it. She shoots a look at the violinist, the worst offender.

"That is indeed how I occupy my days."

"Very good. You were not a little fool, as I recall."

Count Gyllenborg is older than she remembers him from their meeting in Hamburg a few years ago. On top of his head sits a short wig held together by a giant bow at the nape of his neck. His fleshy features rarely distract from a vivacious sparkle in his eye, the seductive curl of his lip. She feels shy before him, eager to stun him with her singularity, the refined quality of her taste.

"I have heard talk of a writer named Samuel Richardson. Are his books any good?"

The count is gulping at his tea as if thirsty, his eyes trained on hers.

"Reading the proper philosophical books should be the first step of your education."

"I would be happy for any recommendations, Count."

She sends Katya for paper and writing utensils, awakened to the prospect of being taken seriously. Here he is, a great scholar and politician, spending his days of diplomacy by her side. Hers! At only fifteen years old, and he at least thirty. A man of letters, a respected Swedish politician, this man with the penetrating gaze. Even her mother hovers around him, ready to shoo away servants and tend to him herself. He tolerates her scurrying for a bit, then Johanna is called away to scold a new maid. They are left to their private corner, the glow of fire, of after-dinner candles. The shadow of Peter has been dispersed, and she is free.

"Even as a young child, you were not stupid," he says, pushing away the tray of sweets, then changing his mind and popping a corner of cake into his mouth. She rued the simplicity of the dessert. Had Peter not been ill and had she access to the Parisian confectioner, she could have commissioned a cake in the shape of the Swedish capital.

He does not look past her like Brummer, Bestuzhev, and the rest of them. He meets her gaze directly, holds it, penetrates it. His eyes are a cool, light brown of new earth.

"I took note of you even then, your quick wit. You were smarter than many of the guests. Your mother never appreciated you."

She is silent, too suffused with joy to speak.

"I remember even as a child you always had a philosophical turn of mind. How are you faring in your new surroundings?" He does a little tilt with his fingers, indicating the apartments.

The empress is right: she has been nervously spending money all over Europe. The chintz upholstery of the chaise is new, she has been replacing the frayed drapes, ordering gold tinsel braid for curtains. Then there is the light blue riding habit on order in addition to two identical dresses from Paris.

"I'm reading books recommended to me by philosophers and friends. In my spare time, I study the language and play the harpsichord."

He smiles, sets down his cup. "I've been watching you here. You have lost something of yourself in this place. Your character is weaker, absorbed with pleasure and luxury and, dare I say it, romance?"

She reaches for her tea, to shield her face behind the rim of the porcelain. He is right, of course. Her impulse has been to celebrate her new position, and she has found herself in a loop of amusements and idle purchases. No romance, however, none of that.

"You must recover the natural inclination of your mind."

His words stir her. A man has not taken her this seriously since George. "If you have suggestions, I would be pleased to hear them."

Katya rushes into the room, her slim hand holding out the sheaves of paper.

The orchestra pauses, and Gyllenborg leans back into his armchair. "Of course you must read Plutarch and Cicero and *The Cause of the Grandeur and Decline of the Roman Republic* by Montesquieu."

"I will send for them at once."

Catherine is wearing her finest velvet, the one that so delicately reveals the neck and, unless she is mistaken, he is taking note of the slope of her shoulders. This is not the first time she has been awakened to the salacious glances of men; they have grown more presumptuous the longer her wedding is delayed. Is it disloyal to inwardly burn while her future husband is possibly dying back in St. Petersburg?

Suddenly Gyllenborg bends before her on the rug. His face is so close to hers that their lips are almost touching. "A pity you will marry him."

"A pity?" she says.

"A great pity. Such an imbalance of talents."

She waits nervously, nostrils flaring. She is aware of the wide hoop of her gown, the artificiality of the tall wig that has recently become fashionable at court, the outline of her still too small breasts. A deep swell rises to wind the clock of her mind. She is wasting time, valuable time.

The orchestra strikes up again, the violinist piercing in his renewed intensity. Gyllenborg seems to observe her closely and decide. His attention returns to his seat and his unfinished cake. "Never mind, Sophia. Forget I said anything."

Just a few short weeks later, Peter and the empress are returned to the Winter Palace and it is cold again, a dreadful cold and empty rooms. She can hear them dropping off parcels in the foyer. The ceremony of intricate greetings floods its way to her, their welcome by the staff, the empress's ringing voice. *We are happy to report that the Grand Duke has made a complete recovery.*

Catherine assesses herself in the mirror, the stray hairs framing her temple, the rash at her neck she tries not to scratch, the freshly applied mauve of her lips. She is looking for what Gyllenborg had observed in her, bright eyes, pink skin, tall, intelligent forehead. This time, she resolves to start fresh, to be more patient with her future groom. His childish smirk is merely shyness, his tiresome drilling of soldiers should be treated as loneliness. With her help, he will outgrow his boyishness. Who knows? Lying day after day in the thrall of death, he may have thought of her too, his imagination darting to the very same places Gyllenborg so admired. She will share with him her new revelation (the happy queen and her consort, Maria-Theresa and Francis, and what about the great love Peter the Great shared with his Catherine in their log cabin?). Already, thanks to Gyllenborg, she is spending her free time reading and weaving tales about who she wants to be.

The rooms are bare of light at four o'clock, and she runs to the reception area, shaking off a deepening chill. At this hour, the shawl barely warms, even her nose is cold. The shadows are so deep, the milling faces almost indistinguishable to her. An influx of spring air wafts through the front door, dispersing the smell of unwashed bodies.

Once the flurry of kisses are concluded, the grand duke is placed before her. She cannot help it—she cringes. His illness has cratered and puckered his face, the oversized wig meant to camouflage his new baldness only emphasizes his bulbous face. The creature is hideous. Only the eyes gazing out from the ravaged landscape look familiar, and they are coldly scanning her for a reaction.

"Am I so changed that you do not recognize me?" he asks, voice raspy, ill-used.

She is speechless. She should be grateful for this recovery. There is no one to challenge her now. The marriage will go forward. The imaginary world of salons and libraries and philosophical discourse is open to her once more. But he is dreadful to behold, unthinkable almost in his scarred hideousness. So far from Gyllenborg, from her uncle.

She sees that in the brief span of time she is absorbing her shock and gathering herself to lie, he has made a decision about her. She watches him blinking rapidly, his jaw set and angry. He spins around to his footman: "Be careful with my purchases, idiot."

"I have been personally praying for your recovery," she stammers. But he is already wandering off in the direction of his chambers, an enormous wig on top of an emaciated body. The hands folded behind him are crossed in warning.

"Aren't you going to greet me, my dear?"

Catherine should have realized the empress would be displeased with the reunion. The empress is always watching but her conclusions alter from day to day.

Catherine allows herself to be squeezed and her cheeks to be pinched. Is it her imagination or is the hug extra long? The empress is breathing down to her, stale from the long trip. "Dearest, I have ordered a portrait of the grand duke especially for you. It should be delivered next week."

She hopes the portrait was executed before the smallpox. "How thoughtful of Your Majesty. I will very much look forward to its arrival."

"It is understandable that you have been worried, as have we all. What is that you are holding?"

She looks down. The Montesquieu tome Gyllenborg recommended, thick, stubbornly impenetrable, is folded at her hip. In her haste, she has forgotten to leave it in her room. "A book, but I do not think I will get through it."

"Good." The empress sniffs. "I never read books of this sort and neither should you. My advisors read and report back only what they think I should know. That is best, don't you think? The print is small and we must preserve our eyes. Now let me tell you about that brave boy's recovery. I sat by his side day and night."

She throws off her furs, winds her hand around Catherine's elbow, and continues in this vein all the way past the construction to the gallery. Outside the back windows, Catherine takes in a glimpse of the frozen Neva stretching beyond end, beyond horizon. She wonders, *When will it finally melt?*

Tanya

The car hugs the edge of a snaking mountain road. I roll down the window and inhale the sea into my lungs. Monaco. If it weren't for my job, for Medovsky's invitation, I would never find myself in a place like this. We pass by a long street with intimidating shops, their white façades, gold letters. Rolex. Cartier. Louis Vuitton. Then back to the hills, fern and lavender on one side, on the other the expanse of turquoise horizon.

My first time in Monaco, I was not at all prepared for the pristine beauty of the coastline at sunset, crisp like a white satin sheath. The undulating blues and whites, toes of yachts wiggling in clear water, the yellow eyes of the hotels, the rectangles of private pools and faces of hotels and glass rooftops. The sight of it, the largeness of attention it demanded. The disparity between my life and that of my clients.

There were my clients, with their hundred-million-euro villas spread out over four floors, shimmering hot tubs right in the middle of living rooms framed by Grecian columns, the rooftop helicopter pad, Turkish spa, 1920s movie theater, a rooftop water slide curved into an infinity pool that gave the impression of falling into the Mediterranean. What a difference from where I grew up! And there were my parents in northern New Jersey, with their two-floor Colonial, their clunky but reliable Volvo from 1999, their gym membership where they snuck in as one another in order to battle senior citizens over empty pool lanes. They could never shed their Soviet tactics of self-preservation. They bought an extra packet of cookies for their friends if there was a two-for-one sale, logged on to their neighbors' open-access Internet, and packed brioche rolls from Russian restaurants into their bags for the following breakfast. How could I reconcile the lucky, middle-class lives of my parents with these people in Monaco, who graduated from the same Soviet public schools, attended the same universities, but here they were with their villas and chunky Winston emeralds and private dancers flown in from Buenos Aires.

How abhorrent my clients appeared to me at first. Women as foreign as aliens, wives confiding while condescending to me: *Tanyechka, talk some sense into him, will you? Do we really need the headache of owning a yacht? Does my daughter really need Taylor Swift at her bat mitzvah when that Selena Gomez would do just fine? Do we really need a custom Lamborghini Veneno?* How Carl laughed when I described the awkwardness of bumping into the singer George Michael in one of the bedrooms trying out a few sentences of Russian in preparation for a bat mitzvah concert.

I take in the Côte d'Azur, the air's orange sweetness and the magnificent view, pushing aside this image of Carl, his funny way of laughing as if only his mouth were involved in the act. *He'll be back soon, he'll be back very soon.* The tablet is open to the profiles of potential clients I'm here to meet—Medovsky's buddies Oleg and David. Their rumored purchases at Sotheby's and Christie's, their trinity of homes in Moscow, London, and Monaco. Their photographs revealing thick necks, crisp collars, hair cropped close to the head. But my mind wanders.

We pull up to a structure that seems to sink into its landscape, seems to be sculpted out of the very rock around it. The wide iron gates pull back to engulf the car into the complex.

From what I hear, Medovsky paid five hundred million euros to tear down a perfectly luxurious villa and build a riad in its place. A Moroccan riad on the Côte d'Azur! Only my clients would think of something like this. The exterior is a plain fortress of mud-brick wall so you think you're about to enter a modest, simple home. In the oligarch's case, the riad's is a useful structure for privacy, but the interior is far from modest.

Stepping into the atrium, through the horseshoe arches and past the interior courtyard, I find myself in front of a fountain that looks suspiciously like a miniature replica of Rome's Trevi Fountain complete with Neptune's chariot with sea horses, the general Agrippa, and the papal coat of arms. The floors are lined with terra-cotta tiles etched with Hebrew, rather than Arabic, calligraphy. Lemon trees in full bloom garnish the voluminous red walls.

I can barely take it all in when the doors swing open and in clicks a tall blonde, the kind who's used to pausing a room with her entrance. She's wearing a floor-length jersey dress speckled with flowers. Her neck is evenly bronzed and a gold clutch is tucked beneath her arm. I should have known Nadia Kudrina would be here.

My former assistant is twenty-five years old and knows next to nothing about Russian or any other art history but her father is PYOTOR Oil chairman Arkady Kudrin, and many powerful men who do business with Kudrin have no choice but to consign with Nadia at Christie's.

She heads immediately for my cheek. "*Privet,* Tanyechka. How are things at Worthy's?"

"Great, Nadia. You?"

"*Normal'no.* Too busy. As usual."

There's no competition on any level with a Russian woman like this: hair ironed flat and combed over one shoulder, robust breasts in danger of escaping her Etro gown, a porcelain leg emerging from an impossibly high slit, unmarked face professionally applied. A pair of expensive sunglasses perch on top of her head. This is the woman whose Facebook profile photo shows her lying on her stomach in a purple lace teddy, heels crossed like daggers behind her, her head tilted to the side, lips glistening purple. Who posts languorous photos of herself on European bridges with men thirty years her senior. Who appears at art openings in head-to-toe fish netting, pens an advice column on how to oversee an armada of domestic staff in *Tatler.* Who's been named by a British gossip magazine as the Russian Kim Kardashian.

"What a treat to see you here." I try to sound genuine but I'm instantly on my guard. Nadia always manages to make me feel like the help she is always hiring and firing for one of her global homes. "Your last sale was pretty impressive. I really love those Chagalls you got. Congratulations."

"The synagogue ones, you mean? The rare oils?"

"I love the stained glass of the Vilna one."

"It's the one always singled out in press. But the others are more interesting, no?"

"I actually prefer the one that's singled out."

I've detested Nadia since she first set foot in Worthington's dressed inappropriately in a white Hervé Leger bandage dress and strappy gold pumps for her first day of work as a summer intern. The girl was everything I dreaded, a lithe, sexual creature, an entitled exhibitionist posting pictures of herself dancing at some Art Basel party or on a yacht in the Maldives or at Reese Witherspoon's wedding. Her very presence announced her as Nadia Kudrina, enfant terrible, fulfilling her global Russian destiny, and no one would stand in her way. When she left the company, I was relieved, assumed Kudrin whisked her away to an internship in fashion or public relations. Except Nadia emerged as the head of Russian art at Christie's and her first auction, a terribly uneven selection from her father's personal collection, raised fifteen million dollars. "The one that got away" is how Marjorie referred to her in my presence. A rueful glance at me as the one who stayed.

"It's a mess out there, isn't it? Are you still managing to pull together auctions? I barely unloaded that Serebriakova for six mil."

"Actually, I've got a great Nesterov for the fall," I say.

"Oh, Nesterov." Nadia takes out a compact, does a quick assessment. "I know the one. Overcleaned, right? After the restorers were done, nothing left of the original."

"And Grigoriev."

"The one that's not an oil?"

I'm so angry, I decide to take the risk. "And, of course, the centerpiece lot. Catherine the Great's Order of Saint Catherine. It's authentic. We've got it confirmed." That is at least partially true.

Nadia looks up from the mirror. "Oh? And where did that come from? How come I haven't heard anything about it this late in the game?"

"Trust me, you will."

A trio of men in hooded dishdashas gesture for us to follow and I eagerly line up behind them. This may be my first moment of triumph with Nadia Kudrina.

"Anyway," Nadia says, swaying behind me, "I am surprised you're even here. I thought I left a message with your assistant, to save you a trip. Maybe it slipped my mind."

"That's thoughtful."

"Tan'. It's like you don't believe I'm sincere. I respect you. There might just not be enough business for both of us. That's a fact."

We're being guided down elaborate open galleries, past the steamy door of the hammam, through sumptuous rooms filled with treasures—vases, tapestries, European masterpieces, rugs—underneath the coffered wood ceilings and drooping lanterns. Palaces like this terrified me at first, but now I appreciate the treasures independent of their owners. We step out onto a garden the size of a city block, through a snakelike trellis, past olive groves and lemon trees, and before a set of gold double doors. We're bidden to take off our shoes and slip on silk babouches.

My first impression is the rose flash of illumination, a room exploding with light. Women wearing elaborate caftans with silk strappy heels and heavy chandelier earrings. Dashing between them are the black spots of occasional tuxedos. The women call out to Nadia, fold her into their circle. I'm free of her, but then there's that moment at a party where you're aware of being very much alone. The klezmer band launches into a new song and, at its head, I recognize the famous violinist Itzhak Perlman.

When I enter parties like this, my initial instinct is to flee, but now I slap the widest of smiles on my face and look approachable. I kiss familiar, nameless people on the cheek, compliment the women on their appearances. I raise myself to my full height and stalk to the bar. But once there, I'm intercepted by a chalky face topped by a beret. It grimaces at me with a wide pair of black-rimmed eyes. Its painted red lips seem to be murmuring something. I try to move away from its mouth but the crowd at the bar pins us together. The sound resembles *muzh. Muzhmuzhmuzh,* the creature is mouthing.

"What's with you?" someone asks, because what must I look like?

Frozen, wide-eyed. All I can see is the red mouth, elaborately outlined. But then it's moving away from me and toward a woman in a long silver gown who's stuffed most of a Pomeranian into a Gucci clutch.

I notice there are more of these white-painted men on stilts and unicycles, bending over to tap guests on their shoulders, drawing them into elaborate pantomimes. Mimes. For God's sake, they're only mimes. I try to still the rattling in my rib cage and pretend to enjoy their pranks. I can already imagine Medovsky's wife, Lena, in that brittle way of hers, saying, "But the Soltukovs had a skating rink and penguins! We can't let them throw the better party."

A glass of pink champagne is eased into my hand and I wander outdoors by the pool where the laser light show is streaming neon onto the Olympic-sized pool and groups of people lounge on cushions under caidal tents. A few of the guests are watching the interplay of light, and I press between them for a view. A pair of tightrope walkers are traversing a taut string over the pool, stacked Louis XIV chairs balanced on top of their heads. This is exactly the kind of lunacy Carl would be fascinated by.

In those days before the book, he would invent day trips for us to Roosevelt Island, to the Cloisters. Inside a basket he packed for us, I would find the strangest things: hummus and sliced turkey bacon, dried currants and shaved ginger and pitted olives. I loved his wacky lunches. When I prepared our meals, they were carefully compiled, a sandwich, a vegetable, a dessert. Practical and composed.

It was that afternoon at the Cloisters that I told him I would take the job. If I don't step up, who would do it? I was the best specialist in a burgeoning field, a field increasingly littered with fakes. Who else will separate the authentic from the forgery? Who else will see to it that Russian art has a future, that the world so wary of Russian politics won't be suspicious of the Russian market?

"Sure, if you love it," he said, as I knew he would.

Follow your passion, live your dream, all those heady American myths. I loved that Carl believed them all.

"My job's so safe now." I was thinking out loud. "That's why I'm not sure. But it's finally the step up in the company I've been waiting for. It's my chance to be a vice president."

"But do you love your job like I love teaching?" He made the question sound so simple. "I can't even tell how much you like what you do. You're always stressed. I can only imagine how much more stressed you'll be after you take this job."

"Being the head of a department's no joke. You're really expected to pull off these insane auctions. And all that travel. But it's an opportunity that won't come by again." I pause, consider, and decide to plunge ahead. "Anyway, it's not like we can afford to turn it down, right? We don't even know if Ditmas will hire you." Carl looked crushed. He took one more bite, then put his sandwich aside. There was the twinge of regret but I wasn't used to the role of breadwinner; there was no room in Russian culture to accommodate it. Each week, my parents asked, "Did Carl get job yet?" and I was never brave enough to say I earned for the two of us.

The Monacan sky has not fully darkened over the Medovsky compound, the smudge of color still a vivid purple. Among the tables laden with food, I catch sight of my client, and next to him are Oleg and David, easily recognizable from their online photos. Before them is an elaborate presentation of shashliki in the shape of a dartboard. They slide the meat off with their teeth, then use the skewer for target practice.

"Gentlemen," I say, hands light on the backs of their chairs.

"Tanyechka, welcome." Medovsky kisses me on both cheeks, exuding genuine pleasure. He is springing with good spirit, the fabric of his Italian shirt already wrinkled, his hair escaping its pomade and poking in every direction. His is a messy energy, the kind that relies on women to contain it. Still, I forget how much I like him, his warmth and eagerness to provide pleasure for everyone around him. He's also Jewish, and there's this link of outsider culture between us—to Russians, we'll always be considered Jews, not Russians.

"Sash, thanks so much for hosting me in this marvelous place. And what a good cause."

The men are rising to greet me, pulling me a spare chair, loading my plate with grilled lamb. I should be glad for the opening; all I have to do now is run the pitch on the steam of all this goodwill. But I'm still shaky from the mimes, as if they were warning me of something. *Muzh-muzhmuzh.* Nadia steps out onto the pool area, surveying the scene, probably preparing a predatory lunge in our direction. I feel my heart zipping again. There's no time to reel them in, to close any deal.

"This is not only a beautiful woman, but an extraordinary art specialist," Medovsky is saying about me. I can hear him praising my eye to his friends, my graduate degree, my learned expertise. Magic, he calls my ability to put forth the most interesting of auctions, items culled for historical importance and also the kind of items not easily found elsewhere. But all I hear behind me is the advance of the stunning twenty-five-year-old Nadia and it seems to me that I'm being annihilated in her wake. Her heels are meant to stamp me out, make me irrelevant.

("Does he have another woman?" my mother asked, delicately. "He's definitely cheating," said Alla. "You don't want to admit it, but it's the most obvious answer.")

I interrupt Medovsky's eulogy with a hasty fanning out of the catalogues, pointing out the most interesting of the lots, chattering nervously about the Order of Saint Catherine, about Larionov, Nesterov, and Archipenko, and even the fake Shishkin from Ramsdale. I'm engaging in an amateur's trap, displaying an overeagerness that will distance the men from me, but I can't stop. Nadia's aura of sickly bergamot is advancing into our space, consuming us all with its aggressive scent. The men sink deeper into their seats, clicking off. In vain, I try to slow down, to bring them back around with my usual tactics.

"Oleg Alexanderovich, do you own a home nearby?"

But it's too late: Nadia is bending over them with her jerseyed breasts and long strands of highlighted hair, her gold snake cuffs gripping her upper arm, and they awaken to her presence. She may be no art specialist, but she knows how to hold attention. They bid me to sit down, step aside, enjoy the show. *Relax. Life is not all work, is it?*

"Hey, Tan'." Medovsky pulls me aside. He's annoyed. "We save our business for tomorrow."

"Okay," I say, shaky.

He taps me in the direction of the party. "For God's sake, at least go enjoy yourself."

I don't know where to turn. Slashes of neon dance across my skin, Céline Dion is singing "If You Could See Me Now" either over a very clear loudspeaker or in person somewhere beyond the lemon groves. The mimes are undulating around me, obscuring me in the final hours before dusk.

Saint-Tropez by helicopter is a blur of land and water. We're escalating ahead of the clouds, shredding through them one at a time. The engine's too loud, the seat belt is flimsy. The dips and jolts of the cabin are wild and erratic. This was not what I had in mind when Medovsky suggested we do business, but you don't argue when you're being led up to the rooftop helicopter pad, and eased into an open door of a whirring chopper.

Of course, now I wish I'd had the courage to opt out of this little trip. After assassinations, polonium poisonings, acid attacks, and murders of journalists in their lobbies, the next most popular method of wreaking vengeance on enemies in this dangerous world is tampering with victims' transportation. How many times have I received the ominous news that a client was shot while getting into his armored car in Luxembourg or died in a private jet crash or simply "expired with no known cause"? How many times have I received phone calls from brand-new widows to cancel the preempt or to suddenly ask me to fly out to estimate estate property?

Outside there's sky, immense and vacant. In the tight compartment, my legs brush against the bare, sculpted calves of Medovsky's mistress— what's her name again? Milla? Malvina? A fair-skinned, red-haired, freckled thing—as she flips through photographs of opulent estates. The stout Realtor with a short, no-nonsense haircut, her neck zigzagged by layered gold necklaces, has been talking the entire time in frilly, pattering Russian. Once in a while, we bend down to earth to circle a property the size of a town in New Jersey.

The Realtor continues, "A professional dance studio can easily be installed if we build into the atrium. And you said you liked fish? An aquarium would be on point right now."

"If we could just do a quick perusal of these other lots," I interrupt, pushing forward the auction catalogue, but the mistress has her head against the windowpane, asking, "Is that fountain the Florentine one pictured here?"

"Yes, yes, the very same. A tycoon from Singapore, I think. One of those rich Asians. He's had the place for eight months and he's fixed the place right up." The Realtor ignores me because she recognizes in me a person in the same position as herself. A supplicant, a salesperson. An outsider.

"I do love a labyrinth," the mistress says, pinching Medovsky's cheek. Medovsky seems hardly the kind to tolerate pinching, but he's grimacing into his laptop, that sloping eyebrow that lends him a darkly quizzical look.

"Then I would love for you to look at a couple of the most exclusive items we have coming up. The Goncharova especially would look great in that space here, and should you decide to donate to a museum show, for example, we can swap in another piece that's exactly the same size."

"I'll worry about furniture and let Sasha pick the art," the mistress says to me sweetly. She's all waves and iridescent hair, a pinprick of a girl. Eager to please and grateful, with flimsy shoulders. I try not to linger on the mistresses for too long; until they turn into wives, mistresses come and go.

Medovsky chides me. "Donation to a show? Getting a little ahead of yourself, are you, Mother Teresa of auction houses? You should have gotten to know the guys last night, Tanyush. I told them you were the real deal. But they liked Nadia because she didn't throw catalogues in their faces."

"Somehow I doubt that was the reason they liked her."

"Are you referring to her tits?" Medovsky laughs. "What do you expect? They're art collectors. Shouldn't they admire the female form?"

I can feel it rising inside me, the same swell I had at my parents' house with the Shishkin. That's all I need, to break out crying ten thousand feet in the air with an oligarch, his mistress, and a Realtor. "Sash, you know I'm an actual expert and she's not, right? Her knowledge of art is as sophisticated as . . . I mean, she's twenty-five and has never even taken an art history course as far as I know. I have a master's degree and years of experience, Sash. I know this stuff."

"Of course you do. That's why when that classless Kudrin ribs me about why I'm not with Christie's, I just tell him that his daughter's a sweetheart but you know your shit. But my friends need a little more connection before they do business."

"I didn't have a chance with Nadia breathing down my neck. Those mimes." I manage to reel in the tears.

"Hey, did you like the mimes? Pretty special. Brought them down from Paris. God, I used to love Marcel Marceau as a kid. Didn't you? I used to cry watching him in that pisshole of a *kommunalka*."

Despite myself, I continue to like him. A softie. I taught Medovsky that English word and he uses it in the press from time to time. "Success depends on personal relations with power, and if you are on the wrong side of this, there are limits to what you can achieve," he told one British reporter. "But I'm not like those other Russian guys taking over your city. I have soul, I am softie." I e-mailed him: "Bravo!" Strangely proud that a word I personally inserted into this man's mouth would find its way into the pages of The *Guardian*.

He closes shut his laptop. "Listen, you're getting me that Order, right?"

The transition in tone is abrupt. This is a command. As if to underline this point, the wings overhead flap a little less vigorously. "You're getting you that Order, Sash."

"Okay, okay. I just want you to tell my competition to look elsewhere. This is no game. You-know-who is expecting it. I made a solemn promise and there is no going back." But then he flashes a charming smile as if to say he was kidding, how could he be angry with me?

"Are you sure you won't consider donating it after all? How great would it look in the Tretyakov across from the portrait where's she's wearing it?"

"Tan'. We're not having this conversation again, yes?" Husky darkness swirls around in his voice.

The Realtor clears her throat nervously. "Now this one right here is terribly sweet and worth a look around. Shall we?"

The domed house below us sprawls along the edge of the water; on the port, a yacht is docked. "Smaller than the last one, but a great view of the sea," the Realtor says. Then begrudgingly, with a sour nod in my direction, from one salesperson to another, "And you'll find plenty of room inside for your art."

"What was all that about, Tanyush? Donate, donate, donate. Why are you on my case, *nu*? Do you get some kind of special tax break or something?" Medovsky is smoking outside the pillars of the villa in a series of rapid huffs. The private beach is speckled with pebbles so white and unblemished, they might have been flown in to populate the shoreline.

"Of course not! It's just one of my goals; you know, more Russian art where people can see it. It's none of my business."

"That's right. It's none of your business. Leave that shit to those bored socialites, the Zhukovas and Kudrinas. You concentrate on doing what you do best."

The mistress's oohs of appreciation waft from somewhere deep inside the house. I've seen enough mistresses to know the phase of the relationship. These women think if they're ensconced in something concrete with walls, their positions will be secure.

"I'm sorry, Sasha. I won't bring it up again."

His shoulders seem to be relaxing, his posture less guarded. I feel bold enough to slip off my sandals and bury my toes in the sand but the texture is not as soft as I expected. Medovsky is inscrutable behind his tinted sunglasses.

After a minute, he speaks. "You have idea why marriage is so hard? It makes no logic, yes? She liked you once. You liked her. Both of you just want to enjoy life and finally have the means to do it. Why do we create this unnecessary drama? Remember when we were in Soviet Union? We had so little but we were happy."

"I was seven when we left. I was a kid." Normally this amuses me, my clients waxing philosophical. They like when I protest that I have a Russian soul just as they do, and I indulge them in their what-does-it-all-mean ruminations. But not now, not on this topic.

"Well, then, I'll tell you. We had nothing. We shared apartment with ten other people including babushka who would always pick up phone and hang up on our callers. We could shit only between ten and ten-thirty. If we had an emergency and failed to clean the kitchen on appointed schedule, we would be forced to do it all month. Take a dirty bath two times a week. We couldn't make joke about our country at a house party without getting a phone call from the police next day. But we were happy. And now, world is all upside down."

A pink, delicate bird tiptoes into the water at the edge of the property. Even after everything I've seen, I can't help but stare. "Is that a flamingo?"

Medovsky doesn't turn to look. He flicks the cigarette to the ground, grinds pebbles on top of it with his toes. "Greater flamingo: pink legs, pink bill, black tip. Imported from Zoo Basel. It is listed in amenities."

The bird submerges its jaw into the wet sand, and it retains the perfect S-shape of the neck.

Medovsky says, "Women are complicated. So many moods. You give and you give but they are not satisfied."

I bristle, defensive. "I'm sure she gives too, probably even more. It's a partnership, isn't it?"

"Marriage? Partnership? Tanyush." He laughs. "You are so American, it's charming. I forgot that about you. Since when is marriage partnership? Even your business partner's not partnership. For God's sake. It is two lonely people who exist in same home sometimes. Hopefully they diddle each other once in a while. Maybe they laugh."

"Isn't that a little . . . depressing?"

"Don't tell me your marriage is partnership. Woman like you who wears pants in family? I don't believe it."

I wrap my arms around myself, suddenly cold. "What makes you think I wear the pants?"

"Anyone can see. You think you are superior. Maybe you are, but let me give you word of advice. Don't let your man know this." He kicks off his shoes too and wades into the water.

Wears the pants. CEO. I'm used to people assuming I'm the alpha in my marriage. Yes, I am more competent, more efficient; taking care of others comes naturally to me. Faster to have me accomplish something than Carl with his lack of attention to details, his indecision. It was during our honeymoon that the terrible thought occurred to me. *Weak.*

We had just arrived in Turks and Caicos. We flung open our French doors to be confronted with the aquamarine perfection of the water, the long stretch of near-empty beach. Our first time in the Caribbean and we were giddy with the transparency of the water. A slick shoreline free of seaweed, free of human detritus. Free of our families and the lives that clung to us in New York. That first day, we ate conch salad tossed with orange slices in our tiki hut resort, treated ourselves to raspberry daiquiris. It was the kind of day that unspooled along with a single narrative in my head—*this is perfect. How did I get this lucky?* Everything Carl said was interesting to me, and I would catch him in the Look.

"We just got here and you've already got sand on your forehead," he would say, brushing it off, his fingers lingering in my hair where I would capture them with my own.

Then we proceeded to the beach. But there were no chairs for us. A shrugging employee explained that the resort ran out of beach chairs and umbrellas by mid-morning. The competition for chairs, we discovered, was early and fierce. We watched jealously as the protectors of their chairs reclined in sweeping shade while we spread our towels on the sand, and shielded ourselves from sun rays with hats.

"Here, take my hat, it's got a bigger brim," Carl said. We kissed, but the furrow between his eyebrows deepened. A vine of anxiety was starting to coil around him.

"Tomorrow, we'll be the ones on the chairs," I promised.

The next day, we woke at first light and ran to the beach to claim our chairs. Too scared to leave them even to swim, we crisped ourselves past the point of sanity, until the sun and reading books brought on migraines and our hungry stomachs growled in protest.

"This is ridiculous, we're trapped here," Carl said from under a precious umbrella as we watched couples like us prowling the sand in search of vacancy.

As the week progressed, we grew bolder, daring to mark our places with towels while we ate breakfast. We consumed eggs and toast in three bites, gulped down coffee and dashed to the beach. It worked, our chairs were left alone. Our places held.

But one morning, a woman was reclined on Carl's chair, reading a paperback against the slash of sun. Carl's towel and mine lay on the sand next to her feet in a crumpled pile. The second chair held the detritus of a companion a pair of flip-flops, a Hawaiian shirt. The woman had the air of neither guilt nor complete ignorance of the situation, her hips flat against the stripes, head propped on her own rolled-up towel. The umbrella we had wedged into the sand was shielding her sun-mottled skin. On the cover of the paperback she was reading was a girl's ponytail, pulled together by a turquoise sash.

"Excuse me," I said. "I think you're in our chair."

"Did you buy it? Does it belong to you?" The woman's voice rose in agitation but she didn't look up from her book. She was prepared for the confrontation, her pose still and defensive. Probably a seasoned vacationer at this resort, accustomed to the morning tussle for resources.

"We saved our place just a half hour ago. My bag's right there."

The woman glanced down. "Shall I reach it for you or will you get it yourself?"

I was aware of Carl at my side, silent, his pale skin scorched by sun or embarrassment or both. He wasn't used to confrontations of any kind. In his world, this simply didn't happen. Yet a Russian part of me, the part ensconced in that patriarchal world, thought, *Isn't this a man's job?*

"Actually, we'd prefer the chairs, if you don't mind," I said when it was clear Carl would not be getting involved.

A field of tanning witnesses turned in our direction, raised on their elbows. This was the show they'd been looking forward to all week. All of them waiting to see how far I would push this, if I would upend the *Lord of the Flies* rules of this resort.

The woman yanked our tote bag off the sand with two pincer fingers and tossed it to me like a football. "Let me give you a little tip, guys. It's yours when you sit in it."

I wondered when Carl would step in. By her logic, we could have claimed the second chair. Even the woman was scanning him, daring him, poised for his response.

"Let's go, Tan," was what he finally said, guiding me away by the elbow. "It's not worth it."

Of course I knew this was the best solution, a clearheaded, practical end to the impasse. What were we going to do—get into a fistfight over chairs? But it took me by surprise, my disappointment in him. I thought I was more American than this. But the thought wormed into my head: *weak.* I had the rest of the vacation to forget this instinct, the rest of our lives.

Now Medovsky tosses his shoes to the side, wincing as he tiptoes over the sharp points of rocks. The flamingo has disappeared down the shoreline. "Tanyush. Be honest. What do you think about Marina?"

"Marina?"

So that's her name. The kind of girl who bruises easily, a peach that can be thumbed with just a little force. The victim of a practical Russian mother who had pushed her toward men like Medovsky since puberty. In a few years, she'll grow cold and wise. The bitterness of being a woman washes over me.

"She seems like a darling."

On the balcony, the Realtor is sweeping at the view for Marina's sake, her hands wafting the landscape as if painting a picture of the future in the air.

"I can't go back, you know," Medovksy says. The water is lapping at the cuffs of his rolled-up pants. "My only desire is to see Russia again, but I've been barred. Do you know what it is to be stranded from home?"

"I thought you were originally from Ukraine?"

"I can't go back there either."

Marina's gold lamé pants provide a focal point for the sun. Her pants may as well be the sun itself. I don't want to know the particulars of Medovsky's exile and it's safer that way. Enough to know that the relation between my client and the president seems to be one of extreme caution bordering on paranoia.

"You were a Jew but you left us," he says. "That's normal. But now at least you can go back if you want to. But I have to buy back in. And even that might not work. I've got some serious enemies, Tanyush. He can fend them off if he wants to, he can keep me safe. But he is not easy man to sway. He has ear of people who hate me, former partners, people I thought were friends. Believe me, I've tried."

"Sash, please don't feel like you need to tell me any of this."

"The Order might be my last chance. You know he has a weakness for Russian history, for making himself a natural heir to Russian aristocracy. He aims to be a Romanov, to pretend the end of Soviet Union never happened."

"Well, for your sake, I hope this will convince him to let you back. I really do." *If the Order's really hers*, I think. *It better be.* But I don't say any of this.

Something in the Turks and Caicos memory is continuing to tug at the edges of my mind. *Weak.* I never wanted to be in that position again, of watching my husband fail. I would rather rescue him than experience that moment of vulnerability. Carl was so used to others propping him up, an entire network of name and money coming to his aid. As his wife, how could I not be one of them?

"Of course, there are a few other pieces I hope will interest you."

"Women," Medovsky says, turning back to the water as if he expected more sympathy from me. "Lena drinks my blood, always dissatisfied. In a woman I prefer simple. But can I divorce her with our two children and properties? Look, Tan'ka, you know men don't leave their wives. It's uncomfortable, inconvenient, and we are creatures of convenience."

"They don't leave their wives? That's an interesting theory, Sash. I wish that were true."

The sun sears high overhead, the blazing heat of it. I feel parched, my tongue the consistency of paper.

He turns back to me, his eyes secreted behind the density of those eyebrows. "It's not too late for you. You are newly married and have no kids, no assets, it looks like. Here's more advice for you: don't marry until you can tell yourself that you've done all you could, and until you've stopped loving the woman you've chosen, until you see her clearly, otherwise you'll be cruelly and irremediably mistaken. Marry when you're old and good for nothing . . . otherwise all that's good and lofty in you will be lost.'"

"What do you mean, Sash?"

"I didn't say this, Tolstoy did." Medovsky grins. "Don't look so scared. This advice is useless. Tolstoy had no clue about marriage. He was a dick to his wife at the very end. And not that it worked for me."

I laugh and the very act of it loosens the tension between us. For the first time since Carl left, I'm filled with a new expansiveness. We will find our way out. We have to. How could there not be a happy ending when a view like this exists in the world?

"We're alike, you and I, don't you think?" Medovksy says, playfully splashing some sea water in my direction.

"You think so?" I shield myself, happy to submerge my ankles in warm water, happy to be back in Medovsky's good graces. "Hey, watch the suit."

"Don't forget there's a little dinner on the yacht tonight. Maybe you'll be more charming to my friends this time."

"I'll do better, I promise."

A series of pattering taps across marble and Marina flies into his arms. I move away, discreetly. They kiss, a long, precise stamp of mouths. "I think this is it," she says. "The one."

The "little dinner" numbers forty people around a geometric white table on the yacht's deck. On the table: morel custard, grilled lobster with ginger vegetable stew, Beluga caviar sushi rolls, Uzbek pilaf with apricots and chestnuts, vintage Château Lafite-Rothschild. I can't help but notice the formality of the setting, the white tablecloth, two glasses centered directly above my plate, the prongs of the fork facing down. A fluttering staff in livery bend next to me with tray and tongs, and off to the side stand three sommeliers: one for wine, one for champagne, and the last for vodka.

The klezmer band with Itzhak Perlman is playing Erwin Schulhoff, Medovsky's friend Oleg is informing me. As a Jew, do I know who Schulhoff was? I'm too careful about making some mistake in protocol to care that I am being singled out as a Jew. We are facing away from the unbroken horizon toward Medovsky's riad built into the cliff, a row of black cars lining the twisted road like ants.

Before he was chairman of an energy investment group, Oleg was a theater director under the Soviet regime, fighting to stage a banned production of *King Lear*.

Do I know the play? he asks me. He begins to recite the Cordelia monologue, and ransacking my memory of AP English, when we had to memorize passages of Shakespeare, I help him finish it. ("Unhappy that I am, I cannot heave/My heart into my mouth. I love Your Majesty/According to my bond; no more nor less.")

"Bravo," he says, clapping.

"I have no idea where that came from." The champagne sommelier refills my glass.

At times like these I feel seduced by the setting, by the men pouring me wine, by the air cosseting my skin. I always go through multiple emotions during a dinner like this: envy, deep intimidation, sadness. But tonight, the world shimmers with beauty as long as I manage to tune out the conversation (*"Hey, Tanyush, did you see Larissa hired Damien Hirst to preserve a bust of her in formaldehyde?" "When you're entertaining in Kensington, do you prefer Ruski's Tavern or Chakana Club?" "She did pick up the gold wallpaper in Dubai, I was with her myself."*) and concentrate on the view. I settle into the dulcet tones of their laughter and the morels are delicious and I think there may be no place more beautiful than Monaco at twilight: the cobalt of the water, the reflected lights of other houses, the distant snapshots of fireflies.

"Why isn't your husband joining us?" Oleg leans over. "A lovely woman like you traveling alone? It's not right."

I'm aware of being drunk, of having the weightless feeling of a Chagall figure, flying high above these people. A tray of sour cherries is being passed, and I heap a cluster of them on my plate. "This isn't really his scene, if you know what I mean."

A female voice inserts itself from across the table. "Tanyush, what's wrong with you? You think you're better than us?" Lena has always frightened me, with her shiny skin-toned lipstick, pursed lips, her spiky, highlighted haircut, her complicated couture combinations: Bulgari and Jason Wu, Chanel and The Row and Topshop. The sharpness of Lena's tone reminds me that I spent the day being an accessory to the Marina affair, the cover, the decoy. The pleasant haze of wine is receding.

"Len'ka, let her alone. That's not what she meant," Medovsky says. Now for some reason the table is strangely silent, even the lapping water seems to have been muted.

But the woman's voice carries over the music. "Not his 'scene'? How dare you judge us?"

The world returns to jarring focus. "I'm sorry, Lena, if it came out sounding that way. I really didn't mean anything by it."

"What do you really know about our scene anyway? You left the country as a child."

"I think you misunderstood."

"You see, you don't remember. You grew up in America so now you can look at us from your lofty perch," Lena says. "Do you know what it's like to be at the mercy of whatever is on the shelves that week? Do you know the feeling of fear that your parents won't be able to feed you? Or the fantasies of wearing a yellow sundress the way they do in the West? Or what about finding out that your favorite pair of shoes, the unique tan ones you splurged your entire paycheck on, were actually shoes they put on dead bodies during funerals?"

"No, she has no idea, she was raised on Cheerios," someone says in the hopeful way of switching the topic.

Memory wriggles to the surface, from the other place, from my childhood. The sickly green walls of the communal apartment, the long hallway where I tricycled back and forth, the dinner parties on one side of the room, my cot on the other. The ice-skating rink in the back of the building, the feeling of your scarf flying about your cheeks, an adult hand sure in your mitten. The first day of school, a day so glorified in books and on television that I stayed up all night staring at the uniform draped over my chair, half expecting it would come to life.

"I remember my mother coming home with a pile of Swedish bras. That was exciting. She left work early because she heard some lady was selling them out of her house. And she waited on line half a day, spent her whole paycheck. But when she tried them on, they didn't fit. Not a single one of them. She had to give them all away to her friend," I say. I have no idea why this is the story I tell.

Again, laughter. "I think I bought one of those bras," says a woman at the other end of the table. Despite the heat, the woman's shoulders are swathed in fur.

"It's funny now, but do you know what it's like when your mother sends you to wait on line for four days because the rumor is they are selling children's coats from Denmark?" Lena says. She gestures to the wine sommelier. "You remember that horrible winter, Ol'ka? We were ordered to buy eight coats when we got to the front of the line. We each got one, and my mother sewed four together to make a single winter coat for herself. Food and clothes, clothes and food, how to get it, trade it. That's all we thought about every day."

Olya says, "I remember. I remember. Who can forget?"

"Come now, we're depressing our guests." Medovsky is looking down at his lap, at the starched napkin draped across his knee.

"And what about when there is no milk for your baby? What about when your baby is hoarse from hunger, your breasts are tapped of all its paltry reserves and there is not a single can of condensed milk in the store?" Lena continues. She takes a few gulps of her wine, striking the table with her index finger for emphasis. The women around her are no longer smiling.

Medovsky waves it all away. "Let's talk of something more cheerful."

"No, she really should know. And what about Sasha? Do you know how he became who he is today?"

"Lena, please forgive me. I didn't mean to offend you." I'm thoroughly sober now.

"Imagine what a hustler you have to be just to survive. Sasha took great risks with a cooperative business at a time when any whiff of capitalism was treason, the KGB breathing down his neck. He didn't know a damn thing about aluminum or business, nobody did. But Sasha never even got a college degree. He was a construction worker, for God's sake, twelve-hour days building dachas for stinking politburo."

"Len, what's wrong with you? This is old news. Are you trying to make me some kind of uneducated Soviet hero?" Medovsky says with a forced laugh. He wipes his mouth with a napkin, methodically, as if to shield from view his mouth. I can see the shame in him, the effort of concealing it.

"No, I would like everyone to know."

"They know, they know."

"Not her. She thinks we're monsters."

I rise from my seat and go over to Lena's chair. The glitter from Lena's eye shadow has speckled down, dusting nostrils and her chin with silver.

"Never. I swear to you, you misunderstand me," I say, searching for the right words. "It's because my Russian is stuck at the seven-year-old level. Can we embrace?"

Lena's jaw loosens somewhat but her eyes remain hard.

"My wife, friends. How did I get so lucky?" Medovsky raises a glass. His face is flushed with wine. Everyone breathes a sigh of relief, a dangerous storm has bypassed us. "To wives. We do not deserve them. I would like to quote a little man you may have heard of. His name was Vladimir Vysotsky. He was an okay singer and songwriter. We all know this personage, I presume?

"Just do it already," people call out. "Turn down the music." Someone whispers into Itzhak Perlman's ear and he lowers his violin. They all strain against the sound of the tide sweeping the shore, and Lena turns to her husband, expectant, a kind of hopeful weariness in her features as if daring him to surprise her after all this time, to gladden her.

"Here we go." He strums an air guitar, affects a growl. He launches into Vysotsky's famous song "I Love You Here and Now."

I do not want the past, the future I don't know.

I love you here and now, with tears and with laughter.

"Beautiful, not half bad," the men exclaim, palms pounding on tables. "*Gor'ko!*"

The staff rush to refill glasses while Medovsky and Lena's kiss unites in the middle of the table.

"We say *gor'ko*—bitter—so the kiss turns it to sweet," Oleg explains, unnecessarily, as if to a foreigner.

My throat feels full. I'm overcome with something I can't pin down— nostalgia, longing, anticipation of loss? "Excuse me a moment."

I lean over the stainless steel of the yacht's railing. Here, away from the stare of the company, the breeze floats cool, the moon shaved to rind. Water laps against the swimming platform at the stern. Up on the sundeck, the glass-walled gym is illuminated, the outline of a man in a very different kind of tracksuit than my father's is walking the treadmill. I'm not sure I've ever felt this alone in the world.

The band, without warning, bursts back into song, Itzhak Perlman's fiddle reverberating up to the heavens. The sea is draped with night, patches of water illuminated by yachts like this one. "Tanya! Tanyusha!"— I'm being called. *Time for dancing!*

Catherine

The empress barges in during Catherine's bath. The water is calm, warm, floating just above the surface of her skin. She has allowed herself to doze. The sun has barely hoisted itself past the horizon, the room still bathed with chill. But the empress's face extends toward her, demonlike. Catherine feels her prune-skinned body examined for flaws or bruises, her collarbone, neck, and, finally, behind the ears. She is deemed satisfactory.

When the two of them move to the settee, the empress takes her hand. She thinks the woman might finally instruct her on what a man and wife do in the privacy of their bedroom. The morning of the wedding seems the ideal time for the conversation. So far, no one else knows or takes the time to tell her what will be expected of her. Katya has no insights, nor do the other ladies. They predict it an act of nature that overtakes you when the two of you lie in bed, naked. Her mother tells her to follow instructions, that men's knowledge of these things is innate. Catherine imagines that if any man has no innate knowledge of such things, it is Peter. Daylight scissors its way into the room, lending the surfaces a feathery sheen of citrus.

"Everything will be wonderful," the empress says at last. She places two jeweled portraits in Catherine's hand, of the empress and Peter. They are miniatures, Peter's small enough to burnish the reality of his features.

"Hold on to these. You need not look at them, but they may be useful someday."

Catherine cannot imagine what use she will ever have of them. As soon as the wedding is over, she will relegate them to her deepest chest. "You have been more than a mother to me."

The empress smiles, the one that accompanies her generous mood. In this humor, her cheeks blushing like peaches, Catherine thinks the empress must be the most beautiful woman in the world. "I hope we have not disappointed you. Marriage can certainly be trying, but husbands can be managed."

"Yet I am so fortunate."

"Not in everything, surely. Peter, for one. His conduct is not always exemplary. I thought he would be a true heir, but his character is not suited to reign. Perhaps with time."

"He is young still."

"Yes, of course. One still hopes he will rise to the task. His mother was so different, I still cannot believe they are of one blood." The empress's periwinkle eyes are moist and Catherine wonders if she was close to this deceased sister. She imagines a young Elizabeth exchanging confidences with Peter's mother against the flicker of candlelight. The way she does with Katya.

But then the doors fling open, and in fly everyone at once. Johanna, the hairdresser, the seamstress, her ladies. They are discussing the best style to hold the crown in place, where to pin the lace cloak at her shoulders. Should her hair be allowed its natural state or should it be curled? Where precisely will the tiara be tucked? Her body is jostled around according to their will, held in place while the gown is draped over her head. She was prepared for its heft but the combination of brocade and lace and the diamond crown affixed to her scalp is like a full suit of armor. It makes her neck throb immediately. They are all admiring her fashionable short sleeves, the rouged sheen of her cheeks, the silver roses woven into the fabric with silver thread. They are deeming her quite lovely, really, as though the observation is one of pleasant surprise.

I am to be queen, she reminds herself. She can hear the metallic sound of muskets, probably the formation of soldiers creating a path to the cathedral. And in that moment, infused by the presence of the empress, by Saint Catherine staring up at her among red ribbon and diamond from the surface of the bureau, Catherine *is* queen. Not someone's wife, or consort or regent, but singular, enlightened monarch. Reader of Plato and the nine volumes of the canon of Saint Genevieve, and *The History of Germany*. Friend to Gyllenborg and Frederick of Prussia. The kind of queen who knows everything pertinent about the Colley Cibbers of the world. It is the role she was fated for, the precocious one in the room, so different than the others, singled out against all odds.

The knock arrives when she is not sure she can tolerate more people around her. She feels the first rumble of hunger from fasting, which she will have to tolerate until the ceremony ends. On the other side of the door stands the grand duke looking equally strangled by his costume. His pocked face is flared with red, fingers dotted with enormous rings. The sword handle at his hip is gleaming with diamonds. The two of them are matching in fabric, and for some reason this realization frightens her, this idea of being draped in identical material.

The ladies coo around him, not entirely convincingly. He blushes deeply at their flattery.

"Take her hand," the empress urges him. His fingers remind Catherine of denuded branches in winter.

"Must I do it now?"

"It's time," one of his men calls out. Brummer? Bestuzhev? The grand duke is shoved toward her.

Peter turns gray with panic. She tries to throw him an encouraging look but he is frozen before the empress's command.

"My hand," she hisses, capturing that branch in her own and the two of them manage, despite her wide hoop skirt, to exit the room. One foot after another, as somnolent as a death march. Somehow they make it out of the palace and into the white heat of morning. A circle of generals surround them, erecting a silver canopy over their heads.

Once seated in the coach, she and Peter stare at the empress across from them, at her purple and gold gown, the sapphires and emeralds cosseting her neck, the candles, the icons. They examine everything but each other. The entire passage to the cathedral takes no more than half an hour by foot, but they are crawling among a hundred carriages, a slow procession that will probably add up to two hours or more. The crown is digging into her skull; she can feel its laceration at the place where hair meets skin. She knows the ceremony will last at least three hours, then there is the banquet, the ball, the dignitaries who will expect dances. She suddenly feels exhausted with the day's requirements.

Soldiers are staring at them with their impassive faces.

"Smile," the empress orders them. "The people expect a little joyfulness from you two."

The horses begin their clop. Soon the carriage is swarmed with people, whistling and calling after them. Catherine does not hear a single utterance of her future husband's name, only the reverberations of her own. Ekaterina! She gathers the strength to do what the empress requests of her. She fixes the crowd with a smile that she hopes is warm and genuine. A little girl perched on a man's shoulders stretches out her hands for connection. Soon, the joy that floods her is authentic, the simple sensation of belonging to others. She reaches to touch the girl's fingers.

"I touched her, Mama," the girl cries.

Her destiny is fractured in two, Catherine realizes. There are the people out there who need her and then the boy at her side, slumped back in his seat in a dramatic pose of resignation. Once he was a being that dictated her unhappiness. Now he may as well be inscribed and embalmed onto that miniature canvas. The empress has aired her doubts about him, which means she is looking into the future toward Catherine.

At the chapel, she and Peter are bent at the waist, going through the motions of the rites as the empress is handing them their rings, as the archbishop intones chants and vows. At last, after three hours, a meek little official reads the decree pronouncing her grand duchess. As the church bells ring and the doors to the cathedral swing open to the square, she feels herself floating and porous and weightless with happiness. She is wed to the cheering faces outside. Not to the tiny figure next to her sweating under all that empty regalia and moaning in her ear, "I'm famished. Aren't you?"

———

At the banquet afterward, she is beyond hungry, but is forced to consume slivers of duck breast on the sly, even if it is the last meal she craves in this weather. She is interrupted in her shoving of the greasy meat into her mouth by congratulations. In order to survive this hot, endless day, the only solution is to uphold an erect carriage and enter into discourse with anyone who desires it. In the far corner, she sees the furrowed mass of Bestuzhev, deep in conversation, and is tempted to interrupt him, to tell him that she has won. She is grand duchess now. But then she is led away to meet some Finnish dignitary, the remains of a solitary grape warm in the palm of her hand. She is aware of words pouring from her, a crinkling, manic laughter. How she dances, tirelessly, from one corner of the hall to the other. Her ladies are worried for her, shepherd water and wine from hand to table. She showers smiles on everyone. For the first time, she feels the surge of being everything she hoped—beautiful, in-telligent, witty, worthy of love. But a quick glance about the giant hall ascertains that Peter is nowhere to be seen (could he have already been deposited in the robing room? Could he already be waiting for her in the state bedroom?). *Byt po siemu,* she thinks. *So be it.*

Everything in the state bedroom is red. Scarlet walls, the sheets draped with rich burgundy velvet. A huge crown with red emeralds is affixed above the canopy. She holds her breath while Katya and two of the younger girls are unfastening the lace cloak. It takes two of them to carry it away to the silver room next door. One by one, the weight is removed, the brocade dress, the corset, the crown. She feels light but also bare, un-protected. The armor is gone and so is the power she felt in the church. The girls are all giggling in a frightened way, either a shared ignorance about what is to come or a modest withholding of their own salacious experi-ences.

"He will probably kiss you first," Zhenia says, when the empress is gone, and the other one, Evdotya adds, "Or maybe he will bow before you, or give you a gift." Katya says nothing, but hands to her the rose nightgown, shipped from Paris for the occasion. It is silk in the latest style, fringed with scallops of ruffled lace. Catherine caresses the fabric. It has the power to make any girl beautiful, even her.

The undressing takes almost no time compared to the dressing, as if she is being stripped of all that made her valuable earlier. The revelry of the remaining guests rises from somewhere beneath the floorboards. She tries to call up Maria-Theresa and Francis again, the love story everyone comforts her with. He is her confidant, her advisor on matters of the state. Many unlikely royal matches end in love, she thinks. But she is afraid.

"Stay with me a while," she begs Katya.

"For a little bit, if you like." But the empress is outside the door shooing the girls out.

"You too, girl," the empress chides. "Do you want the grand duke to find you here instead of his bride?"

A squeeze of the hand and her friend slips away. Catherine is alone. To stand or lie down on the bed? She resolves to try both positions. If she were Peter walking in, which would be the more enticing vision? She decides to recline, then props herself up on one elbow. She wonders if anything in the act will surprise her; she had heard it favorably compared to bloodletting. Pain, she can handle, she has proven that. The initial act will probably end quickly, with the initial sting of a needle's insertion. She leans back against the pillows. The ceiling is a simulacrum of a blue sky, sloping upward into the heavens. George is with her by the lake, hiding behind her favorite elm. She can feel him pressed against the other side of the tree, about to frighten her when the time is right. He is ready to pounce, to collapse her in his arms.

Footsteps slice through her reverie, and her body tenses in preparation for Peter's entrance. But no, it is only her headache, the dull pounding of it from the removal of the crown. The steps, if they existed at all, dissipate. Downstairs, the merriment grows rowdier. Glass shatters. She sinks back down and returns to the lake, the carefree feeling of being young, when nothing much is expected of you apart from a few hours with tutors and your governess. When you are resplendent in grass and sky. From time to time, she glances at the shade of the evening light. An hour passes, probably two. George had this way of kissing her, engulfing her lower lip with his own, pressing stray hairs behind her ears.

She startles to a presence standing above her, outlined in the murk. It is the gentle curve of Katya. "Are you awake?"

"My dearest." Catherine's voice is hoarse from sleep, from the mental travel to another time. She reaches for her friend's hand. "Is everything all right?"

"I was told to inform you that the grand duke has just ordered supper in his rooms and he is waiting for it to arrive."

She nods, slowly, still confused. Her pink nightgown is creased with her sweat or the August dampness.

"He is probably nervous with anticipation," Katya says, untangling the twisted curtains around the bed. "I would be if I were him."

Here she is, a queen-to-be, and her friend pities her. Her heart turns solid. "You're probably right," Catherine says. "Go to bed."

"Leave you?"

"Yes, of course."

The girls embrace, and Catherine feels a larger gulf between them. Despite everything she has shared about Peter, her friend is envious. Oh, to be simple Katya, would that not be preferable? She returns to the softness, a state of half dreaming, half dread. George jumps out from behind the elm and she screams. Babette calls out from beyond the slope of the field, "Figgy! Where in the world are you ambling to?"

It is the smell that wakes her, not the footsteps. "So be a man, stick it to 'er," someone is saying in the hall, a chorus of rough laughter. Around her gathers a cloud of wine and smoke. Peter is standing at the room's entrance. He is free of his heavy garb, his blouse stained with blots of red. He continues to hold a goblet. She wants to cover herself, hide her nightgown out of sight.

"Wife," Peter says, moving toward the mantel. Then he doubles over with laughter. "Isn't that funny?" The sour reek of wine.

She gathers herself into a pose of dignity, having forgotten which position she has chosen as the most seductive. "Why is it funny?"

"Imagine if they could see us now? My servants would get a kick out of this. You and me in bed. Isn't that amusing?"

The silence is long and heavy. He looks up at the imperial relics. "Ha. The crown, that's funny too. Watching us like some kind of hawk."

He is nervous, bravado layered over trembling. Neither of them moves, waiting for something to happen. Her heart pulps at the base of her throat, taking away breath or voice, a patient at the mercy of an apprentice doctor. Just let it be concluded quickly, efficiently.

"Welcome, my husband," she says. *Welcome?* The word hangs between them, a heavy cloud. In one flowing motion, he climbs into bed, fully clothed. She takes his goblet away and reaches over to extinguish the candle. When she turns back, she finds him splayed lengthwise, asleep.

Tanya

PRESENT DAY

As the train plunges deeper into Brooklyn, the population changes. Suits and slacks and blouses give way to families, nannies. Immigrants, just like we were thirty years ago. This is Carl's route every day to his newly full-time job at Ditmas College. A pair of Bangladeshi women are hysterical over some picture on their phone, an Orthodox Jewish family loops around a bag of chips, an older woman, face pulled back by a too tight bun, completes a crossword puzzle. I follow the weave of female high schoolers in backpacks and neon-colored hot pants as they rotate around the center pole.

Tan'ka, you know men don't leave their wives. It's uncomfortable, inconvenient, and we are creatures of convenience.

He's not cheating. The very idea is still ridiculous but I'm here to placate my mother and Alla. He's been gone over two months now. Two incomprehensible months. The way he used to look at me.

The train slides into its final station and, outside, I navigate the dangerous constellation of Flatbush Avenue and Nostrand, cars whipping by from all directions. The Ditmas College campus is shoved into an urban mass of Target and Applebee's, its gates high and fortressed, as if protecting its square of education from the danger of its surroundings.

Once past the security booth, I emerge onto the wide expanse of the quad where two pairs of Georgian-style buildings face off over a lily pond dappled by elm trees. Students, coffees in one hand, linger in circles, a sprinkling of booths are advertising petitions for protests—budget cuts, politically contentious speakers. The campus is a bucolic pocket tucked behind gates, the English department housed in a gray-winged façade closer to the pond. There have been few improvements to the building since I was here last. I recognize the faded tread of the staircase, the utilitarian hallways of a former public high school. Carl's office is the first on the right, shared with two colleagues, their books heaped on one another's desks, coats jumbled on a broken rack, a yellow rotary phone passed around on the rare occasion a student calls. What was once scruffy and romantically academic, I now clearly see as the shabby fringes of budget cuts, a stripped-down battle for supplies.

Suspect number one for any affair is, of course, Victoria Henriques, Carl's eternal graduate student. She first arrived as a Ph.D. student in the history department, then, because of her interest in the Soviet Union, was introduced to Carl and creative writing. "Troubled" and "brilliant," and "probably too thin-skinned for the profession," was how Carl described her. She was a mélange of Dominican and Jewish, a prodigy unable to meet deadlines, whose work erupted out of her in unreliable spurts. He would often be reading her drafts, red pen in hand, slashing entire sentences, writing "Vivid!" in the margins.

There was a shorthand between her and Carl, an intimacy of hidden scholarship once she decided to ditch history texts and the Soviet Union to write an updated, wildly ambitious feminist version of *Fathers and Sons*. Long afternoons of advising, of poring over ideas and sources, Turgenev in Russian and English splayed everywhere. He never avoided the topic of her, but there was an implied intimacy in the way he said her name, the long drawn-out vowels of it—Vic-to-ria.

She was in the audience during Carl's lecture on "Catherine the Great and the Case of the Russian Female Sovereign." The talk was smart and confidently delivered, about how foreign diplomats, and even Catherine herself, would attribute her successful rule to possessing masculine characteristics like force of mind and ability to carry through a plan. It was the first time I saw him perform like this and the vision was thrilling. It was Carl as I meant him to be, forceful and knowledgeable, making deliberate eye contact with the smattering of academic types in the rows of the auditorium.

"Ironically, compared to its Western counterparts, eighteenth-century Russia was comfortable with its female rulers," he was concluding. "Hard to imagine this kind of matriarchy in the contemporary context, of course. But for Russians, a *gosudarina*, or empress, was an extension of the Motherland. Nevertheless, Catherine the Great felt she had to publicly align herself with a male predecessor like Peter the Great rather than associate herself with the less than impressive accomplishments of Empress Elizabeth or Empress Catherine the First."

My heart burst with pride for Carl. I was in the throes of that new wife's awe of one's spouse as an intoxicating stranger on an upward trajectory. In the lecture's drier moments, I scanned the faces gazing at my husband. Victoria was sitting in the first row, wrapped in diaphanous silk scarves, their skeins rippling over bare shoulders. Once in a while, she shook out her hair, thrust her hand into the density of her curls as if to air-dry them. An empty notebook lay open before her, but she took no notes.

After the talk, Carl was besieged by questions. Once the crowd thinned, we exited to a city immobilized by snow. Flatbush Avenue was eerily empty of cars. Outside the gate, we saw a hooded form smoking in the dusk, a series of loose black curls, languorous limbs over forlorn eyes. It might as well have been Anna Karenina herself.

"Is that Victoria?" Carl said. *Of course,* I thought, this *would be Victoria.*

"The very one." She turned to us, her bright red mouth open, exhaling steam. The vintage coat she wore was thin, fraying. She was clearly frozen in it, this big luscious head on top of a pair of hunched shoulders. Her eyes were rimmed with kohl. "That was brilliant, Carl. Your novel's probably amazing. You have a way of making all that dry history so accessible."

"Thanks, V."

He was pleased. I could see him hiding the extent of it in the swirl of the snow. He introduced us.

"What are you doing standing out here in the middle of a storm?" he asked her.

"Nothing. Breathing."

"Breathing, huh?"

"That's right. Just breathing. Call me Lady with a Lapdog." The girl punctuated the answer with an actual breath. She was blinking furiously against the torrent of wind, her Persian scarf undulating at her throat. She appeared lost and very much alone.

I could feel Carl's reluctance to leave, his body poised to continue the conversation. *Jesus,* I thought. *Breathing? Lady with a lapdog?* But something alive wormed in his voice, an attraction maybe or a terror of being left behind. Victoria was me once, the dreamy, younger, exotic me before I could no longer afford to be dreamy. ("You're making a mistake by letting men see your strength. Men like helpless women," my mother used to say when I was entering my late twenties and was still unmarried. "Look at Alla. Does she ride the subway at night? Does she pick up her husband at the airport? That's right. Because she knows it's the man's job to take care of her.")

"We should go," I said. "Nice to meet you."

Carl tightened the scarf around his neck. His cheeks were red from the cold. People were waving to him from the gates, calling out, "Great talk!" "*Russian Review* will want it."

"Yeah, thanks for coming. I'm sure I'll get your usual candid opinion on Monday."

"You always do, Carl," Victoria said with a theatrical wave. The way they kept saying each other's name for no reason saddened me, all that clichéd young female effort and men too susceptible to flattery. I felt oddly robbed of my own time as the subject of impossible longing, but I was busy climbing, achieving, becoming. And when we were out of earshot, I said, "So that was the famous Victoria."

"She casts quite a figure, doesn't she?"

Is it possible to see your husband whole by the longing in his voice? To hear in it desire for what you no longer are?

Now that I'm outside his office at Ditmas College, I don't know what

I expected to learn. Did I think I would catch him with Victoria in erotic abandon? The door is firmly shut, Carl's office hours scrawled on a sheet of notebook paper. I rap lightly. Out from the main office, young women exit with forms and manila envelopes. They are unformed, with gangly limbs, hair knotted messily with rubber bands, striped V-necks over low-slung jeans, or encased in childlike rompers. They move easily from conversation with each other to tapping on their phones. The overhead lighting turns their complexions yellow, not at all the young beauties I imagined Carl intertwined with behind his desk.

"Mrs. Vandermotter? Waiting for Carl?" Out from the main office, as if conjured out of air, comes Victoria.

She appears to be eight months pregnant and, by his wrist, she holds a toddling boy in a broken-in baseball hat. An adjustment takes place in my mind, realigning the romantic heroine in the snowstorm with the tired mother before me. But there's no doubt; it's Victoria Henriques in her early thirties, her curls gathered into a practical ponytail, her face bare of makeup, filled out. The gaunt, faraway look ("Just breathing") is gone, replaced with an exhausted directness.

"I know," Victoria says, glancing down at him. "He's why I'm on the twenty-year plan. You know classes ended last week, right?"

"Right, right." Of course. It's already May. My mind hasn't worked on an academic schedule since school.

"You don't take my job seriously," Carl said once, when I'd joked about his cushy summers off while I toiled toward auction deadlines. "You think I don't even work."

"That's not true," I'd protested, even as I tried to quash the thought, *Does he even have a job?* Then, *I will always work harder than he does.*

Victoria is resisting the boy's tug of her hand. "I'm almost done though. Defending next week, then I'm finally out of here. M.F.A. and Ph.D. Didn't he tell you?"

"Congratulations, Victoria." I can afford to be generous. Tired mother or not, the ingénue will finally be gone.

"I want Wheels on the Bus I want Wheels on the Bus I want Wheels on the Bus."

"Okay, Smith, I heard you," she says. I can't help but smile at the equalizing power of age; the ethereal beauty with an unruly child named Smith. "You've probably already checked Urban Writers offices? He might be there."

"Urban Writers?"

Victoria is being jerked down the hall. She calls back, "Urban Writers Space. In Manhattan. He's always there these days. Our theory is he's moonlighting in another teaching gig," before disappearing around the corner.

I feel unexpectedly stung. A second job? That's how it begins, Alla warns, men hiding things in sock drawers, materializing in secret locations.

Outside by the lily pond, administrators unwrap sandwiches from parchment, purses resting against their thighs. The fish bob to the surface, mouths ready for an influx of crumbs. I watch them compete for food, glide over one another in their eagerness to be first.

The Urban Writers Web site is sleek and popping with color. It promises a communal working space, private offices for meetings, a fully stocked kitchen with tea and coffee, and a small library. The photos show serious people huddled around tables, stacks of paper spread out before them. They are staring intently at the gray-curled leader at the head of the table who is articulating her comments through elegant flourishes of the hands. None of it makes any sense to me. When I'm at work, Carl had our apartment to himself, not to mention the Queens apartment and his Ditmas College office. And why would Carl take an extra teaching job that probably pays nothing?

But the woman who runs the operation looks out from the screen with her oceanic eyes, soft black hair caressing sculpted eyebrows. She is stunning in the same mysterious way as young Victoria and her name is equally offensive: Hermione.

"Medovsky," Regan says, and I snap back to my desk at Worthington's, to the ringing of the telephones, the hallway kitten-heel patter of the interns.

"Sash." I pick up. *"Privet."*

"Listen, can I can buy it before sale? Preempt it, or whatever that's called? I can't go into details, but situation is urgent."

It takes me a minute. "The Order? I can raise it with my consignor but I know she wants to offer it to as many buyers as possible. Sash, just sit tight. Everything will turn out for the best."

"How can I sit, Tanyush?" He sighs. "The world, it's speeding up. It changes with every blink. Time, it is fleeing me." A wild animal growl erupts in the background. I imagine him calling from a rooftop garden of some over-the-top party featuring tigers and their trainers. ("Sasha had those mimes and acrobats in Monaco, remember? Let's bring in a few cats from the zoo.")

"What do you mean?"

"Even at *gymnasium* he was stubborn, secretive. He's vengeful when he does not get what he wants. You know the man—he starts a war on a whim. He says, 'I want the Order. Get me the Order.' Or else, or else. One of my old enemies comes to him and says, 'Do we have your blessing?' and he might say, 'Well, I didn't get the Order, so why not? Who am I to stop you?'"

"Sash, who are you talking about?"

"The president, of course. Tan, haven't you been paying attention? The president!"

On the screen, I'm examining the curve of Hermione's mouth, the gentle rise of her thin lips. Hermione and Carl stepping out for ramen between work on their ambitious novels, the two of them melding into the midtown crowds.

"It'll be yours. And when it is, I'm sure he'll love it," I say, vaguely, before hanging up.

"What the hell was that? Lions? I could hear that all the way from my cube," Regan calls out. Today she is dressed like a prim Dita von Teese, hair curled into a coil, fingernails painted black.

"So I'm not crazy. You heard it too."

Regan comes around to my desk, leans a chin on her forearms. "We're working for some real creepers, aren't we?"

But I regret having dispatched with Medovsky so quickly and have the impulse to call him back and listen to him. The more he calls, the more it becomes clear that he needs me. And I like his booming voice on the other end of the line, projecting the kind of masculinity I didn't know was lacking in my life.

"Who's that little hottie?" Regan asks, pointing to my screen, and I remember Hermione, Carl and Hermione kissing between bites of ramen. I wipe her face away with a single click.

Catherine

MAY 1746

For the third day in a row, she asks for Katya but flinty Madame Krause appears instead. Madame Krause has been making many unannounced entrances lately. She first showed up the morning after the wedding night, flickered over the preserved bedsheets, a delicate, "Have you perchance inspired love in His Imperial Highness?" She appears when the empress is most displeased with Catherine, in order to explore the cause of late-night revelry with her friends or the provenance of a dress that competes too closely with one of the empress's twelve thousand gowns.

"Where is Katya?" Catherine demands.

"Which Katya?" Madame Krause is neat and prim, her darting eyes scan the room for details to fill out her report. "If you have a question about a particular lady, you will want to speak with the empress."

Wedged into a corner is the wooden leg of one of Peter's puppets, flung over the folds of the covers. Madame Krause takes this in. Everyone at court is engaged in the frenzied question of consummation. Has it happened? Is Peter even capable of it? In some quarters, the joke is that the puppets are fulfilling the grand duke's responsibilities. Of course, the reality is not too far off. Peter prefers puppet reenactments to the sight of her disrobed.

Catherine raises herself to full height, glaring down at Madame Krause. "I would like to see my lady Ekaterina Vassilievna Zhukova immediately."

"I'm afraid that will be impossible."

"Must I remind you it is the grand duchess herself inquiring?"

"The lady you are referring to is gone."

"Where has she gone to?"

"Sent away. By the empress herself."

An understanding blooms inside her. She can picture it—the hours before dawn, a huddle of men lighting the way with candles, Katya bundled off into a waiting carriage. She would have meekly asked to see Catherine, to simply say farewell. The hairbrushes, pins, and ribbons she left behind were given away to servants. Catherine's eyelids prickle.

Immediately following the wedding, it was made clear that until an heir is brought to term, all distractions of the grand duke and duchess would be excised. Slowly, the empress began prying confidantes away from Catherine. First, her mother was sent packing back to Zerbst.

How Johanna had lingered beside the carriage, arranging Catherine's necklace, smoothing her brows, the mournful way she whispered, "And so it is done." As the carriage containing her mother pulled away, Catherine realized she would probably never see her family again. And now Katya is gone. She looks down at the Order across her chest, the one she wears daily. The saint is the only friend she has left.

She had expected marriage to lend her security at court. Free of the pressures of her uncertain position, she imagined unfettered hours with Katya and the cheerful Zhenia, the only other of her ladies she truly trusts. But instead she and Peter are confined in a royal prison, their every move monitored by spies. She has heard that Bestuzhev has advised removing the last of her independence and the empress finds fault with her on a daily basis. "Why are you wearing that? Take it off," she said about a newly commissioned emerald necklace, and Catherine looked up to find the empress's own neck draped in emeralds. She wonders if the empress has informants who know about her empty nights with Peter, when they slumber as far away from each other as possible.

She is not a terrible person, this Madame Krause, and in her eyes Catherine spies sympathy. After she completes the inspection, she turns back to Catherine. "It is no good, you know. Your friend won't be brought back and you will find no news of her. I assure you she is in a hospitable place back with her family. They want it that way, for you to focus on your tasks." Her tasks, Catherine thinks bitterly. If only they all knew her husband curled back at the thought of touching her. She is pretty sure they have to touch in order to produce an heir.

The woman sits on the edge of the bed, yanks one of Peter's puppets by its ankle. Sniffs: "Your husband is neglecting his duties."

"Please, Madame Krause. He needs them."

Despite herself, she feels protective of Peter, of the puppets he loves like his friends, the toys that respect him more than anyone else at court. If they fail to follow military command, they are reprimanded, always with cause. It is the one domain in which he holds any power.

She expects a flinty, a huffy, "We'll see." These wardens have the ear of the empress, they can wield it to garner favors for themselves. But to her surprise, Madame Krause only smiles, presses a finger to her lips, and says, "Shhh. It will be between us."

Luckily there are still the other ladies, Zhenia and Vika, who plait her hair and share her suppers late into the night. Zhenia is the pretty but peasanty one with a shadow of dubious paternity, a mother who was once a serf and managed to marry the widowed landowner. Her laugh is too brawny and explodes at inappropriate moments, but she never complains, and these days, good humor is the difference between survival and despair. Vika condescends to Zhenia by speaking only in French and reminding them all that she hails from one branch of the Rostovs, one of Russia's oldest and most noble of families. They are grumpy with each other, but vie for Catherine's attention, Zhenia with her anecdotes and gossip, Vika with her knowledge of European fashion and court intrigue. With them, she can talk girlish things, mocking Bestuzhev's lumpy nose or the strange dress of inexperienced visiting dignitaries. They pull apart the most recent balls, who arrived later than seven-thirty, who bungled their entrance by passing through a door meant for another rank.

Their hands are brisk with needlework, their mouths full of pleasing stories. They are available for her amusement, and when the absence of

Katya crashes into her, gripping her by the neck, they smooth it away with their silly chatter. Without them, her rooms are hollow—the upholstered French armchairs lack bodies, the dressing table looms ghostly in the corner, the daybed remains undented. They pile on Catherine's new jewelry and imitate the empress's appearance at a ball, her grand, horselike entrance. When her rooms are too quiet, when solitary night descends, they bring with it the music of their voices.

"What a beautiful ring the grand duchess wears, perhaps too beautiful." Zhenia flutters around in character as the empress, as if to say, *We are safe here, you are among friends.* But the enemy may be stalking the halls, sniffing around for wrongdoing. To avoid her wrath, she may just want to remove that ring.

"I will return it to you as soon as the birthing pains begin," Vika chimes in. But it is the wrong thing to say. Catherine is all too aware that the empress waits, ready to fly into a rage. It has been almost an entire year since the marriage.

"Be quiet, you fool," Zhenia snaps, red-faced. "The grand duchess has plenty of time."

Vika seems to shrink deep into her dress. And they all return to their needlework.

Then Vika is whisked away. With Russia's new strained relationship with France, orders of French brocades have been canceled.

No amusement until an heir materializes!

Even the balls are made intentionally dull. Catherine loves to dance, but the guests are at least thirty years old, moving stiffly and gracelessly around the floor. Out of pointed spite, the empress made sure no young people were invited and Catherine is forced to listen to the dull observations of the ancient countesses and princesses. Will this be a good riding summer? Will Chulgakov win at draughts again? Zhenia and Evdotia are kept at a distance, flirting with ambassadors and officers over glasses of fermented juice.

The entire dance mimics performance, the simulacrum of merriment. It may as well be marriage itself. Catherine wanders around the halls, the smoky card games, the boozy circles of the foreign diplomats, the first flashes of fireworks. There is no one for her to talk to.

She is drawn into a game of spillikin, the ivory samovar handed to her with the hook. Everyone too scared to breathe as she nears the pile of playing pieces, watching her try to remove one without dislodging the rest. Her hand, bored and unsteady, topples the structure right away. She moves on.

The dances are lively at least, the Russian folk dances, the Polish minuets. In the past, she would have acted as centerpiece to the constellations of others, but she can take no pleasure from the watching or the participating. These dances used to be suffused with romance, intrigue, flirtation, the sensation of being nimble and daring, pretty. She is still being congratulated on her marriage, and the men sharp enough to notice her detachment from Peter aim to dazzle her with their attention. But she concentrates on providing the proper, appropriate responses.

She and Peter dance the first minuet, and she is aware of the empress's impatient eyes roaming their forms, as if trying to answer the court's most pressing question: have they or have they not? What is the delay? Rumor at court is that Elizabeth is hoping to bypass the ridiculous Peter altogether, to groom Catherine's future child as heir. In spite of the half-hearted daily guidance of the dance coach, Peter garbles steps, bungles most of the figures, rises when he should plié, missing the beats entirely. The fate of an entire nation rests in her womb.

"You might want to make more of an effort, at least in public," she says over the music. She is bolder now with her suggestions to him.

"What do you care?"

"Everyone is watching," she points out. Obviously. She enacts a pretty turn of her heel, to distract the audience from this pitiful lurching.

The dance is endless. On one of the final turns, she thinks she sees the sympathetic eyes of Katya, and whirls her head to find an old crone who looks nothing like her friend.

"Who cares if they're watching? God, why do you?"

"Because we are married now, and there are expectations."

"So what? You know Zhenia and I are in love. Everyone knows I prefer her. I told Count Devier that one could not compare the two of you. He disagrees. We fought bitterly about this, when it is obvious that Zhenia is much, much prettier."

She forces her legs onward into the dance, entering the sideways position. There is no sensation in her fingers. It can do that. She can remove the responsiveness from the hopeful valves of her heart, like a surgeon.

"Is that so?"

"What? Tell me you did not guess."

She is certain that he is no more aware of the intimacies of love with Zhenia than he is with herself, sure that his feelings are the confused fumblings of an adolescent. But still this news cuts her. Zhenia's betrayal, Peter's ability to have companionship, and her own gaping solitude have become snarled together. She gathers the remains of her pride.

"Everyone knows about you and Zhenia? Then I suggest caution in whom you confide."

"She is beautiful, for one, which you are obviously not."

The hollow in her throat grows deeper, sharper. His limp hand on her waist is pressing the sharp star of the Order against her hip. Every time she looks at the medal's face, the saint taunts her: for love and for the fatherland indeed. Those saints had high expectations of mortals. And just when she wishes it to be over so she can escape to the privacy of her bedroom, the music spurs them onward.

Is it only a week later? The frost of January. An eternal winter here, the kind that pierces your head and enters your very pores. It seems to her that winters back home were less stinging and gray, cold but not intent on extinguishing a person. They used to have a variety of sky at least, whereas here it plods on, merciless and gray. But the fire warms the room, bathes it in supple glow, and Catherine is in a good mood today. It is one of the few afternoons she has to herself, the empress just risen from sleep and ensnared in counsel with a Scottish dignitary. In the morning, Catherine kept the man company for a while, interested in the exciting details of Bonny Prince Charlie and the failed Jacobite rebellion. But just as the story was reaching its fascinating conclusion with Bonny Prince Charlie fleeing Scotland, the empress's lady-in-waiting interrupted them and sent her away.

Now she is playing herself in chess. At the same time, the Bayle dictionary is open before her as well as the novel *Tirant lo Blanc*, and she moves back and forth between all three when boredom strikes. She makes notes between moves: "Banishing serfdom is inevitable. Man must not live in fear of authority."

But just as she grows sleepy for the night, sunk into the recesses of her daybed, she hears footsteps. Peter's footsteps are easy to discern from the others by the way they slap against wood, erratic and ungainly. She shoves the books he always views with suspicion under one of the embroidered pillows.

He bursts inside. "You had her sent away, didn't you? You didn't want me to be happy, you selfish girl."

The news is hardly surprising, but she still feels a stabbing ache of solidarity. She too had so recently liked Zhenia. "You should have been more discreet," she says. "I warned you at the ball."

"But we were all friends, at least we thought so. We all played together." She has never heard his voice choked with feeling, even as his childishness persists. We all played together? What a shame, she thinks, that we experience the same thin isolation yet we cannot take solace in each other. She has lost Katya and now he has suffered his first major loss.

She approaches him in sympathy, but her hand is violently swiped away.

"You betrayed us, and I trusted you," he says, with a strangled voice. His pupils are dark, eyes bulging. He looks as though he might strike her.

She spits out, "I keep your hateful secrets."

"Who else would be responsible if not you?"

"Think, you silly child! If your efforts with discretion extended to others, it could be any one of a hundred people."

The truth drips into his features as they assess each other. For once he has no retort, no sarcasm to offer. A cloudiness leaves his features, and something suppressed and brittle behind them rises to the surface. He understands the full extent of their situation. They are alone, trapped together for life. Outside the window, a frozen, vast nation is to be divided between them.

Tanya

"Cece, over here," I call out, as if running into my mother-in-law on the street is a moment of serendipity. In fact, I know her schedule so well, it's easy to intercept her form glistening in the sun at just the right moment. Frances Vandermotter's gym is around the corner from Worthington's on Second Avenue, and she often power walks past the gold-stenciled revolving doors at around ten forty-five, blond hair tucked away under a cap, eyes hidden behind raccoon sunglasses. "How's Armand's torn meniscus?"

"He's better, much. Well, where have you been? It's been weeks after Greece." Frances walks into the kiss, arms pumping.

I've been avoiding the Vandermotters' calls. What would I say? Your son left me, at least I think he left me. Do you know anything? Is he coming back?

The rain has succumbed to unblemished sky, the kind of cerulean day that renders even overflowing garbage cans charming. Men in ascots idle by their cars in front of Worthington's, the streets are a blur of suits and hospital scrubs. Exposed legs flash everywhere.

"How was Greece?"

"Oh my goodness, who doesn't love the islands? Everywhere you point the camera, it's utter perfection. And you? How are things in the office? Isn't your auction coming up?"

We step into the tide of lunchtime flurry, women in practical and impractical shoes holding plastic squares filled with kale or leaking containers of soup.

My in-laws' passion for travel is secondary to the pleasure they take in recapping an itinerary. Their hotel, their meals, an elaborate recounting of each attraction, sights that they insist are omitted from guidebooks, hidden gems discovered thanks to pointed questions to locals. It took me some time to understand that Carl's family funneled all their fear, love, and affection into two or three subjects. Travel, the Foster Children's Alliance, Recollections of a Superior Past. Their firm place in the world blinded me to ways Carl must have been unhappy.

"You must come by this weekend, Tanya. No excuses. Armand is making old-fashioneds. A few of the ladies of the Foster Children's Alliance should be coming later to discuss business. We're in terrible financial shape. Terrible. We might have to close. I don't know where we can get money on short notice."

"Let's discuss that more this weekend. I might have an idea," I say. I'm thinking faster than I'm talking. But in noting the shift in Cece's expression, a warmth melts deep into my stomach. I'm worthy of them means I could be one of them.

"Tanya, that's incredible, I don't know what to say," Frances says after I made my insanely bold promise.

"It's really no problem. A client might be looking for a cause."

"Well, wouldn't that be the eleventh-hour salvation? I'll call Miggy. She'll be thrilled. We all are."

How frail Carl's mother looks, how reedlike under the muscle of her strength. All our years of marriage, she has alternated between drawing me in and keeping me at a distance; I never knew if she was friend or foe. I guess I'm about to find out.

In the evening, Carl and I emerge onto a busy stretch of Queens Boulevard. There must have been some kind of parade or concert because we pass real Russian women resplendent in their belted coats, walking arm in arm with their families. As we pass them, I feel their eyes flickering in judgment. They are all whispering to me at once, a harmony of female

Russian voices in my head. They are chiding, affectionate, maternal. *You failed, but maybe it's not too late*, they seem to be saying. *How did you overlook the most obvious thing Russian women have known for centuries?*

They walk, these true ladies with lapdogs, swollen with power, fueled on memory, swathed in fur and Lycra, dreaming. How romantic they still look to me, these women, full of secrets and longings. Queens—in its sprawl, its anonymous brick high-rises, its confusing tangle of streets—hides their secrets well.

"So this is where you're living."

"I like it here actually," Carl says. He seems to have undergone a physical transformation in the months we've been apart. His style has become younger and hipper, a faded T-shirt peeking out from an open short-sleeved button-down, low-slung jeans and sneakers as opposed to his neat chinos and loafers. The overall look of this change strikes me with a blunt force.

"The place hasn't changed at all."

The old Rainbow store, the same crappy city supermarket that used to house Waldbaum's, Uzbek bodegas, Bukharian shish kebab joints, Russian pharmacies. We are walking awkwardly, arms out to our sides. Usually, I would link my hand through his arm. Evening is a time for strolling, the genders divided. Men walk in front with their friends, women behind. Both groups laugh and talk about their own concerns. Once in a while, the men turn around and address the women. Once in a while, the women pretend to gossip about the men as if they weren't in hearing range. It occurs to me that the world I sometimes occupy is more fluid than I'd assumed. I had dismissed it, latched myself on to the new world with the assumption that what I was leaving behind was already dead.

"You look great," I add. The trick is to always flip your fears into their opposite, to unearth the kernels of confidence.

"You do too. But you always do."

"Have you been hard at work on the book?"

"I've been thinking mostly," he says, rolling his lower lip back and forth between his teeth. I have no more dominion over these small habits. "I'm trying to figure out why I'm so angry. No, more like surprised. You know?"

"No, I don't. Tell me."

The man next to me starts to blur. Almost to ascertain that he's still there, still my husband, I stop him so he will face me. We're in front of a Bukharian restaurant, the communal tables noisy with merry toasting. It's started to rain, a thin spitting kind of rain, almost imperceptible on the skin. Once in a while, the door opens and the smell of smoking meat is expelled into the air.

Carl reaches over to pluck some feathery substance from my hair. "I think I need a few more weeks, actually. I feel something different every day. I'd like to get it all sorted in my head."

"Why?" I say the word. There comes a time when the word must be said. I watch him flick away the speck, the instinctive husbandly act still wired into him. "Honey, talk to me."

Carl squints down the street as if he is hoping there is some wormhole through which to vanish. Talking about feelings was never his strong point; he would contort himself in order to avoid it.

A couple leaves the restaurant, exclaims at the turn in the weather. The man leaves the woman under the awning, promising to return with the car.

"At least come with me to your parents. While we're still ironing things out. Do we need them asking questions?"

"You're right. For now, we should keep up appearances for our families." He looks miserable, creased and in pain.

So many wives passing us, in groups and alone. In too tight sheath dresses with high heels or baggy housecoats and high heels, their hair dyed and pulled back, gossiping or staring ahead, rushing forward with purses and satchels and granny carts.

A Russian anecdote: A wife is training a new puppy. Her husband looks on dubiously. "My dear, I'm afraid you're not getting very good results." The wife says, "Don't you worry. It's a matter of patience. It's not like it was easy with you at first either."

I take Carl's hand. "Can you tell me if you still love me? I still love you."

A car is slowly parallel parking in front of us. The man turns off the ignition and comes around to the passenger side to open the door, then guides the woman from her place beneath the awning, shielding her hair with his jacket. My mouth fills with something gritty and pebbly.

"Of course I love you. I'm just trying to figure out a way to be seen. Does that make any sense?"

"A way to be seen? No," I say, sadly.

Then I point out that we're late to his parents' house.

We trample into the Vandermotter apartment, disheveled, wet, and out of sorts.

"You certainly look like you've dressed for the occasion." Frances greets us in a sleeveless white shift, cherries decorating its borders.

Today I realize that the Vandermotter apartment no longer holds magic for me. The items within it have lost that foreign mystique: that dreadful Puritan portrait inherited from Aunt Vivian's Virginia horse farm, the framed Yale fleeces from Armand's alma mater, the schooner proudly displaying the date 1793. The splashes of orange everywhere as a testament to Dutch heritage. The Vandermotter and Mortimer framed family trees extending their fruitful branches through generations.

Over time, the deterioration of the Vandermotter home became more and more evident, the sleights of hand to give it the veneer of polish while hiding its fissures. Cece sorted her décor into two categories: the items displayed for guests and those slated for daily use. Antique Limoges china and good silver in the armoire and Target plates and Broadway Panhandler cutlery on the table, Tiffany lamps on view but Crate and Barrel lamps actually ignited, pressed lace bedding in the cupboard, Bed, Bath, and Beyond sheets on the bed.

When I first met Carl, I thought it all terribly prudent, the flashy taste of my own parents coarse and undiscerning by comparison. *At least an immigrant has a healthy relationship with stuff,* my mother said once after a tense dinner party at the Vandermotters' where we ran out of conversation before the entrée was plated. *We know it's all expendable, that we might have to abandon it at the drop of a hat. These people are just holding on to ugly things.*

But maybe it was just self-protection, having been forced to part with heirlooms, disentangle yourself from the objects that define you. Leaving the Soviet Union, my parents had to winnow all their belongings to suitcases weighing a ton. Precious room was made for toilet paper and homeopathic textbooks, items they were convinced did not exist in the new country. Left behind was my father's stamp collection, valuable and lovingly collected over a lifetime, a passionate hobby he never did take up again in America. My mother feared her gold Soviet jewelry would be worthless but those phantom necklaces and rings still loom large in her mind. How she would love to see that one ring again, embedded with the tiny sapphire sickle.

My parents' Ramsdale house also displays this lack of reverence for tradition. Furniture is moved from room to room depending on my mother's moods, new cheap rugs are bought and the old discarded, curtains alternate with the seasons. Everything is bought on discount. Nothing too precious or valuable, nothing that would ever tug at my mother's heart again if she were forced to part with it.

By contrast, the Vandermotter residence remains perpetually unchanged over the sixty years it has belonged to the family. There's the sepulchral feeling of being inundated by furniture, the sense that none of it belongs in the same room together, that the paperweights and other knickknacks are only ever moved by the cleaning crew. If one slides aside a painting or the leg of a desk, one will find the imprinted blankness of its original piece of wall or floor, the certainty that you're the first person to have dislodged this item from its eternal rest.

Carl brushes past me to the kitchen and there's the lament of an open beer. How I want to touch his back, the soothing measure that works so well when we visit his parents.

Armand strolls in, drink in hand, Miggy by his side. Miggy is an incomprehensible creature to me, birdlike with a craning neck, the kind of expression that either signals confusion or a need for eyeglasses. She is divorced, the state evoking such exaggerated sympathy from the Vandermotters that she's always invited over in the evenings. "Did Frances tell you about Santorini?"

We're forced to sit down and endure a detailed observation of Greek islands, the particular minerality of the white wines, the Cycladic island landscape, Byzantine monasteries. They'd prepared for the trip by reading Aeschylus. Miggy nods owl-like from having heard it before, but gives a convincing impression of renewed interest.

"How are things going at the alliance, Cece?" Carl has even less patience for vacation recaps and I slip him a conspiratorial smile.

"Terrible. If our new round of fund-raising doesn't come through, the agency might have to be shut down," his mother says, stacking plates for the crackers.

Over the years, it became apparent that this charity is the one cause Carl and his mother have in common, their one source of bonding. In planning its galas, sending cards to the kids, and attending meetings with its president, mother and son have unleashed their quiet love for one another.

In the early phases of courtship, I was Frances's enthusiastic pupil, accompanying her to meetings and fund-raisers and luncheons. From the outside, it all looked so exclusive and important—I'd seen those photos in the *New York Times* Style section, those slick, floral people gathered in museum clumps, wearing elaborate hats at garden parties. I was fascinated with how unattractive the people were given license to be, how pleased they appeared in one another's company, how their ease probably came from this status they were born or married into, and I wished this ease on myself.

"You have to make an effort. People just need to get to know you," Frances counseled at one of those luncheons, where I was seated among Miggy, Clara, and another woman with smooth, slicked-back hair who took turns disclosing in great detail their meals for the day. The conversation was mind-numbing.

"I find if I combine avocado with a sprinkle of lemon juice, my body can really absorb that monounsaturated fat," Miggy was saying.

"Oh, I never touch avocado. As silly as it sounds, I'm scared of it."

"But that's absurd. It balances your potassium-to-sodium ratio. You should really rethink it. I eat an entire avocado every day."

"I know. I know. My nutritionist says the same thing. It's irrational."

"At least you recognize that."

My mind would wander in the middle of their chatter, grateful that Carl didn't require this life of me, that he'd shunned it for himself. He loved the kids but never the parties, and when I described my evenings at the functions, embellishing them for comic effect (The Attack of the Killer Avocado!), he would say, "Poor Tanya, what a bore." In any case, there was never a way to penetrate those round tables with drooping orchids, their plates with slivers of raw fish drizzled with a complicated oil foam. Now that I've appeared in the *Financial Times,* and those women have been e-mailing me nonstop since the article was published, it seems even more silly to have tried.

I realize Frances has been talking for some time. "It's been an uphill climb since the financial troubles. In fact, I've had to pare down on other demands so I could concentrate on the organization alone. I'm treasurer now." Armand bends down to serve what I now recognize as Eastsides, lemon rind contorting around the rim of the glass. I can picture an entire closet consisting of multiples of that navy jacket with gold buttons that he wears.

Miggy pulls the flaps of her cardigan tighter. "Cece's understating it as usual. We've had a change in board leadership. It's actually been a mess. No matter what we try, we can't get our numbers back to where we were in 2008. And those poor kids! We've barely got enough caseworkers to handle half their load."

"It's tragic is what it is," Carl says. "We should do another fund-raiser. I'm up for helping in whatever way."

"I think two in a season is a bit much, don't you?" Frances says, eyebrow raised. "It's diminishing returns after the first."

A flutter of terror—he's talking about himself in the singular—and a long-hewn instinct kicks in, the need to preserve, to stop a client from defecting.

I clear my throat. "I may have someone interested in contributing to the organization. I was telling Cece."

"Really?" Miggy sits up straight, her neck elongated, at attention. Carl raises his chin. "Isn't that great news?"

I can tell my husband's listening, and this inflates me with fresh courage. "A new client actually. He's interested in one of my lots—the Order, Carl—and I think the cause would really speak to him. A lot of my clients are becoming important philanthropists."

"Yes, so this has been the one spot of hope," Frances says, brightly.

"You don't want their money. They're criminals," Carl says.

"Why not, darling? We could use it and they've got it."

There have been encounters between her world and the oligarch world, but they've been brief and bumbling. My clients have a perverse desire to inject themselves where they're not wanted, but then grow bored with the protocols of other social systems. They like to be wholly themselves, certain that those "sticks up their asses" will loosen up eventually after a few resounding toasts. Meanwhile, the "sticks" are allergic to an overt display of money; like repelling batteries, the two groups occupy opposite sides of any fund-raiser.

I sit back, confused. Carl's never said he had moral objections to my job.

"I agree with Cece, Carl," Miggy says. She appears energized by the news, raising her glass in the air as if in Russian-style salute. *Za zdorovie!* "If they're willing to help, who cares what their motives are or where the money comes from? There's no point turning away donors when children are at stake."

"Well, I for one would be happy to meet the man," Frances says. "I don't care what people say. One has to do what's right." This is definitely not her first drink of the evening. She crosses her leg, heel dangling. What never fails to astound me is how different these people look from anyone else I've met, less the result of the decent clothes as the indifferent way they're worn on tapered shoulders.

"Great. I'll set it up." I'm still holding the drink in my hand, but I notice it trembling. I will have to call Regan and check in where we stand with the Catherine historian. We should have had some preliminary word on the final authentication. "And my clients have really changed, honey. They're not the same guys from the nineties. They're discerning.

They've developed an eye. They want to make a positive impact with their money."

Carl examines me, inscrutable. I'm sure this is an elaborate test he's forging for me, and I refuse to fail it. It's only a misunderstanding of what I do. A misunderstanding. I wrap my tongue around the word until it develops its proper shape.

"You guys are so attractive together, have I ever told you that?" Armand says. It's his way of sending private messages to Carl, addressing us both, broadcasting his love in public announcements. "We were like that once, weren't we?"

"Oh God, not again."

"I'm serious. We were damn attractive. We just lit up a room, you know? Everyone said so."

"Were we attractive?" Cece smiles. "I can't remember. It was just so long ago."

Catherine

"Are you so hard-hearted that you do not believe in love?" Sergei repeats.

Catherine squints around for elusive hares. They are riding side by side, the others far ahead of them. The earth is mottled with the debris of summer, trees drooping like canopies. All around them is lushness, fecundity, an endless field peeking white with daisies. Even her dogs are indifferent to the chase at hand, sluggish and drooping as if tuned in to the sumptuous cloud of torpor that surrounds them.

"Who says I am hard-hearted?"

Catherine knows she should drive her horse onward, join the others as soon as possible. But Sergei Saltykov's horse is lingering beside hers, perilously close, his scent redolent of fragrant, dying petals. His voice gently rides the breeze. "If I am not being impertinent, may I ask if you have known the pleasures of love?"

"In fact, you are being impertinent."

He showed up at court the year before, this bored and drowsy man, married to one of the empress's ladies-in-waiting, a beautiful girl always in search of her missing husband. Catherine noticed him right away, and who could avoid noticing him? Ripe at the perfect age of twenty-six, dark-haired, pretty, the kind of eyes that squeezes its prey until it succumbs, who believes himself smarter than his peers. But still he is unafraid and amusing and the first man bold enough to parry with her. He knows how to distract the crowd in order to capture her attention, and when the others are off performing some silly game he devised, he is nearby, hovering, red-lipped, waiting.

"I imagine you must know the pleasures of love with your wife," she reminds him primly. Her heart is flapping, the wings of a butterfly. She hears the sound of flaring guns in the distance, but otherwise is pleased to note that no one has returned to check on their whereabouts.

"All that glitters is not gold," he says with dramatically downcast eyes. "Marrying Matryona was a foolish decision. I caught sight of her on the swing, high in the air. I thought it was love. I was impulsive back then."

"By 'back then,' you are referring to two years ago?"

"Two years is a long time for youth. Now, of course, I can see gold among less precious metals. As soon as I laid eyes on you, for example. Your good nature, your thick hair, your beauty."

"Quite a list of my finer attributes." She knows she is encouraging him, this long-lashed charmer. She should have shut him down months ago, a severe and definitive turning away. Not that Peter would notice or care, but the empress is still sharp, plying suffocating affections one min-ute, vengeful the next. But when Sergei enters a room, a flutter brushes through her sternum, and when he stalks over to her with that private smile of knowledge, she finds herself forgetting to breathe.

He is as close to her as two impatient horses can be, his boots brush-ing her ankles. "May I hope then?"

"'Desires change their objects: that which one used to love, one loves no longer.'"

"Montesquieu?" He pauses, impressed. "You have not been idle, Grand Duchess. Then let me respond to you with Montesquieu: 'Man is a creature that obeys a creature that wants.' Allow me to believe you are not indifferent to me after all."

She is pleased, but makes the gesture of being resigned to a fate be-yond her will. "Who am I to rein in your imagination?"

He smiles. His lashes fan longer than any man's, framing his eyes like slivers of imported citrus. She urges her horse to a trot.

"Surely you like me best of all the men at court." In a breath, he has caught up with her. How foolish he is, how unrelenting. But her mind is being colonized by the roiling force inside her and then there are eyes that pin hers down.

"You please me fine," she says.

"I can tell you are far from indifferent."

"Not indifferent, perhaps . . ."

"I may hope then."

Another sound of gunfire rings out past the domed Japanese pavilion. There is a call of triumph and the barking of dogs. The successful capture of hares. She thinks she hears the cry of her name. *Ekaterina Alexeyevna!*

"We should go. A private counsel like this will only draw suspicion."

"Ekaterina Alexeyevna," she hears again, her adopted name easily carried by the summer breeze. The island is still for all the noise in the distance. She feels exposed by its boundaries.

His hand strikes out before she can sense it, their horses side by side again. He is gripping her by a cleft of the elbow. "Then tell me right now I can hope. That I will be tolerated."

The flutter has spread into fever spasms through her body. He believes giving voice to her desire will be her subjugation. So be it. But she is capable of manipulating his desires as well as her own; she has learned this much in court. There is the pleasure of the private knowledge of one's superiority while pretending to the opposite, making the decision to yield while not giving anything up of value.

"Yes, yes," she says, at last, the words as if tumbling against their own volition. She has timed them to her own pleasure. The sensation is a tingle coursing up and down her sternum.

"I take you at your word then."

"But you must leave now. I can see them returning for me."

His fingers unclench. "I will consider this a solemn vow." He spurs his horse and rides into the swell of cheering voices.

"Wait, I meant no," she cries, the dapple of light falling warm on her cheeks, her shoulders. The sun hovers directly above him too, so he blurs into a shimmering brown speck, disappearing into the field. Suddenly she doubts her powers to control desire.

"No, no, I meant no," she says again, moving closer to the hoots of

men, the baying of dogs, the row of hares being carried in satchels. Upside down, bleeding.

She keeps him at bay as long as she can. In public, she refuses to take part
in the amusements he organizes until he complains that the grand duchess is simply too cruel. Afterward, the others busy with a silly singing
game or other, she allows Sergei to catch up to her between walls and
doorways where he whispers that the very heavens have charged him
with great responsibility. His lips say they love her.

"For all you know, my heart may belong to another," she says, knowing this will only inflame his desire. He insists she is far worse than
the Tatars in her ravages. He grasps, she slips out of them. They eye
one another in darkened corners, her hair flat against walls. There are the
touches of affection—he rights a snagged necklace, rescues an earring
from possible ejection from her lobe, she adjusts a crooked bow in his
hair. She takes pleasure in burning his letters full of misspellings, watching their edges singe and curl.

One night, she leaves the door to her bedchamber ajar. And waits.

This time, the steps down the hall are firm with intention. When he
rounds the corner, a candle glows iridescent between his palms. He is all
smiles and slit eyes, an actor gauging his audience, testing out poses to
create the most dramatic effect.

"My Katya," he says with bowed head, as if the act were already completed, his rights to her secured.

She startles. "You must never, on any condition, call me Katya. That
name belongs to someone else."

She is wearing the wedding-night nightgown, its pink rose fluctuat-
ing in the light. Next to her bed she has draped the Order for strength.

"Whatever my beloved commands. Catherine, then." He places the
candle on a table and reaches down to stroke the curve of her jaw. His
chin: first receding in shadows, then back in the light, orange. The stones
of his rings are cool against her clavicles but her heart is a hot thing. She
reaches for him, trembling with fear. The scent of him, overly perfumed,
fills the room. She tries to match fantasy and this very striking reality in

her mind, the bent-over form of Sergei wedging himself beside her, the lowering of his mouth on hers. His lips are as soft as she imagined them, goose feathers undulating up and down her face. His tongue sinews between her teeth, the bristles of his hair scrape against her skin. It is not a George kiss, but close, very close, like being submerged in silk.

He is performing some act of careful kneading, circling, teasing, awakening some nascent seamy surface. But even as she is bursting into new portals of sensation, a small part of her continues to calculate, to compare the two of them, to weigh her strength against his own. Or her weakness.

The next morning, she rides like a man in full view of the empress, grasping the shanks of the horse with her ankles. She can feel the woman's eyes on her, following her progress out of sightline, and she does nothing to alter to the sideways female position. The sound of hooves against earth, her scalloped breath, the high heat of the day pressing against her constricting clothes. She is rushing headlong into what little wind unsettles the air, aware of only the seismic connection with the horse.

And afterward, not immediately changing out of her man's habit, she simply strolls up to the empress, who is fanning herself, bejeweled as always despite the occasion.

"I have been watching you ride," the woman says, tight-lipped. Her knee has been bothering her, and now it rests grotesque across the lap of one of her ladies.

"Has my form not improved?" Her face is throbbing from the sun, cheeks burning. She feels as though the empress must know that they are now equals in womanhood. Finally, she has her own Razumovsky.

"I suppose we have discovered the reason for your childless state after seven years of marriage. It is unhealthy to ride that way." She leans to her ladies. They cluck in agreement as they fan.

She wants to burst out laughing—let me tell you the reason for my childless state. Your nephew has not once penetrated me in seven years—but instead says, "But surely not. Not all women are equally graced with easy fecundity."

"When we imported you from your provincial German town, we had every expectation you would be one of the graced ones, my dear."

"I am grieved you consider me a failure."

"A failure, not entirely. But you have fallen short, my dear. I cannot lie."

In the full blaze of day, it is apparent the empress is getting older, the folds of her skin drooping under all those precious stones. More often, she loses threads of conversations, her mind turning inward to some faraway place. The blue of her eyes has dulled opaque, a film of sweat loosening the uneven mat of face powder, grotesque where once it was flawless. Even the empress must realize that her reign is nearing its end.

Love is a secret, a series of hushed confidences and exchanging salacious memories and planning for glorious futures. It is a temporal condition in the mind as well as a visceral one in the body. There is a clear separation between Sergei and everyone else. He is now Seryozha to her, and his voice booms while the voices of others are easily ignored. He is elegant and sweet-tongued where his rivals are bumbling. His laugh rings strong, fills the empty space around them. She could be blindfolded and her skin would prickle if he were in the vicinity. When contemplating their last encounter, she could only think in silly metaphors—the first drink of water, the melting of wax, the flicking stem of fruit. In the evening, she makes an extra effort to tuck silver roses into her hair.

Daily life goes on, the move from Summer to Winter Palace. Her attendance is needed at the ceremonial blessings of the canal in Kronstadt, a swirl of masquerades. She and Seryozha toss innuendoes to one another from behind masks' sanctuary.

"Perhaps you are unduly fatigued today," she might say between minuets.

"Up too late perusing Cicero again, Grand Duchess?" he might rejoinder.

Peter knows all and encourages them because to him, the affair is an elaborate game. He considers the empress—rather than himself—as victim to their deception and believes himself to be on the inside of a great prank.

"Why are you so solitary? Perhaps you should see what Seryozha is doing," he would prompt her during a dinner with a tittering laugh. Practically pushing her in the direction of her lover.

Later the same night, Peter sneaks up on their tête-à-tête with a knowing look. "How are my turtledoves this evening?"

She grimaces, sets aside the remains of her unfinished, too soft peach. Her husband's idiocy should not be encouraged. But Sergei turns to Peter with those limpid eyes of his, those sculpted brows. "We were speaking about that special exhaustion that follows nocturnal pleasures. And what about the grand duke? Has he ever enjoyed the thundering frisson of love with your lady?"

Peter looks genuinely confused. Thundering? Frisson? "I have never experienced anything like that," he admits.

"Is that so?" Seryozha pretends at shock. "Perhaps a doctor might examine you for defects or obstacles? I see no reason you should miss out on these sensations."

"You think I should see Lestocq?"

Under the table, they are locking knees in silent mirth. It would be just like Peter to undergo some unnecessary surgery in search of feelings he will never experience.

"I can arrange it," Seryozha says, grandly. His fingers are adorned by rings; the gold cameo is a gift from Catherine. "I can even accompany you."

"Maybe you are right," Peter says, chewing on his bottom lip. "If you would accompany me."

Fool, Seryozha mouths when Peter turns away.

Still, through the gauze of infatuation, she is aware that public eyes settle on them, that judging mouths are busy at work. Sharp twitches of the eye darting from her stomach to her face to ascertain the truth.

When it finally arrives, the sensation in the belly reminds her of tainted food lodged deep, unmoving. Most of the time she forgets about it entirely until she feels a faint tug, a turning. She cannot stand the scent of pickled meat or hair powder. Only the ladies closest to her take note of her changing shape, dresses altered to accommodate an expansion. Her mind cycles through a thousand worries: will the child be recognized as heir? Will she be removed from court? Will Peter let slip that he has never completed an act that could result in this?

In Moscow, she tries to discuss the matter with Sergei, to seek his counsel, but these days he extricates himself with dainty excuses. When she enters a room, he swears his days are suddenly filled with meetings. His appearances at the palace have become erratic. When she manages to ensnare him in private counsel, he admits everything about court life has begun to irritate him. Travel to the palace is becoming inconvenient, Bestuzhev is against him, his political viewpoints are not being taken seriously.

It is weeks until Catherine finally catches him alone. He is rushing from the palace with a sheaf of papers in hand, probably inserting himself into meetings where he is not invited or agitating for jobs he does not deserve. She surprises him behind the wooden pillar, leaps out at him with a roar, and his terror equals that of encountering an actual lion.

"You frightened me."

For a minute, she just wants to gaze at those eyelashes, the way they quiver nervously at her.

"I have news," she finally says.

Sergei is impatient. He had clearly hoped for an undisturbed exit. "Must we discuss it now? The carriage has pulled up." The hall is not empty, far from it. The British ambassador is exchanging pleasantries with a young Russian officer, a housekeeper rushes up the stairs with fresh linens. But she must seize her moment.

"I'm afraid so."

"What is it then? You know how I hate all this secrecy."

She has practiced this but the silkiness of the words elude her. "It is not unexpected. A natural consequence, shall we say. But the doctor says only a few months remain."

Her Seryozha blanches; even his nose is drained of color. A servant carrying a tray of raw pheasant shuffles past them. They wait until the man is out of sight.

"My God. You know what this means."

"That we can be together?" She allows herself to hope. That she has misinterpreted his coldness, that he has been yearning for the simple life of a real marriage. Will he ask her to leave the palace with him? They could erect a modest country home for the two of them, the baby sleeping on top of duck feather pillows. The first Peter and the first Catherine, the cabin, the twelve children, the great city of St. Petersburg built in their shared vision.

"We will have to arrange for his surgery then. Immediately."

The country house, the wrinkled baby on a blanket, the easy bustle over a simple masonry stove. All of it is gone. A blade spirals inside her and she steels herself for this new reality. "Will he consent to it?"

"The fool will be relieved! At last, the world will trust the problem has been solved. He will be let alone, his blasted task fulfilled to satisfaction."

Madame Krause emerges from behind a pillar. She is an unexpected vision with her wide hoop skirts, her too wide face framed by girlish ringlets. "May I speak with you?" She directs herself to Catherine, ignoring Sergei.

"Farewell, then." He rushes away before anyone can stop him.

Oh, Madame Krause with her impeccable timing, with that twisted face of intrigue. She affects a martyred air for playing a crucial role in the royal drama. Catherine wants to slap her for interrupting them. "I will be straightforward, my dear Catherine. I am privy to some delicate information."

"What is it?" She feels it again, lower this time, a churning.

"I do not doubt that you fancy someone. Someone that is not the grand duke."

Catherine sighs. "What makes you say that?"

The woman rushes on, a handkerchief wrung between her hands. "You may think I am here to reprimand you but you will see that I will not make difficulties for you."

The last of Sergei's footsteps disappear in the front hall. She forces her attention back to Madame Krause. "I do not understand. What is it you are implying?"

"I believe you fancy one of the Saltykov brothers, I am not sure which.

What I am saying is that the empress has decided not to put obstacles in the way of such a relation. If I am making myself clear."

"No. Not exactly."

"An heir is an heir after all. Her Majesty is very eager after all this time. If it is to be him"—she nods in the direction of Sergei's departed form—"no one needs to be the wiser."

The woman does not even bid her farewell, as if she wants to spend no more time than necessary on an indecorous task. She is on to the next errand, a dressing-down of the forgetful housekeeper. When her wide back recedes, Catherine runs toward the entrance, the wide-open doors. "Seryozha, come back."

How he will laugh when he hears this: they are free, they are free. They can do as they like, undisturbed. The baby nestled between them. A samovar boiling water in the kitchen. Their own small bedroom fragrant with the heat of love and warm milk. They can erect a wooden house on the grounds of one of the lesser-used palaces (Oranienbaum?) and no one can stop them. An heir is an heir, and Peter has taken himself out of the picture.

But Seryozha's carriage is gone.

The labor stretches deep into the night, the mattress on the floor pointy as rocks. In her pain she is alone, forgotten. *I am giving birth to the heir of a great empire and nobody cares,* she thinks in a kind of numb disbelief. The midwife has left long ago but has not returned. Her call for water is ignored. The pain starts in a single toe, then sears its way up the leg, exploding in her midsection. She holds her focus on a single ceiling plank.

When the child, a beautiful, slippery boy, is born, he is instantly whisked away, exchanged for a pouch of money, a hundred thousand rubles and second-rate jewelry brought to her by a businesslike chamberlain. She hears her son is to be named Paul.

"May I see him?" she asks, but the message never seems to reach the empress. Day after day, there is no sight of the child. In the immediate aftermath, she is celebrated. Sumptuous furnishings are wheeled in for congratulatory visits from the court—a pink daybed embroidered in silver, upholstered French armchairs, fresh brocade curtains fringed in gold. She eyes them indifferently. Which is a good thing because a few days later, the footmen return to sweep it all away, and collect what is left of her money when the last of the visitors depart. Outside the window, she hears fireworks, the splashing water of a fountain. The midwife told her it sprayed beer.

Apart from performing the necessary ceremonial rites, the empress has sent not a single kind word, and there has been no missive from Sergei, who is busy packing for his Stockholm post. Her son is far away, sequestered somewhere close to the empress. Her breasts leak, throb, then dry up. Peter has moved on to the least attractive and most repulsive of the maids who hates her. Most of the day, she faces the wall; when the door opens and shuts, she does not care who enters. Alongside this deadening of nerves, she feels a smoldering anger.

Then one day, she rises. She asks for her books, her Voltaire and d'Alembert, and her maps. She sits in her dressing gown, tracing a line from the Caspian to the Black Sea, following a possible route of trade. She finally puts ink to paper: "I would like to feel fear, but I cannot; the invisible hand that has guided me along a very rough road will never allow me to falter." In the distance, she hears a low, insistent cry, but by now it sounds to her like the drumming of grouse, nothing more.

Tanya

PRESENT DAY

"How can you not know the reason your own husband left?" Alla says. "Unless you don't want to tell me, which is completely understandable."

We're the first to arrive in the boardroom, waiting for the other members of the Jewish Community Center committee to file in: the topic of the day is how to market Judaism to cynical Russian-Americans. A Regina Spektor fund-raiser concert is at the top of the agenda.

She's immaculate as usual, my best friend, sporting a pale pink manicure, her hair a refreshed blond. On the days she meets me for lunch at the office, the old-money codgers do a double take.

I flip through our agenda. The downside to good friends is the way they keep poking at your most tender spots. "Carl's the kind of guy who needs to think. I'm trying to give him space."

"Sounds like bullshit to me. Space? Who gives her husband space?"

"Maybe he's angry," I concede. "Maybe he has new-husband buyer's remorse. I don't know. He's not talking."

"If that's true and something's going on with that Hermione woman or someone else, then you hope it's a phase. There are worse things in a marriage than affairs. But be ready to find out something you don't want to know."

Alla's speaking from experience. She discovered one affair by accident (by picking up Greg's phone after a text), and one on purpose (her brother hacked into Greg's work e-mail), but she never confronted her husband about the information. This last time, she went on a covert domestic attack, booking them for theater around town, dropping the kids off with her parents so they could launch into spontaneous vacations. When they returned from a trip to Sardinia, she announced to me that the other woman was definitively gone.

Before us is a tray consisting entirely of carved melon: honeydew, cantaloupe, and some kind of Persian variety with a dark green rind. Their surfaces glisten with slimy veneer. On the wall is a series of photographs of hip Jewish bands singing to appreciative seated audiences.

"He's so moral, so black-and-white. I knew that marrying him. He judges me." With a twinge, I think about the Order displayed in luscious four color, in *ARTnews,* Artnet, *Vidimosti,* and the *New York Times.*

"Moral? I thought he would have grown out of that by now."

"Maybe he's right. I didn't even want him to see the Order."

"Why not?"

"I don't know. The book, I guess. It might bring all that back."

"His book? About the queen? I thought it did well. Though I don't blame him for moving on. Between you and me, I couldn't finish it. Be honest, it was boring, no?"

A few dutiful JCCers file into the room—*privet, privet*—take their seats. It's a good excuse to drop the whole subject.

"Oh God," Alla says, flipping through the mimeographed packet. "Russians are never, ever going to become better Jews, Regina Spektor or not. This agenda is a waste of our time."

"Why? I think it's possible. There's got to be better outreach. We're just people who've been taught to be suspicious of organized religion, to be suspicious of God. Marketing spirituality is like marketing anything else. There have to be incentives."

"And Regina Spektor's our incentive?"

"Sure, why not? She's one of us who made it. It raises morale."

Alla puts on the breathless, squeaky voice of the *Kultura* anchor. "'Regina Spektor is just one of our people on the move.'"

The new president of the organization is getting started at the front of the room, booting up the computer. A diamond-studded Star of David is dangling between her breasts. "Thanks, everyone, for being here so early in the morning. And I want to thank Tanya Vandermotter again for arranging for us to use the Worthington's galleries for our Spektor event."

"They're clapping for you," Alla reminds me. Now, the woman is calling up a PowerPoint presentation on the projection. Myth no. 1: Russian Jews are not spiritual people. Myth no. 2: Russian Jews are resistant to organized religion. Myth no. 3: Russian Jews have negative associations with Judaism. Myth no. 4: We don't need volunteers to spread the message.

Alla leans over. "Please tell me you will not be the one to spearhead this initiative."

"Why not? I think they need me, don't you?"

"My God, haven't you got enough on your plate? You've got to work on your marriage."

"Okay, I get it. I'll let someone else run this show. I've got to be back in the office anyway."

"My point exactly."

The most powerful New York Russian-Americans are seated around the long table. All the varieties of melon and minimuffin are consumed and the meeting begins.

Instead of returning to the office, I stop in front of a squat, airless building near Penn Station, take a key out of my bag, and unlock the front door to the Urban Writers Space. The application had been easy, a few questions, a deposit, and Hermione Tarling, lovely and vague and completely disinterested in my identity as Carl's wife, handed over the code to the building.

Earnest heads bow before flickering screens at each cubicle. There is the languid mewl of music expelling from someone's earphones. I scan one body after the other for the particular shape of Carl's back, for his narrow shoulders, for his classic profile. For all the things that were recently so beautiful and foreign and self-contained and reliable, like the flamingo I saw with Medovsky. But he's nowhere. The kitchen is occupied by a trio of commiserating writers sipping tea and comparing overburdened teaching loads.

Incomers choose cubicles, and when they are full, the overflow writers pile on the couch in front of the offices. Several lean their heads back to sleep. The ridiculousness of what I'm doing—playing hooky from work by pretending to work—doesn't elude me. But I boot up my computer anyway and wait for the familiar step. A jasmine scent curls down from ducts in the ceiling. Hermione Tarling checks on us all, a queen surveying her domain.

All those words being written, I think, looking around. All those books on laptops struggling for the light of day. The tormented tap of keyboards, solitary struggles waged in every cubicle. Soaking in the neurotic air of all these writers, I wonder if I should have listened to Carl's struggle more, acknowledged the difficulty of the creative enterprise. I wonder if I couldn't stand the idea of him being diminished, less than I needed him to be. That maintaining his proper role in our relationship meant doing whatever it takes to get that book written and published.

For the first time in almost a year, I Google *Young Catherine*. It takes some effort to retrieve the memory of how the book's publication stirred our household. It was a time of great tension, like right after a glass is flung from the table but before it explodes. It was a time when neither of us said what we meant, when we awaited the next piece of news with stilled hearts. Each day, reviews of the book were forwarded to us by Carl's agent, and they were mostly good and I tried to massage into Carl some sensation of joy. They praised the male author's insight into the emotions of a girl forced to adapt to a foreign culture, the disappointments of romantic love, the pressures from different factions and the way young Catherine adroitly navigated them. I read one of the more glowing reviews to him out loud but he begged me to stop, saying he couldn't even listen, and what did I think I was proving by reading each customer's online assessment? *(I'm not sure I even liked her all that much or wanted to follow an entire book about her. She was not as likable as I wanted her to be. The history stuff was slow going.)* Nothing, I'm not trying to prove anything. Even when his department chair called with the long-desired job offer, he wasn't thrilled.

The book's unexpected triumph unsettled Carl and he began losing sight of daily details even more than usual. Slips of paper fluttered about unorganized, items of clothing were professed missing, meals were forgotten. Just when I hoped that everything that arrived with the book's success would lend Carl the validation he'd been waiting for, he surprised me with an uncharacteristic shortness of his temper, his fruitless pacing, his rejection of all interviews and prizes. He took the job at Ditmas College but only after much convincing from me.

He would flare up without warning, on the subway, in bed, wandering through the Central Park Zoo. "My editor's already asking for the next book," he would suddenly blurt out, apropos of nothing, koalas calmly blinking at us from wobbly branches. "What the hell am I supposed to do about that?"

"Honey." I would try to soothe him, my arms around his body as if I had the power to eradicate his pain even when a part of me wanted him to stop his wallowing. "Just focus on this one. On enjoying this one."

Even his agent called me on the sly. "Is it me or is he losing it? Talk some sense into him. It's a real shame to squander a once-in-a-lifetime opportunity. I've got authors like that. Can't handle success and their careers die on the vine. Tell him to call me."

So again, I was forced into action. Late nights after work, between trips to visit estates and research potential inventory, I worked a second shift in service to Carl's exploding career. Translations accepted, e-mails answered, permissions decisions made, requests for blurbs rejected in Carl's name.

Hadn't my parents insisted that being an immigrant taught me to handle things, be the kind of person who has her life fully under control? How often has it been made clear to me that when you immigrate as a child, you cease being a child? You suddenly realize your parents are struggling while you're gaining in power. The new world makes more sense to you than to them, who are still dripping with the dew from the former life. You start to separate friends from enemies, dangers from safety, you start to understand the limitations but also the license granted to you as a foreigner.

Your parents begin relying on you in large ways and small until your competence is assumed. You become the person who sets up phone service, who negotiates directions with pedestrians, orders Chinese food, explains odd American customs like wearing green on St. Patrick's Day. Once you do it long enough, others start to depend on you too. In school, your less academically diligent friends expect you to know the homework assignments. Later, they'll assume you'll be the one to book vacations, walk up to the maître d' and ask about tables, host the bridal showers. And it gives you a tingle of power to take care of things for others, to be relied upon so completely. The world is an easily negotiated field of logistics to you, but to others it's a quicksand of unpleasant duties where impossible decisions must be made every day.

"You are so great at this, Tanyechka," my parents said. An expert who so easily can figure out where to eat, how to take out a mortgage, find an accountant, an orthopedic surgeon, a lawnmower, a handyman, the proper dress for a birthday party.

"Don't worry, this is only temporary," they said from their patriarchal perch of the Old Country. Once you marry the right man, he'll take over the responsibilities of handling, ease the burden of your competence. I said I didn't need any of those things—the American model is about the division of labor, not about the protector and the protected. There was Carl, who from outside was so perfect for the task, his family name thrusting him into the former category. What my parents didn't know was that he didn't mind my aggressiveness in the world. He preferred it.

Carl liked my booking restaurant reservations and vacations. "Two tickets, please," I'd say at the movies, and he would linger back, allow me to take the tickets and lead us into the theater. He liked that I ordered food for both of us, organized our birthday gatherings, told him exactly what I wanted for a gift, surprised him on our anniversary. He tried to please me a few times in the very beginning, buying me a chrome watch or gifting me a subscription to a magazine I'd never read. But after a while, he was happy to give up the effort and allow me to manage the minutiae of our celebrations.

There was only one area in his life where he wanted no input, no direction. It was his one zone of mastery, and since I knew nothing about creative writing, barely wrote a thing apart from painting titles and descriptions, it was a relief to abdicate expertise, to allow him jurisdiction over his one circumscribed domain.

That novel.

He finally placed his completed manuscript on my pillow one evening as I was rushing to dress for the company holiday party. When I emerged from the shower, I could see the pile of paper neatly held together by leather string, a sprig of thyme plunged between its coils. It felt as though my husband had plucked out his own heart, wrapped it in a bow, and nestled it in the cotton of our bed. I was too afraid to lift it, to touch it. A quick perusal told me that there would be some heavy history right up front and that he had got some Russian expressions wrong.

"I want you to be honest," Carl said. He was wearing a tuxedo, on his way to a fund-raiser for the Foster Children's Alliance. He was so elegant, so easy in tuxedos.

"Hey, did you hear me?" he teased, grabbing me on my way to the closet. His mouth tracing the hollow between my breasts, then playfully pulling away.

"I'll tell you the truth. I'm sure it'll be great."

But I didn't want to talk about the book, the pressure of judging all those years of work. I hoped it would all somehow be resolved without me, that he would take command of his area of expertise and leave me out of it for once.

I returned his mouth to where it began its journey. "I think you missed a crucial biographical detail right here."

"Seriously, tell me. Have I got any talent?" He flipped me onto the bed, hair falling diagonally over the tip of his nose.

"You definitely have talent," I murmur.

"I mean it. No joke. You'll tell me, right?"

The bridge of that nose was burnished pink by the sun. And how could he not have talent? It was times like this I was reminded of how easily he slipped into the coils of my projections.

"Of course I will," I said, losing myself in the way he looked at me, suffused with all that adoration.

By the time I close the Web browser at the Urban Writers Space, the praise for Carl reverberating through my head, it's midnight. The offices are dark, empty of people. There's no way I'm returning to an empty apartment and another anguished night.

Luckily the time translates to eight in the morning in Moscow, a respectable start to the workday. Scrolling down my phone's history, I find the right number. Igor Yardanov picks up on the first ring.

"Good timing, Tanyechka. I just landed at JFK."

The company allows us to sneak high-profile clients into Worthington's after hours, but there's still something illicit in entering the dark monolith of your corporation at one in the morning. Considering how many billions are cloistered within these walls, the act of penetration is made surprisingly easy. A single revolving door is kept open, the two security guards on duty trust you and never check in your guests.

Igor and I breeze by one of my favorites from the overnight shift—Juan—who blows me kisses. "That one is a special lady, my friend. Cherish her," he calls after us. Igor looks bemused, his hand on the curve of my back. He's a man accustomed to entering empty buildings in the dead of night, of being whisked by security to spots available only to him. In a cashmere sweater and shoes that make no noise on the parquet, he glides toward the elevator with the nonchalance of an employee.

"I imagine you are adored by many men," he says.

"Juan's nice to me because he doesn't have to live with me," I joke.

Igor looks down at me from all that height, that curved precision of his features. "I'm sure he is very, very sorry about that." And my heart springs forward.

On the floor, I lead him past dark galleries—a collection of Jewish artifacts consigned by an old Philadelphia family—past my and Regan's cubicles and into the viewing room. I flip the lights, aware for the first time that the room is windowless, carpeted, and I'm alone with this man. The fake Burliuk is occupying the same lowly position on the floor, its face turned to the wall as if in shame.

"Why don't you have a seat? I'll bring it out at once." The back of my knees are clammy with sweat. "The consignor was very strict about who can touch it, but I've got the clearance from our president to name you as a serious buyer."

Looking behind me, I see his spread legs in that fine Italian wool, arms crossed behind his head. He smiles. "Good call."

I stride past offices of individual specialists, surrounded by the proof of their obsessions. Their desks mirror mine—digital printouts of Chinese porcelain or rhinoceros horn carvings on Robert Chen's desk or Iranian calligraphy on Liliane Goncourt's. Once we were all having a drink together after work and I asked them if they were ever bored of their specialties. Didn't they feel hemmed in by the narrowness of their expertise? Didn't they too long to break free, to start over, to swap fields?

"Beautiful," Igor says, when I return with the Order on the velvet tray. His fingers are unnecessarily brushing mine, neither taking the object out nor giving it up. "I can feel it was truly hers."

"Can you?" It slips out, a hopefulness. I almost say, *Me too.*

What about you? Liliane shot back at me. Do you like being a Russian specialist? I didn't know how to answer. Why did I take the job if I fantasized every day about having nothing to do with anything Russian? I wanted Russia's hold on me to loosen, for it to be merely an ominous country growing only more ominous on the other side of the world. But Carl never understood that I know more about Russian art than anyone in the world, and there's a responsibility to make sure the world does not misinterpret the Russian intention, that it is correctly understood.

I find myself lecturing to Igor, a long string of information he probably already knows. "The Order first left the country in 1926. The Soviet Union was in a financial crisis after the revolution and Stalin was desperately trying to obtain any foreign capital he could. The royal jewels were his most valuable commodities. An American diamond merchant bought it and displayed it at Wanamaker's in 1935. Imagine Catherine the Great's regalia on view at a Manhattan department store. That's where my client's grandfather saw it." *At least we hope it belonged to Catherine*, I think but don't say.

"Interesting, yes. I imagine many valuable things were allowed to leave Russia this way."

I look away, quickly. "Can I ask what you would do with the Order if you won it in the auction?"

He pulls me down on the couch next to him, a man who likes people to inhabit the spaces he expects of them. "I know what you are worried about, Tanyechka. Trust me, I am good man, not like Medovsky and the others."

"I'm not implying . . ."

"I made money honest way, by making smart financial decisions. I want to give this back to my country. It is most important to me that the Order is viewed by the people. It is our heritage."

"Oh. Well, that's great, that's exactly where I would love it to go."

"But I want it to be in museum, for people to see the history of Russia. This belonged to the greatest empress in history."

It's not easy to maintain professional decorum in your workplace at this hour. There's no Regan to rescue me now, no phone calls to offer diversion. Just me and a man who might be carrying a gun, or worse.

"I have met with Nadia Kudrina at Christie's but I would never consider working with an amateur like her. What I see in you is the proper intentions, a clean heart."

He is pressing all my buttons. I'm embarrassed to feel a flush of gratification suffusing my cheeks. "Thanks for saying that. You know Nadia Kudrina is hardly an expert in the field."

"Exactly. You are the only specialist to trust."

The hairs on my arms are pricked, at attention. A rarefied aura of privacy surrounds us, the unrelenting tick of the Sotiau mantel clock. It seems like the perfect time to broach the subject. "You say you're a good man. Should I assume you're active in philanthropy?" I choose my words carefully with meaning.

His eyes never leave mine, steady, unblinking. "Surely you must know I am one of Russia's premier philanthropists."

"So you must care about the New York Foster Care Alliance."

No pause, no space for even a breath. I'm pretty sure he has no idea what the New York Foster Care Alliance does. "Yes, I do. Very much."

"My mother-in-law's on the board." My mind snaps to Carl, of the poignant way he never forgets to ask about the kids. How he would rush away in his gym clothes, later admitting he'd been out with one of them, playing basketball in Chelsea Piers or renting bikes or devouring ice-cream cones. I have waited and waited. *To save your marriage*, I think, *you need a large gesture.* "They do very important work with at-risk kids."

"Please say no more. We understand each other."

I don't hear the door swinging open, because my eardrums are pounding. But it's Stasia, my favorite from the cleaning crew, a tough Polish lady who considers art a great "scam," thinks Picasso's nose obsession is a result of excess masturbation, and brings in homemade potato-filled pastries when I work late.

"Good evening, Ms. Vandermotter. I will leave this room for last."

"Thanks, Stasia. We won't be much longer."

"Vandermotter." Igor chuckles. "A nice Russian name."

The sound of the vacuum outside drowns further talk on any topic. I feel frozen on the couch beside him, the Order directly between us. What would I do if he kissed me? But Igor rubs his chin with a thumb, lost in thought. "Shall we?" he says, looking directly at me. When the thrumming inside me subsides, I realize he means for us to leave.

Catherine

The hallway is long and dark and no one is accompanying her to this particular ceremony. As is the case so often these days, she is left alone until her official presence is needed. Day after day, she is nudged to the side. She does not mind. Her job, now that the empress is dead and her husband has been crowned Peter III, is to wait and see. Not a day goes by that he does not blunder or offend some dignitary. To the horror of many, the rules of the palace have been loosened. Drunk courtiers are pissing in daylight, flopping about like fish in the courtyard. The churches are ransacked for valuables. Foreign dignitaries are leaving the capital by boat and sled.

She is seven months swollen with a third child, Gregory's this time. Now that an heir is firmly in place and the old empress gone, no one bothers to take notice of her wider skirts and draping shawls. She is biding her time, her body given over to yet another somersaulting creature inside her, slowing the progress of her inflated ankles. If only she could spend days resting in bed, but the atmosphere is treacherous and requires alertness.

In her hands, Catherine holds the box that contains the Order of Saint Catherine, the one she has worn slung across her chest on countless occasions. The one that kept her company during her first night with Sergei. Once in a while, during a dull moment at a ceremony or opera, she would look down at its face, her spirits momentarily bolstered by the woman in its center. Catherine and Catherine and Katya, the triptych of Catherines that rule her life. Saint Catherine, the beauty, the scholar, the brave soul ready to battle an emperor for the lives of persecuted Christians. The woman who insisted she would stay a virgin until she found a man worthy of her. When it is too painful to remember her friend Katya, Catherine turns her thoughts to Saint Catherine. No wonder she stayed a virgin; a worthy mate is no small feat for a woman whose entire scope is the world. Who knows that more intimately than she?

But now she must close her heart to Saint Catherine in order to hand her away in a farce of a ceremony she hopes will end mercifully, quickly. Perhaps if she slows her pace, one leaden foot in front of another, she might delay in reaching the abrasive sounds of birthday revelry that greet her from the palace mouth. But too soon, she is waiting outside the hall, fingering the box's brown satin for the last time.

"*Ma stoicienne, charmante princesse.*" The French ambassador Breteuil greets her when there is nowhere else to go but inside, where bottles will litter the tables and barely lucid men gamble. "I must commend your noble conduct in the face of such arrogance."

She does not want to meet his eyes, to confront his pity.

"We, the right people, are all on your side," he whispers. "None of us can tolerate that conduct, the disrespect to you."

"I appreciate the sentiment, Louis." She wants to have him removed—his blather could easily get her into trouble—but there is no one left to do her bidding.

Instead, he edges closer, the heavy gold ring on his scaly finger scraping the fabric taut against her belly. "You are as much loved as the emperor is hated."

Brushing by him, she manages her escape, but there is still the business of entering that room. The laughter on the other side of that door is ghastly, the braying sound of her husband and that mistress of his who has risen in power by catering to his weakness. The court is aflutter with gossip as to whether the two have completed the love act, whether Paul will have a rival heir. Bets are being called. She tries to shut her ears to the tither. All she knows is that her former lady-in-waiting, the dreadful

Elizabeth Vorontsova, is currently occupying Catherine's seat beside Peter. She swings open the door.

A half-filled goblet and a nest of chicken bones are arrayed before that horrible woman. A gnawed-on tendon is tossed to the side. She and the emperor sit perched with their arms interlocked.

"Finally," that woman says by way of greeting. "How long are we supposed to wait?"

Catherine's hands quiver with rage, but she coolly watches her husband's mistress or whatever she is—the woman described at court as a "pothouse wench," a woman possessed of a "broad, puffy, pockmarked face and fat, squat, shapeless figure," as she has heard it said—bend her head in anticipation. The table is stilled by her presence. No one picks up any food.

"What are you waiting for? Come closer," Peter insists. He is wearing a blue Prussian uniform pinned with the Order of the Black Eagle. He may as well be a visiting ensign, not the monarch of Russia. The guests are a smattering of Vorontsova's family, the lowliest of Peter's flatterers, but also an aggrieved Panin, Razumovsky, and other diplomats and men she respects. They are examining her, waiting for her reaction. Panin, mortified, examines his nails.

Deliberately, coldly, she launches herself past the rouged grimaces. Up close, Vorontsova emits an astonishment in her features that she has pulled off this unlikely rise in fortune. Catherine drapes the ribbon around the neck of the odious woman. It is no easy task to keep her face still, hiding her revulsion at the woman's foul breath and body odor.

Nikita, the jeweler, could have easily made Vorontsova her own order, but Peter said, "Why don't you grant her yours?" For Love and the Fatherland indeed. She looks one last time at the beloved face of the saint, the one she had admired daily since first being awarded the honor sixteen years ago, when she believed there would be love between her and Peter, that they would be partners on the throne, fingers interlaced like Maria-Theresa and Francis. Now from the center, Saint Catherine emanates sisterly support, one she cannot hear at the moment. All she can take in is the deafening boiling of her blood, the child heeling her sternum.

"We are very pleased to confer this honor upon such a worthy person, a dear friend of the court," is what Catherine says instead, muttering through her teeth but with the perfect air of bruised pride. The hearts of those watching must reach out to her. When the child inside her is finally removed and the proper time comes, their allegiances will be fixed firmly with her. That too is marriage.

After the proceedings, she discovers Panin in her chambers. He is emerging out of the shadows in scarlet velvet and rubies strung along his fingers. His chin cascades into multiple folds, sinking into the silk of his collar.

"What are they saying?" she asks.

"He plans to imprison you in the fortress," Panin replies, gloomy. "That is the latest talk. Or at least send you to a monastery. Either way, he plots to rid the court of you."

"I see."

The two of them are murmuring in the privacy of her chamber; his breath smells not unlike Vorontsova's. The room is increasingly turning into a moat of protection, shrouded by tightly pulled curtains. Only her friends enter it, so she has fewer visitors than ever. She barely throws the curtains open anymore, preferring the void of light.

"We have little time is what you are saying."

Count Panin bows, but his eyes never leave hers. She has often wondered if he is not jealous of Gregory Orlov, if he is waiting for her to tire of him so Panin can step into his place and her bedroom. In each of these tête-à-têtes, he seems about to embrace her. His cheeks are two yeasty loaves of bread.

"What do you recommend should be our course of action?"

"It would be easiest to elevate the young Grand Duke Paul of course," he says, waiting for her reaction.

She is silent. The other day, she received a note: "Give the command, and we shall place you on the throne." She threw it into the fireplace. These days, she is receiving advice from all directions. *She should be regent. The opportunity for her reign has gone. The opportunity has not yet arrived. She should rule in her own name.* The Orlovs and the rest of them keep flinging their own opinions regarding the matter. Wasting time.

"Which do you advise?"

"My recommendation? His Majesty can be arrested when he returns to the city. I assume the Orlovs have readied the Guards for the possibility." Again, Panin pronounces her lover's last name like a particularly tart rowan berry.

She hears footsteps in the hall and they freeze, waiting for the rhythm of them to pass. There is a long pause, then a knock, loud and insistent. Their sharp intake of breath is simultaneous. Panin retreats back into the shadows but it may already be too late. She may be headed to Schlüsselburg Fortress, imprisoned next to that poor, slow-witted Prince Ivan. Her heart is dangerously close to fleeing her body. She feels incapable of movement of any kind. The knock repeats, lighter this time.

"A moment, please." She forces herself to creak open the door, hand lingering on the knob. In case this is her last day of freedom, she checks her coiffure.

On the other side stands a frowning Nikita. He is stretching a necklace out to her, and in her breathless confusion she thinks it may be the Order being returned. She feels a wave of gratitude to Peter who must have changed his mind. He knows how much the Order means to her. But the court jeweler clutches in his hands an adornment she had sent to him for fixing, the emerald one with the broken clasp.

"I'm afraid I must return this to you on His Majesty's orders. His Majesty insists I only repair Elizaveta Vorontsova's trinkets," he says under his breath. He does not fully confront her gaze but none of them do these days.

She flashes him one of her more voluminous smiles. "Oh, it does not matter. Thank you for informing me. Please relay to His Majesty that he has bestowed on me so many generous gifts that I will certainly not want for this particular one."

She pushes shut the door, hand pressed to the palpitating skin above her breast. Panin is watching her. He is following the course of that hand, its indentation on her skin.

"So what now?"

"In the meantime, you are still the king's wife," he says. "Attend balls, concerts, play your role. And wait. Let us do the rest."

She nods, the slightest of motions. The backing away of the sun flings the room into near darkness. She thinks this might be the day Panin finally makes his desires known. He is edging toward her, the chicken odor almost unbearable between them. But then, just centimeters from her face, he halts. They are breathing in unison, nose and mouth. She thinks he will press his lips to hers. Then he is gone.

Peter plays the violin at Oranienbaum. His eyes are closed, the bow moving with surprising grace. There is a melancholy to the way he gives himself over to music for which he has no talent. His bowing technique has improved, Catherine decides, but then the Italian singers and the court orchestra muffle any unique sounds he is able to extract from the instrument. His entire upper body sways to the music, his jutting chin even more pronounced than usual. Vincenzo Manfredini, the composer of the opera, claps politely.

If the plan were not under way, and there were no turning back, she would have found it unbearable to be at this hateful palace at all. Peter has brought a coarse decorating touch to the grounds, defaced it with a ridiculous citadel, the "Joke" castle where he frolics with his soldiers. He has made Oranienbaum a giant playroom with Vorontsova, who is now fanning herself in the front row, whispering to a cousin between arias. As is the norm these days, Catherine is a minor guest in a public display of demotion. The solo drags on, Peter never one to leave a stage gracefully. The entire scene feels unreal to her, ossified into the past. Encased in glass, a relic of another life.

But with the trap for him ready to be sprung, Catherine finds it a relief to be blending into the background. The night before, she doubted whether she should even bother making the trip for this fiasco, but Gregory agreed with Panin. She must act under a pretense of normality. In the meantime, the officers will be told the time is nearing. Everyone knows the arrest of the emperor is imminent.

"We cannot arouse suspicion. Besides, you love the operas of Manfredini." Gregory was splayed across her bed, fully dressed, boots and all. How the uniform suited him, as if molded to his body. She loved the decisive movement of his hands, so much more serious and ambitious than her other lovers. He lacked Seryozha's prettiness, but she had outgrown the need for simple, picturesque beauty in a man.

She leaned a chin on his shoulder. Her womb was just barely settled, the boy so recently whisked away in beaver fur. "How can I enjoy Manfredini's music when that louse will be destroying the music on the strings of his violin?"

Gregory's own interest in music was fleeting. Frivolity! he comments when cultural subjects arise. But he has a sharp instinct for political tactics; it was his idea to become promoted to treasurer of the Artillery so he could palm money and vodka onto the well-connected soldiers.

"By this time next week, you may even be sole autocrat," he mused, lowering himself to her lips, lingering there, proceeding to her neck along the valve of her collarbone. His cheeks were incredibly smooth, a soft dome of flesh. His weakness for cherries meant he often smelled of the fruit.

"Sole autocrat," she murmured. She allowed the words to persist on her tongue. "And they tell me I should act as regent."

Peter finishes the violin solo with a flourish of the wrist. He appears not to know his whereabouts, still in thrall to the notes. The crowd gathers itself to standing. His face is irrigated with pleasure from the applause, not realizing that the appreciation is polite, desultory. The singers wait for him to exit so they can turn the opera back into art.

She rises to clap until bewildered faces turn to her, and when the applause dies down, she continues clapping with feverish enthusiasm. Peter looks at her in grateful surprise, a face wiped of spite. It is the face of the needy boy she once knew.

"Bravo," she cries, trying to engage the rest of the audience. "Was that not fine?"

Her enthusiasm brings with it a fresh wave of ovation, and now Razumovsky, Panin, and even Manfredini are on their feet again. Brilliant, Your Majesty, just brilliant.

Her husband appears miniature holding that drooped violin in his hand; with those pink cheeks, he resembles one of his puppets. Grinning widely, he is absorbing praise into his skin. When she feels doubt for what is about to occur, she remembers a typical afternoon the week before when he accused her of growing intolerably haughty. These days, the very glimpse of her sets him off on a tirade of insults. She had simply been taking a turn about the gardens after a morning at the chapel. She was bothering no one.

"You walk around with your back all erect. Who do you think you are?" As usual, he emerged from nowhere, startling her. His dwarf, who was always at his side when Vorontsova was not, cackled.

"Should it please you if I walked around bent over like a serf?" she retorted. The tulip trembled slightly in her hand but she was learning how to steady her emotions.

"Is that a way to speak to your king?"

"Treason," the dwarf said.

"Shut up, dwarf."

She said, "Pardon me, Your Imperial Majesty. I had somehow forgotten you were the king."

"Then maybe you need a reminder." He drew his sword, an impressive instrument mostly used in role-playing and military drills. His dwarf moved closer for a better view. The entire scene was ludicrous, among the full bloom of apple and orange trees. But she dared not smile.

"If we mean to fight, I'd better procure one for myself," was all she said, coolly, before walking on.

Now she thinks, *Your turn to meet the tip of my sword, Your Imperial Highness.*

Tanya

PRESENT DAY

Moscow is a place of no limits, no boundaries, no control. What once seemed exhilarating in this country of awakening potential has now solidified into wariness, the constant possibility for danger.

First of all: the traffic. Beyond any traffic I've ever encountered. As soon as the driver pulls away from the airport, I resign myself to spending anywhere from the next two to five hours alone with the man in a coiling snake of cars. Once I finish answering my e-mails, setting up meetings, and briefing Regan on Skype, I'm aching for freedom from this vehicle. The man at the wheel tends to be overly chatty and pessimistic. He complains about how the former mayor has destroyed the historical architecture of the city's buildings or whether the president will reassemble the Soviet Union piece by piece or how his ex-wife incessantly calls his mobile with the most meaningless requests or how at least under communism, he could have counted on a pension.

Second: the people. As soon as I enter the orbit of my clients, I'm instantly exposed to a faint halo of danger. Once, while I was in the middle of dinner at the restaurant Oblomov, a restaurant where my meal is brought to me in bed, a man was shot on a backroom mattress by someone who calmly walked out the front door. I screamed, my client shrugged, the police were called, but an hour later, the sheets of the dead man's bed were cleared for the next reservation. Even without the possibility of murder, there's the absurdity of scenarios in a country where rich men can realize their most esoteric desires. Once, a client insisted I accompany him to a nail parlor. There I sat reviewing lots in an upcoming auction trying not to stare at the breasts of the topless technician while my client received a "special menu" pedicure. Yet another time, while visiting the penthouse of one of my most powerful consignors, I crossed paths with a woman in a leopard-printed miniskirt on towering heels holding a painting under her arm. She didn't greet me, but dragged the frame to the elevator and disappeared inside it.

"Who was that?" I asked my client.

"A prostitute," he said simply, ushering me in. He was dressed for the meeting in a crisp formal suit, only the hair at his neck revealed a recent shower. It was then I noticed the blank square of his wall where the most exquisite Pirosmani had hung just the day before, the same Pirosmani I was counting on as a centerpiece for the fall auction.

I proceeded to the kitchen, past the Doric columns, past the swimming pool with a mysterious pair of women in black cut-out bikinis. "Do you know how hard it is to be a Georgian in South Ossetia?" he asked.

"I can imagine." I reached for the proffered glass of wine.

"She told me her whole life story. Bombed the shit out of her village in '04 and '08. And let me tell you, Tanyush. It raised the hairs on my arm. Separated from her parents, her mother in camouflage fighting alongside the soldiers. Horrible."

"A tragedy over there."

He held up a bottle of wine. "This is actually from her family's vineyard. Such shame we can't get good Georgian wine in Russia anymore."

"So you gave her a Pirosmani?"

The man shrugged. "I felt bad for her. Wouldn't you do the same?"

Oh, yes, I have personally redefined professionalism, the need to keep my face neutral before the unbelievable.

Arriving in the center of wealthy Moscow I steel myself. For women wearing ruched evening dresses in the cold light of morning, for prostitutes loitering at my hotel bar, for paying eighty dollars for a movie that comes accompanied by cocktails and rocket salad, for the babushki guarding the entries to art galleries who berate me for seeing a show out of linear sequence. I steel myself for being yelled at, because unwritten rules of the Soviet period are being broken, and the babushki have to punish someone for their change in circumstances, for the end of the security they had once been promised.

My one oasis of solace after an exhausting auction preview is the Park Hyatt Hotel, a sleek sanctuary where the staff have taken a rare course in customer service, one of the few places no one yells at me, pickpockets me, or charges me a different amount than was listed on the menu. The city looks magical from its roof, where I am summoned toward a seat ("Would you prefer a blanket or a fur coat?") and a mohair blanket is wrapped around my legs. Women under fur coats warm themselves by chrome space heaters, sipping champagne while their companions swirl cognac and rust-colored liqueurs. We are all facing the cupolas of Red Square, flashing against the purple of the night. The iconic spires poking at the sky, the perfect, globular red. I imbed myself into the blanket and count the days until I can leave.

On the Park Hyatt roof, I settle into my usual lounge chair, the one pointing directly at the majesty of nighttime Kremlin. I send for tea but a bottle of rosé Dom Pérignon arrives instead. "A little gift from your friend Igor," the server says, with a slight smile. As if, *Don't worry, I know what you are so don't think you're anyone special. All the women here have an Igor.*

I start to tell him not to bother uncorking it when a flash of blond hair says in Russian, "Bring us a second glass."

I look up into the taut, glittering skin of Nadia Kudrina. The young woman is entirely swathed in white—a skintight white shift dress that looks like an Alaïa, white silk strappy sandals that she flings to the floor next to the chair. As if on cue, the majestic tips of the Red Square spires recede behind the opacity of cloud.

"I'm here to pick up a Shishkin," Nadia says. "Can't stand to look at them, can you? Bubbling brooks and those itty-bitty forest animals. Blech." She motions to the server. "Bring us sushi. And a stool for my handbag. Where do you expect it to go? On the floor? On my lap?" The fact that designer purses can expect their own chairs in the best Moscow restaurants is another charming detail of the city.

Our glasses are poured, champagne the color of the palest of petals. As I'd expect, it's dry and delicious. I plan my escape strategy: one drink, then plead a headache.

"Oh, no you don't," Nadia says. She's taken note of my wary expression. "No way we are going back to our rooms before five in the morning. You are I are going to skip the Garage VIP gala and head right to Krysha. Live a little, right?"

I pretend I too was invited to Zhukova's gala. Oh, well. I would have liked to stroll the Rem Koolhaas building at night.

She's polished off her glass, popped a single California roll in her mouth, and rises to stand in those towering heels, with that cascade of hair. "Let's go, *idem*. Get up. It's getting late. Let's just go straight to Krysha."

"I don't think so." I drape the blanket more tightly about my legs.

"I know, I know. Krysha's so five years ago, I prefer Strelka, but it's Krysha's birthday tonight. We're supposed to wear white."

"Ah, well. I've got nothing white. Next time." White is a color for the young, the wafer-thin. But now we are attracting attention from guests in the other chairs, probably because Nadia is a high-profile Moscow socialite on par with Zhukova and Sobchak, constantly photographed by the Russian media, her outfits dissected on entertainment talk shows. She protested against the president when it was fashionable and then got engaged to a top-level politician in his administration when protesting became passé and is separated from the man now that protesting is back in vogue. Someone snaps a photo of us with a cell phone.

Somehow the bottle is empty, the evening chill wrapped around my shoulders. More phones are raised, and Nadia pulls me toward the exit, down the transparent elevators, the lobby with its black and wood, its geometric lines. We spill out on the streets toward a chauffeur opening the door of an idling sedan.

"Wait a minute," I protest, but I'm being shoved into the car, and someone introduced to me as Pyotor is driving us along the slick streets of Moscow night.

"This baba's got something against fun," Nadia tells the driver. And it's only after she pulls out the lipstick in her purse and checks the messages on her phone that I'm calm enough to be convinced this is not a kidnapping. I can enjoy the view out the window.

It can be beautiful too, Moscow. Roads like unfurling carpets, the stony, august illumination of the statues of poets, squares so clean and regal, the magnificent golden caps of churches, the gold moldings and imperial eagles of the restored Bolshoi Theater, the GUM department store. We are riding over sloping bridges, past soaring cathedrals and libraries. We slow down in front of an apartment building and four more women pile in to arrange themselves in pairs. They're draped entirely in white, in knee-high patent boots, ribbons in their plaits; one is decked out in a Vera Wang-ish wedding dress. They're a swirl of twittering voices. One exclaims over my black ensemble, not to mention my conservative cowl-neck top and jeans, complaining that getting past face control with me in tow will be a bitch.

Nadia says, "Ladies, ladies. Our next stop is TsUM." And they quiet down.

Purses are splayed open to reveal a spread of cosmetics, lavender powder exploding on leather surfaces.

"I've got a client to meet tomorrow. I should get back to the hotel."

"Oh, quit your whining, old lady." Nadia rolls the window down, expelling the curl of cigarette smoke. "The Art Twins will be there."

The entire night has taken on the logic of dream, a succession of events in which I've no agency. Squeezed next to Nadia and her friends, I'm reminded of my first year at Worthington's, my first years in America even, when I was simultaneously inside and outside its rules. How little was expected of me in both situations—my teachers assumed I spoke no English or Hebrew and never expected completed assignments; at Worthington's I was an invisible junior trainee with no connections, no claim to its insider privileges. And now, in Russia, among the real Russians, I'm an American imposter. The girls speak in rapid-fire slang, passing around a canister of pills, chasing them down with the contents of a flask.

"You didn't hear I'm launching a fragrance?" Nadia answers somebody. "It's going to be called Muza. Hey, Petrushka. Crank up the tunes, will you?" Her blond hair is plastered prettily to her forehead.

The others congratulate her and chime in with updates on their own projects. One is hosting a reality show, another anchors a political program, someone else is starting a denim line. The driver turns up the music, Nadia is congratulated on her father's new acquisition. An entire Greek island or just a portion of it? Everyone is buying Greek islands. What parties they'll throw when the deal is finalized! I turn my attention back to the streets, to the blur of streetlamps. When Carl comes back home, after the auction is over, we should take a vacation.

"I'm also thinking of starting a gallery. What do you think, Tan? You and I leave our auction houses and go into business together. The pressure of auction is exhausting, no? With our contacts and your expertise, we can do private business for ourselves. I can get us nice modern space in Chelsea, maybe near Pace."

Momentarily, I'm flattered. I even allow myself an image of it, the hush of a gallery on a weekday morning, the bare white desk, the walls waiting to be arranged to my taste. No meetings with Marjorie, no ominous fruit bowl upstairs. No consignor kickbacks or corporate machinations. Of course, now's hardly the time for shaking up my life but the idea is tempting.

"I really like my job."

"Well, think about it," Nadia says, returning to her texting. "We'd make a good team."

Pyotor turns up the music and the entire backseat vibrates with the swirling of hips.

We pull up in front of a darkened department store and Nadia spills out, dragging me up the steps behind her. The place is shuttered, but Nadia punches into her cell phone and the door swings open. A man ushers us inside. One by one, the floors erupt with a brilliant radiance. I'm greeted with a museum of clothes organized by color, sloping racks of draped garments in blues and reds and pinks, on the walls paintings of dogs in bathing suits, chandeliers low and ripe, recamier chairs piled with scarves. Under the gaping skylight in the back of the store hangs a row of silks and jerseys and corsets, white as winter.

"Isn't an empty store the only way to shop?" Nadia says, combing through the white Martin Margiela section.

"Are you kidding? I'm not going to buy new clothes for this one party." I avoid not only the topic of money but even glancing at the exorbitant prices. But Nadia is flinging hangers onto the chair, crinkled blazers and silk pants and a white bustier.

"Quick, they're waiting. Try this on." Nadia shoves me behind a velvet curtain.

I stand among pants and bustier, half in, half out of the clothes. Outside the dressing room, Nadia and the man are exchanging friendly inquiries about one another's family and beyond them are floors of emptiness, piles of unseen clothes. A kind of rabid energy overtakes me. I start to frantically try one thing after another. A hand reaches in to me behind the curtain and I follow its directions until I'm zipped into some complicated Comme des Garçons thing, a Marie Antoinette–type gown to the knee, a silk blazer of white flowers draped over my shoulders. I look like some bold projection of myself at twenty-five, convinced I would have time for multiple reinventions.

"Perfect," Nadia says, giving me a quick survey.

I finally read the tag. "It's over four thousand euros!"

But I'm swept out of the store with the same stealth, my own clothes draped around an elbow, and the man in the sunglasses waves and tells us to have a nice time. In the backseat, my hoop skirt engulfs all the girls, and they're all giggling, pinned by my taffeta.

"Now you look like somebody," they say with approval.

"She *is* somebody," Nadia says. Her tone, to my surprise, seems sincere.

We climb the steep staircase to the roof. In front of me, there's only night, only the flash of white leather leggings, a buffed heel at my nose. Each window is murky, exploding with light and flesh. The bouncer hurries us inside to avoid photographers. "Have good time, *devushki*."

The club is a series of windowless rooms with bursting music and a bald DJ swaying to his beat. A fuzzy drink that smells of peaches appears in my hand and next time I look down, it's gone. There are clumps of men standing around the fringes of the dance floor watching Nadia and her friends undulate. The women are whispering to each other, pointing their phone cameras at Nadia. In the whirl of the strobe, they're a sea of colorless creatures dipping in shades of blue. This is the new Russia: technology and hair and the frisson of danger.

Onstage is a woman who looks like Medovsky's Marina, a blaze of red hair, bony limbs flailing. They call out to me, drag me inside their circle ("All hail the queen!"), and I shock myself by being capable of this still, sweaty gyrations to a mindless beat, hands electric in the air among the socialites of Moscow whose toothpick bodies hide mine from the onlookers, open only to the cool white lights of Krysha, the DJ at his turntable, cuing the awaiting track on his headphones, waiting for it to burst out onto the speakers.

"Great news, my dear," Regan says. Her voice seems grainy and far away. I jump up in bed, my mouth sandy, dry. I manage to separate myself from the white taffeta but not my corset. What time is it? My head feels like a bowling ball but fragments of memory are coming back. Yes, there was the ride home from Krysha. I was belting "When You Believe" with Pyotor, whose voice turned out an impressive Mariah Carey alto. I don't remember the last time I had that much fun.

"What is it?"

"We heard the final word from Natasha's Catherine historian. He says that sources assumed it was lost sometime before she actually became empress, but he agrees with Natasha that the other orders from that period are spoken for and the period matches. Plus we've got the catalogue from Wanamaker's. I think we're good to go."

I leap up. "Really? Oh, thank God."

"I know, right? It was cutting it close."

I turn on the light to the cool hotel room, the tan sheets, tan wallpaper, elegant writing desk, a black bowl of lemons on the counter meant to remind guests of an alternate, civilized home. How beautiful it looks now, how safe.

"What an immense relief."

"Better to have covered all our bases," Regan coos. "Now we can go into that auction and not worry."

I look at my watch. Tonight, I'm supposed to meet Igor at the new Bulgari store. I pour a glass of water, guzzle the entire thing, and stare at the invitation.

Gerri Halliwell and Igor Yardanov invite you to a special opening.

"Thank you, my dear. See you on Monday."

I feel porous. I didn't realize how the question of the Order was weighing on me, pulling me down. Reaching over to part the curtains, I am sprayed by the Moscow morning sunshine. To press my head against the pane of the glass, to absorb it most fully. For a long time, I don't move. It feels so good, for a change, not to move.

Gerri Halliwell is strutting around in thigh-high boots, giving the impression of fellating the microphone. She's wearing too much of everything but clothes, awash in makeup and bleached hair. Pale skin folds around her middle, her breasts are pressed into a bouquet of her leotard. An oversized replica of a chunky diamond engagement ring rotates behind her.

The Bulgari shop would be a strange place to meet with a client, but this is Moscow we're talking about. Most of the crowd's engaging in some kind of deal closing, the passing along of business cards. Women older than me lurk with sharp slits in their skirts, vertiginous silver heels that match their purses too precisely. All that effort reminds me of how American I truly am: Russians never tire of considering every detail of their appearance, from nail polish to pattern of stocking to shape of earring to shade of mauve.

"You're from where? Sotheby's?" a man asks me, screaming over the music.

"Worthington's," I correct him.

Igor escorts a tall brunette into the room, and the crowd parts as if for monarchs. The woman looks down at us all, regal and icy in her beauty. Her pouty lips and long, feathery tresses brush against an arm lightly entwined around Igor's. A man I faintly recognize as a guest at a recent client dinner is whispering in my ear, "Is that Igor Yardanov?"

And we're all a bit in thrall to him, that faint mole imprinted right below his eye, not an ounce of excess fat. He floats and pauses, kissing Gerri Halliwell on each cheek and shaking hands with Moscow's mayor and a flock of Bulgari executives.

"Toast, toast," the crowd chants, and the microphone is handed to him. I tune out his speech—something about being honored to partner with such a prestigious brand once again, opening another location in Moscow proves the city is one of the most cosmopolitan in the world—and wait the proper amount of time for the well-wishers to disperse.

"You missed the preview. And I've got a plane to catch in the morning," I say when it's my turn to step in front of him. The nervousness from our late-night meeting at Worthington's returns. He really is unblemished, like a canonized actor in his prime. His gaze is unwavering. If Medovsky wants everyone else to feel relaxed in his frantic presence, Yardanov is the opposite.

He holds up a finger. Wait, wait. Until the flow of supplicants in front of Igor completely ebb and Gerri Halliwell stops singing and the flashes of cameras recede. The revolving diamond ring glints against the dimming crystal of the chandeliers. The lights are dimmed into nightclub mode.

Igor pulls out his phone. "Bring it around," he says.

I follow him outside where the air is fresh and bright with recent rain. The line at the velvet rope snakes around the block. A group of flashy women are being turned away by the bouncer and their cajoling and name-dropping is failing to gain them entry. Karaoke? one of them suggests to the others, resigned. They're not getting in here.

Igor is leading me to a waiting BMW town car, one that looks like many of its neighbors, the streets clogged with unmoving, identical black bulletproof vehicles. The field of parked cars is so wide, it's as though people dropped their cars off in the middle of the street and abandoned them.

"Why don't we take the metro?" I suggest, but Igor finds the idea preposterous.

"Metro? *Ty shto?* What for?" He looks so offended that I give up, having long ago stopped arguing with my clients on the issue. In Moscow, if you have a car, you use it no matter that you squander years of your life in traffic. The whole point of massive wealth is the luxury of amnesia that you ever rode the metro next to people just like you, whose futures were equally drab once, whose clothes were bought at the same state-owned stores, who had only their pensions to look forward to. Miraculously, the car makes it down an entire city block before finally being stilled by traffic. I rack my brain for suitable topics of conversation, the intimacy that will earn me his trust. I settle on his parents.

"Igor, you never mention your family."

There is a tranquility to Igor that contrasts with Medovsky's frenzied nature, a self-contained ability to watch, to listen. In the car, away from the crowd, he appears to relax. He pulls at the knot of his tie.

"Why should I mention family?"

"I was just wondering how you get along. If they live here or in the States."

"You are not first person to ask me this. Why is Igor Yardanov not married? That is thousand-dollar question."

"Oh, I didn't mean that."

Or did I? Igor, famous for his shifting array of beauties, never a repeating face, the rumor that he hires them for functions where he will be photographed.

"I like women. I'm not family man," he says, annoyed. "What more do you need to know?"

"That's not what I was asking, but okay."

The car's come to a complete stop; the driver lets out a series of terse blasts. I'm aware of staring at the same statue of some long-dead writer for twenty minutes now. Suddenly Igor says, "Let's get out of here," and we're out of the car and rushing through a park. I'm trying to keep up in heels and the restrictive dress, past pensioners on benches and teenagers in punk attire peeling the skin of smoked fish and tossing beer cans on the ground. Packs of dogs that belong to no one follow our path with interest. The sun is still high in the air, and it occurs to me how rare evening is here this time of year, this land swabbed in eternal daytime. I can imagine Igor as a Soviet boy here once, with Medovsky, the two best friends with their satchels, their Lenin pins, the city crumbling inside yet orderly on the surfaces around them. The two of them racing after school just like this, socks pulled up to their knees.

"Wait, slow down," I call after him, out of breath. The air is stinging my cheeks. I feel utterly free, the vista refreshingly clear. Maybe there was something in the Nadia night that woke me, a portal to a world I was overlooking. For the first time since Carl left, I can see beyond the two of us as individuals, the individuals the two of us thought the other was, each of us entrenched in where we came from and where we thought we were going. If it weren't for the heels, I'd run like this forever. And scream with joy.

Then we're in Lavrushinskyi Pereulok in the magnificent courtyard of the Tretyakov museum complex. I've never paused to examine the actual structure of this grand edifice, but now I feel like a princess dropped into a Russian fairy tale. The red façade calls up ancient Rus', a time of wood sprites and Rusalkas and witches roaming among enchanted birch trees. The intricately carved doors are beckoning us into a gingerbread house.

"Have you ever been here after dark?" Igor says with a wide smile, a boyish exuberance. "It kicks Worthington's ass." He holds my hand tighter in his and I feel that nauseous sensation of vulnerability that could be the thrill of forgotten desire.

He makes a phone call and the red doors spring open. A chiseled man, every starched detail in place, bars our way. "This is Sergei," Igor says, and the man appears to bow only with his eyebrows. He has silver-white hair and a dancer's physique, the proud neck, regal head, muscular legs. The tuxedo, white silk bow, cravat, cummerbund, all fit him perfectly. He steps aside, the two men exchanging a particularly long glance. A hallway explodes with light, then another, then the one after that. The three of us are alone in the temple of Russian art.

The Tretyakov Gallery's selection anoints the canon of Russian art; it's the final arbiter of what's truly national and what is foreign. My favorite galleries display portraits of the female rulers of the country—the plump figures of Empresses Anna and Elizabeth, regal in their flaring skirts. There's Empress Anna standing stiff and erect, wrapped in ermine and surrounded by the attributes of her power. Nearby, Empress Elizabeth stands ornate and resplendently bejeweled, the fun-loving twinkle in her eye. Then the portrait that appeared on Carl's book cover—young Catherine the Great as grand duchess, the Order of Saint Catherine pinned to her side. I like the future queen's direct glance at the viewer, the intelligence inscribed in her long, oval face. *I'm smarter than all of you,* it seems to say.

"Amazing, isn't it, that this object can still exist, that this two-dimensional thing can be touched," Igor says. I think he's referring to the Order. His hands are light on my shoulders, the tendrils of his odorless breath spiraling close.

"Remarkable." I feel a surge of triumph. The Order is real. The Order is hers. I can focus on directing it where it wants to go. And what it wants is to be reunited with Catherine.

We walk from room to room, the Nikitin portraits of Empress Elizabeth, the paunchy belly and weak, empty gaze of Peter III upon coronation, the Antropov portraits of Catherine the Great in her prime, the lively one where she wears the ermine cap shaped like a tidal wave, wields an intimidating scepter, and the more stately image, where she sits in profile, a Greek goddess on her throne. We pause before the Torelli ones, Catherine the Great dressed like Minerva surrounded by muses. One could never accuse Catherine of being underrepresented. The queen knew the importance of marketing herself.

Igor stops, gestures to the wall. "How can you say her Order doesn't belong among all these people of her court? Picture it right here in the middle of the room for all to see."

"It would be perfect." My clients are wily, I must remember that.

"Then we must work together to make it happen."

I can feel the excitement in him too, energy vibrating off his skin. We're stopped before Shibanov's *Celebration of the Wedding Contract*, showing the rite of joining Tatar peasants in matrimony. I've always loved the painting for the rich color and detailing of costume. But it's the bride in the center that strikes me now, her body central in the frame, controlled by male hands.

I'm aware of Igor's grip on my forearms. A steel pincer holding me in place. Up close, his skin smells of wooded musk, a sanded piece of new furniture. A scent of menace. I pull him toward me in a single movement, run a finger across the smoothness of his jaw, the cleft of his chin. I think he might take the opportunity to kiss me, but when he doesn't move, I kiss him. The sensation of being single returns in a flash: fear and risk and blind, foolish hope, the feeling of needles pricking at my skin, the throbbing at the back of my throat. The new persona required for a kiss, the peril of believing in that persona once the kiss is over. The yielding and jabbing and play of it, the suspense about its choreography. Everything buried, forgotten.

The way he looked at you.

I realize that the barest of lips met mine before they were withdrawn and when I open my eyes, Igor is farther away than before, a face set square. Mortified, I fixate on the Shibanov painting, examine the woman at its center, her face stony as she faces her inescapable fate.

"That was a mistake. I'm sorry." I feel like a seeded shame is worming its way inside my belly. "Forgive me."

"Nothing to forgive," Igor mutters. But his response is not a moral reluctance or hesitation of temptation. It's empty of charge, of any yearning.

I follow Igor's gaze toward Sergei flitting in and out of the gallery in the crispness of his suit. He is carrying a wide array of items across his arm: a coat, a tray of amber beverages, a candelabra. He is preparing for a party about to launch. As he passes, he measures Igor with his eyes. It's in the particularity of the collusion between them that is visceral, bodily. There's an invisible string that connects them that I didn't feel between Igor and the latest brunette at the Bulgari store. A turning of a key inside me yields to a click. I think of the rotating cavalcade of long-haired women. I think of the laws in Russia banning homosexuality, but really they're not so new. Homosexuality is always a target of the utmost disgust here and, law or no law, it will probably stay this way. My exhilaration is fading. I'm ensnared in a secret I never needed to hear.

"Nothing to forgive," Igor repeats carefully. He's back looking at the Shibanov, hands clasped behind his back. "Just let me have a real shot at the Order in the auction. That's all I ask."

I sense the oily mechanics of manipulation, a forced complicity. "Someone else is interested."

But he's back to being Igor, charming, graceful, flirtatious, but this time with an undercurrent of warning. He probes in his pockets and emerges with a pack of cigarettes. "I've already helped you solve that problem. I hear the Order is not authentic. Have you ever met Natasha Mikhailovna at the Hermitage? A lovely older woman, real Soviet variety, slightly bitter. Can you blame her? Poor seventy-eight-year-old lady works with men like me every day and barely makes two hundred rubles a month. I've ordered her a monogrammed Bottega Veneta tote. You can imagine. She is over the moon. What is it to her if the Order is real or not real?"

Through gritted teeth, I say, "How generous of you. But it's authentic. It's been proven by experts beyond Natasha."

"Tanya, Tanya." His voice is softer, as if we finally made it to the precipice together, and our only viable route is down. I can almost swear the tone of his voice is confirming my hunch. He's gay, an unthinkable thing for an oligarch to be.

I'm being eased down the stairs toward the exit. The first of the hired staff, young, leggy creatures dressed as 1920s flappers, are stepping through the threshold pushing trays of china and heavy glass. It is yet another party to which I was not invited.

"You see what is at stake, don't you?" Igor moves aside to welcome the women and snaps them toward Sergei. When they are out of earshot, he lowers his voice. "I am putting my very reputation in your hands as you are putting yours in mine."

"There's nothing I can do. I can't manipulate an auction. Our calls are recorded."

"Let's not be starting from scratch as if we just met each other. Don't forget, if I get the Order, a check will be immediately wired to your mother-in-law. New York Children's Foster Alliance, yes? We are good in business, you and I."

Deals like this are made all the time at the higher levels of Worthington's. When clients are wealthy or powerful enough, contracts are broken for their sakes, binding confidentiality agreements are ignored, enhanced-hammer deals mean the seller waives all commissions. In the gallery's gardens, I remind myself to put the entire thing in perspective. The decision has been made; only my marriage matters, not an auction. Carl and his family will be grateful; it will be a new beginning for us all. But as I walk to the Tretyakovskaya metro station, a tendril of doubt is worming its way inside, circling, before dissipating again in the red glow of a Moscow night.

Catherine

"*Matushka, matushka,*" a voice repeats. Catherine protests on the fringe of sleep, trying to remember where she is, what circumstances she is entering. A quick glance around the room confirms that it is Alexis Orlov, her lover's brother, inside her private chambers at Peterhof, where her husband has practically imprisoned her. She notes the worn paisley chair by the window, the outdated curtains, the dead empress's gold easing stool, that particular quiet of an underused palace. The empress insisted on bringing all her furniture when she changed residences, not noticing when chairs arrived broken, amputated of legs.

"What is it?"

Alexis's face is either blanched of color or overly powdered but his eyes are inflamed. The entire thing is too intimately close to her own, projecting a spray of spittle on her cheek.

"*Matushka,* the time has come. Everything is ready."

"Today? Right now?" The sun barely tipping over the sky, and her mind is still glued to the confusion of horses, the voluptuous ride of it, then death. Her dreams lately are a series of fragmented scenes in which someone gets hurt.

Alexis is trying to hurry her along with a steady drilling of words. "The time to act is now. Right now. Passek. He's been arrested."

She attempts to rise as the consonants continue to fire at her. Passek, a guard they've secretly informed of their plans to overthrow the emperor. Why would he be in custody unless he's confessed something? She quickly understands that it will be a matter of mere hours before news of the conspiracy leaks to Peter. For now the emperor is still at Oranienbaum, which leaves the capital wide open. By the end of this day, she might be either regent or empress or dead.

She unlatches the window. The remnants of the nightmares are gone and she shoots up in bed, calling for her maid. Alexis excuses himself, an embarrassed squint at the ceiling before darting out. For a second, she is alone, frozen in the middle of the room. Then her girl arrives with a dress, corset, toiletries. She is a skinny slip of a thing, all jutting bones, but loyal and asks no questions. There is brave determination in her eye, a spark of coiled action.

"I thought this one would be right for the special day," she says. Among the fold of clothes, Catherine glimpses dove gray with pink silk.

"No, not this one." Her mind is racing now and she calls for the simplest in her closet: black, unadorned. She can almost hear her mother's voice advising her: *An appearance of strength and seriousness will be required before the masses, Figgy. You must fulfill your destiny, Figgy.* The girl returns with the correct dress with an urgent alacrity as if Catherine is already the empress.

She allows the gown to be fastened upon her, and when the girl approaches with makeup, she rejects most of it.

"Everything must be simple, honest. Do you understand me?"

The girl blushes, bites her lip, and Catherine reaches toward her to reassure them both. What she would give for the girl to transform into Katya, but Katya is dead of smallpox, dead at least five years now. They informed her when she finally found the voice to ask.

The palace seems to stir to life, a parade of feet rattling its floors, the sound of pouring water. She examines herself in the flimsy, grimy mirror. "There. That is fine." The age of thirty-three suits her, and black lends her the perfect austerity.

"I'm ready," she calls out the door, to Alexis lurking somewhere on the other side of it.

Through the gardens, along the main path, a carriage is waiting. In front of it, the horses already look exhausted, heads hung low to the ground. The carriage cramped with little legroom is far from the luxury she has become used to. This one lacks a berth for reclining. But Alexis is waving her inside, the driver already in his box.

As they clop toward the capital, Alexis is recounting a string of recent events. The cause of Passek's arrest was some idiot soldier who confronted Passek with rumors of a coup d'état. Of course, Passek denied everything, but the soldier went ahead and ran to his superior anyway.

"The grand duke is foolish if he denies the threat, but surely his advisors will make him see sense," she agrees. "You were right to fetch me now."

Alexis, pleased, pulls the cabin's curtain aside. A spray of voluminous sunlight fills the carriage, masking half his face. It is far less handsome than his brother's, crude and rough where Gregory's charm and good humor soften his asymmetrical features.

The carriage slows its pace until it barely moves forward. Then it stops. They are stuck on a dirt road on the fringes of a forest. Alexis springs out the door.

"What in God's name is going on?"

She can hear the outline of an exchange between him and the driver in the box. *What can you do? Ustali,* she hears. *You try traveling all night and then are forced another ten kilometers in the morning.* She smooths out her tousled black skirts as she climbs out onto the soiled tan of pebbled road.

"He said the horses will not move and that's that," Alexis says, bulging with frustration. He is battering the side of the carriage with his fists.

Entire lifetimes, it seems, have been crammed into this moment.

"Castrated piglet," he keeps cursing, either at himself or the driver. She wipes her brow from the heat. The horses are breathing deeply beside her, their eyes impassive. They have no idea that the fate of an entire country rests on their spasming backs. She pats the smaller one's flank, his rounding, rasping barrel.

"Maybe once they have regained their strength," she says. "Poor things."

"But we are losing precious time. We can be arrested any minute. All will be lost."

Men, she thinks. Always panicking, impatient, all that unbridled melodrama at the most crucial of moments. She misses her lover, Stanislaw, how the world simply flowed through him, how cheerfully he greeted obstacles. He had no stamina for something like this, had no illusions about his own limitations. The body of the carriage is starting to buckle beneath Alexis's fists.

"Stop it, Alexis." He is infecting her with his mounting hysteria. "For God's sake, we have to think."

"My brother will hire a carriage if we do not arrive. He knows the situation."

"There," she says, soothingly, a maternal pat. "Resolved. We have no choice but to wait."

All this unexpected heat and smog, and here she is in somber black under the broiling sun. Alexis drops his fists, and they both listen. For what? The word of God? Her lover? Salvation? She looks up. The light filtered through the thick mass of trees creates shifting shapes on the grass. She watches them dance and dissolve.

For a while, she tunes into the whistle of flirting cardinals, to the rotation of the world and not much else. Then they make out the sound of horse hooves, a musical symphony of metal against ground, its rhythmic elegance. A cart rolls into view, trotting with brisk nonchalance.

"Wait here."

She can see Alexis through the spiral of rising dirt. He is impressing a cartful of peasants with his uniform. He is pointing in her direction, calling her grand duchess and then empress, and insisting that they need the means to enter the city. To fit the name of empress, she channels Elizabeth. She forces herself to rise tall and imperious, haughty. The peasants look her over. They are doubtful, hands folded over their chests in self-protection. At last, Alexis engages in the final acts of bartering, and the amount of financial renumeration escalates. There is also the exchange of horses, the peasants' fresh ones attached to their carriage.

"You will remember us, when you are *gosudarina*," the elder of the peasants calls out to her. It is the first time she hears the word "empress" in relation to herself. If nothing else, he probably thinks he lucked into the best deal of the year.

"Of course I will," she says. "And you will be generously compensated."

The group splits a laugh among them. She is not sure if they doubt her identity, her future possible status, or if they have given up any hopes of benevolent monarchic intervention in their daily lives. They are piled back on the cart now, peeling apples.

Alexis climbs into the box alongside the driver and she is left to her own excited thoughts. She slices the remainder of the day into pieces, rehearsing each individual chunk, branding it into her brain. She does not allow herself to think of her old self, little Sophie, the comet, a stranger in a foreign land.

Just as the first cupolas of the capital come into view, a carriage is speeding toward them. Gregory, with Prince Bariatinsky at his side, waves to them from an open door. They are resplendent in full Guards regalia as if on their way to a coronation.

"Get in, get in," they call to her.

She and Alexis are enfolded into their carriage, and they are traveling briskly on the road. Wedged among these three men, their scent of perspiration mingled with perfume, she realizes this is real. It is happening. Her fate is about to be realized.

Gregory can barely settle in his seat. He alternates blowing into his hands, staring out the window, and gazing at her with fiery excitement. At first, everyone is talking at once, adding his own interpretation to Passek's arrest.

"Stop," she commands. "The past is history. Let us go over the future instead." The men had forgotten her; they seem ruffled at her interruption as if the plan did not culminate with her at their helm.

"Forgive us, *matushka*," says Alexis, and they become men again, plotting the contours of the day. They would start with the soldiers, of course, then move to church and palace. The Guards are theirs to be seized; Gregory has prepared them for the coup. The archbishop of Novgorod would anoint her in front of the cathedral on Nevsky Prospekt. She should stick to the narrative they have prepared, her ironclad reason for rule—her life and, more important, that of the heir to the Russian throne are in danger. Deposing the emperor would have to be done for her son's sake, as well as that of the country. If necessary, she can point to many of Peter's disastrous foreign policy decisions: the absurd war with Denmark that everyone decried, the sentimental return of hard-won Prussian territories.

As the carriage rolls into the city, she rehearses the plea, gradating her voice with the proper modesty. *It is not for my own sake, but that of my country and its holy Orthodox belief that I throw myself at your mercy.*

"Perfect," Gregory says. He plants a fervent kiss on her hand but it feels like he is kissing an idea not a woman. Already, she can feel her very hand becoming less tangible, less fleshlike. The steeples of Moscow burst into view, strips of bright colors and bulbous shapes of cupolas.

They are barely in the soldiers' barracks, when she sees men running toward the carriage, as if timing their footsteps to the drummer boy's instrument. They are batting their hands on the side of the carriage, howling her name.

"I should be on a horse," she breathes to no one in particular. "High above them so they can see me."

Before she knows it, she is climbing out to a fresh wave of cheers, a mass of uniforms engulfing her. She feels hands wrapped around her feet and ankles. Rows and rows of eyes and mouths are working in unison. A tide of affection rises in her and the correct words tumble out, mellifluous, directly from the heart. *I throw myself at your mercy.* Applause erupts and there are a few hearty shouts of *Gosudarina!* The colonel pushes his way toward her, bends before her with his cross. He is calling her by yet another new name: Catherine the Second of Russia. There is no reversal now, no sending herself to Zerbst. She will die on this land, and all these men inflate her with a feeling akin to immortality, a rising, impenetrable fullness. She is hustled onto a horse. A queen in black must be in full view as the leader of armies.

The wide plaza of the Nevsky Prospekt is already filled with onlookers who must have heard the news. Children are being raised onto window frames, the elderly hoisted up for a better view. Benedictions are being flung at her from all directions. Now in addition to the blue of military uniforms, there is the black of priests, chaplains, the ordinary curious. She can feel Gregory and Alexis firm behind her, the wall of their bodies pushing her onward to the church. The ringing in her skull turns out to be church bells, bringing with them more people. She feels herself floating above her own body as if an observer to another's coronation.

Inside the church, the archbishop Dmitry is already awaiting her, his eagerness no less urgent than her own. She can barely hear his voice when he pronounces her sovereign—*gosudarina*—for all the bellowing in the aisles, and outside the church. She surveys them all, the soldiers shedding the hated Prussian uniforms Peter imposed on them, onlookers stumbling in from the street, women with babies pressed to their chests. Behind her, the wall of icons gleams gold, saints nodding in approval. The archbishop is administering one oath of allegiance after the next, a few dissenters are reprimanded. She is an actor on the largest of stages, aware of her appearance—free of makeup, lacking in adornments, her hair unpowdered. She affects the right pose, humbled yet deserving. A true *gosudarina*. A deserving *gosudarina*. A *gosudarina* selected by God himself.

"The heir, *matushka*," Alexis whispers when the ceremony is over. She nods. From now on, they communicate by muscle memory, like a string of dockworkers emptying a vessel. To capture a country, one needs to complete each step: military, political, divine. The Winter Palace is next. She must publicly enact the reunion with a son she never sees, to confirm the final image of ascension. To play it safe, protect herself against dissenters who will point to her foreign birth, she decides to hoist up Paul and declare herself regent, the caretaker of the country until he comes of age. As a German with no dynastic right to the Russian monarchy, this will be the moderate route. No one will dare argue with Peter's deposing.

Once she leaves the church, order breaks down at her horse's side. Pushing hordes are creating panic in the streets. A man screams as he is trampled. It frightens her, how quickly revolt can be stoked when masses

of people gather. She gulps away dread—what if she is torn to shreds?—
and proceeds down Nevsky Prospekt.

She had never been more than a guest here, she thinks when the familiar palace comes into view. The sight of it tweaks at her insides. The
empress thought her invisible, a silent womb. She stops before the front
staircase, taking in its small deteriorations. Then she begins to climb.
Once inside, her eyes adjust from throbbing morning light to the palace's
dank interior.

"Where is he?"

But he is already being brought to her, the boy in nightdress, frantically blinking off sleep. She can see he has been briefly informed in the
warm nest of his bed, but he still looks terrified at the human swell surg-
ing behind her. He is craning his neck nervously for a glimpse through
the gates. Her son is frail and bony and overwhelmed. She reaches for
him.

"Come, Paul, come to your mother." How odd to say the word. None
of her pregnancies, successful or otherwise, inspired in her the idea of
mother. And he may as well be a stranger, this eight-year-old child quiv-
ering away from her, clutching at Panin.

"Take him," Panin says, unfurling the boy's fingers from his arm. He
barely looks down at Paul, his gaze firmly on Catherine, on the outline
of her black dress, the sweep and color of her natural hair. "You are very
regal today, very beautiful. You know the world awaits you, don't you?"

"Yes, I know." And she does believe it. They are dragging the child
toward the front windows, his feet almost elevated off the floor.

Panin is firm. "Then do what you need to do. What we need you to
do."

She grabs her son in a bearlike embrace and thrusts him out onto the
balcony. For a moment mother and son are conjoined breath, open-
mouthed, flaring nostrils, chests rising and falling in rhythm. Her name
is being yelled down below and she yanks herself out of this alignment
with Paul. Remember, she tells herself, the people are branding you into
their memories—each move, the very tiniest of acts, declares your intentions. She must make them unambiguous. She glances up above the heads
of the crowd into the vastness of the sky as if in search of that comet to

tell her what to do. The quiver in her arms reminds her that time is passing, and if she does not act, a choice will be made for her. She must decide right now. Regent or queen, queen or regent. Or dead.

Instead of raising Paul ahead of herself, instead of triumphantly holding him aloft, she drops him to the ground and remains standing alone, framed by the balcony. A fresh wave of cheering erupts. The message is clear. It is not her son who is emperor, but she who is *gosudarina*. She will be ruler even if she spends the rest of her days convincing the country that she belongs here. She feels the boy clawing at her dress like a puppy who has been briefly loved and discarded. He is trying to scramble to his feet. His muscles are tensed under the white shirt, she can feel the ropelike ripple of them. But she keeps a hand on the windswept peak of his head, both as a calming mechanism and also to keep him down, out of sight. It is not yet his turn. She alone must be mounted in their consciousness.

"*Ura!*" they shout in approval.

She waits a few beats, then retreats into the palace. Her mind is already settling on the next act—gaining the unequivocal support of the administration—but then notices that he is still out there, her son, cowering on the balcony planks. She feels a momentary ache. An ancient instinct awakens in her of protection, the desire to wrap him, swaddle him into a cocoon. He looks pitiful in his fetal curl, hands squashed at his ears. She turns back, starts to say, *Do not be frightened,* or at least perceive the plump curve of his jowl, offer a pat on the shoulder. The residue of his childish freshness remains on her fingers. But Panin gets there first, bending over the boy.

"Wait, let me speak with him," she tries. But he is being shuttled away, out of sight, the faintest blur of white nightdress before he is gone. And Gregory is back at her side.

"The Senate and Holy Synod are waiting."

He directs her toward the rows of waiting men. A lump in her throat persists, and cannot be budged. She experiences a feeling of overlooking something, and she flattens the folds of her dress in search for it. A stinging prick of the chest? A momentary anxiety? Little Paul is long gone now, his voice too.

Her hand is being pressed, a surge once again pulling her, this time into the cabinet. In that meeting, she will repeat the words she rehearsed in the carriage. That she, guided by divine forces, decided to sacrifice herself for a country being steered in the wrong direction. Because no one else can accomplish this task, it has become her divine duty to save Russia from its dangerous course. *Overcome by the imminent peril with which our faithful subjects were threatened, and seeing how sincere and express their desires on this matter were: we, putting our trust in the Almighty and his divine justice, have ascended the sovereign imperial throne of all the Russians, and have received a solemn oath of fidelity from all our loving subjects.*

There, that is done. She turns to her lover. What next on today's agenda?

Oh, yes, she remembers. Inform her husband that he is no longer the emperor.

Tanya

As a specialist, you never sleep the night before an auction. Your mind constantly revolves around opportunities you may have missed, clients whose bidding power you've overlooked, bidders who need extra prompting to get into the fray. The day has barely cracked when I hail a cab to the office, standing outside in ridiculously high heels, Central Park tinged a hooded blue.

Before seven, and I'm already at the office checking faxes on who has registered to bid, which lots are amassing interest. The business day has long ago opened in Moscow and I'm busy working the phones, wheedling clients into bidding. The trick is getting the players on the phone. I entice them with the possibility of a deal, knowing that once they register, they won't be able to stop. There's a primal instinct of competition pumping through their blood. Once they've set their minds on a particular lot, a client can go up two and a half million in five minutes.

"Maybe there's a good reserve on the Nesterov, Vitya," I say, casually. "You know I can't tell you the number, but trust me, it's worth getting on the phone for. Shall we try it?"

For example, I know Vitya's personal tics, his rivalries with my other clients, his impulsive decision to grab at yet one more thing. He wants to be wooed and enticed, because he's itching to enter the game and win. I offer him a buyer's premium as an extra incentive. And behind my shoulder stands the specter of Marjorie, holding the sheet for last season's underperforming auction. If I don't succeed in roping in Vitya, I'll probably lose my job. Luckily, he trusts me.

"If you think so, Tanya," he says, and agrees to go higher.

And I'm forced to do the same for Volodia and Grisha and Borya and, finally, Sasha Medovsky. But with Sasha, I do something I've never dreamed of doing in the past, something that goes against the very instincts of an auction specialist, not to mention one who has just received the unequivocal news that a client's desired lot is bona fide authentic. I insert a seed of doubt.

I call him on my cell phone. "I've been meaning to touch base about the Order, Sash. Between you and me. It might not be such a hot idea."

"What the hell is going on, Tanyush? I just got a call from Natasha at the Hermitage. Is what she saying true? Are they starting to question the provenance?" His voice is looming larger, this time for a good reason. What I'm implying is unnatural, unprofessional under any circumstances.

"I'm afraid so. But you know what? We just don't know for sure. It's a wonderful piece."

It's not too late to leave matters in the hands of the open market, to back away as I'm supposed to do. But would I ever lie to a client? And hasn't Medovsky become more than a client? Hasn't he become a friend?

"You said you were a hundred percent sure," he snaps.

The business manager runs by my cubicle with an iPad, on his way to meetings inaccessible to me. Upstairs, there's a boardroom for vice presidents. Up there, the table is mahogany and oval-shaped, and it's always topped with trays of grapes and berries. The walls are adorned with art from the upcoming sale; right now, it is the Goncharova. This is where the chief executive meets shareholders, where the vice presidents do their debriefing. The room is all windows, but veiled behind frosted glass. In Worthington's, I was told again and again, you either move up to that room, sit around the table with Dean and eat his fruit, or you collect your things and go.

"Can we trust Natasha? I'm pretty sure we can," I say. "And let's not forget her original assessment. I'm just telling you what I know, that there are a few missing pieces of information."

"I can't believe I'm finding out now that it's not one hundred percent." His voice is flooded with disappointment and, if I'm not mistaken, with fear.

"I'm sorry, Sash. I just found out myself. But you know we wouldn't sell it unless we were ninety-nine percent."

Your clients have done shady things, some of them have killed or had enemies killed, and because I'm focused on Carl, on making certain I do everything I can to patch us, I don't want to think about that. In any case, Medovsky is no angel, and I remind myself that money laundering was one of the only charges against him that saw the light of day. They've come of age inside a vortex of amorality, my clients, just as I did. Their brains are wired to beat the system in order to survive its daily absurdities. They've suffered too. They were schoolchildren in the Soviet system, weaned on a single television station, they played piano and ice-skated in the winter. They were victims of Jewish quotas, turned away from schools because the "nationalities" in their passports screamed "Jewish." Earnestly pinning their little Lenin decorations to their chests, reciting, "I am entering the team of the Soviet Union Pioneer Organization, in front of all my comrade mates, I solemnly declare: to love and to protect my country, live as the great Lenin advised, as the Communist party guides, as the Pioneer Laws require," their red kerchiefs tight around their necks. Like me, they fervently believed their words, put all their faith into the truth of them, lived with the certainty of a united, single-minded society for many years. Marching and singing with a clear voice, hair smoothed to one side. But I left. They stayed to watch the dissolution happen outside their doors, tuning into news one fateful August to watch Nureyev performing *Swan Lake* all day long. Knowing that the government only clogs all the channels with *Swan Lake* to distract people from some national calamity. In this case, it is the fact of tanks approaching Red Square.

Still, these clients touch me, they pull at my heart despite myself. Is it their fault they're good at what they do? That they saw the door of opportunity, an unprepared country with countless pathways to new money? That they watched as Russia was cracking open its hidden gold and they seized it?

"I don't understand. You said it belonged to Catherine the Great. You said there was no doubt."

I waver. "It is. There isn't. You know what? Forget I said anything, actually."

"But the fact it's Catherine's is important, crucial really, symbolic in this case. The president has made that very clear. You know where he receives foreign diplomats, don't you—in the Kremlin's hall of Saint Catherine. This order would go there, on display. He's counting on receiving it, I have already promised him. He would not be pleased if it turned out to be fake, and not pleased is an understatement." His voice slurs into cloudy film.

"Oh, I completely understand. And it is not fake. I'm sure of it." I allow my heart to harden, picturing the president showing off the Order to his courtiers. The final sentence lies there naked, with no additional reinforcement. "I'll call you a little later from the room."

Now they're filtering in, the rest of my groggy department, to their desks. They're wearing their most polished unstructured shifts, their crispest ties, prepared for their roles in the public spectacle. An auction is like a movie, the specialists its high-grossing actors. At the phone bank, you must exude control, be calm but urgent enough to instigate competition. You do not smile too much. *You look ridiculously hot up there,* Carl used to say. Our best sex may have been after auctions.

Regan places a coffee and mixed berry muffin on my desk, eyes bright behind the red rims of her glasses.

"I love this shit, don't you? Are we going to make serious coin or what?"

"It's exciting." I don't sound my usual peppy self.

"What's wrong with you today? Someone better drink coffee right quick."

It's eight in the morning, the fax machines spitting paper. The business manager swings back from his meeting with crossed fingers and, in the distance, I see Marjorie returning to her office, phone balanced on a shoulder, fingers searching her desk for a writing implement. I take the opportunity to steal into the storage room, unlock the safe, and pick up the Order for the last time.

"Good-bye, Catherine." I feel silly chatting with a medal. "I hope you wind up at the place that deserves you."

And Carl never did get to see it. At the museum, wasn't the Order the last argument we had?

"Tanya, where are you?" I hear. "Tanya, the phones!"

I freeze. Is it possible that it's not another woman? Not Victoria, not Hermione? Is it even remotely possible that Carl left me for Catherine?

"Tanya, Vitya Kharkov's calling again."

There's no choice but to return her. All the lines are ringing. Clients are ordering skyboxes at the last minute. Reporters insisting that this year they want actual photos of the purchasers, the men always hiding behind agents, murky voices over the telephone, swathed behind the an-onymity of skyboxes. Time for the oligarchs to come out with their bids! Demands from all directions are being hurled at me. There's no time to think, to make any sense of it. I start to lose the thread of the connection I made in the storage room. The very idea, whatever it was, seems ridicu-lous in the very immediate chaos.

The flurry of the day gives way to six o'clock, and the auction regulars take their seats in the room, flipping through marked-up catalogues. Nigel sits cradling his gavel, eyes closed in preauction meditation. It's pure theater. Whatever details remain must be left to chance. I take one last look at myself in the mirror, a swipe of lipstick, an expression of poised urgency, and step out to the phone bank. I'm the Specialist again.

In the back, by the elevators, client reps pluck secretive men and briskly escort them to skyboxes before the reporters can make note of their presence. The dance is seamless, everyone where they should be. Igor arrives with a quick scan of the floor. He slinks along the side walls and disappears into his box.

Then to my surprise, the Vandermotters walk in. Frances in her pearls, her vintage Chanel, Armand in his special-occasion Brooks Brothers head to toe. What are they doing here? They make rounds at the important rows, bend down to kiss the Nahmads' cheeks, shake hands with Larry Gagosian, who came with one of his Russian artists. Carl's parents have never attended a Russian sale before. They wave vaguely at me, a brief glimmer of gold bangle. I monitor them from my place along the telephone bank as Nigel rattles off the conditions of sale. Then their presence makes sense. They must know on some level that this auction is tightly linked to the future of the Foster Children's Alliance.

"A very warm welcome to tonight's sale of Russian art," Nigel announces. And it begins.

One final survey of my bid sheet, then the phone begins to blink furiously. Medovsky is calling on line one.

As an auction proceeds, I remind myself to breathe. *Focus. You have committed to nothing.*

"Someone's just exceeded her high estimate," the business manager whispers as the Goncharova is whisked off the dais. "This is going to be a landmark sale for Russian art and we're not even up to the Order yet."

"Great news."

"Are you kidding? This is more than great. It puts yours as the highest-grossing department at Worthington's." He sings. "Someone's getting a promotion, Ms. Vice President."

I knock on wood, three times.

"Oh God, you Russian Jews." He rises, an exasperated ceilingward glance. "Can't ever take any pleasure in victory. The Cossacks are coming, aren't they?"

"The Cossacks are always coming," I sing after him.

The Vandermotters are sitting diagonally across the room, calmly directing their attention from catalogue to art to me. I can feel a moist spot spreading under the elastic of my tights. Returning to the phones, I find that on line two, Medovsky's friend Oleg is playing hardball, trying to trick me into revealing the reserve.

"But how much is it approximately? Come, Tan'ka, I might have to give up if it's too high."

"Why don't we try for the Aivazovsky? That reserve's not bad at all. All the energy has been on the Goncharova and Larionov. I think you should get in there."

Line one is blinking, a cold red eye. In the audience, Frances stands out from the crowd with her looming bowl of blond hair and black-rimmed glasses, her tight face, her paisley scarf, the square of her chin. It takes effort not to glance up at the appropriate skybox where Igor must be facing the podium.

"Tanyush," Medovsky says. "How's it looking?"

"Great, great. The Order's next." My throat is almost caulked shut. I am fully aware of each word I'm uttering; our phone calls are taped by Worthington's. If there's any dispute, the slightest doubt about a specialist's deportment, someone in Dean's office will meticulously go over the recordings.

"What we talked about earlier. Just give it to me straight. Is it hers or not?"

If you can't juggle tones and people, if you can't make the right snap decisions, you shouldn't be sitting at the telephone bank. You're moving between souls, between bank accounts palpitating with desire. I think of Medovsky at his own party. How small he looked by the vastness of the sea, the squeals of Marina in the empty house above. How we stood shoulder to shoulder, two dealmakers before the razor slip of shore.

"Sure it is, Sash. How's Lena?"

"The Queen is fine, her kingdom intact, thank God for all of us."

"Give my regards. Thank her again for the splendid dinner. I'd like to host you guys in New York next time you're in town."

"We would love that, Tan'ka," he says, warmly gracious in spite of it all.

The Order is displayed on the screen, magnified so the saint is projected onto an entire wall in her peaceful stance, her blue cape. An order rarely excites this much interest, but its aura of Catherine the Great animates the crowd. They lean in closer. It looks identical to the way it appears in that portrait at the Tretyakov, the red of the ribbon against the canary of Catherine's dress, the silver of the diamonds reflected in the white lace of her sleeves. The saint examines us all, gauging our worthiness. And it occurs to me: they're all here for this. Gagosian, who never goes to Russian sales, the Nahmads, the Vandermotters, they all want to witness the passing on of an imperial relic. Its powerful feminine magic did its work on me, on Carl, and now it has infected everyone else. I meet Frances's eyes and can almost be sure I detect a nod, a license to move forward, as if the deal I made was not just with Igor, but larger, some kind of covenant that encompasses all women.

When the bidding tops a shocking twenty million, I begin to tell Medovsky that our phone connection is terrible. May I call him right back from my cell phone? Then I proceed to a series of gentle nudges that quietly imply disapproval. "Sash, I don't have a good feeling about this. Maybe we should stop here. If it turns out not to be hers, you would be in a vulnerable position." My voice is as low as I can make it without drawing suspicion. The bank is chaotic for eavesdropping; Regan and the others are deep inside their own negotiations with future bidders.

"Twenty million. Shall we do one more?" Nigel coaxes.

The room is too hot, the air-conditioning broken and the fans are pointing in my direction. The secondary bidders have long ago given up and now the Order is ricocheting between Sasha and Igor, as I knew it would. When my picture appears in the art blogs that evening ("Landmark Sale for the Russian Department at Worthington's, Exceeds Christie's") it will probably be of a glistening chin and faded lipstick.

"Are you sure I should stop?" Medovsky says, doubtful. "Who the hell's bidding against me? Lazarenko? Yardanov?"

"I just want you to realize how high we are in this moment. The competition's not backing down, and you know I'm only thinking of you."

"I need it, Tan'. I need it and I need it to be authentic beyond any doubt."

I cup my mouth with a palm as if for Medovsky's benefit. "I know, but do you really want to spend this kind of money on an order, especially one whose authenticity is in question? It could go up and up. Think of Lena, would she approve?" I was saving the wife for last, the specter of aerobicized Lena, her scowl, her future vengeance.

He puts up a fight, cycles through a few more rounds as I expect. Twenty-three million. I see Igor's line blinking: a warning. I choose to ignore it. Thirty. The room is squinting with anticipation; the reserve had been seven. This is going to be a blockbuster sale, especially during these volatile times. I can almost visualize my own hands prying open Medovsky's grip, finger by finger, until he releases the Order.

"If you don't think so, Tanyush," he says, a plaintive, uncharacteristic bowing to my expertise, and I remind myself that it's only one more acquisition for a man who has too much, who wastes too much. My marriage is worth more than one more house for his mistress, one more bribe to a president.

"Between us as friends, I think it's the wise choice," I murmur, a butterfly beating its wings inside my rib cage. And I can feel them, fingers wrenched, a man letting go of his prize. The Order plummeting to earth.

"My God," the business manager says when the gavel falls, the Order awarded to Igor even if no one in the audience knows that yet. "This is pretty damn nice for the Russian department." Hands are descending on my shoulders, kisses disembodied from lips.

"Sasha? Sasha? You there?" But the phone is dead.

I scan the room for Igor's descent from the skybox, but as soon as I step down from the bank, I'm surrounded by reporters, and forced to regurgitate the usual postauction platitudes: "I think what this auction proves is that the market is looking for quality, not quantity." "If only every sale featured an order from Catherine the Great." "I'm pleased to see the value of Russia's imperial treasures is still recognized."

I push through them in search of the right skybox, flinging open one door after another onto empty, utilitarian offices. My clients make rapid exits, often before the end of the auction, and I shouldn't be surprised to find the skyboxes empty. Yet I am. I lean my forehead against the glass, staring down at the kisses, the handshakes, the hordes below. What kind of closure did I expect from Igor? Thank you? The Vandermotters' charity is saved, the Order encased in a museum, safe for future generations. It had been a business transaction, nothing more. So why, I wonder, does this doubt persist?

I take the stairs slowly, and I'm back on the floor, along with a smattering of leftover reporters and lingering observers. I find my way to the Vandermotters, kiss in the proximity of Frances's cheek. She's thanking me for inflaming Igor's interest in the organization; thanks to his contribution, they'll be able to hire an administrator, establish a delivery of monthly care packages to all the kids, and revive plans for a Foster Children's Alliance Center in Tribeca.

"I'm so glad," I say.

They're different, Carl's parents, more effusive, and this new attention frightens me.

"My dear, we'd love to honor you at our next gala," Frances says, not letting go of my arm, two hands warming both sides of my hand. "As a Russian-American who's done so much for the art world."

"That sounds great." Hadn't I once dreamed of being embraced by her like this, the ultimate proof of my belonging in their family? But now all I want is to hear Carl's voice. "I should get home."

"Of course. We'll see you soon anyway."

Leaving the glowing grandeur of Worthington's behind, I'm once again on the windswept streets of midtown. It's late enough that the majority of passersby consists of dog walkers or postcollege kids stumbling to the next Irish pub down in Murray Hill. Behind me looms that square glass building infused with light, with the rosy sheen of money. Oh, the price of admission, I think. The high price of admission.

Catherine

She is the mistress of the palace, of an entire empire, and she finds it suits her, as if she has been practicing the role for decades. One could even say she is fulfilling an ancient destiny inscribed on her very tissue. Private plans she cradled inside while she was grand duchess threaten to emerge all at once. She wants to fill the library shelves with Montesquieu and Voltaire and Diderot and her beloved volumes of Bayle's *Dictionnaire historique et critique,* meet with Starov to build a pavilion extension onto the Winter Palace, hire a French chef, rearrange the furnishings to accommodate the work of the state rather than the frivolity that permeated the reign of the former empress. She remembers Count Gyllenborg's expression, his pity for her distance from the cultural center of Europe. She will buy whatever European art is best then, and a lot of it. She wants to immediately draw up plans to erect side panels in Moscow churches in honor of Saint Catherine, to build a throne in the martyr's name, order an icon of Saint Catherine with the likeness of her own face. It is crucial everyone believe that she and Saint Catherine are one, that her right to rule has been ordained by the saint herself.

When the Orlovs burst in for the meeting, she is still giddy with the fact that it is in her power to grant meetings, that she is in fact an actual empress with whom people want to meet. The brothers are grave countenanced as usual; Alexis roiling with common sense, Gregory not so different in conducting the crown's business than in manifesting efficient ardor in the bedroom.

"We must discuss the *gosudar*," Alexis says.

She groans. "To what end? Is he not in comfortable confinement until his room at the prison is ready?"

The matter of her husband deadens her fresh elation every time. Peter being held at the stone house at Ropsha, surrounded by the glittering fishing lake, preparing—even if he does not know it yet—for incarceration. She tells herself that she takes no real pleasure in the reversal of fortunes but he has become a problem to be solved. During the first four days since his abdication and arrival at Ropsha, he has sent at least three letters addressing her properly as Your Majesty. Always ending with the same request: he will make no further claims to the throne if he is reunited with that kitchen wench Vorontsova. That he has no realistic idea of the fate that awaits him should not surprise Catherine, but it galls her. Those letters have gone unanswered.

How could she forget the many times he has humiliated her in the past months? Calling her *dura*—"idiot"—in the middle of a large dinner, parading that Vorontsova as her successor, forcing her to relinquish her own beloved Order of Saint Catherine. Each slight was a dagger's parry. *I beg Your Majesty to have confidence in me and to have the goodness to order the guards removed from the second room as the one I occupy is so small that I can hardly move in it.* She has ignored his letters that begged a return to Germany, a rendezvous with his mistress. But she did fulfill the more reasonable desires: the transport of his favorite bed and his loathsome dog, the arrival of his doctor. When she thought of him, it was with the sharp pull of guilt and most of all a longing to eradicate all traces of his memory. She most preferred imagining him at peace, wandering the Ropsha grounds among sparrows and starlings and cranes. *Also I beg you to order that no officers should remain in the same room with me since I must relieve myself and I cannot possibly do that in front of them.*

"Why must we speak of the *gosudar*? I suspect he is secure at Ropsha," she says.

"We hear he is ill."

"Is that so? How does he fare? What is the cause of the illness?" She hopes her voice is not too seeded with hope.

The brothers exchange a brief glance. "A severe headache, it is reported, stomach ailments. His Holstein physician has been sent for, as you requested."

"I am relieved to hear it."

She is aware of a carefulness to their dialogue, all three of them waiting for a dictate, a final decision of some kind. Alexis is pacing the rug, Gregory's palms curl the back of the chair. Now that she is empress, she views her lover differently, through the affectionate lens of a mother loyal to an impulsive child.

Gregory blurts, "But surely he must be rendered harmless. How do we know he has permanently abdicated his right to the throne?"

The day is hot despite the flung-open windows, her lover always made uncomfortable by his uniform's restraint. The chair tumbles back, and he hastens to readjust it.

"How do you propose we accomplish this harmlessness?"

Dura, she hears Peter's mocking voice. He was seated alongside Vorontsova, and the guests pretended not to hear the word, busying themselves with the contents of their plates. They darted glances to express their private sympathies, but she was certain they were titillated by the prospect of a fiery reaction. *Dura*. The trigger had been a minor one as usual. She had refused to rise for some inane toast he proposed to drink to his Holstein uncles because it was a politically idiotic, unpatriotic act. But to her surprise the word *dura* unraveled her. She wound up openly weeping in front of all those guests, the shame of the epithet mingled with a quiet spite of playing the victim. Peter threatened to jail her for the slight against his uncles. Only at the last minute, someone convinced him to retract, to have mercy for her. That person saved her life.

Would it not be convenient if Peter were gone, vanished? To be utterly free of him in body and symbol? But she remembers the boy she first met, her childhood friend with his wooden soldiers. She recalls entering the palace for the first time in the dead of night, his shy greeting (*I could not wait*), their games of blindman's bluff. Walking in on Brummer beating Peter with a branch over the railing of his bed, the look of hopelessness on the boy's face when it was clear she was repulsed by his cheeks distorted by smallpox.

"If you will allow us to come up with a solution," Alexis says.

She hesitates. "Propose it."

"You would not even have to trouble yourself with the details."

"The prison should work fine. There have been no disturbances with the crazy Ivan."

"Allow me to remind you of your meeting with Panin, Your Majesty." A voice floats from the other side of the door. She recalls the rest of the morning's agenda—landlords insisting she draft a decree on hard labor for impudent serfs. It is one of those acts she has no enthusiasm for— had she not once argued against the institution of serfdom altogether?— but the first lesson of reigning such a vast realm is that compromise is necessary even when it contradicts your personal beliefs.

"I suppose I can leave this in your hands," she says. "But now I must meet with Panin."

"Of course, *matushka*. We will take care of it," Alexis says, bowing. The brothers are so similar in many ways, but Alexis has more hair overall, bushy eyebrows set over his eyes. They are filing out of the room now, but she is unclear on what had been decided. Should she call them back, be clear in voicing her opinion? It has been the most exhausting week of her life and the heat renders her limp. Musing returns her to Peter, the day he cut out a hole in the wall to peep in on the empress getting dressed. In his efforts to stretch to the opening, he overturned her mother's toiletries, spilling powder all over her dressing gown.

In the bowels of the palace, she hears the cry of a baby girl so recently inside her belly. The sound of an eight-year-old boy's feet running up the staircase. On her desk, a mountain of paperwork awaits, silly Peter manifestos to be undone, laws revoked, revised. She can push him further down the priority queue, let him enjoy the freedom of a still lake. A more resolute plan can be carved out later. There on top of the pile lies his most recent letter, and she pushes it to the side. *Once again, I beg you, since I have followed your wishes in everything, to allow me to leave for Germany with the persons for whom I have already asked Your Majesty to grant permission. I hope your magnanimity will not permit my request to be in vain.* She turns back to the Holy Synod documents, requesting a return of relics to the Church that Peter had seized when in power. The boy, her husband, is forgotten.

She rises to a day of great industry. There are letters to be written, a stream of visitors and well-wishers to be greeted. A few cheerfully accompany her to prayers. She moves easily from task to task. There is a stimulating variety of errands—discussing the erection of the library, conferring about the Poland problem, seeking a southern cavity to the sea, the imperial dinner menu, informing foreign states of her position as sole autocrat. Her former talents for pleasing others are put to good use. People who enter her chambers are immediately set at ease, the visits all ending in the kissing of her hand, a satisfying stream of gratitude.

Simple meals are delivered to her: cold sturgeon and soups. During the day, she socializes little, a quick dispatch of the meal, then back to work.

For the first time, the faces that greet her in the halls are uniformly benevolent. She sees no condolences in their expressions or distress or wickedness. They bow to her, call her *gosudarina* or Your Majesty even if she begs them to do away with formality. She is no longer at the margins of the court, but is the axis on which it turns. In between meetings with senators and ambassadors, she takes a moment to breathe, to sip at her tea. If she does not attend that night's opera, there is always the quiet game of piquet. She has written to her friends in Europe, and to her old lover Stanislaw, inquiring about art she can buy in bulk. She can already picture it—Russia holding the world's greatest art collection. No more shame about not knowing Colley Cibber and whether or not his is the dullest play of the London season.

Only the thought of Peter pulls at the fringes of her contentment. At night she sleeps lightly, ready to defend herself against the slightest sound. Once she used to lie in bed waiting for his footsteps, for some kind of turn in their relations. This passive expectation for the boy to enfold her in his arms. And now she waits for footsteps of a different sort, prepares for the possibility of revenge from his allies. She hears his hic-cupping, mocking laugh in her dreams, and awakes bathed in sweat.

Matushka, *Little Mother, most merciful* Gosudarina, *sovereign lady, how can I explain or describe what happened?* The rider, cap in hand, hands her the paper scrawled with erratic ink. The expression on the man's face is of terror. Catherine tries to suppress her own panic, to give the impression of a monarch in control.

"What is the matter?" Catherine asks. Her mask is strewn across the table with its pair of excised eyes. Still in her ball gown, still recovering from hours of feverish dancing, she scrutinizes the page. The handwrit-ing does not appear to belong to Alexis Orlov but to a drunk man, a man out of his wits; she can barely make any sense of it.

Matushka, *he is no more.* She almost does not need to read on. There will be many questions regarding her complicity, so she forces herself.

"I was handed this to deliver to you right away," the man chatters as she scans the lines. "I swear, that is all I know."

To her surprise, she feels herself go cold, the tips of her fingers numb. She stares out the window. The masquerade's revelers are tipping out of the front gates to their carriages. Drunken laughter swells the corridors. A speckled house sparrow tangled inside the curtains is fluttering for its freedom. She releases the bird into the night sky, an act that soothes her, and also buys her time.

Her first reaction is one of logistics. If it was indeed murder, Alexis was too smart to poison Peter and leave any residue. A knife wound would look equally bad. Then it must have been suffocation, the brute force of hands on Peter's tiny, hapless neck.

How could any of us have ventured to raise our hands against our Gosudar, *sovereign lord. But* Gosudarina, *it has happened.*

"Any word back, Your Majesty?"

She finds her voice. "No. Thank you for your prompt relay."

Back to Alexis's jagged scribble: *We ourselves know not what we did.* She can imagine the fear on Peter's face, his weak wrists batting away his attackers. The muffled screams, high-pitched and unnatural. His lifeless body would resemble one of his puppets. A flood of relief follows remorse inside her, the two sensations alternating in waves. She considers burning the letter, then realizes its disappearance would throw suspicion on her. It remains under her pillow for the night. In the morning, points of ink stab the white linen.

Gregory arrives at her cabinet at first dawn with a hasty peck on her cheek. He peers at her warily, meaty hands limp at his sides. *Murderer,* she now thinks, unsure if she is addressing herself or him. Neither of them speaks.

"I see you have his portrait," he says. They both glance at the floor where the face of an enhanced version of Peter III scrutinizes them, frameless. She had it wheeled in hours ago, just in case. Its stare trails her from shelves to love seat to window. She is also wearing the jeweled portrait of Peter the empress gifted her on her wedding day. The empress had promised it would be "useful" on certain occasions.

"In his letter, your brother verifies it was an accident," she begins.

He looks as though something oppressive has been removed, as color returns to his cheeks. He probably expected her fury or, worse, arrest. A glaze of cloud seems to depart, replaced by a cast hard and bronze. "It was no accident. It was God's will."

"A stroke."

"Hermorrhoidal colic, if you like."

She swallows.

"It affected his brain, then."

Gregory nods, slowly. "The delirium was followed by exhaustion, and despite all the assistance of doctors, he expired."

"Inflammation of the bowels."

"Stroke of apoplexy."

"They can attest to this?"

"We will acquire their verification. They will find no poison," he says quickly.

"Of course not. I trust you are telling the truth." They are heaving a cumbersome load back and forth like a child's ball. "Thank you. I must compose the statement now."

"We can attest you were completely innocent of the matter. The man was deathly ill. As he was dying, he demanded a Lutheran priest. You might include that in the report."

She turns away. "Thank you. You may go."

He loiters as if torn between attempting an intimate display of regard or one more professional, then decides on an awkward bow. As if to say, *We only did what you wanted of us—your supremacy is now uncontested.*

"We found this among his belongings. I believe it belongs to you." He drops a square box on her desk. Brown, velvet, with scalloped edges. She knows its contents like she knows the pathways of her own mind. Wrapped in a delicate silk chamois lies the Order of Saint Catherine.

It is she at that stone house at Ropsha in her dreams, not the Orlovs. Just Catherine and her husband, and they are children again. She is fifteen, not thirty-three. It is a time before childbirth, before disappointment with love had settled into her bones. They are playing with his soldiers, her husband lining them up in formation, dressing some down, promoting others. She slumps in an armchair with one of her books, recalls that sense of unbroken boredom she once suffered when days were an unreasonable length, and the sun did not descend fast enough.

Peter suddenly rises from play. "Something's wrong? Fetch the doctor." He is doubled over in agony, looking to her for salvation.

She is slow to unwind herself from the tufted arm, reluctant to respond to that voice, the one that never aged or matured or developed in it any hint of affection for her. Like the strangled croak of a wounded dog.

"I cannot help you. I don't want to help you."

"Dura," he says, his face changing. "Fetch me a doctor. Fetch me Liza who loves me." He is spread on the couch, the three-tipped hat cascading off his brow. The pillow beside him is soft enough, big enough.

"Do you suppose your Liza is already on her way to help you?"

"And who loves you? Orlov? Paniatovsky? Saltykov? You are nothing, some minor German princess. You are not beautiful. You are not smart. You don't belong here. I am the grandson of Peter the Great. I am the real heir to the throne. Only prison is good enough for you." He is fading away into his pain.

"Stop whining already. I've had enough. Twenty years is too long for our ill-fated union."

She collapses the pillow on top of his face, making sure the corners are tightly pressed to block the flow of air. The thought occurs that the pillow is too valuable for the task, specially ordered by the empress from Spain for its colorful embroidery. But it is too late to exchange it with a more disposable item. She is physically stronger than he; that has always been the case. He buckles with the surprise of her attack, hands flailing at her. She straddles him with her thighs, the most sexual position they have ever undertaken during all those fruitless years of marriage. He is trying to unseat her by a frantic gyration of his hips. He mumbles what is probably a string of curses, but soon the sound is thinner, weaker. All she has to do is hold the position and she does, keeps pushing down long past when he has stilled. His body is limp. She continues to thrust and to clamp down until she is absolutely sure. For a marriage to thrive, sometimes the husband must die.

Catherine, the eternal dreamer, and this is the most honest dream of her life.

When she awakens to the dead of night with a palpitating heart, there is no returning to sleep. Instead, she dresses in the black of her victory, a veil over her head, the Order of Saint Catherine around her neck. It is surprisingly easy not to be recognized out on the streets slick with leftover rain. A common carriage ferries her across cobblestones. She is a black figure darting among shadow, a shroud of lace obscuring her view. The Alexander Nevsky Monastery is empty apart from the mosaic of Jesus staring at her from above the gate. She pushes open the heavy door. The interior of the church is also empty. There are no crowds of mourners like there were for the former empress, no persistent sound of female keening. Unlike the corpse of the empress that was hidden from view, Peter's body is on stark display atop the stand, a shriveled figure in a foreign Holstein uniform and hat too large for his body. Even the extinguished candles are cold, their wicks had been barely touched by flame.

A faint hint of moon strains through glass, making more silver the grand sarcophagus of Alexander Nevsky. It is one of her favorite places. It had been no hardship to spend entire days here in public mourning for the passing of the empress, not only because it placed her in a sympathetic light with the right people but also because it allowed her to escape the embarrassment that swirled around Peter's crowning.

She nears the stand. As feared, her husband's face is purple, distended, marked by the struggle of his final minutes. His neck has been covered, but even the darkness cannot disguise the bluish ring radiating from beneath his chin. There is a kind of bafflement in his repose, as if he were meant for an entirely different fate, far from the world stage. As if his authentic life had taken place in some imaginary land of eternal childhood filled with simple pleasures and amusements among companions who loved him with no judgment or expectations.

She lifts the Order of Saint Catherine from around her neck and slides the medal inside Peter's uniform. It is safer in the grave with Peter. The power it confers on its wearer is strong, magical; had she thought to lend it to Katya, her dearest friend would have doubtlessly lived to share in the triumph of her coronation. But the gift of supremacy is dangerous in the wrong hands. Vorontsova wore the Order when it did not belong to her and now she has been reduced to irrelevance. Catherine has already asked Gregory to find a suitably odious soldier to marry the woman and transfer them both to some far-flung village. *She Is to Her Husband Compared.*

She kneels to pray, a hasty string of sentences that morph into unexpected spasms of sorrow. If anyone caught sight of her now, he would assume to be witnessing the grieving of a wife praying for the soul of her beloved husband. And in a way, she is. Because her heart is still soft and pliant, and she can afford one last burst of sadness for the man. But she is also praying for herself: *Gosudarina*, Queen, God's anointed sovereign.

She leaves the monastery the way she arrived. Solitary, solitary autocrat.

Tanya

When I was a child, and my parents wanted to instill culture in me, they dragged me to every New York City museum except the Metropolitan. According to them, it was a temple not fit for the bedraggled Kagans from the humble reaches of Rego Park, Queens. The other museums we could handle: the MoMAs, the Museums of American History, the Cooper Hewitts. But the Met? It's not a place for immigrants, my mother insisted, only for those worthy of entering a palace. Take a look at it! Stretching across blocks of Fifth Avenue with its superb Beaux Arts façade, so imposing it is a constant reminder of how small the human is who makes its way up the Grand Stairway.

But now, impossibly, all these years later, it's actually me flying up the broad staircase of the Metropolitan Museum in a ball gown, past the black-suited blur of security. For the first time, all the splendor once so out of reach for poor Russian Kagans is actually inviting me inside.

I push through the front doors as summer tourists stream out for the day. Breezing past the ticket office just closing its window, I find the welcome table tucked away in the Egyptian wing. A row of girls holds reams of printed names in manicured hands. They say, "Oh, you're one of the honorees, aren't you?" and apply a sticky tag to my chest. Can this be real? Can I make any sense of it? Tanya Kagan of the immigrant Kagans, whose face was once pressed to the glass globe of Manhattan, who stole soap from bodegas, who fended off bullies in yeshiva and roamed the streets of Rego Park alone. Here? Now?

Regan pops out from behind a pillar. "You look amazing."

She's wearing the most conservative outfit I've ever seen on her: a soft powder-blue Alberta Ferretti wisp cinched at the waist, a pair of suede closed-toe pumps.

"I probably went a little over the top. But, hey, look at you," I say.

But Regan's back to business. "Have you been picking up your voice mail?"

"What's up?"

She is leading me through the lobby, where the day's final tourists are milling, contemplating their next move. They stare at Regan in all her height, at my own layers of black silk and lace, trying to match our faces to a mental Rolodex of celebrity. Crowds disperse, the Egyptian tombs and sphinxes displaying their ancient flint knives of battle.

Regan is scrolling through her messages. "Medovsky," she says, ominously.

"What about him? Is he pissed Yardanov got it?"

"They're calling it suicide, as usual. Oh, yes, here it is. *The Guardian*: Inconclusive cause of death, quote unquote. Wife found him in the bathtub in London."

"What?" We're stopped short by security. "He's dead?"

Hands are inspecting the entrails of my purse for suspicious materials, its contents exploded onto the table. I stare dumbly as compact and perfume and a ring of keys are being tucked back away by anonymous hands. I feel like the entire hall has been sapped of air.

"Have a good time, ma'am." The guards wave us inside but I can't move. A strange sensation of utter grief washes over me.

I slowly turn to Regan. "How do you know?"

"Like a thousand oligarchs calling all afternoon, fishing for inside info. Why weren't you picking up? God, I'm so sick of our clients. They're always dropping dead." She holds up her phone, showing a picture of an inflated blonde, the Order of Saint Catherine draped between her pixelated breasts. She scrolls down. *New Hudson Yards Owner Igor*

Yardanov's Beauty du Jour Flaunts Pricy Gift. Regan appears to be waiting for a comment, an assessment. "Classy, right?"

"He was a decent guy." I'm close to bursting into tears. The guards are staring at me.

"Which one? The one who got the Order?"

"No, the other one."

"Sucks. You liked him, right? You stayed with him in Monaco?" Regan's concerned hand rests on my shoulder. She's gently pushing me away from the table.

"I did," I say.

"Probably that old gang of his from Ukraine. That's the gossip. Too many enemies and not enough friends. Anyway, we're late. *El mayor* may be up on stage already. I had no idea he would turn out to be such a little guy but still kind of sexy, don't you think?"

"Regan, wait." My fingers are leaving a pink imprint on my assistant's flesh, but it suddenly seems crucial that the words are said out loud. "Do you think, maybe, had he won the Order and gifted it to the president . . . Do you think he would still be alive?"

Regan scans me. (For signs of culpability? Verifying my involvement? Or is she just worried?) "No, Tanya, you know what? I don't. I'm pretty sure it was bound to happen one day."

"But maybe not. He sounded so desperate the other day on the phone. He wanted to preempt, and I never even asked the consignor. I wanted to get us more money."

Regan holds my hands until the shuddering subsides, then opens her clutch—sequined in the shape of a kitten—for a tissue. "Don't do this to yourself. You'd never have gotten that kind of money if you preempted. None of us have any idea about the crazy lives of those people. But they hardly revolve around us and our art."

I take the tissue. For a minute, I forget what one does with a tissue. "How can you be so sure?"

Regan wipes at my face, flecks of foundation streaking her fingers. "Look at us standing out here when the superhot mayor is inside."

"Oh, Regan."

"What? I like powerful old dudes who run New York City. Oh, look at you. You want me to say it again?" She holds my gaze. "Don't worry. It's not your fault."

We're greeted by women in red floral folk dresses with enormous shimmering *kokoshniks* on their heads. They're holding out bowls with bread and salt, traditional Russian folk rites of welcome.

Regan sweeps by them. "They're taking the Russian thing way too seriously."

Rows of sarcophagi, masks, tusk figurines line the exhibition halls. Limestone statues of kings, hands stiff at their sides, peer at us, eyelids like hardboiled eggs without centers. All I can think about is Medovsky, his thick eyebrows and trimmed moustache, Lena, the mistress, his friends reminiscing on the yacht. I remember my friend smoking before the precipice of the Mediterranean, the flamingo delicately tiptoeing in the background. I hold the image in my mind. But there's no time.

My hair, I think, my makeup, I'd been running. But the mayor's voice is reverberating along scalloped ceilings, the introduction to the ceremony under way. The wing opens up to a large party milling around the bar. They're forking mini chicken Kievs in their mouths, petite slivers of toast pyramided with red caviar. The women wearing a shade of somber red as if they were instructed: adorn yourself like a Russian! In one corner, by the wall of glass, prances a folk ensemble in Siberian attire, a circle of socialites urging them on. Nadia from Christie's is working the crowd, flinging a genuine smile in my direction. I notice Alla standing next to a few other JCC folks, glass raised to me in proud salute. I look around for any glimpse of Carl.

In the center of the room, past the dappled rectangle of the pool, looms the Temple of Dendur, its yawning sandstone gate with its two fringing walls, its carvings of lotus plants and Egyptian gods. A Met employee helps me up the steps of the dais. When I take my place behind the podium, I think the structure must be stretching high behind me as if I were Cleopatra or a queen at a coronation.

At the microphone, the mayor is rushing toward the end of his speech. He is enumerating the many accomplishments Americans from the former Soviet Union have contributed to the country. Russia's loss was our gain. Their names are rattled off like a chant: Mikhail Baryshnikov, Regina

Spektor, Vladimir Horowitz, Sergei Brin, Maria Sharapova, Mila Kunis. They have enriched us in the arts, in sciences, in technology. On stage beside me stands an ambassador to Israel, a hockey player, and to my surprise: Igor. No one told me he would be one of the honorees and the unexpected sight of him makes me aware of a boiling inside my body. That bronzed skin, gelled hair, those symmetrical features that add up to a face that is more superhuman than human. I feel myself flushing with anger.

"Darling, your hair," I hear my mother-in-law whisper delicately. "Pat it down."

The mayor is calling us to the podium, a handshake frozen for the benefit of photographers.

To Igor, the mayor says, "For your role in supporting one of our greatest sports teams and for your contribution to the New York Foster Children's Alliance, an organization that is bettering the lives of foster children not only in this city but across the entire country." Igor nods. He must be used to honors like this, must receive a few of them a week.

When it's my turn, I realize the mayor has edged into my palm a silver teapot. "Congratulations," he says to the cameras.

I examine the trophy. *TV* is engraved on the pot's front in sloping letters, the finial shaped like a pineapple, a fluted straight spout with a scroll wood handle. *TV?* I think. *TV?* But then I'm gently guided back to the row of honorees and struggle to balance this curious item for the remainder of the speech. When one hand can no longer prop it up, I transfer it to the other. Igor's just two people away from me.

It was bound to happen, I tell myself. They're killed for so many reasons, men like Medovsky, they all have so many enemies. Regan's absolutely right. It would be foolish to assume I played any tertiary role in the murder. Would he be alive if I hadn't steered him away from the Order?

The tall brunette in the front row, the one who is now wearing the Order of Saint Catherine between the scooped décolletage of her nonexistent breasts, was Igor's date at the Bulgari event. There's nothing remarkable about this girl taking pictures of Igor with her phone except she looks bored, as if fulfilling a task required of her. She is interchangeable with all the others at his side, pouting, inflated lips, beautiful Asiatic cheekbones, the kind of striking perfection you see in every bathroom of Moscow nightclubs, at every hotel bar. The Order is draped incorrectly, I notice. Not the way Catherine would have worn it at the side of the hip, but as if it's a gaudy pendant. The fraying ribbon has been removed, the star of the Order dangling on a thick gold chain.

After the ceremony ends, I'm attacked by a thousand cold imprints of lipstick, by anonymous handshakes. I look for a place to deposit the tea-pot, to free myself of its weight. Nadia Kudrina sidles in beside me. She's wearing a low-cut pink gown, a strip of velvet fabric stretched across her breasts. Some man's arm is attached to her waist. "Congratulations, dear. Just so you know, I'm serious about us starting a gallery. I think it's the perfect time to get out of the auction business. We'll make more money and so much less stress."

"Okay, I'll think about it," I say, vaguely.

"Soon, okay? *Poka*. Kiss, kiss."

Others are touching my arm, shaking my hand. A Russian man with a camera is following me, encouraging me to smile for the show *Kultura*. Your relatives in New Jersey are watching, he says. Smile!

I slice into the belly of the crowd and find Igor in conversation with the mayor, the girl leaning robotically at his side. The mayor is trying to talk Igor into donating to the New York library system.

"I suppose the Order is on loan from the Tretyakov." I insert myself between them. The mayor is taken aback at the intrusion, but politicians know how to quickly recover. "Congratulations again, Ms. Vandermot-ter." He rattles off an abbreviated version of his great admiration for Russian-Americans.

I ignore him and point to the Order, unabashedly sticking my finger in the girl's chest. "You'd better be careful, honey. This thing's going to a museum."

"Have you lost your mind or what?" the girl says in accent-free Brit-ish English. Handlers whisper into the mayor's ear, and he is expertly eased away.

"Don't be naïve, Tanya," Igor says. He too ignores his date. "Have a glass of wine. Relax."

"I won't relax. Why do you people always tell me to relax? Do you have any intention of carrying through with what you promised me? Do you know how historically important this piece is?"

The girl's shocked and I don't blame her. Apart from wives in the privacy of their homes, no one speaks like this to men like these.

"Maybe I'll still do it. I'm surprised at you. I had no idea you were such an idealist."

"I suppose you've heard what happened to Alexander Medovsky." I know I'm on thin ice. Danger aside, the thwarted kiss aside, a specialist knows when to press her case and when to remain silent.

"A tragedy."

"And I don't suppose you had any idea it was going to happen. I suppose it was a case of serendipitous timing."

Igor looks bemused. He presses a finger to his lips as if to say, *Shhhh*. But he doesn't go through with the sound and it is the implication of the gesture that chills me. The president could have protected Sasha, I think, but he had no Order, no incentive. I gave it away to the man standing in front of me.

Igor says, "Remember when you said it was open market? I think you would agree with me that even an open market needs a nudge in right direction."

"Maybe your ladies'-man reputation needs a nudge in the right direction." I must be out of my mind to be threatening a man like this.

But his face is frozen. "Maybe your job needs a shove in the right direction."

Behind him, Marjorie is waiting her turn to join in the conversation, ever harried in an unfortunate acrylic pantsuit. I quickly swallow my response. My boss wears the polite smile of client relations, of bringing an important person into the fold. "What a pleasure to finally meet you, Mr. Yardanov!"

A thick male cohort of admirers is pulling Igor toward the Siberian dancers. The room is pressing in on me, the glass walls leaning at a dangerous slant.

Marjorie turns to me. "Tanya, we have really underestimated this market. You're so incredibly good with these clients."

"Thanks, Marjorie. That means a lot to me."

"This auction has made me and Dean think a bit deeper about your role in the company." She sips at her wine with the awkward slant of someone avoiding transferring their lipstick onto the rim. "I was going to talk to you about this on Monday but the good news is this: we want you out in the field."

I force myself to pay attention even as I watch Igor and the mayor in a huddled group with other suited men. "The field? What field?"

"Where these new clients are. Kazakhstan, Azerbaijan. You could have Moscow as your base, of course. It's an incredible opportunity for a newly minted vice president, don't you think?"

The shoulders of the men become one blue smudge. I force my attention to Marjorie. "You mean leave the New York office? I don't understand. Was this Dean's decision? You know my husband's job is in Brooklyn."

"Let's just discuss this on Monday. Make an appointment with Karen. But smile, will you? It's a promotion. Don't pretend it's not what you wanted." Regan slides past with catalogues and Marjorie follows to flag her down.

Tiny sparks of light invade the edges of my vision. I can barely linger on the prospect of living in Moscow, much less visiting the compounds of Azerbaijan billionaires. Medovsky, Medovsky. Sasha. I picture his purple body, strangled, in the bathtub, a rope he never used dangling over the porcelain rim. I picture Lena sobbing, doubled over.

The faces of the guests glow grotesque in the greenish-silver light of the slanting windows. All those white teeth, the manes, the veneer of powder.

"Do you like the teapot?" It's Frances, face shining, hair slicked back behind her ears. Without her ubiquitous sunglasses, her face looks exposed, kinder. This time her Chanel suit is paired with a somber navy top.

I look down at the object in my hands. "I was wondering what that was."

"Darling, it is a very good reproduction of a Paul Revere teapot crafted in 1762. Well, don't look so stunned. I remember you admiring the silverware when you first came with Carl all those years ago. This is a little tribute, or just call it a promise. You know, one day the Paul Revere will be yours. And your children's."

I raise up the teapot again, the inscribed *TV*—Tanya Vandermotter. The two words together don't make sense at first. The light sharpens into full focus and I feel something melting, then expanding in my rib cage.

I embrace the woman, a long grateful squeeze. "Thank you, Cece. You can't imagine how much this means."

"And don't your people like tea? Think of it as a samovar."

"Yes. 'My people' drink tea. You're so thoughtful."

"Nothing to keep thanking us for, dear. You are a Vandermotter. It's as simple as that."

"I'm a Vandermotter," I repeat.

Miggy appears to pull Cece away. "Can I grab this lady? We've got another possible donor out here." They're swallowed into the milling crowd. I make my way to the bar for a drink. The air is fragrant with a frenetic kind of gulping, scent and manicures and the steady din of networking. Through the lattice of my thoughts, I'm aware of being smiled at, approved. By the rim of the motionless pool, Alla is gesturing meaningfully at her empty glass.

"Please jump ahead," someone says, ceding his place in line. "You're the star of the night."

I encounter the bottles of vodka, the pitchers of juices, the curling tails of lemon peel.

The bartender waits for my order, then prods, "Can I offer you a beverage? One of our herb-infused vodkas?"

"Okay," I say. A burning engulfs me, a grasp of an idea that has eluded me until now. Now the immensity of it is distilling into a kind of clarity. Medovsky's wife was right after all. I'm no different from my clients, no different than Marina and the other mistresses. I ate their caviar, drank their expensive wines, dined on their yachts, and yet I thought myself different from them. If Carl didn't know me, wasn't that my fault? Hadn't I transformed myself long past recognition? I was Tatiana Kagan once, letters written in a careful first-grader's Cyrillic.

I'm aware of a long line of people waiting for my response, a glass ready to be filled in the bartender's hand.

"Actually, I've changed my mind, thanks."

His face relaxes, and he leans forward. "Hey, don't let these Russki cocktails intimidate you. Let me make you something more familiar. I bet you just want an old-fashioned martini, don't you?"

A commotion is rattling in my head. There's no Sasha now, no job, no Carl.

"Gin and tonic?" he persists.

Okay, I think, turning away. Okay, okay.

I find Alla and wordlessly hand her the teapot. "Hold on to this for me, will you?"

"But where's my drink?" she calls after me.

Igor's fake girlfriend is standing by herself next to the pool, immersed in the screen of her phone, hair falling over the perfection of her sloped cheekbones. She's taller than me, yes, but the Order is surprisingly easy to yank over her head. It slips off willingly as though it were waiting for me. All I can see before stuffing the Order in my purse and running for the exit is that pair of dreamy eyes, the round globes of them. No one calls after me, no security guards block my way. It's probably taking the girl time to process the theft. She's paid by the hour, probably thinks it no more than a novelty trinket. By the time the girl calmly relays the news to Igor, I'm flying down the red-carpeted steps of a museum that was never meant for me. Now I grasp what my mother meant by keeping me away from this: a palace is something you earn.

I'm hailing a screeching taxi, giving the driver instructions to midtown. My calls are being forwarded to Carl's voice mail, but I redial every couple of blocks just in case.

As we leave the borders of Central Park behind to plunge into the maelstrom of Times Square, I allow myself to muse on Nadia's idea, the possibility of a quieter life in a gallery. Where a specialist is most needed, where my client relationships would be meaningful. No more juggling people's fates at auctions. And no more nudges in the "right direction." Me and Nadia. Who knows? It might work.

"What do you think of this much-ballyhooed novel your husband's working on," Carl's department chair asked at his Christmas party. "Between you and me. Is it as brilliant as we think it is? I'm on the personnel committee, you know. I've got to know if we should offer him the tenure-track job."

The entire drive to this town in western New Jersey had been confusing, with contradictory directions, and Carl was your typical New Yorker—a terrible driver. He lurched us from lane to lane in search of the right exit. Once off the highway, we drove by the main streets of adjoining towns, men smoking outside bodegas, shuttered movie theaters, dollar stores. A sign directed us back on a highway and we were plunged into the smudged neon of chains: Hooters and Fuddruckers and Outback and Loews movie theaters.

I'd tried to keep the tone light. "Let the Jersey girl drive."

"They'll ask about the novel." He squinted at the splitting road, green signs of incomprehensible highways: ONE, NINE, ROUTE FOUR.

"So why don't you tell me what you want me to say?"

"That you love it, of course. Darling, you know my whole life depends on publishing this thing. As it is, my parents think I'm this massive disappointment."

I was trying to look at the bright side of an expanding pool of dread. Carl's zigzags of self-confidence depressed me and I hated the contours of that feeling. I couldn't understand all those tortured nights Carl spent staring at a blank screen, deleting and adding, pouring himself countless cups of coffee, complaining about the agony of the craft, of the ticking tenure clock and his own lack of talent. His protests of how soul-racking writing was, how I could never truly comprehend the extent of his torment. Privately, I hoped his anguish pointed to some kind of authenticity as an artist. What I was ignoring was a transformation before the prospect of failure, my placid, life-coasting husband shrinking before me. But it was clear that the months I remained quiet about his manuscript were slowly chipping away at him.

"I can do that," I said, cheerfully. "I'll say you're brilliant."

The house, when we finally pulled up to it, was at the end of a country road. Elegant but deteriorating, chipped slate tiles on the roof, frowning stone fireplace, ironic posters of Mao. The department chair's original specialty had been Chinese literature before he settled into the

English department. It still amazed me, these academic parties, how different they were from Worthington's functions. The brown loafers, corduroy dresses layered over turtlenecks, dog-eared hairstyles. Even the parsley garnish wilted on silver trays, the sparse food already gone and the crowd still hungry.

"So what do you say, Tanya? Is it a masterpiece?" The beginning of the night, and the Ditmas College department chair was already swaying on alcohol, with heavy eyelids.

"You should have no problem getting behind the project. I've read it and it's brilliant," I said, cool and confident, indignant on my husband's behalf that his career was always up for scrutiny by this scruffy crowd. There was Carl across the room, his paper plate of cheese cubes, a kindling pile of toothpicks at one corner. He was laughing with Victoria, who was dressed, for some reason, in a bright fuchsia sari. The whole sight infuriated me.

"That's what we thought. We've all got such hopes for him. We all have a novel in a drawer, of course. But I'm sure with Carl it'll be different. He's a real thinker, an intellectual. But we need name recognition to hire, you know. Everything's about undergrad enrollments these days."

The department chair gravitated away, his duty of conversing with me completed. One relief of being a faculty spouse was the assumption that my career was too foreign to be comprehensible, and I was often left alone at these functions after the most cursory questions about my profession. I proceeded with drinking.

"You look great," Victoria slurred to me from her protégée's pose on the carpet. "Always so polished. So perfect. So voluptuous. So Russian. I hope I look like you when I grow up."

"That's ridiculous," I said. "You are grown-up."

"Just give us some pages." The chair managed to return to Carl's side. He was sloshing the mouth of the beer bottle in my husband's direction. "A chapter?"

"Oh, no, you'll just have to wait," Carl said, straightening. "It's a complicated project that covers forty years. I'm trying to tease out the history so it'll be comprehensible to the layperson."

"We won't be waiting too long, right?"

"Hey, I'm all too aware you've got pressure to do a national search. Don't you worry, Mike."

"Not too long, Carl. Just get a contract and you know the job's yours."

We returned from the party too drunk to gossip, to do much of anything but drape ourselves across the couch. Downstairs, on Broadway, a car was blocked in by a double-parked van, the horn emitting a series of resolute gasps. I toyed with the idea of initiating sex or at least tossing off a few e-mails to my Moscow clients, but then looked up to find Carl staring at me. *The way he looked at you.*

"Why don't you just say it. You hate it."

I'd hoped never to have this conversation. I figured if I didn't say anything, it would be skimmed past, avoided. "No way. I love it. It's almost there. I mean, another draft might be necessary. But it's really very strong."

"'Very strong,' oh, please. That's how you describe one of your fakes before you break the bad news to your clients. Let's just get it over with. You hate it. I wish you'd just speak the words. God, do you know what a relief that would be?"

I felt instantly sobered by this unusual display of directness. There would be no skimming then. I steeled myself, and plunged. "Okay. It's boring. It has no life. No suspense."

"Great. Thank you. At least now you're not avoiding me."

I tried to soften the damage. "Look, it's no big deal. You just wrote it like a historian and, I hate to say it, from a man's perspective. Why don't you just turn it into an academic book or history text or something? Wouldn't that be easier?"

"I don't want to write an academic book. You know that. I've been working on this novel for so many years. It's got to work."

I took his hand. "You know what? We can get it in shape."

"We?"

I warmed to the idea. "Sure. I've got some thoughts on how to bring it more to life. I'll help you." Our eyes met and I thought he recognized my sense of purpose.

"It's pointless," he said. I've never seen his face so collapsed, so blurred with panic. "I'm not a writer, I guess. I don't know what I am, actually."

I knew it was the wrong thing, but said it anyway. "Honey, you're a Vandermotter."

Carl leaned his elbows on the table. "That's a terrible thing to say."

"No, it's not." I grasped my husband's palms, pulled them away so his eyes were visible. "We can do this."

How often have I seen this expression in my parents' eyes? *Fix it, Tanya, fix it. You speak English so much better than we do.* The plea in their eyes for me to weave the seams together, to close the gap. To translate the new country for them. The expectation that I can make any crisis go away to keep a family together.

He inhaled. "Unfortunately, this is one thing you can't take care of."

"Why not?"

"This is my field, my specialty, my issue, okay? This is a novel, not naming a painting. Just let me handle it, no matter what the fuck it means for my job." He took a beer into the bedroom and slammed the door. Whatever he was doing was drowned out by the television, a hysterical exchange between reality show contestants. My head ached, but a solution was pushing its way to the surface.

His laptop was charging on our coffee table, light blinking green. I struggled to remember the dull beginning of his novel, a history lesson about eighteenth-century Russia. The document floated on the desktop like a disengaged limb. I opened it. A few details of the book contained interspersed wisps of interest. There was a famous comet, wasn't there? Wouldn't the young Sophie have seen it on her journey to Russia? I saved a new version of the document, and moved the comet section to the front of the novel. A young girl arriving in a foreign land. A young girl who imagined herself selected for an extraordinary purpose.

I started to type.

I presented my version for his birthday a few months later like an ornate gift, slipped him the wrapped, bow-tied package across the table. We were celebrating at the same Brooklyn restaurant of our early dates. What had

once been the sole fine-dining destination of a grizzled block in south
Carroll Gardens was now surrounded by newer places, trendier ones, glass
awnings stenciled in black and gold, reams of people waiting their turn
on the sidewalk. Our restaurant, on the other hand, was settled into its
dotage, the menu unchanged, the bricks above the fireplace chipped, the
booth that was once so romantic and enclosed, now drafty by its wood-
framed window. There was a smattering of couples drizzled between
bar and dining room; no one would be waiting for our table tonight.

"We should get the tiramisu for dessert. It was good that time, wasn't
it?" Carl said, scanning the menu, and when I didn't immediately answer, "*Kotenok?* Did you hear what I said?"

I reached into my bag for the present, set it on the rickety table. "Surprise. Happy birthday."

He accepted the wrapped pages with a grin, perhaps mistaking it for
something else, thumbing at the corners while skimming the lines.
"You're so goddamn sweet. What's this?"

"I did a little work on the book," I said, pretending to examine the
wine list. A quick skim confirmed that the bottle of wine from our last
visit was still on the menu. I ordered it.

"What? My book?"

As a deep part of me feared and dreaded, Carl didn't seem pleased
with my gift. He kept turning the envelope around as if this were a gag
gift and a real present would be hidden within its folds.

"Most of the novel's completely unchanged," I lied. "I just perked up
a few places."

"Perked up," he said. "In other words you rewrote the whole thing.
My novel." The bread arrived, cold under a shroud of napkin. I dug into
it with relish.

"I wouldn't say rewrote, that's a huge overstatement." In reality, after
consulting some self-help books on writing fiction, and getting carried
away with the story, I turned my attention to it during lunchtime at work.
Once I began, with Carl's research as the foundation, words flowed freely
out of my own memories of those early years in America. The foreign
streets of Rego Park, the kids at school who detested me for being geeky
and Russian. That endless solitude of my room with the fantasy of a sin-

gle best friend, a beloved confidante. All those disappointing boyfriends of my twenties who never grew up, never stepped up to the plate, who were never strong enough for me. Didn't I also believe I was destined for greatness merely because I was transplanted from one place to another? Wasn't I surrounded by incompetence? Wasn't I also considered my parents' salvation, great-but-not-too-great things expected of me? The bread was as cold and dense as it looked, but I made a show of enjoying it.

"Let me get this straight," Carl says, looking at me in that rare dangerous way he had, an unblinking glare. "You just rewrote in five months the novel I've been working on for six years. And you think this will get me a job."

"I told you. Whatever I did was minimal. You really did most of it."

I didn't tell him that for me, there was nothing tormenting about funneling a life story through this marvelous woman. I found the words streaked across the page as if by their own design, carried forward by my anticipation of Carl's relief. There was the feeling of satisfaction at solving a problem, at jiggling a key into a recalcitrant lock and hearing the click.

"That's totally fucked up," Carl said, picking up the pages. "I have a doctorate in Russian literature. And you just decide to write your own version of my book?"

"Sometimes a doctorate gets in the way. I just pruned some of the hedges, or whatever. Make your intentions clearer."

Our lamb arrived, congealing between us on a plank of potatoes. He flipped through the manuscript, skimming it through to the end.

"Oh, and I see in your version, she has him killed. I never wrote that. No texts verify with absolute certainty that she was responsible for Peter's murder."

"She's not, she didn't," I said, flushed. "The Orlovs killed him on their own. In my tweak, they just took her silence to mean she was onboard with the plan. I can make it less ambiguous if you don't like it. Or you should. I mean, it's yours now."

"It's mine now," Carl repeated.

"Is everything tasting okay?" The server in her white apron hovered. "Didn't you like the lamb?"

"It's delicious," I said sharply. The woman retreated.

Carl folded his hands on the table. "How interesting, your creative choice. Killing the ineffectual husband."

"Darling, you're reading way too much into it. He's not ineffectual."

"Give me a break. That's what you think of me. In your mind, I'm Peter."

"Of course not. That's ridiculous."

"Why don't you listen to me for a change? Think about why you do things. You're afraid. If I don't get a job, your perfect life's ruined. I'm a terrible reflection on you."

"Nice try, Mr. Ph.D."

"Oh, so I'm wrong again?"

"Catherine feeling guilty about the murder was for drama's sake. Not to mention many sources say she condoned his murder. But that's not the point." I tried to bring my defense back on track. I was afraid of where all this was going. "Let's talk about your ending."

How could I say this tactfully? Nothing interesting happened in the end. In his hands, Catherine was superhuman, a fortress of wisdom and strength. An angel without flaws. It was as if he'd spent six hundred pages giving her the Look.

A specialist's job is to understand your client's psychology better than he knows it himself. You need to know the kind of person he is, whether he cannot stand losing, whether he will back away at the first sign of conflict. Some people can't stop bidding. They need to win. Of course, often, it's the specialist herself who needs to win.

Carl was silent the entire subway ride home. That night, for the first time in all our years together, he slept on the couch. I wondered if I'd gone too far this time, but waited to see what would happen next.

In any case, I told myself later, Carl could have chosen not to publish *Young Catherine,* he could have not accepted the Word file I e-mailed him, he could have forwarded it directly to trash. He did not have to send it to an agent who'd taken an interest in his work from a short story he'd published in a literary journal the year before. He could have decided not to sign with that agent when she offered representation. He could have kept the book out of submission. But too many people were waiting for it and his career depended on it. In going forward with the book, didn't Carl settle with me into a tacit agreement? Didn't he give me permission to solve the problem? I hoped my apprehension would pass by our simply going on with our lives, the exchange buried inside us. He would be a star and I, a happy ghostwriter. In taking care of him, I've taken care of our little family.

We never spoke of the creation of the book again. Until the Order arrived in my office and it was actually hers, the entire dangerous subject of Catherine the Great was closed between us. And I was all too happy to absolve myself of any involvement and graft the book onto him. Because in my mind, the novel belonged to him in the same way a gift belongs unequivocally to its recipient. Wasn't this what Russian women did every day? Pass off their own accomplishments onto their husbands, so the men remained above them as saints to be admired? The rightness of it was etched past my collarbone, into the moral center of my heart.

A few sleepy writers look up after I punch in the code for the Urban Writers Space. They clearly didn't expect a woman in a long black ball gown, a floral silk clutch, a diamond-encrusted relic wound around her neck, to burst into such a space. They gape at me curiously from the rims of their laptops as I inspect all the cubicles one by one, rule them out for Carl. A triangle of women freeze over their microwaved dinners in the kitchen. "Can we help you?"

Hermione peeks her head out of her office. "Are you looking for the workshop your husband's taking? It's just ending."

"You mean the one he's teaching?"

"No," Hermione said, cautiously. "The one he's taking. He's a participant, a student."

I feel that stab of intuition, the kind where the outcome only needs to be verified. I walk down the hall and peer through the window at the class. Among people spanning their twenties to sixties, Carl sits around a long table, listening. The very same animated, gray-haired instructor from the Web site is wrapping up a point and the class is following along with her in their own paperbacks, a few underlining a cogent phrase or two. On the board is a map of a novel structure. Why would my husband, an M.F.A. from Columbia, author of a best-selling novel, be a student in this introductory writing class? I focus on Carl again, at the careful way his pen etches across lines. Then, of course, it crystallizes. Carl is here to start over. Learning to write again to cobble back what's left of his shattered self. The self I helped shatter.

I step away. My entire bag is vibrating, it seems, has been vibrating almost the entire cab ride downtown. Without looking at the phone's face, I turn the device off. In the classroom, papers are fanned out on desks with markings in the margins. Laptops are shutting down. I rap on the window a few times until he looks up and realizes it's me. Then I press the face of the Order against the windowpane. I'm gesturing like an idiot from the Order to Carl, then back to the Order, raising the absurd gold chain in a pantomime of a ceremony, a commemoration. *Touch it,* I'm trying to mouth. *Let's share its power.* Also as if to say, *I'm sorry. Now you know who I am.*

I can't delay the call to Marjorie for long. If the police are not already waiting for me at the apartment, then as soon as I push into the revolving glass doors of Worthington's, I'll be stripped of my ID and keys to the safe. I'll be detained until I produce the thirty-one-million-dollar object.

The class is a mixture of well-meaning confusion, as everyone looks around. *Is she waving to me?* But Carl's blinking at the Order. I can see him making sense of what I'm showing him, tabulating—didn't the auction happen already? Aren't I risking my job? I think I can make out a flash of worry on my behalf. Our eyes latch and I ransack them for the famous Look.

Here's what I find in his eyes: a woman torn into two pieces as a child, then scattered further into the tiniest of shards. A woman fighting her innate pessimism, her innate Russian-Jewish soul. A woman who thought that hoisting her husband above her would even the playing field between them. A woman who believed in even playing fields in the first place. For Catherine, there was a fate inscribed in a great comet. So what if my fate may contain only sky sprinkled here and there with the faintest of stars, and nothing more extraordinary than that?

He smiles, and I remember the complicity of marriage. It's an unfamiliar peace, a present-tense, radiating, explosive peace. I have no idea what will happen next, and it is this I've never allowed myself: operating without a larger plan, not stretching toward the next rung on some mythical ladder. Embarking on a path that simply meanders at will, and then might—maybe, possibly—lead me back to him.

Acknowledgments

I was extraordinarily lucky to have so many generous friends who read early drafts of this novel. Many thanks to them: Allison Amend, Sonya Bekkerman, Gabriel Cohen, Katie Crouch, Angie Cruz, Laurence Klavan, Phillip Lopate, Claire McMillan, Lynne Sharon Schwartz, Lizzie Skurnick, Peter Trachtenberg, Joel Whitney. Karen Kettering at Sotheby's provided me with crucial details pertaining to the Order of St. Catherine on its journey from Empress to auction house. Professor Marcus Levitt at the University of Southern California helped resolve a question of politics surrounding the young Sophie in Empress Elizabeth's court.

I wrote a lot of this novel at the Brooklyn Writers Space, a welcome refuge from all the noise.

It seems as though the road from your first to your second book is as rocky as they say. Time and time again, many friends offered a hand or talked me back into the light. There are far too many to list here, but special thanks to Paul W. Morris, as well as Kim Beck, Jessica Anya Blau, Mitch Hoffman, Stephanie Hopkins, Skip Horack, Jonathan Hsu, Dana Levin, Dawn Lundy Martin, Maud Newton, Karolin Shoikhet Obregon, Daphne Retter, Anya Ulinich, Natalia Vayner-Heyraud, and Josh Weil. Thanks to Gary Shteyngart, who is finally making up for not inviting me to the seventh-grade dance.

Kim Witherspoon and David Forrer at Inkwell are incredible champions of literature. I feel so lucky to have them on my side. Thanks to

Laurie Chittenden, who buoys my Russian soul with her cheerful passion and fierce talent. Also at Thomas Dunne, many thanks to Melanie Fried.

This book is dedicated to Sonya Bekkerman, best friend and muse for thirty-five years now. This book could not have been written without her.

Without the love and support of my parents, Mark and Gina, I would never have had the courage to pursue the writer's life. I thank them for urging me to embark on any road of my choosing. My sister, Elizabeth, inspires me daily; when I grow up, I want to be just like her. Thank you to my grandfather, Yakov Kreychman. Thank you also to the other half of my family, for all of their support: Ed Lowenstein, Paula Friedman, Jane Lowenstein, Ron Wendt, and Noah Lowenstein. This book carries within it the memory of dear relatives who have passed away, who have indelibly shaped me.

Finally, thanks to my beloved husband, Adam Lowenstein, whose unflagging love and support nurtures me and sustains me through any challenge, whose daily presence by my side is the greatest adventure of my life. And to my tiniest guiding genius Simone, a master storyteller in the making, who is up every morning before dawn in expectation of a glorious new day.